DEATHWORLDER
AN ASTRA MILITARUM NOVEL

DEATHWORLDER

AN ASTRA MILITARUM NOVEL

VICTORIA HAYWARD

BLACK LIBRARY

A BLACK LIBRARY PUBLICATION

First published in Great Britain in 2024 by
Black Library, Games Workshop Ltd., Willow Road,
Nottingham, NG7 2WS, UK.

Represented by: Games Workshop Limited – Irish branch,
Unit 3, Lower Liffey Street, Dublin 1,
D01 K199, Ireland.

10 9 8 7 6 5 4 3 2 1

Produced by Games Workshop in Nottingham.
Cover illustration by Igor Kieryluk.

See Black Library on the internet at

blacklibrary.com

Find out more about Games Workshop
and the worlds of Warhammer at

games-workshop.com

Printed and bound in the UK.

For bad birds, everywhere. And for those who love to see them fly.

For more than a hundred centuries the Emperor
has sat immobile on the Golden Throne of Earth.
He is the Master of Mankind. By the might of his
inexhaustible armies a million worlds stand
against the dark.

Yet, he is a rotting carcass, the Carrion Lord of the
Imperium held in life by marvels from the Dark
Age of Technology and the thousand souls sacrificed
each day so his may continue to burn.

To be a man in such times is to be one amongst
untold billions. It is to live in the cruelest and
most bloody regime imaginable. It is to suffer an
eternity of carnage and slaughter. It is to have cries
of anguish and sorrow drowned by the thirsting
laughter of dark gods.

This is a dark and terrible era where you will find
little comfort or hope. Forget the power of technology
and science. Forget the promise of progress and
advancement. Forget any notion of common
humanity or compassion.

There is no peace amongst the stars, for in the grim
darkness of the far future, there is only war.

CHAPTER ONE

There is a particular smell to a dying world. It comes after the stench of rotten meat and decaying vegetation has faded away, after the acrid burn of a warhead or sulphurous smog has dissipated. It comes only when the immeasurably vast lifetime of a planet has shivered down to days, or hours or minutes, when the final clouds are clearing and when life is so scarce as to be inconsequential. It is a smell of ending, cold and clean. Of nothing.

Lazulai is ending, but it is not quite dead yet.

Major Wulf Khan looked out over the battlements of Cobalt Fortress, a smoking cheroot clamped between her teeth. Another dawn was breaking over this doomed planet and somehow, she was still here to see it. The noctis watch was coming to a close and she was making her final rounds.

The sky above looked like an abscess, purpled and engorged with the writhing mass of xenos that thronged the upper atmosphere. Khan was reminded of the Catachan vein-worm of her home world. The pitted flesh-wound where it laid its eggs would swell as the larvae grew, and discolour to the unhealthy hue of Lazulai's skies. That parasite could be dug out with a knife. The tyranid infestation, which had reduced this world to a carcass, could not.

She slowly exhaled a plume of smoke. When her regiment had made planetfall, there had been great cities visible, built from the wealth of the gems mined on Lazulai. But this world had bred soft, indolent people who hadn't realised the galaxy was at war. Who had themselves let in the aliens, and doomed their own planet. They deserved to die. It was a shame she and her troops would die with them.

The battlements of Cobalt Fortress zigzagged away into the weak morning light. For about a mile in each direction from where Khan stood, crenellations jutted like fangs along the battlements, with watchtowers rising every thirty yards. The fortress took its name from the great cobalt pits in the mountains at its roots, but the stronghold itself was built of something like black obsidian, wrought long ago by forgotten architects. When her regiment had arrived to join the fight, they'd been thousands strong, but the relentless attrition of the xenos had ground their number down to mere hundreds.

Three hundred feet below Khan's viewpoint, the razed ground smoked, scorched after months of siege. Human and tyranid carcasses lay where they had fallen, heaped around the fortress for half a mile. They were waist-deep in many places. You became accustomed to the stench after a while, and the occasional crack of gas-bloated aliens rupturing. In recent weeks alien fauna had begun to erupt overnight, seemingly from nowhere. Fanged pumps that spurted out spore-clouds, polluting the air. They had tried to destroy them when they'd first appeared before learning that this only served to release a sudden, choking blast of deadly spores.

This morning was quiet, although the lull would be temporary. The monsters swept past in waves, their destination and intent unclear. Khan knew in her bones there wasn't much longer left now, for Cobalt Fortress, or for Lazulai. An old soldier's instinct for a terminal trajectory.

All she could do for her remaining troops was to keep them fighting, make sure they died like soldiers, not like grox in an abattoir. The ending would be the same, but she wanted them to believe the Emperor was still watching, that this fight still mattered.

Khan cast an eye along the ramparts. Two of her soldiers from the 903rd Catachan 'Night Shrikes' were on patrol and loomed close in the spore-dimmed dawn haze.

'Anything to report?'

One of them leaned against the battlements. Her hair was tied away from her face with the ubiquitous red bandana of Catachan. 'Nothing to report, major.' She grinned, gesturing at the corpse fields. 'But the weather up here's just like home.'

'Don't get too comfortable. You two just cycled out of ground-watch?'

The Catachan nodded.

Khan glanced at the weapon slung at the trooper's back. 'Not much use for a claw up here, Trooper Lief. It's the aerial variants the bastards send after us topside, and by the time they're close enough for you to use that, you'll be dead.'

The soldier laughed. 'Gotta show the pretty little Cadians how Catachans do things.'

'Catachans do things by surviving,' Khan said. 'You'll have a better chance of that with a lasgun in your hand. Understood?'

'As you say, sir. As long as I frag myself some xenos.'

Khan grunted. 'Just don't frag yourself, soldier.' She turned to continue past them, along the ramparts. Every regiment dealt differently with the stress, she thought. Some were lost to denial, others to despair. Catachans tended to become more Catachan, aggressively so, as Lief had.

'Sir!' the trooper called.

Khan glanced back to see Lief gesture in the direction she'd been heading.

'Looks like xenos-bait at the north tower.'

Khan turned and squinted. She made out a small human figure at the base of one of the gun emplacements, slightly closer to the edge of the battlements than was comfortable. 'I'll check it out. Continue your patrol.' She took a drag on her cheroot and strode back the way the soldiers had come.

It was said that psykers felt the xenos shadow most acutely, but no one was immune to it. Khan couldn't see how anyone living in this nightmare of constant, chittering dread wouldn't go mad. Many of Cobalt's defenders already had. 'Xenos-bait' was soldier's slang for any trooper who'd retreated far enough into their own head that they became impervious to the reality around them, or whose disregard for their own safety in battle became fatal.

She saw him as she rounded the corner. After a time, some people couldn't resist the screaming call of the ground, the final embrace of the distant earth below that would silence the xenos cacophony forever. A young Cadian, he looked barely more than a child to Khan. He stood at the edge of the battlements beneath the stolid, black gun tower, glassy-eyed, gazing up at the roiling sky, his white knuckles gripped tight around his lasgun.

'Trooper,' she said. 'Anything to report?'

'No, sir. All's well,' he replied, still staring upward.

Khan grunted and leaned against the battlements beside him, resting her broad forearms on the obsidian parapet. The temperature was rising, and the black stone was already hot to the touch.

Her skin had tanned darker than its normal brown over the months-long burn of the topside watch.

'And you, soldier? All's well?'

He turned his gaunt face to her. 'Yes, sir.'

She noted the name stitched onto his uniform. 'Tell me straight, Trooper Greiss.'

'We can't win, sir,' he said, avoiding her gaze. 'We can't do it, and there's no reinforcements coming.' He shot her a glance. 'I know there aren't, sir, or they'd be here.'

'Lazulai's the gateway to the system, son. Do you really think the Imperium would let it fall?'

'But sir, the fortress can't hold out much longer...' He trailed off.

Khan squared up to the man. 'This battle is for the world, trooper. We're stationed here because command needs their best at the hardest posting and General Kvelter tells me the Cadian Two-Thousand-and-Twelfth are the best the Emperor has. Do you want to prove her wrong?'

'No, sir.'

'Then you keep those skies clear for me.' She pointed along the wall. 'When was that gun tower last inspected?'

'Yesterday, sir.'

'Do it again. We need to be ready for the next round.'

Greiss nodded, stepping back from the edge and proceeding to the tower.

Khan grimaced as she watched him leave, the lies bitter in her mouth. But he had stepped away from the brink. And what was an officer's business if not saving soldiers in order for them to die in battle? Lazulai's grinder was going to take every scrap of meat they could throw at it and there were no more coming. Throne curse the day she'd been nominated to lead.

'Major,' came a tense shout from Greiss. 'Incoming!'

Khan turned and saw the xenos immediately, still an airborne speck on the horizon. The warning siren started up a dull blare and across the obsidian walls soldiers scrambled to respond.

'Magnoculars,' she ordered.

Greiss jogged over and passed his across. Raising them to her eyes, Khan focused on the flighted monstrosity: a chitinous horror the size of a Valkyrie, with a broad keel of fluted bone and a tubular protrusion extruding from its vast maw.

The creature's very motion sent a prickle of horror through Khan, a deeply wired response to something so inherently alien, something so clearly designed to devour. It was an instinct all humans had, but which, in order to survive their home world, Catachans were acutely attuned to. Although even that hadn't been enough to prepare them for this tide of monsters at this end of days.

Khan noticed the alien was listing slightly, as if injured. But it still headed directly for the fortress. She frowned. How in Throne's name had it come up on them so quickly?

Khan's vox buzzed. *'Major, this is control. Lightning Strikes are ready to deploy on your order.'*

'Hold,' Khan said, raising the magnoculars once again.

The troops called this form a 'skyhunter'. It carried aircraft-killers under its wings, hideous lumps of flighted gristle that drained the power from engines and sent planes tumbling from the sky. Khan squinted. This monster's wings were tattered and all but empty. From here it looked as if just one bubonic war-head remained. Perhaps the xenos had encountered resistance at another outpost. She pushed away the glimmer of hope that arose at that thought. Cobalt was the last of the surviving fortresses for hundreds of miles.

'Sir,' control voxed again. *'Wing-Commander Lennard has the pilots ready to scramble.'*

'Stand them down,' Khan said. 'We'd only be giving it a chance to take down a fighter. And I'm not about to give it what it wants.' They could ill afford to lose any more planes.

The monster was coming in hot and would be above them in seconds. She stubbed out her cheroot on the obsidian-glass battlements.

'Towers E and G,' she voxed. 'Incoming hostile. Ready las-cannons.' Illogical as it was, her hands itched to draw her knife on the abomination. 'Hit the bastard from both sides, on my count.' *That should be enough from this range*, Khan thought.

There was a groan of hydraulics from Tower E, which stood closest to her, and then the snap of las-fire. The ruby beam smashed into the chitinous hide, shearing one leathery wing away entirely and sending the alien wheeling down towards a jutting bastion. It crashed heavily into the defensive outcrop, smashing a chunk of walkway and sending soldiers spinning out over the drop to their deaths.

'Clear the walls!' Khan roared. Tower G hadn't fired. One shot hadn't been enough to kill the monster, and it hung by one bony wing spur, dangling over the vertiginous drop.

Khan strode towards the battlements, drawing her chainsword as she went. Why hadn't Tower G fired? She could see half a dozen Catachans and Cadians already concentrating lasgun fire on the beast over the edge of the ramparts. If the skyhunter pulled itself up onto the battlements they would be in trouble.

The hideous thing started up an unholy drone that set Khan's teeth on edge. Its throat bulged before a rapid, projectile blast of sputum issued from its maw, jetting into the row of defenders and dashing them against the battlements like fallen leaves. She could hear their screams as the corrosive fluid began to melt their skin. Those still standing held the line and continued to fire with grim determination.

'Frag it! Aim for the head,' Khan called over the vox.

She saw the first grenade sail out over the edge of the battle-ments and skitter off the monster's back, detonating harmlessly as it dropped out of range.

The second slammed into the place where the horror's wing had been, gouging a human-sized chunk of flesh and splin-tered bone.

'I said, aim for the head,' Khan growled again, adrenaline thumping through her veins.

The target's obscured, sir.'

They were right. To guarantee a direct hit they would have to come right to the rampart's edge, back into the beast's range.

Impossibly, the monster was starting to climb, slamming its massive jaws into the sheer black stone as leverage, and dragging its huge body up by the wing-stump. It was seconds away from clearing the ramparts and being able to ram its way inside the fortress. The damage it could do to the remaining defenders inside the enclosed space was unthinkable.

Khan was closing on the damaged bastion, close enough now to smell the tell-tale ozone stench indicating it was about to discharge an organic missile. She was not, however, close enough to stop the Catachan who was even now taking a run-up to dive over the edge, Devil's Claw blade raised above her head.

'Trooper, no!' Khan barked. It was Lief, the idiot from the morning patrol. Khan swore to herself. She should have realised – the Devil's Claw, the talk of fragging tyranids? Lief was far further gone into the tyranid-madness than she'd realised.

It was too late to stop her. Lief was already in motion. The xenos snarled as the soldier soared above it, and almost too fast to see, the final aircraft killer shot out from under its wing. It smashed directly at the diving Catachan, bursting her head in a bright halo of blood on impact, the mercury-weighted blade she had held bouncing uselessly away, down to the ground far below.

The remainder of the watch squad had already formed up with lasguns as the wounded tyranid began to claw its way up the battlements again.

'Shoot the maw!' Khan shouted over the vox. They needed to disable the fleshy cannon in the aberration's distended jaw before it climbed up high enough to immolate them.

The defenders sent a volley of lasgun fire at the hideous beast as its head emerged over the top of the crenellations. There was a sickening burst as they ruptured its gullet. Strings of lurid viscera trailed from the shattered exoskeleton and floods of ichor gushed from the uselessly pulsing oesophageal valve. But still it kept coming, clawing its way inexorably up over the fortress' edge with its remaining limb.

The troops fanned out in neat formation across the ruined walkway where the xenos now squatted, positioning themselves to hit it from multiple angles. The monster suddenly lurched forwards, slamming its bone dorsal cage into the stone. There was a judder, and a section of the battlements gave way, trapping two of the soldiers on an island of stone, and in the line of fire directly behind the monster.

'Cease fire,' Khan said, readying her chainsword. There was only one way of ending this without losing more of her troopers. The walkway was slick with ichor, and she stepped carefully across the rubble, approaching the monster's head.

There was a sudden movement as the beast lashed its barb-tipped tail around towards her. Khan dodged a fatal hit to her skull, but the bludgeon glanced against her arm, gouging a lump from her bicep and sending her stumbling. As it raised the barb again, a boltgun shot boomed out, smashing the tip of the tail away before it could dash her brains out. Without hesitating, Khan plunged in close to the monster's rearing head and snarled her chainsword into its neck. The weapon's teeth screamed as they ground into the chitin plating around the horror's skull, biting deeper into whatever was inside its head. Growling, Khan leaned her full weight onto the blade, which juddered and bucked in her powerful arms.

She felt the chainsword throw a tooth at the effort, but she kept going until the revving sword roared clear, and the body collapsed forward, spewing unknown fluids.

A ragged cheer came up from the defenders, but Khan raised a hand, expression severe as she caught her breath.

'There is nothing to celebrate here,' she said, fixing each soldier with a hard gaze. 'This' – she gestured at the alien with her befouled chainsword – 'should not have made it onto the fortress walls. This didn't cost us soldiers today. We did.'

She let the troopers take in the sight of her, veteran of a thousand battles, legend of a dozen systems, bloodied and angry. She glanced meaningfully at the dead, their skin sloughed away by xenos bile.

'Not all of you are Catachan. But where you came from doesn't matter now, because you're all serving on a death world. If we don't carry each other, we're all going to fail. And I will terminate any soldier who does not carry their comrades. Is that understood?' She slowly met the eyes of every trooper in front of her. 'When you pray tonight, ask Him-on-Terra to grant you another day to repay your comrades. Because every tomorrow is bought with blood. Do not waste it.' She exhaled heavily. 'Now, who was in command of Tower G?'

A Cadian stepped forward, chin up. 'Sir. I was.'

Khan eyed the soldier. She didn't recognise him. 'Have you held this command before?'

'No, sir,' he said. 'It should have been Trooper Adair, but she didn't report for duty.'

Khan frowned. Adair was one of hers. 'And where is Trooper Adair?'

'I can take you to her, major.'

Khan turned to see her orderly, Sergeant Rutger Haruto, boltgun still smoking in his hand, bionic eye glinting. She should have known it was Haruto's shot that saved her from the skyhunter's tail. He stood head and shoulders above the Cadian troops even though his demeanour was habitually hunched, dark brows beetled low in an expression of perpetual frustration.

She glanced at his gun and gave him a nod, then turned back to the troops.

'Burn this abomination, and the bodies. We don't want to leave any meat out.'

Haruto led Khan off the battlements and down into the labyrinthine depths of Cobalt Fortress. Even in the humidity of Lazulai, once you were deep into the miles of identical passages that ran under the mountain, it was cool. It was also claustrophobic, but it was preferable to standing watch under that unholy sky. Khan felt a little tension lift from her shoulders. You could almost pretend you weren't surrounded by abominations down here.

Aides from different regiments moved swiftly and quietly past them in the ebon gloom. There were mostly Cadians and Catachans left now, interspersed with the occasional preacher or tech-adept. The corridors were hushed, darkness filling the voids between the cold pools of lumen light. The gloom dimmed the whorls of colour in the gemstone walls. The precious stones beneath Lazulai's skin were what had made the world affluent, and the xenos-cultists had inveigled their way into the weakness cultivated by the greed of the planet's custodians. Embarrassingly, the Adeptus Ministorum had been the most powerful presence on the world before its downfall. Khan suspected that even now, the Church was having to explain why its priests had been preaching heretic gospels of four-armed Emperors, whilst overseeing the manufacture of the majority of the sector's gem-encrusted shrines, altars and devotional relic cases.

Haruto walked beside Khan, his shock of dark hair tied back into a messy rat-tail. Her sergeant was sharp. He could pull at things in ways she had only seen the finest strategists or enginseers do, although to most of the Imperium's non-Catachans he looked closer to an ambull than an adept, and he was habitually treated as such. He was also stubborn as a grox, a trait which had both served and inconvenienced her in the past.

'Give it to me straight, Haruto,' Khan said, rolling her neck. The adrenal flush of combat was already ebbing away to be replaced with aches and pains. 'What's happened with Adair?'

'She's being tried.'

'What?' Khan spat.

'For violation of regulations.'

Khan clenched her fists. 'Who?' she growled.

'Captain Bligh. He's holding the proceedings in the lower briefing room.'

'That bastard cost me lives today. What was he thinking, pulling a soldier off duty?'

Haruto cleared his throat. 'I believe he was thinking that in the absence of a commissar, he was responsible for delivering the Emperor's Judgement.'

Khan broke into a run.

Haruto kept pace with her easily. Soldiers flattened themselves against the walls to let them past, Khan barrelling ahead, shorter but more muscular than her sergeant.

She slid to a halt outside the briefing room and, finding it locked, hammered on the door.

'Captain Bligh, this is Major Khan. Open this door now.'

After a moment a nervous-looking adjunct swung the door open. 'Sir,' he said, clearing his throat. 'Captain Bligh has asked me to remind you–'

Khan swept the man aside and strode into the room. Bligh stood up on a dais at the opposite end, behind a lectern. His uniform was pristine, but his cheeks were gaunt, sweat glistening on his pallid skin. Rows of Cadians stood ranked down each side of the room.

Trooper Adair was on her knees in the centre, hands cuffed behind her. She had her broad back to Khan, but she somehow still radiated insolence. Half a dozen soldiers had their lasguns trained on her.

'Weapons down,' Khan barked.

The Guardsmen obeyed the senior officer immediately.

'Captain Bligh,' Khan said through gritted teeth, her patience for diplomacy run very thin. 'In the interests of continued good relations between our regiments I am giving you ten seconds to explain what in the name of Terra is going on here.'

Bligh gripped the lectern in front of him. 'Trooper Falke Adair has been found guilty of infringement of discipline, breach of the disciplinary code and insubordination.' He spoke Gothic with the clear, clipped intonation of the Cadian's officer class.

Khan looked at him expressionlessly. 'That's all? You've not commanded Catachans before, have you, Captain Bligh?'

There was a stifled snort from somewhere in the room. The tension was dissolving, but Captain Bligh's eye twitched.

Khan leaned forward, and lowered her voice. 'Captain. The walls are being beaten down by monsters as we speak. Are you certain any of this is a priority?'

'We need to hold the line, sir. If we don't have standards, we don't have anything!'

'Get up, Trooper Adair,' Khan ordered.

Adair stood and turned. She had biceps that could crush a man's skull and a face that could launch a thousand recruiting drives, with a broad, strong jaw and pict-friendly cheekbones under a crop of white-blonde hair. She'd have been the archetype of military perfection were it not for the smirk twisting her otherwise noble face. Khan could spot trouble a mile off, and Adair was the kind of trouble that left broken hearts, teeth and formal warnings in her wake.

'What did you do, trooper?' Khan asked.

'Took some trophies, sir. Didn't fancy Captain Bligh's request to take 'em down from the mess wall, so I put them up where he couldn't reach 'em. He's had it in for me since.'

Khan heard Haruto trying to stifle a snigger behind her. Adair was a brute, taller than the average Catachan, and Bligh barely came up to her shoulder. She could easily have put him under her arm and carried him if she wanted.

Khan turned to Bligh. 'That hardly seems to warrant a hearing. Catachans take trophies, captain. It's appropriate to allow for regimental traditions for the sake of morale.'

'That's not in fact why Trooper Adair is here, major,' Bligh said through gritted teeth.

Khan inclined her head. She felt the muscles in her neck twinge. Throne, but she was too tired and angry for this. 'No?'

'Yesterday she disobeyed a direct order to remain at her post. As a consequence, four of my soldiers died.'

Khan glanced sharply at Adair. The trooper's face had dropped to a sullen blank. 'Is this true, Adair?'

'Sir,' Adair said, her voice toneless, her earlier braggadocio gone.

Captain Bligh shook his head, lip curled. 'This is the kind of disregard for command that will defeat us before the xenos. She abandoned her comrades without even knowing who they were, what they were worth.'

'No,' Adair said quietly.

'No?'

'No, sir. I know who they were.' Adair looked up. 'They were Sergeant Clay, Trooper Dakor, Trooper Vance and Trooper Colm.' A muscle in her jaw twitched. 'They died fighting, but they died because I wasn't at my post, it's true.'

Bligh turned to Khan. 'Now that you appreciate the situation, major, I must strongly insist that this hearing is concluded and that Trooper Adair is punished appropriately.'

Khan rubbed her eyes. 'If you insist, captain.' She could do without Adair being in the brig, but perhaps a rest would do the trooper some good.

'The execution of Trooper Adair will take place at dusk,' Bligh continued.

'What?' Khan growled.

'It is clearly the punishment commensurate with the infraction.'

The soldiers in the room muttered and shifted. Haruto swore.

'Sir,' one of the other Cadians said, a red-headed Whiteshield. 'Requesting permission to speak?'

'Denied,' Bligh said.

'Granted,' Khan countermanded. 'Step forward.'

The young soldier pushed her way to the front of the crowd. 'Sir. I was loader on a weapons team at the north wall yesterday. My gunner was shot down and ours was the only heavy bolter left.' She swallowed, the strain of defying her commanding officer evident. 'Sergeant Adair moved from her post on the south wall to operate the weapon until reinforcements arrived. Without her, the xenos could have gained ingress to the fortress via the north hangar.'

Khan could picture the entrance to the external battlements, wide enough to allow the largest tyranids in. What they would do if they gained access to the fortress required little imagination.

'It wasn't her decision to make, soldier,' Captain Bligh snapped. 'Her choice resulted in the deaths of the squad she had been ordered to cover. If a soldier cannot hold their post, they cannot be trusted.'

'I've heard enough,' Khan said. Her feet ached and she was fairly sure the xenos filth on her fatigues was starting to eat through the fabric. She summoned her last reserves of patience. 'We all have to be more than our posts in this war, captain. I understand your anger, but this is an emotional response, not a logical one. Trooper Adair did the right thing. If she hadn't done what she did, we wouldn't be here to argue about it. I'm sorry about the deaths of your soldiers, but we don't have enough fighters left for you to start shooting them. And for what it's worth, I'd order Adair to do the same thing again.'

'Major...' Bligh said, fixing Khan with a hard stare.

Khan held his gaze. 'You caused Adair to be away from her post this morning, captain. That was an action that nearly cost me a squad too. Let's call it even?'

Bligh was silent.

'Trooper Adair,' Khan said, still maintaining eye contact with Bligh. 'You'll write a chit to the families of the Cadians to tell them they died as bravely as Jungle Fighters. And you'll start treating your commanders with more respect, or Throne help me I'll beat that lesson into you myself. Understood?'

Adair nodded. 'Yes, sir.'

'Captain Bligh,' Khan said, 'I recommend you take a break this morning. This hearing is over.'

'No,' Bligh said, then repeated it more loudly. 'No.' His face twisted. 'Commissar Schuto won't stand for this.' He drew a las-pistol and aimed it at Adair.

Khan made a small motion to halt whatever action Haruto was planning to take in her defence. 'Commissar Schuto is dead,' she heard him mutter.

'Put the gun down, Bligh,' said Khan.

'Discipline must be enforced!' spat Bligh. 'If we are to pre-vail, we must behave like soldiers. Don't move,' he snarled at Adair, who had been positioning herself to attack him despite her still-cuffed hands.

Khan gave her a warning glance and began to walk towards Bligh.

'Stay back, major!' Bligh snapped.

'No,' she said, moving forward softly, one step at a time.

Bligh aimed his gun at Khan. 'I said, stay back!'

Khan kept inching forward. 'You won't shoot.'

'I will,' Bligh said, hand shaking.

'You won't. Because Cadians are good soldiers. You follow orders even when you're half mad.'

She was right in front of Bligh now. She placed one of her massive hands over the laspistol's barrel. 'Let go of the gun, sol-dier,' she said soothingly, as if reassuring a frightened animal.

'Things need to be done properly. It's the only way we can win,' Bligh said, jaw set.

'Then let's take this to General Kvelter. She's fair. She'll make the right decision.'

Bligh nodded slowly as he considered this, and with her left hand Khan gently pulled the weapon from his unresisting fingers. Then she shot up her right fist lightning-fast and punched the captain, hard. He jerked backward at the force of the blow, then crumpled to the floor, eyes rolling back in his head.

'You,' Khan said, gesturing at a Cadian lieutenant. 'Take your captain. Put him somewhere he won't do himself or anyone else any harm.'

'Sir...' The lieutenant frowned, biting back what she wanted to say.

Khan sighed. 'Out with it, soldier.'

'Captain Bligh is a hero, sir.' The lieutenant's distress was visible. 'He led the last patrol out of Cobalt. He was wounded holding the line while the tank column withdrew. Carried back three injured soldiers himself.'

Khan nodded. 'And that, lieutenant, is why I didn't kill him. I suggest you get him to the infirmary sooner rather than later.'

Adair watched the Cadians carry the captain out and folded her arms. Kill bullets were tattooed onto the rippling muscles of her biceps around a crudely inked regimental crest of a monstrous Catachan Shrike.

'They talk themselves up, but the Cadians can't hack it here, sir,' Adair said. 'Not like us.'

'Us?' Khan repeated. 'You mean Catachans like Trooper Velope, who broke out of the fortress to try to "save" his squad a week after he saw them die? Or Lief, who just tried to take out a skyhunter with a knife? Neither of them is still here to hack it. Everyone is going their own variety of mad, trooper. Assuming you're above that is the quickest route to it. Stay watchful.'

'Sir.'

'And Adair,' Khan said, gripping the woman's massive bicep. 'You did the right thing yesterday. Do you understand?'

'Yessir. Thank you, sir.'

'Good. Now get topside and help clean up. I've got a meeting with command.'

General Kvelter was an old-fashioned officer. Even as the world was ending, she insisted on briefing the senior staff in her office – a formal, wood-panelled room lined with paintings of notable Cadians. Today, Khan found herself the only senior officer there. She was quite possibly, she realised, the only one left. Kvelter sat at one end of a long table while her orderly, Lieutenant Bose, served her recaff.

'Ah, Major Khan,' Kvelter said. 'Take a seat, would you?'

Sergeant Haruto poured recaff into the cup placed beside Khan, then took up post behind her chair. Lieutenant Bose prided himself in ensuring things ran as they should in the general's office, and that Kvelter was always immaculately turned out. Not a silver hair on the old officer's head was out of place. In contrast, Khan was aware that she was dripping blood and gore onto the general's carpet, and that half of her uniform would probably need to be burned. Haruto and Bose already detested each other, and this was unlikely to help. Although Khan suspected the business of maintaining their low-level feud was perhaps one of the small things still keeping them sane.

'Quiet morning topside, I hear,' Kvelter said briskly.

'I've had worse.'

Kvelter nodded. 'I appreciate your leniency with Captain Bligh.'

'News travels fast.' Khan sipped her scalding recaff.

'He's a good soldier.'

'They're all good soldiers in bad positions, sir.'

Kvelter nodded. 'Just so.'

The old Cadian was sharp as a knife and Khan had come to respect her. Cobalt would have fallen months ago had it not been for her shrewdness. She ran the operation like clockwork, and it was to her credit that the cracks were only recently starting to show.

Kvelter cleared her throat. 'I'll get to the point, major. You have new orders.'

Khan placed her cup down. 'Sir?' There had been no new

orders from sector command for months, not since the xenos cast their blanket of silence over Lazulai. *Hold and fight* was all they'd been told.

'We have reports of an incoming swarm – something larger than we've ever seen. Spotter planes are going dark across the continent. Before it hits, you're to take a small infiltration team deep into the eastern regions to recover an asset. You'll be aware that in recent weeks a number of units have been deployed from Cobalt Fortress, and that all have been neutralised. Most recently a squadron of Lightning Strikes.'

Khan raised an eyebrow. 'And before that a tank column. I see the wreckage daily on my patrol topside. Sir, sending an infiltration team out into that environment is a suicide mission.'

Kvelter allowed herself the shadow of a smile. 'Possibly, but not necessarily.' She gestured to Bose.

The lieutenant placed an open file in front of Khan.

'You will take your team to Opal Bastion,' the general continued. 'It is located approximately fifty miles east of Cobalt Fortress. There will be a liaison officer from the Cadian Eighty-Second waiting there to guide you onward to the asset you are tasked with recovering. That asset is of immeasurable value.'

'What is it?'

'Classified. Above your clearance, and mine. But you will be escorting an agent-adept of the Adeptus Mechanicus who will oversee the extraction. She just arrived via orbital lander with the final orders from sector command.'

'They want me to take a cog-worshipper on a tour of the apocalypse?' Khan pinched the bridge of her nose. 'And what will you be doing whilst I'm out getting my squad ripped apart by xenos, sir?'

'Losing the fort.'

Khan stared blankly at the general. 'What?'

'Losing the fort,' she repeated.

Cold uncertainty gnawed at Khan's guts. 'With all due respect, sir–'

Kvelter cut her off. There was a thin smile on her face. 'Major, I can confirm what you already suspect. There are no reinforcements coming. As far as command is concerned, Lazulai is lost. But there is one shred of use the Imperium may yet take from this planet. One shred of use that you and I might yet be. You recall the failed operations we spoke of a few moments ago?'

Khan regarded her silently.

'They were tasked with the same mission. Go east, recover the asset. We dispatched tanks, aircraft, infantry. None of it worked. The xenos became aware of them immediately.' She leaned back. 'We've tried throwing our weight around, and it didn't work. We need them not to notice us. So, we're going to send a core of our best Jungle Fighters into the jungle.'

Khan frowned. 'There's no jungle on Lazulai.'

'Things have changed in the past few weeks, major. But it's less about the terrain, although that will present a challenge.' She gestured to the file. 'Of all of us left, your people are the best equipped to navigate the hellscape the tyranids have wrought here. You'll find everything we know about the current situation in that file.'

Khan slid the file across to Haruto. She wasn't much for reading, but she had already felt him craning over her shoulder to get a glimpse of the picts and maps.

'And whilst you head east,' the general said, lilac-hued eyes glinting, 'I'm pulling every asset we've got and moving north. I want the enemy to think we're heading for Jasper Fortress. I'm going to give the bastards a light show. Provide sufficient cover that you have a chance of flying under their auspex.'

'And give the troops a last fight. A proper one,' Khan said.

General Kvelter nodded.

'Still, it's a damn high butcher's bill for a recovery mission.'

'Yours is the last mission, major. And one which we must accomplish by any means necessary. The order came from Lord Commander Stone himself.' Kvelter placed her hands on the desk and lowered her voice. 'This could be it, major. This could be what we've been waiting for. Something that could stop the bastards, not just on Lazulai, but across the Imperium.'

'You think we're recovering a weapon?'

'What else could be such a priority for command?' Kvelter pursed her lips. 'And if it is, it's worth the price.'

Khan regarded the general. There was no fear in the wiry Cadian's eyes. Her will was so hard it could slice bone. 'It'll be a good death, sir.'

'I doubt it,' Kvelter laughed dryly. 'But we take what we're given. Now, if you'll excuse me, I have an assault to plan.' She rose to her feet. 'It's been an honour, Wulf.'

'Likewise.' Khan saluted and made to leave, then turned back and extended a hand. 'Cadia stands, sir.'

Kvelter gripped her hand and gave Khan a hard smile. 'She stands. Happy hunting, major.'

CHAPTER TWO

Lieutenant Kaede Anditz drove his power sword into the cultist's shoulder, past her collarbone and down into her heart. She hadn't seen him coming, had been too focused on holding her post. She'd been kneeling in the sand beside her heavy mining laser, tracking Anditz's squad on the other side of the bluff when he had stealthed up behind her. Her back arched as she tried to breathe, despite the slender adamantine blade splitting her torso. Anditz withdrew the sword slowly. Sound travelled in the dust-bowl valley that cradled the entrance to Var Mine, and Anditz couldn't be sure how many traitors remained. The crackle of the ancient weapon's disruption field and the haemorrhaging liquidity of the woman's final breaths was loud, although discreet relative to the crack of a laspistol.

His platoon was at this moment, with characteristic Cadian efficiency, carefully eliminating the enemy defence positions around the mine's entrance.

As the woman slumped forward beside her weapon, Anditz

noticed a purplish flush on her skin that tracked up her neck. He hooked his boot under her body and turned her over. Her nostrils flared for a moment as she looked at him, but the light in her eyes was already dimming. Streaks of blood and bubbled saliva smeared her face, which was unmistakably degraded. An inhuman distortion of the skull and the undulating patterns of bruise-hued bone deforming her forehead marked her as a corrupted xenos-worshipper. She was also inexperienced, as the other defenders had been.

Anditz wiped a bead of sweat from his forehead with the back of his hand. It was still early in the day but the humidity was already closing in. He pressed his comm-bead. 'Sergeant Dolor, you are clear on the northern vector.'

'*Message received. Corporal Barette is dispatching guards. Sergeant Morton is completing his final sweep. Expect his rendezvous shortly. Breach team holds the mine entrance.*'

Anditz watched Dolor's team move into defensive positions around the fortified lift cage marking the mine's entrance. It stood lonely in the dustbowl, an isolated portal belying the labyrinthine network of tunnels and chambers below the ground.

This was it, he thought. It had taken months of attrition, but they were finally in a position to assault the cult's nerve centre. How many years the xenos-worshipping bastards had been planning their insurrection for, he didn't know. But on the day of revolt, thousands of them had risen from underneath Lazulai's cities and attacked. Generations of monsters with half-human faces that had been nurtured by the very world they sought to destroy.

Exactly how it happened, the precise nature of the heresies that bastardised human flesh with xenos chitin, was known only to the agents of the Holy Ordos – sanctified wielders of such fearful knowledge that would drive lesser minds insane. Ordinary soldiers were protected from such horrors. You didn't need to know *why* a thing existed to understand that you had to shoot it. That said, the troops had all heard the rumours. Whispers of a dark embrace and an alien kiss. It'd be the Emperor's Mercy for anyone heard speaking of it in front of a commissar.

Anditz glanced down as the xenos mutant at his feet died. Whatever life force animated her left and she became inert, lying awkwardly on the sand, a pool of red spreading out from her wound like a flowing shroud on the ground. Strange how her blood looked so like his, he thought, when it had come from something so inhuman.

Anditz looked up to see Sergeant Morton approaching from across the scrubby hill.

Morton was as sound a soldier as you could hope for. He'd been under Anditz's command since the start of the deployment on Lazulai, when they had been tasked with quelling the initial planetary uprising. The traitors had infiltrated everything from the Ecclesiarchy to the local Astra Militarum regiments and had entirely taken over the extractive industries across Lazulai, meaning they were well-equipped with mining charges, vehicles and industrial tools that cut flesh and bone just as efficiently as they cut garnets. Fighting well-armed locals in a warren of mines across the industrial deserts was one thing, but the war had become something quite different when the cult's monstrous kin had arrived from the stars.

'Sir,' Morton said softly as he approached.

'Report,' Anditz ordered.

'Three guards eliminated. All relatively easily. I'd venture that they're running out of experienced fighters, sir.'

Anditz looked down at the corpse of the cultist at his feet. Young and inexperienced. That was what the enemy was left with now. Or at least the humanoid forces. There were plenty of the nightmare xenos that they'd called down.

'Do you think it's what they expected, sir?' Morton asked.

'What do you mean?'

'The cultists, sir. Do you think they knew it was tyranid monsters they were bringing here?'

Anditz shook his head. The aliens that had fallen across Lazulai hadn't discriminated between humans and cultists in their attack. 'I don't know. Captain Nkosi still thinks there's a chance they could be controlling the aliens from the mine.'

Morton remained respectfully silent. The idea that anyone or anything could control the tyranids seemed preposterous. They both knew it, and they both knew that Nkosi knew it too. But to the troops, the chance that this strike could do something big mattered. After grinding months of war and dwindling supplies, hope was their most powerful motivator.

'Whatever the case,' Anditz said, 'today we'll destroy the last cultist stronghold, and any leaders along with it.'

Morton nodded.

'And if nothing else, it'll stop their blasted broadcasts.'

Morton gave a half-smile. 'Worth the odds in my book.'

'*Lieutenant Anditz.*' Sergeant Dolor's voice buzzed in Anditz's comm-bead. '*Corporal Barette has reported in. No further sentries found. We are clear to breach.*'

Anditz and Morton made their way down the bluff towards the rest of the platoon. Spore eddies chased around their ankles and the air tasted gritty and organic. Anditz noticed purple spikes of plant growth extruding through the sand at intervals. It didn't look like native Lazulaian flora.

'That felt too easy, sir,' Morton said.

Anditz grunted. 'I know. But remember, Opal Bastion's pinned. The enemy won't be expecting us to come at them with a full platoon.'

'They underestimated the captain.'

'Nobody ever does that more than once.' Anditz smiled wryly. Born and raised in Cadia's crucible, Captain Nkosi was a woman unfazed by overwhelming odds. But although she had taken the gamble of launching the assault, it was now down to Anditz to make sure it paid off. As he and Morton approached the platoon, the waiting soldiers stood to attention. Even after the months of fighting they were disciplined professionals. Each one of them worth ten of any other regiment, Anditz thought.

'Troops,' he addressed them, meeting the eye of each Cadian. 'We will now descend into Var Mine to neutralise the leadership of the xenos cult. Sergeant Morton's breach team will clear a path. I will then lead the assault team to eliminate our targets. Corporal Barette's support team will defend the rear and facilitate evacuation. Understood?'

'Sir,' the soldiers barked in unison.

Anditz nodded. 'This mission will be dark. Voxes off.' Then he moved into the large box-cage of the lift, his soldiers filing in behind him. There would easily have been room for another platoon in the cage, designed as it was to carry workers and machines into and out of the mine. Not that they had another platoon.

They had found early on in the war that when they were underground, the resonances of Lazulai's mines not only twisted communications, but also the frequencies could alert the enemy to their location. For this mission they would be reliant on visual signals, along with their recollection of the mine's layout – every soldier had memorised the plans ahead of the mission.

Barette strode into the lift last. She was young and wiry with a shock of red hair she bound back tightly. She gave the terrain outside one last scan, then slid the heavy mesh door across. The lift juddered and started to descend. The open walls moved past them, the impossible striations of diamond and emerald casting soft washes of colour across his comrades' faces beneath the lift's lumens.

A long time ago, whoever lived on this planet had done something unnatural to Lazulai's mantle to force the growth of rare minerals. A kaleidoscope of jewels had thrust their way through whatever indigenous rock had originally formed the earth, bursting seams for themselves like crystalline worms tunnelling across the planet, forcing aside duller geologies in their gaudy wake.

Magos Reiner Stuhl had called it geoforming. He had amused himself by saying that Lazulai was the Imperium's only gem world. The mad bastard was probably dead now. He'd refused to evacuate his archeotech excavation site when Captain Nkosi's battalion had fallen back from the xenos-infested eastern territories several months ago. He was most likely now rotting in the ancient dome he'd guarded so jealously.

Sergeant Dolor cleared her throat. She stood beside Anditz, hands clasped behind her back as the lift jolted downward. She was a tough soldier, experienced and brash. A scar that would have made a Catachan proud ran up her jaw and onto her cheek.

'Quiet down here, sir,' she said. 'I don't like it.'

She was right. You could almost feel the tons of minerals above, the thickness of the silence oppressive. The air was damp, but cooler than the surface.

'No noise, no spores,' Anditz said.

Dolor gave a throaty laugh. They were all increasingly irritated by the matter that drifted like mycelial shoals across Lazulai's surface, but some suffered worse than others. Dolor had been in and out of the infirmary with chest infections the past month, like many of the others.

'Something to be thankful for, sir,' she said. She glanced at the rockface moving past. 'Why'd you think it's all gems, sir?

You'd think if you were picking what the world was made of, you'd have picked something useful. Crude promethium, something like that.'

Anditz understood Dolor's point, but Lazulai's Ecclesiarchy had certainly found the gems useful. The planet was famed for its devotional ornaments and liturgical jewellery, and its soaring cathedrals of rubies and emeralds attracted pilgrims from great distances. Life was easier here than on other worlds, or had been for many, at least. Perhaps that was why the xenos had struck, infiltrating the miners and the Church, not to mention the gemworkers. It was a perversion, that the filthy hands of xenos mutants and collaborators had wrought the bejewelled thuribles and pendants exported to the cathedrals of a thousand Imperial worlds.

Anditz's eyes had just been starting to adjust to the dark when the lift cage started to slow, grinding to a halt as they reached the entry stope. Corporal Barette pulled the mesh door open and gave a silent signal.

Sergeant Morton gave Anditz a nod, then led the breach team out into the darkness. In a few moments, Anditz would lead the assault team after them. Morton's team would be sweeping ahead, disassembling any explosive traps left out by the xenos-worshipping cultists. The enemy likely wouldn't have left anything too serious for fear of damaging their own command, but given prior experience, they were likely to have left a few unpleasant surprises for trespassers.

Anditz gestured for his assault team to take their positions, and he moved out of the lift with them fanning out ahead. He positioned himself where he had visuals on his soldiers. They crouched in the pools of shadow between the stark strip-lumens that hung at intervals along the cavernous space, waiting silently for his signal. Back by the lift shaft, Corporal Barette's support team held the entrance cavern to the second level. They had plenty of cover back there from the towering mining machines that stood silent, drills and grinders idle. Without exception, the hulking juggernauts of steel had been defaced with cultic symbols that had turned Anditz's stomach.

He crouched with his back to an impossibly striated wall of diamond and emerald. He was acutely aware of every one of the Cadian 82nd under his command, each of those human lives a diminishing and precious resource on this benighted world. Each of them on this mission his personal responsibility.

There was a brief flicker of lumen-light from the tunnel ahead, the signal from the breach squad that they were clear to proceed. Anditz felt a flare of adrenaline. He'd led his soldiers through the long months of conflict against the enemy in the open field, but this was different. Anything could be around the corners here. The cultists had been relentless opponents, and many of them twisted in form, but Lazulai was now infested with other, more unnatural things. Things you did not want to be trapped underground with.

Anditz gestured for his squad to follow. Eight silent shadows detached themselves from the darkness and padded down the corridor in tight formation, lasguns aimed ahead.

The breach team crouched at the entrance to the first chamber. Rising through the quiet, the muffled sound of the cultists' conversations and laughter was just audible on the other side of the metal section wall. Anditz thought he could hear music. He pulled on a rebreather and his team followed suit. If their intelligence was correct, it would not be cannon-fodder on the other side of the door, but the leaders of the operation, grown complacent since their push to apparent victory. Whatever heretical celebration was taking place was about to be brought to an abrupt end.

Anditz pulled a smoke grenade from a webbing pouch and nodded to the trooper positioned by the door. Grim-faced, she slid the hatch open. Anditz tossed in the grenade, which was already gouting out noxious clouds of grey smoke. He glimpsed a brief flash of figures backed by purple hangings and jewelled shrines before he ducked back, and the trooper slammed the hatch shut.

Anditz gestured the location of the targets he'd sighted to his assault team. They slipped into the confusion and began to systematically neutralise the cult's elite members.

Anditz moved forward through the chamber, ignoring the screams and shots either side of him. His own objective was to take out the leader, a swollen-headed twist with a honeyed tongue. He'd studied enough intel-vids to recognise the shadowy figure at the back of the room, holding court on an emerald throne.

The remaining cultists were screaming in fury or terror, running amok in their flowing finery or various stages of undress and knocking over glasses of amasec. Anditz advanced on his target methodically, weapon raised. He shot a few cultists who hove into his line of sight – a spindly figure in cerise velvet who brandished a needle pistol and a bulky man in gunmetal taffeta shouting something incomprehensible about bloodlines. He aimed his weapon at the target's ridged cranium, but before he could fire, something barrelled into him from the left, knocking him to the floor. He rolled onto an embroidered carpet and ducked up into a crouch. His assailant hurled herself at him again with a snarl of silk and a hard knuckle-full of diamonds. Anditz brought the butt of his laspistol up and struck his dark-haired attacker in the temple. She collapsed, unconscious, a slim dagger dropping from her fingers.

Anditz scanned the room for his target, but the leader was

nowhere to be seen. He must have retreated back to the second chamber, now firmly secured behind a heavy blast door. The smoke was clearing, revealing the opulent wreckage of the cult's inner sanctum. Glasses of amasec sat undrunk or broken around the damask-covered benches. It was a far cry from the torn overalls and grimy goggles of the miners they had fought elsewhere on Lazulai. These were the planet's elite, the people who would have had the power to lower the world's defences and cut off communications when the day of rebellion came. He saw that one of the corpses was wearing the gold-fringed general's epaulettes of the planet's home regiment, all fallen to heresy. They had been at the top of the pile, and now they lay dead in their own blood and effluvia. Anditz's lip curled. Good.

'Emperor's Teeth,' muttered Sergeant Dolor, stepping up behind the lieutenant.

'Language, sergeant,' Anditz said, and turned to see what she'd been looking at.

Dolor was staring at a huge, hideous statue that leered over the chamber. Inhuman in aspect, it had four arms outstretched, and was rendered in pale moonstones and purple sapphires. The eyes were picked out in black onyx, and at the end of each limb were long, savage obsidian claws. Piles of jewels had been placed at its feet with colourful flowers and still-smoking incense.

'That's what they worship?'

One of the troopers spat. 'Doesn't look much like the ones that actually dropped out of the sky.'

'Focus. Clear the room and move to breach chamber two,' Anditz ordered, dragging his eyes away from the profane effigy.

'Sir, do you want this one dead or alive?' asked Sergeant Dolor, rolling over Anditz's unconscious attacker with the toe of her boot. The woman's painted, fine-featured face was familiar.

Anditz frowned. 'I recognise her. That's one of the propagandists.'

'The one from their broadcasts?' Dolor sneered. 'I'd be glad to shut her up for good.'

'No,' he said. 'She's been on the inside since the uprising.' He looked down at the familiar face. This cultist had appeared early on, urging Lazulai's human population to rebel against the Imperium. It soon became apparent that she'd just been a human front for the xenos cult, as more warped and shadowy propagandists emerged from the shadows with vox-scramblers and comm-hackers and powerful, persuasive words that turned people to their will. But she could be a source of tactical information.

'Have the support team evacuate her for interrogation,' Anditz ordered.

'Sir,' Dolor acknowledged.

'Eyes on me,' Anditz ordered. 'They're expecting us now. Clear for breach team.'

The assault team formed up, guns aimed at the heavy door as two of the breach team advanced, carrying a melta charge between them. It clunked as they mag-locked it to the metal section door's lock. One of the troopers cranked the start handle, and the other pulled the ignition pin.

'Clear!' shouted Anditz as the soldiers beat to cover.

There was a hiss as the activated melta boiled away the water in the air, then the blast came. The charge punched through the lock, smelting a skull-sized hole in the door, which swung loosely inward.

Anditz moved cautiously forward into darkness. Above him soared a cavernous ceiling, glimmering with sprays of emerald stars forming unfamiliar constellations. The chamber was lit by candles grouped in their dozens, each as thick as a human neck. Blinking, Anditz's eyes adjusted to the flickering light. A jade trough stood to one side of the chamber, the exquisite stone cradling a charnel horror of glistening offal. Embroideries of the cult's standard draped the walls. Anditz's target stood in the centre of the room, breathing heavily and leaning on a gold staff.

'You desecrate the true emperor's temple,' he said, his voice deep and melodic.

'A little more blood won't hurt,' said Anditz, raising his gun to the heretic's swollen brow.

'You would kill me so recklessly?' the heretic said. 'Don't you wish to know our secrets? Learn our objectives? Gain some tactical advantage?' He paused, looking into Anditz's eyes.

Anditz wrestled with the question for a moment, his thoughts fuzzy in his brain. Gain tactical advantage. That was the right thing to do. That was why he was here. He noticed a spatter of blood at the man's feet, strangely reflective in the flickering light. He must have been clipped in the firefight.

Anditz gestured for his troops to hold position. They flanked him, weapons raised. He forced himself to focus. His thoughts felt slow.

'If you have any secrets, witch, you'd better share them now. And don't think about trying anything. There are twenty lasguns aimed at your head, ready to blow you straight into the warp.'

The leader made a moue. 'Come now. I only sense nine little souls in here, lieutenant, including yours.'

Anditz gripped his gun more tightly.

'Despite this,' the leader continued, 'I feel sorry for you. Because you cannot hear them.'

'Who?' Anditz asked through gritted teeth.

The man smiled. The flickering candlelight revealed strange architectures of bone under his skin. 'The star children. Their voices are so beautiful. They have shown me the light of distant stars, the resonances of other galaxies.'

'You're talking about the xenos destroying Lazulai?' The monsters who had slaughtered whole regiments of his comrades.

'Destroying?' The man seemed amused. 'The Imperium does that quite well enough itself, I think. No, they are rebuilding.'

'Why are you collaborating with them?'

'We are brief. They are eternal. Through their eyes I have walked on the shores of metal seas and danced under diamond rains. Can your Corpse-Lord promise such ecstasy?'

'Sir,' Sergeant Dolor said from behind him. There was disgust in her tone, undercut with fear. Anditz shook himself. There was something irresistible about the man's words, something compelling in the harmonies.

He adjusted his grip on his gun. 'What is your function in the cult?'

'A humble servant. One of many.' His smile was ghastly, his fleshy lips flecked with blood. 'I am not afraid of death. For them, there is no such thing. This is why your agonies are futile.'

There was a sound like a sword being unsheathed, then a stifled scream.

Anditz spun, gun raised. He saw Dolor drop to her knees with her hands around her neck, blood gouting from in between her fingers. Her eyes were wide as she gasped for breath.

The breach team were already firing into the cavernous ceiling.

'What was it?' yelled Anditz.

''Stealer, sir,' one soldier replied.

There was a creeping stench of ozone, and Dolor fell forward, beyond help. Anditz felt his hair stand on end, and instinctively he turned back to the leader.

The man stood twenty feet away, his hand raised towards Anditz. His jaw hung loose in a silent scream and his eyes had misted over. Greasy coils of smoke roiled around his ankles, and the edges of his robe had started to scorch. Anditz pulled his trigger, but nothing happened. A misfire? He frowned and pulled again. Nothing. He glanced at his hand as he fired, and despite what his brain told him his fingers were doing, they were immobile. Through the chill of the mine, sweat beaded on Anditz's forehead as he strained to fire his gun, but his hand was frozen motionless. He glanced beside him to see his soldiers staring at their guns in confusion.

Filaments of light sparked around the leader's hands now. The witch was manipulating them. Anditz started sprinting towards the psyker a split second after the troopers beside him had the same thought. The two Cadians slammed into the psyker first, knocking the wounded abomination to the ground. As soon as they touched him, there was a popping sound, and simultaneously their heads peeled open like seed pods. The skin and skulls opened instantly as if they were segmented flowers, their glistening brains revealed inside like an obscene fruit. The soldiers didn't scream, just toppled to the floor silently, their open skulls presenting their encephalous harvest to their horrified comrades.

Anditz felt the fog of shock start to descend. The psyker lay on the floor, howling, apparently wounded by his own attack. Smoke rose from his eye sockets now, his mouth a smear of blood. As if in a dream, Anditz raised his laspistol and fired. Now the freak's line of sight was broken, the weapon cracked readily, burning a fist-sized hole through the distended cranium. The cultist shuddered to a stop immediately and lay still.

Anditz felt his heart pounding in his chest. He tried not to look at the profane remains of the soldiers. 'Back out of the chamber, slowly.'

The star lights above them flickered. Anditz glanced up. There was the hint of a dark shadow moving above them. Instinctively, he swung his weapon up and fired.

There was a strange hiss, almost like the absence of sound, and something dropped on the ground six feet away from Anditz, rolling into a crouch with its scythe-claws raised and needle-teeth bared. It was humanoid in shape, but with too many limbs and a hideously distorted skull. It was unmistakably a genestealer.

Its worshippers had placed garlands of perfumed flowers around its neck and set bangles of hammered gold and diamond around its purple limbs. Its talons were still reddened with Dolor's blood. Anditz saw all this in a brief flash as the horror launched itself at him. He barely had the chance to dive away to the left before a searing cone of fire blasted past his right-hand side.

With a roar, one of his troopers was advancing on his attacker, flamer gouting burning promethium. The xenos thrashed in the flames. Ignoring the pain where the flamer had licked near to his ribs, Anditz raised his lasrifle and joined the rest of the soldiers firing at the genestealer. They continued to shoot long after the thing had stopped moving, until Anditz gestured for them to stop.

'You nearly cooked your commanding officer, Kai,' he remarked to the trooper wielding the flamer.

'Apologies, sir,' she said, wiping away a bead of sweat on her forehead.

He glanced at the charred remains of the 'stealer. 'None required. Now' – he pitched his voice to the rest of the assault team – 'prepare to move out. Get me the support team. We're taking Sergeant Dolor's remains with us.'

'What about Brynt and Rugman?' a trooper asked, nervously gesturing at the remains of the Cadians desecrated by the psyker.

'We can't risk the witch-taint. We'll cremate them here. Kai, give me your flamer.'

Anditz caught an expression of relief on the soldier's face that the duty wasn't going to fall to her.

He turned so that she wouldn't see the grief on his.

Anditz was leading the troops back through the first chamber when a burst of static came over the vox. He frowned at the break in protocol. He'd not lifted the prohibition on communications.

'Breach team reporting. There's something coming up the far lift shaft, sir,' came Sergeant Morton's voice.

'Do you have a visual?'

'No, sir. Support team is clear, breach team moving to intercept.'

'Direction of attack?'

'The lower sump. Throne, it sounds big.'

'Take cover, sergeant, my assault team is incoming.'

'Sir, I think it's the Old Hand.'

Anditz detected unfamiliar concern in Sergeant Morton's voice. 'The Old Hand' was the nickname the troops had given to a massive xenos that had been captured on surveillance picts from the uprising.

There was a burst of lasgun fire and screaming. Anditz heard it both through the vox and echoing through the cavern up ahead.

'Prepare for contact,' he called to his assault team. 'Follow my lead.' He drew a grenade. 'Frag out,' he said, scudding the explosive around the corner. It detonated with a roar somewhere in the lift shaft ahead.

There was a tremor that they felt rather than heard, and a rush of dread. Anditz gritted his teeth. It reminded him of the everyday horror of Lazulai's churning skies, but amplified. This was cold, directed hate, vast and ancient.

'It's coming out of the shaft!'

He readied his laspistol and charged around the corner.

The breach team was assembled, facing the lift shaft, positioned in whatever cover they could find. Anditz did his best to suppress the rising horror in his stomach.

The xenos was emerging from the lift shaft in the sickly flickering of damaged lumens. An elongated skull rose from the darkness, damaged on one side where the frag grenade blast had hit, but still with one bright yellow eye glowering at the assembled soldiers.

'Do not make eye contact!' Anditz yelled over the vox. But it was too late. Two of the soldiers closest to the lift shaft froze under the power of its psychic glare and the alien easily batted them over the edge to their deaths.

After a split second of shocked silence, the remaining soldiers began to fire. But the xenos had already leapt, its huge bulk soaring out of the shaft with hideous agility. Anditz had a brief impression of veined, leathery flesh and a chitin-bladed spine before it landed in the corridor, loose diamonds skittering beneath its claws. The thing was three or four times the size of a regular 'stealer. It exuded cold implacability. Anditz would much rather it was snarling or growling like a normal animal rather than moving towards them with the inevitability of a drowning tide.

'Flamers, advance!' roared Anditz.

Troopers Kai and Tyren stepped forward, their weapons spitting furious gouts of burning promethium at the xenos. The gems on the walls glinted in the sudden flare of firelight and the flames licked at the monster's chitinous lower limbs. A stench of burning hair and chemicals permeated Anditz's rebreather, but the alien seemed unperturbed. It slashed at Kai, almost lazily, with obsidian talons as long as a human's arm. With one casual flick it disembowelled her. She dropped onto her knees, flamer stuttering out as she vomited blood. Tyren screamed in fury and roared forward with her weapon, the heat of the promethium blast raising bubbles in the monster's chitinous plating. But it was too fast. It leapt easily over her head, evading the flamer fire, and impaled Tyren before she could turn. It moved like an aquatic predator underwater, not in a way that any land creature should be able to move, certainly not with the bulk and armour plating this creature had.

'Breach team, hold the line! Assault team, fall back!' Anditz shouted. If any of them were going to get out alive, sacrifices would have to be made. He was going to get as many of his soldiers out as possible.

Anditz turned and ran back to the mine's entry cavern, where the digging machines stood silent.

'What are your orders, sir?' asked one of the troopers who'd followed.

Anditz turned. He was already halfway into the cab of one of the mining engines. 'Get out and wait with the support team. If you hear anything coming up the shaft that doesn't sound like a soldier, blow the whole mine and get back to the bastion.'

'Understood, sir.'

Anditz slid down into the cockpit of the battered machine. Even from inside the heavy vehicle, he could hear the screams and desperate shots of his soldiers up ahead.

'Focus,' he muttered to himself and examined the controls in front of him. The vehicle was a rockgrinder, designed to crack mineral seams and bore through bedrock. It was also the favoured transport of the cultists, who had adopted it as a war machine. Fortunately, this meant that the ever-ready Cadian command had briefed their soldiers on its operation.

Anditz urgently spoke the few words of awakening he'd overheard tech-priests use and the machine growled into life at his touch. Despite the cult's defacement, its spirit was apparently on the Imperium's side. Anditz spun up the grinder array. The saw-toothed drilldozer columns on the vehicle's front ram began to ramp up to speed, each standing almost as high as a person.

Anditz sent the machine snarling forward, slowly at first, then faster.

'Get clear!' he yelled over the vox to his platoon. There was no room to manoeuvre as the corridor narrowed on the approach to the shaft entrance, where the xenos was dismembering his remaining troopers.

The rockgrinder's lumens cast the gruesome tableau ahead into sharp relief. The xenos turned at the vehicle's thunderous approach. It reared, roaring a silent blast. Anditz saw Sergeant Morton flatten himself into a narrow crevice small enough to shelter a human from the mining vehicle's path, but insufficient for the Old Hand. The monster was trapped now. Unless Anditz reversed the rockgrinder, the xenos' only means of escape from the vehicle's serried saws and grinders was down the vertical mineshaft. He was going to drive the monster down the lift shaft and send his vehicle hurtling down after it.

'You and me are both ending here, you bastard.' He gritted his teeth.

The xenos knew it was trapped. Anditz could feel something scratching at his consciousness. He knew it must be the thing in front of him, but it felt somehow vast, and as cold as the vacuum of space, a malign tunnel into infinity. It was trying to find a way in, and Anditz knew given time, it would. He felt a warm drip of blood from his nose as the psychic pressure built in his head.

He threw the vehicle forward at top speed. There was nothing more he could do. It was in the Emperor's hands now.

Time seemed to slow as the vehicle approached the yawning lift shaft. The xenos turned, its motion fluid as it threw itself back down the yawning chasm from where it had emerged to escape the rockgrinder. The vehicle tilted forward as its wheels ran out of solid ground and tipped over into the blackness.

Anditz felt detached from the violent end he was about to face, although he wished he hadn't studied the mine's plans quite so closely and wasn't quite so aware of exactly how many yards the fall would be.

And then his head cracked into the console as he was thrown out of his seat. Dazed, he raised a hand to his nose. It was bleeding, but the pain suggested it was now from the impact rather than the incomprehensible will of an alien mind.

Warning alarms blared and rune-lights flashed around the vehicle's cabin as the engine choked to a halt.

He wasn't falling any more.

He scrambled over to the vision slit's duraglass screen. The xenos was pinned between the rockgrinder's ram and the several tons of plasteel mining lift that had rushed up to meet it. It was writhing, powerful limbs thrashing as it tried to free itself. It didn't express pain or make a sound, but moved with an unnatural, horrible focus that a living thing so terribly crushed shouldn't have been able to muster.

Anditz's stomach flipped at the sight of it. It was far, far too close to him for comfort. He moved to the controls. He had to work quickly. He wasn't sure the extent to which the lift was solely halting the vehicle's descent, or if the bulk of the rockgrinder had wedged itself in the narrow shaft. Either way, he was about to restart the bone-shaking engines that could risk rattling it loose. At least if he went, he knew he was taking this monstrosity with him.

'Suffer, beast,' he growled and once again called on the machine's spirit. After a nerve-wrenching stutter, it roared to life and its enormous drilldozer blades started to grind into the alien's chitinous flesh, spattering the vision slit with ichor.

Anditz was turning to clamber out of the vehicle when a huge talon smashed through the duraglass and into the cabin.

'Throne,' he swore, scrambling skyward and up and out through the vehicle's rear access hatch.

The back of the rockgrinder was lodged about five feet below the lift shaft's mouth. The roaring engine and sound of pulverising flesh and gristle beneath filled the shaft, along with the putrid stench of xenos offal and greasy smoke.

Anditz was scrabbling for a handhold to climb out when the vehicle lurched downward by another foot. He urgently ran his hands over the stone, feeling for any texture to grip, but the walls were smooth. How had the monster done it? He reached for the hilt of his power sword to act as a piton.

'Sir,' came a familiar, clipped voice.

Sergeant Morton appeared at the opening, arm outstretched.

'You took your time,' Anditz remarked, gripping the soldier's hand, and relieved his ancient weapon had been saved the indignity of acting as a foothold.

'Is it dead?' Morton asked as Anditz scrambled over the edge.

'By all rights. But I want to be absolutely certain. We're going to blow the mine. Any other survivors from your team?'

The sergeant shook his head.

Anditz gripped his shoulder. 'We'll burn this place for them, and for the Emperor.'

'Yes, sir.'

Corporal Barette and the remainder of the support team waited on the surface, grime-smeared and grim-faced.

'Get clear!' Anditz yelled, as the assault teams started pulling krak grenades from their packs and proceeding to the mine's mouth.

'Opal Bastion isn't responding, sir,' Corporal Barette replied as her troopers began to move the unconscious prisoner and the body of Sergeant Dolor.

'Leave the sergeant,' Anditz said. 'There's no time. Get clear and attempt to make contact again.'

Barette nodded.

'Ready?' Anditz called to the assault team. 'Drop.'

The soldiers pulled the pins of their grenades, tossed them into the mouth of the mine and then turned and sprinted.

Behind Anditz, there was a roar as the krak grenades erupted. He flung himself forward, hands over his head as the explosives collapsed Var Mine onto itself, burying its horrors forever, and taking Dolor with it.

Anditz glanced around, ears ringing from the blast. As his soldiers picked themselves up, there was a sudden, long scream. Anditz raised his gun immediately, adrenaline pumping. The propagandist prisoner was conscious and was howling in apparent agony on her hands and knees, and other voices were joining hers from across a nearby ridge.

Anditz gestured to the troopers on their feet to follow him. Just on the other side of a rough scree, half a dozen cultists lay on the ground, some apparently catatonic, but all having dropped their weapons. Some shook, others vomited, and as the Cadians watched, one plunged his fingers into his eye socket and wrenched out his own eyeball. Another writhed on the ground like a worm, blood and saliva foaming from her mouth, before retching up a lump of her tongue.

'Cadia's Gate,' muttered one of the soldiers.

'Shoot them,' Anditz ordered.

'Looks like they were planning an ambush,' Sergeant Morton observed, gesturing at a heavy mining laser as he and Anditz walked back to the mine's entrance, the sound of las-fire cracking out behind them. 'What do you think happened, sir?'

'I'm not sure. 'Their...' Anditz hesitated, but was unable to find a better word. 'Their priest. Before I shot him, he said something about being able to hear them. The tyranids.'

'Was the Old Hand giving them orders?'

'If it was, it's not any more.' He looked at the propagandist prisoner. She sat quietly now, arms wrapped around her knees, staring expressionlessly ahead. 'Corporal Barette,' he said. 'Any word on the bastion?'

The corporal looked up from the vox-unit, grim-faced. 'Yes. They're being hit hard, sir. And surveillance says there's another aerial wave coming in. Orders are to beat it back to base.'

Anditz's heart sank. This had been a bittersweet victory. The cult might be in disarray, but the xenos monsters were still fighting and Opal Bastion had already weathered so much. Whatever was driving these monsters, they had yet to destroy it.

'Good work, troops,' he called. 'But there's no time to rest. The corporal tells me they're flailing around back at base without us.'

There were a few laughs at this, but Anditz could tell the remainder of the platoon was shaken.

'We've cut the cult's head off today. There's more fighting to do, and it won't be easy, but you've done what no other regiment could. You've gone into the enemy's lair and survived. You've done Cadia proud.' He nodded. 'Move out.'

It wasn't the homecoming that Anditz had hoped for his troops. The march back to Opal Bastion had taken half a day across what had previously been cult-held terrain. It was a slow trek through track-churned spoil and the ruins of former mining settlements.

They had seen a number of cultists along the way, some dead or unmoving, others frenzied, some attacking. None of the activity appeared especially coordinated.

The approach to the bastion revealed the extent of the onslaught their comrades had weathered. The trenches around the encampment were slick with blood and viscera, human and alien. Dead Cadians had been left where they'd fallen. Anditz felt uneasy. It was bad for morale, and not in line with Captain Nkosi's usual protocol. Nobody was even trying to recover the dead. What had happened?

The mood in the bastion was grim, the corridors all but empty. The soldiers' faces were hollow and grey. An attendant told Anditz that Captain Nkosi had been wounded. He led Anditz to the medicae bay where she was being treated. Someone had rigged up a makeshift screen to provide some privacy, and Anditz was ushered behind it.

He narrowly avoided baulking at the sight of his commander. Nkosi had lost an arm and a leg, the stumps wrapped up in stained bandages. Her skin was blanched and she breathed shallowly, but she held him with a sharp gaze.

'Sir,' he said.

'Lieutenant. Your mission to Var Mine was successful?'

'Yes, sir. We eliminated the cult's figurehead, and the xenos known as the Old Hand. The cult now appears to be in disarray. We also captured the propagandist known as Lamya DeShay.'

'Not the one who sings?' Nkosi shifted herself upright, grimacing.

Anditz didn't know if her expression was a response to pain, or the thought of the cult's constant, maddening vox-casts in praise of their heresy. 'Correct.'

'So, we've struck a blow against the cult, at least. The xenos invaders, however...' She cleared her throat and spat a small clot of blood into a dish beside her. 'You can see how that has gone. Going by the last attack at least, it seems that the inhuman aggressors are unaffected by the loss of the figurehead.'

'Can we request support from Cobalt Fortress?'

Nkosi made a wet sound that could have been a laugh. 'No.

General Kvelter has her own problems. Although she has sent orders for you personally, lieutenant.'

'Sir?' Anditz frowned. He had never served under the general directly.

'Well, technically any soldier who served in the eastern detachment. But as I understand that Sergeant Dolor was lost in action, and the other is myself, you remain the only sensible choice. Your orders are to escort a covert infiltration team to Magos Reiner Stuhl's excavation facility.'

'The tech-priest who refused to evacuate?'

'Yes.'

'Sir, I believe the working assumption is that he's dead.'

'Correct. He is not of interest, but an asset at his facility is. I can't tell you anything more because I don't know anything more.' Nkosi paused. 'But I get the impression that this asset could change the fate of the war. Perhaps even this world.'

'Sir?' A little thread of hope wormed its way through Anditz's heart. If there was something they could do, something that would allow them to fight back – that would change everything. 'It must be a weapon,' he said, frowning.

'All I can tell you is that we've been issued these orders from sector command. And that there's no greater priority operation.'

'Understood.' Anditz nodded. But he saw a glimmer in the captain's eyes. He was sure she suspected the same as he did.

Nkosi coughed, her lungs bubbling. 'Surveillance suggests the xenos are massing. There's something like a wave sweeping across the continent. Communications from spotter planes have been going dark as it reaches them. We're anticipating it will arrive here in the next few hours. Based on the current trajectory, command thinks it will just clip us and it's going to hit Cobalt directly. But I'd rather be ready for the worst.'

'I'll brief the troops, sir.'

'Lieutenant.' Nkosi gave him a hard stare. 'You are this outpost's most important asset now. Do you understand what that means?'

'Yes, sir,' Anditz said, although the idea was jarring. No one soldier ever mattered more than the rest, they were all simply parts of the Imperium's war engine.

'Do you?' The wounded captain struggled to raise herself up. 'Because even if command is right and this wave doesn't hit us, another one will. This bastion won't last long, but you can still be of service.'

Anditz felt a twinge of dismay to hear the formerly indefatigable Nkosi speak this way. 'There's still a chance, sir. We can hold on, support could still make it from elsewhere.'

Nkosi ignored that. 'If there is any sign that the bastion might fall, you are to secure yourself in the vaults. Do you understand?'

The vaults were barely ten feet square and had originally been built to protect the highest-grade gems from potential shaft collapse or theft. The Cadians had used it to store volatile munitions, and currently it was where the cultist prisoner was chained. It was secured by two heavy blast doors built to withstand rockfall.

'Yes.'

Nkosi grunted. 'That order supersedes all others.'

'Understood, sir.' It rested heavy on him, but the stakes were higher than the honour of one soldier.

His captain suddenly looked exhausted. She lay back and nodded. 'You are in command. Do Cadia proud.'

'Sir.'

'And Anditz? Take what you find in that trunk with you.'

Frowning, he bent to open the trunk. His breath caught when he saw what was there. His regiment's greatest treasure.

'Keep it safe. Keep Cadia alive,' Nkosi said.

'Always, sir,' Anditz said.

He saluted and left his commander to take what rest remained to her.

CHAPTER THREE

'You'd think,' Sergeant Rutger Haruto said, 'that by now we'd have had a little more intelligence on the xenos.' He was sitting at a large table in the fortress' strategium examining the spread contents of the file General Kvelter had handed Khan. 'This is nonsense, and half of it's redacted anyway.' He threw the sheaf of parchment he had been reading down onto the table.

Khan regarded her sergeant with a wry smile. He tended to be most cantankerous just before he solved a problem. Haruto carefully removed his eyeglass and held it delicately in one massive hand as he wearily rubbed his remaining organic eye. Without wearing a lens, his bionic defocused when he read.

'Have you selected the squad yet?'

'Mostly.' Khan placed down the knife she'd been sharpening. 'I've one slot left. It has to be the right balance.'

He nodded. 'Still just bringing six?'

'Yes. We've got to keep it small if we're going to stay under the xenos' auspex. And don't forget we'll be carrying the cog-whisperer too.'

'Adair still on the list?' he asked.

'I know you don't rate her,' Khan said. 'But she's the kind of trouble we're going to need.'

'She's trouble full stop.'

'It's my call. I say she's what we need.'

Haruto shrugged. 'Fine. But Kvelter's set march-out for tonight.'

'I'll have my team by then.' Khan pulled out a cheroot. 'Do you have our route yet?'

He gestured at a map amongst the papers. 'Given the geography, we won't do better than this. We'll march out with the main convoy, then break off here and follow the canyon east out to Opal Bastion to rendezvous with the Cadian liaison officer. The remainder of the force will continue north, as if they were heading to reinforce Jasper Fortress.'

Khan rose from where she was seated to examine the map. 'Kvelter said something big is moving in our direction. A mega-swarm. Do we risk them cutting us off?'

'I disagree with the extrapolations that command has made about the trajectory. If we follow their estimates, I reckon we'll lose a day.' Haruto tapped the map. 'We have to get out in front of the wave, and I think we should go this way.'

Khan nodded. The stakes were as high as they could possibly be, the price of failure unimaginable. But she'd take Haruto's instinct over the scryings of a quill-pusher far from the battle-field any day.

'The xenos will hit Kvelter's force while we're down in the canyon,' he continued.

'And then we're out into the open?'

Haruto gestured noncommittally. 'It was open when these

picts were taken. But the last scout reports suggest there's been significant shifts in the terrain. They mentioned abnormal plant growth.'

'No further specifics?'

'No.'

Khan nodded. She'd seen enough of the enemy's spore growths to imagine what might have happened elsewhere. Perhaps Kvelter wasn't exaggerating when she said there'd be a jungle. Serrated corruptions of native flora had begun to thrust themselves out of the field of corpses outside the fortress.

'Xenos cult activity?' she asked Haruto.

'Concentrated around industrial areas. Opal Bastion's last dispatch stated there'd been further disruption to cult activity. We should expect them to be less coordinated but more unpredictable. No clear estimate on numbers.'

'So, we're striking out into unknown terrain against unknown forces?'

'In brief, yes.'

Khan grunted. 'Beats sitting around here.'

There was a knock at the door.

'Enter,' Khan called.

The slight woman who swept into the briefing room was unmistakably of the Adeptus Mechanicus. The red robe would have been clue enough, but the mechadendrite cables coiling around her thick locs of hair confirmed it.

'Tech-Adept Nefeli Wrathe?' Khan asked.

'Yes. And you are Major Wulf Khan.' Wrathe's voice was toneless and high, slightly distorted by the vox-grille covering the lower half of her face. 'Catachan veteran and decorated recipient of the Eagle Ordinary, the Triple Skull, the Ribbon Intrinsic and the Merit of Terra.'

'You've read my record,' Khan said.

'Preparation is imperative.' Wrathe cocked her head and moved towards Haruto's movement plans.

Haruto gave Khan a look.

'However, the projections sent by your command inaccurately describe the arc of enemy attack and additionally do not factor the ongoing effect of terrain differentiation caused by the xenos. You will need to make calibrations.'

Haruto folded his huge arms. 'I already did.'

Wrathe leaned forward to study the papers more closely. Khan wondered how she could see. The tech-adept's eyes were milky white, as if she were blind. A constellation of what looked like communication studs dappled her face – perhaps they allowed for visual input. She was just as superior as Khan had expected her to be.

Wrathe's vox-grille crackled in what Khan interpreted as a grudging grunt. 'Your calibrations appear to be within acceptable tolerances.'

'You're even more effusive than I expected,' Haruto said.

'How gratifying for you,' the tech-adept replied, and turned to Khan. 'I would brief you now, major. Alone.'

Smiling, Khan sat back and crossed her arms. She could play the role of diplomat when needed. 'Sergeant Haruto is my second. Given the risk of this undertaking, my preference would be for you to include him in this briefing.'

Wrathe nodded. 'In the interests of efficiency, I accede to your request, major.'

'Lazulai's dead,' Haruto said. 'Why the secrecy?'

'I would rather not disclose that.'

Khan watched the tech-priest closely. She was certain the adept knew more than she was letting on.

'The general mentioned an asset,' Khan said. She intentionally hadn't mentioned the word 'weapon' yet. She wanted the adept to tell her the truth of her own volition. 'An asset of significance to the Imperium. Something that you'd assume would have been removed long ago, before this world was beyond rescue. But it wasn't. So, I'm going to hazard a guess that your people didn't know it was there until recently.'

Wrathe didn't reply, but she held Khan's gaze.

Khan grunted. 'So, I'm right. This is salvage.'

Wrathe's vox-grille crackled. 'It isn't salvage. The riches of Lazulai pale into insignificance compared with what we seek.'

'Oh, I don't doubt it's significant. But significance is decided by bureaucrats.' Khan grinned coldly. 'My question is, is it *worth* it? Thousands of soldiers are about to give up their lives for it. My soldiers.'

Wrathe blinked. 'They are all soon to die anyway, major, along with this world. Any additional value they can leverage is evidently worthwhile.'

Haruto barked out a laugh and turned to the hooded woman. 'I'll put it differently. Is what we're recovering useful?'

She hesitated.

'Would I think it's useful?'

'Yes.'

'Really?'

Wrathe gestured frustration. 'You have been issued orders, major. I anticipated this briefing would merely comprise instructions regarding our progress and destination, not a discussion of the merits of the mission itself.'

Khan tilted her head to one side. 'Catachans are rather less like machines than you might imagine, Adept Wrathe. We don't simply follow instruction. We've got to believe that what we are doing makes sense. Just as our leaders are only those we believe that it makes sense to follow.'

'Your regiments are peculiar in this regard.'

Khan wasn't sure if it was a question or a statement, coming as it did from Wrathe's toneless vox-grille. 'Other regiments aren't like us, no. But then no other regiment could get you to where you want to go. Trust is everything where we come from, adept. If you're trusting us to escort you, then you can trust us with the truth.'

Wrathe looked at Khan for a moment with her strange eyes, then slipped a hand under her hood and a hum of white noise started up.

'What's that for?' Haruto asked.

'A precaution.' Wrathe spoke over the low sound apparently being generated by something mechanical inside her head. 'The xenos infiltrated deep into this world. Who knows where their agents placed vox-thieves?'

Khan waited patiently.

'I will tell you what I know. Then perhaps you will accept the significance of what we do. Perhaps this is a necessary condition for your operational success.' She smoothed her robe with her delicate silver-spindled fingers. It was a strangely human gesture. 'My mentor, Magos Reiner Stuhl, has been operating an excavation on Lazulai for a number of years. He was researching the geological phenomenon known as geoforming that took place on this world.'

'You mean the gem strata of the planet? That was all engineered?' Haruto asked.

'Yes. A work of mechanical genius.' There was a brightness to Wrathe's strange eyes.

Haruto watched her intently. 'Go on.'

'There is no natural geological process that would account for the particular strata of minerals evident here. Furthermore, Lazulai's precious stones show evidence of design. The absence of nitrogen in its diamonds, and the presence of synthetic inclusions, for example.'

Khan cut in before Haruto could ask any more questions.

The tyranids would have devoured all of them before he tired of exploring a new puzzle.

'And during excavations Stuhl found the device we're recovering? What is it?'

Wrathe turned to her. 'Uncertain. Magos Stuhl communicated to us that he had discovered something ancient, older than the world in its current form. After that, communication was lost.' She twisted a cuff at her wrist and held her hand palm down over the table. A weak hololith flickered onto the surface.

'What's this?' Khan leaned forward. The Martian glyphs depicted meant nothing to her.

Haruto was already craning over the image. 'Something to do with spores?' he asked the tech-adept.

'Yes. Magos Stuhl continued his experimentation after the xenos emerged on this world. He noted that certain operations of the archeotech resulted in the death of tyranid spores surrounding his compound.'

'Almost immediately by the looks of it,' Haruto said, tracing the symbol with one finger.

'It has anti-tyranid properties?' Khan said. This was significant by anyone's measures. She felt a sudden thrill. If they could hunt this device down, it could change everything, everywhere.

'I must stress that the message was brief, and the data not quantitative.' Wrathe hesitated. 'But there is a possibility. It was at this juncture of possibility that he contacted our faculty requesting extraction assistance.'

'When?'

'Six standard months ago.'

Khan crossed the room and picked up Haruto's map. 'The facility is in the eastern territories? There were troops stationed there six months ago. Why didn't he request assistance from the Astra Militarum?'

Wrathe inclined her head. 'Magos Stuhl was still working on decoding the working of the device. Had human soldiers learned of its properties they may have attempted to seize it and damaged it beyond repair. It was too significant a discovery to risk.'

Haruto frowned. 'He hid a weapon that could have saved Lazulai?'

'It is unclear as to whether it is a weapon, or indeed whether it could have changed the fate of this world at that point. What is more probable is that it could have been destroyed if exposed.'

'And you don't think he should have tried?' Khan said.

'No,' Wrathe said.

Haruto grunted. 'I agree.'

Khan raised an eyebrow at her sergeant.

'Think about it, sir. What it could mean for the Imperium. A weapon that could destroy the tyranids? It's worth a planet.'

'Your commanders also agreed,' Wrathe said.

'I see why command made this our priority. But I still don't agree with the call Stuhl made. He'll have to explain himself when we get to his compound.'

'That is unlikely.' Wrathe gripped her wrist again and the hololith flickered into non-existence. 'He has not made contact since his initial missive. Our working assumption is that he is dead.'

Her voice didn't change discernibly, nor did what was visible of her expression. But Khan felt something shift in her demeanour.

'So we don't know the status of the device?' Haruto said.

'No,' Wrathe replied.

'If we can get to it, what do we do with it?' Khan asked.

Wrathe's vox-grille crackled. 'We get it off Lazulai, to safety. Magos Stuhl will have had transport at the excavation site.'

Haruto gave a thin smile. 'That's an uncharacteristically simple answer, Adept Wrathe. It relies on us actually getting to the site alive, on the transport still being there and being functional, and on us being able to move the artefact.'

Wrathe regarded him. 'Yes.'

Khan shrugged. 'Like I said before, it's better than sitting around here.'

'I would ask that you keep the nature of this conversation in confidence,' Wrathe said as she reached inside her hood and quieted the vox-blocker. 'This is a sacred thing that we seek.'

Khan nodded. 'We're moving out at nightfall. If you'll excuse me, adept, I need to address my soldiers before we do so.'

'I will prepare,' Wrathe said, and left the room.

Khan and Haruto exchanged glances.

'Anti-tyranid properties,' Haruto said thoughtfully. 'Has to be a weapon.'

'We can't assume anything. I'll bet the adept knows, though.'

'Come on, sir,' Haruto said. 'Why else would command send us after it?'

Khan sniffed. 'Every order command sends down makes perfect sense, does it?'

Haruto shook his head. 'We might just have a chance, sir. This could change things.'

'We've got to get to it first, sergeant.' She pushed down the hope that had flared in her stomach. Anything that wasn't a gun in her hands was false optimism, and she was experienced enough to know that naive hope could kill just as quickly as the enemy.

The courtyard of Cobalt Fortress was full of life for the first time in months. Despite herself, Khan felt invigorated by the sights and sounds of battle preparations. Dozens of mighty war machines were being rolled out and attended to by tech-priests, who were anointing them with sacred unctions and oils and intoning prayers to slowly wake machine spirits. The thrum of engines and promethium haze within the soaring basalt-black of the fortress' crenellation-fanged courtyard made a mighty pulpit from which priests sang war-hymns.

The soldiers preparing to sally out were mainly Catachans and Cadians with a smattering of more obscure insignia and regimental standards on show. All troops had turned out as neatly presented and pressed as they could after siege conditions, proudly flying their colours. There was a buzz of conversation that brought everyone to life after the stultifying months of siege. Did these troops truly believe they were fighting for victory? Or, like the Catachans, were they simply invigorated by the thought of fighting? Khan passed a Cadian Sentinel unit, nodding to the commander as she strode by. Perhaps it didn't matter.

A cheer heralded her arrival at the Catachan line. At the head, ready to roll out, was a mighty Baneblade emblazoned with the colours of the Shrikes. Captain Thorne stood and saluted, and four hundred Catachan Jungle Fighters followed his lead, standing to attention in unison as Khan approached. Each soldier stood straight and true, chin up, chest out, dressed lightly in fatigues, red bandanas tied according to the custom of their home territories, each staring ahead.

Khan grinned. She could feel the bemusement of the other regiments around them. Until a moment ago, her Jungle Fighters had been behaving just as the others might have anticipated according to their various prejudices or expectations – smoking, fighting, laughing. But what the other regiments didn't realise was that Catachans could snap to just as well as any Cadian when they wanted. But nobody was entitled to this. You had to earn it.

Khan clambered up onto the Baneblade and Haruto handed her a vox-caster.

'Every one of you knows what it is to face death, and every one of you does it with the relish of a fighter forged on Catachan. The jungle made us, and the jungle will take us. But we'll give it a bloody good fight first,' she roared. 'Remember why it is the galaxy fears us, and the alien quakes in its boots as we approach.' She grinned. 'A Catachan Devil once stung our people's hero, Sly Marbo. After five days of agonising pain...' Khan let her words hang and gestured expectantly.

'The Catachan Devil died!' howled the Jungle Fighters in delight.

Khan laughed aloud as the Catachans cheered and slapped each other's shoulders, then she raised her hand and allowed her face to settle into a determined scowl. The Jungle Fighters fell silent.

'You all knew this day was coming.' She surveyed the faces in front of her. If she was going to send these soldiers to die, she'd try her damned hardest to look each one of them in the eye. 'And if today is the day the jungle calls us home, we will die with the enemy's blood on our teeth, with their guts in our fists and the stench of their fear in our lungs. Catachan Jungle Fighters!' she roared. 'Today you will show the God-Emperor Himself why you are the greatest warriors in the whole of His mighty Imperium! Today you will show your sister regiments why our people are feared across the galaxy! Today you will show the xenos what it means to die in terror!'

The roar of the Jungle Fighters thrummed in Khan's heart. She was proud of her soldiers, proud of their bravery. She looked out at the sweep of troops in front of her. They were far, far better than this damned planet deserved.

'Him-on-Terra is watching!' she shouted. 'Bring Him a blood tithe. Troops, dismissed.'

She handed the vox-caster back to Haruto and slid back down

the mighty tank. As her boots hit the ground there was a sharp crack next to her ear. She clapped her hands over her head and turned. A las-burn smoked in the side of the Baneblade, and sliding down the tank's side from the impact point was a half-melted xenos about the size of a fist. Frills of livid tissue hung out from one side, and it stank. Khan grimaced.

'Lucky miss,' Captain Thorne said, nodding at the mess. 'Those things started dropping about an hour ago. They eat directly into whatever they hit.'

'Who fired the shot?' Khan asked, glancing around.

'That would be Sniper Hasan, sir,' said Captain Thorne. 'Call-sign Ghost.' He pointed to a distant tower.

Of course it was, Khan thought. Nobody else in the regiment could have made that shot.

Occasionally, a person found that for one reason or another, they didn't quite fit into the community settlements on Cata-chan and preferred to take themselves into the jungle and face the horrors of the wild alone. Catachans were innately pragmatic, and if such a person survived and returned to society, their value was such that they were allowed to serve wherever they'd be of use. Hasan was one such Catachan who served his community by existing outside it.

'Find him and tell him to report to Sergeant Haruto. I have a job for him.'

Captain Thorne nodded.

Khan slapped the side of the tank. Ghost would complete her team. There was nothing more she could do now. She had the right people in the right places, and the dice would fall as they may.

Night fell quickly on Lazulai now. Whatever the xenos were doing in the atmosphere was causing the penumbral veil of dusk to drop with indecent haste. Braziers had been lit around Cobalt Fortress as the Astra Militarum forces made their final preparations, throwing the polished black stone into sharp chiaroscuro.

Khan sat atop the mighty Baneblade with her infiltration team. As far as anyone else knew, she'd be leading the Catachans from the front. But as soon as they reached the drop point, she'd quietly slip away and Captain Thorne would take control of the regiment, leading the troops into the great battle against the xenos. Thorne was a good leader and the soldiers trusted him, but if her troops were going to die, she should be leading them. That regret would sit with her for as long as she lived – although prevailing conditions on Lazulai suggested that wouldn't be long.

She caught Sergeant Haruto's eye and he nodded briskly, stony-faced as usual.

The tech-adept sat stiffly beside him, face unreadable behind the vox-filter that concealed her nose and mouth. Khan wondered how old she was. From what she could see behind the implants, her skin was smooth. She could be young, but you never knew with the Mechanicus. She looked fragile surrounded by Catachans, but then most humans did. Her skin was deep brown, unlike Haruto, who had burned badly when they first arrived in Lazulai's bright summer. She already suspected the two of them shared a common obstinacy of character. However, as much as Khan had clashed with her sergeant, at least she knew he was on her side. As far as Khan could tell, whose side the cog-worshippers were on depended on what suited their unknowable agendas. She'd have to watch their Mechanicus charge carefully.

Hasan, the Ghost Catachan, sat perched at the rear of the tank, camo shroud draped around him. He looked pensive, cheeks hollow. He reminded her of a captive raptor, tethered but never truly tame. Khan's own brother had been like Ghost, but he had gone out into the jungle and never come back. Perhaps he was still there, or perhaps it had swallowed him up. Khan knew Hasan would be uncomfortable with the crowds, with the machines that surrounded them. If Lazulai had really grown a jungle, the sniper would be more at home once they were in it.

Khan lit up a cheroot. The general discouraged the use of lho-leaf, but it seemed futile to consider quitting at the end of the world.

'Sir?' Trooper Adair's grinning, crew-cut head appeared from behind a sponson. 'Permission to come aboard?'

'Granted,' Khan said, one eyebrow raised.

Adair vaulted easily up onto the Baneblade, eschewing the ladder placed against the side.

'Reporting for 'nid-fragging duty, major.' She cracked off a sharp salute.

Khan took a drag on her cheroot. 'You faced down the enemy in the open field yet, trooper?'

Adair grinned wolfishly and flexed a powerful bicep to show the scratch tally tattooed there. It was sizeable. 'These are all vermin I crushed in the open, sir. I reckon it's not as satisfying if you're taking pot-shots from a wall.'

Khan blew out a plume of smoke. 'What counts is the killing, soldier. How exactly you frag 'em is a detail for the historitors.'

'Yessir!'

Khan jerked her head. 'Talk to the sergeant about getting read in on the mission.' She watched as Adair clambered over to Haruto and wondered if she'd been that much of a pain in the arse as a young hotshot.

The xenos in their locale had been suspiciously quiet over the past hours, she thought. Perhaps they were gravitating towards whatever wave of forces they were massing. Although how they coordinated themselves, nobody knew. Was it just a stampede?

A massive wave of predators following one another? Inaccurate as command's projections about the exact trajectory might be, to see the lights winking out across the continent was disconcerting.

In the velvet night sky, Lazulai's constellations were diminished by swirling rivers of light. They played across the firmament in curtains, shimmering green to white to pink as they eddied across the upper atmosphere. Soldiers who hadn't been posted topside might find the display beautiful, even sublime. But as soon as you realised what it was...

Khan tore her eyes away from the lights. This was no normal planetary aurora, but trillions of bioluminescent xenos spores flowing in shoals across the skies, an oppressive reminder of the enemy's pervasive presence. The lagoons of darkness that pooled in between the vivid billows of light provided moments of blessed reprieve, a small space where aliens *weren't*.

The hiss of static from a nearby vox-skull preceded the amplified blast of a clarion trumpet calling the assembled forces to attention. Flood-lumens illuminated General Kvelter as she strode out onto the courtyard balcony in full dress uniform. All eyes were on the commander, the steely Cadian whose resolution in the face of impossible odds had remained unshakeable. She leaned forward, lilac eyes burning, and bellowed into a vox-caster.

'Soldiers! He who gives His life for you on Terra today demands yours in return. Shall we allow our enemies to violate the sacred territory of humanity? Will you permit heretics to carry terror into the heart of the Imperium?

'You will not,' she roared. 'You will march to meet the xenos enemy, and you will tear victory from its jaws and show the galaxy what happens to those who dare defy humanity!'

A thump of fists and feet started up in the crowd, alongside a drumbeat.

Kvelter nodded and walked along the low battlements to ensure that all of the assembled troops could see her.

'Outside these walls lies death or glory. The enemy sweeps towards us, and we heed the cry for aid from our comrades at Jasper Fortress. They have fought well, but they do not have what we have.' Kvelter leaned forward, gripping the battlements, and bellowed out at each assembled regiment in turn. 'They don't have the Arcadian Forty-Seventh, the Cadian Two-Thousand-and-Twelfth, the Catachan Nine-Hundred-and-Third!'

Kvelter paused while each of those regiments raised their weapons and cheered before she continued.

'The Rigan Fourth, the Vulturine Eighteenth or the Savlar Twenty-Second!'

Each regiment shouted in turn as Kvelter called them out, some of the cheers larger than others depending on how many survivors remained. Kvelter pulled the vox-caster close to speak over the noise.

'Sisters, brothers, siblings. Hold the line. Stay with me. Today, the enemy awaits. We will drown them in a tide of blood!'

The troops roared, and for the first time in many months, the huge gates of Cobalt Fortress began to grind open.

Their blood or ours? Khan wondered. Kvelter had done a good job, the job she had to do. She needed to make the soldiers believe they were going to win. But it twisted Khan's gut to know it was a lie. A lie to send these fighters marching out as a shield for Khan's own squad. She felt alone amongst the cheering regiments, their battle cries a mortification on her conscience.

Focus on the fight ahead, she scolded herself. *Complete your mission, then you'll have time for guilt.*

A pack of Hellhounds growled out ahead of the force, arcing great gouts of fiery promethium from their inferno cannons to burn away the mess of corpses and dead xenos obstructing the crusade's path. Khan's Baneblade snarled to life, the ancient engine growling with a righteous thirst. Even though they were riding desant atop the mechanical leviathan, the power of the engine thrummed and rattled Khan's squad as they rolled forward out of the mighty gates.

Khan knew from experience what it was to crew such a beast. The sound of the engine, the clatter of shells and blast of the cannon were so powerful it almost manifested as a physical presence. It might seem oppressive to outsiders, but through the chaos of the sound, the stifling air heavy with sanctified oils, you found a harmony.

Ahead of them was the black sweep of night, glowing red with the rear lumens of the vehicles in front.

She noticed that across from her, Wrathe had closed her eyes and was gripping the handholds on the Baneblade tightly.

'What do you think of her?' Khan asked, pressing her commbead and speaking directly to the tech-adept.

Wrathe took a moment to reply. 'Sublime. The spirit of *Rising Devil* is strong and vengeful. And she is of the superior Mars pattern.'

Khan smiled. 'Catachans have earned names, so she does too. We call her *Ofelia's Fist*.'

'I noticed the dedication on the engine block. A former commander?'

'A driver. Trooper Ofelia Layke. Four generations ago, a Donorian clawed fiend gained ingress to her turret. It did not leave alive.'

'Such a beast could have done great harm to the machine.'

'And the crew. It killed Layke, but she buried her knife in its throat, stopping it from destroying the tank.'

'Then she will have earned the Omnissiah's favour that day,' Wrathe said. 'Will the vehicle's earned name ever change?'

'When someone does something better than Ofelia did.'

'And your earned name is?'

'Tusk,' Khan replied. 'Sergeant Haruto next to you is Viper, Sniper Hasan back here is Ghost, and Trooper Adair is Jet.'

'I predict there will be a lengthy, semi-mythologised narrative associated with each?'

Khan smiled. 'I see you're already getting to know us.'

A movement caught her eye. A squadron of Sentinels strode past in Cadian colours, flood-lumens coldly illuminating their path through the darkness. Their thumping, backward-jointed legs easily outpaced the slow, tracked grind of *Ofelia's Fist*. They were to scout ahead with the Hellhounds and establish a route for the main force. To *Ofelia's* left spread out the hundreds of soldiers and vehicles still remaining of the Cobalt Fortress Crusade Force, tiny stab-light beams each indicating the position of a soldier. Down to the right swept complete blackness, the ravine that Haruto had identified – the route by which her squad would, at the appropriate juncture, leave Kvelter's force. Khan's regiment led the right flank of the crusade, with *Ofelia's Fist* positioned on the far edge by the ravine so that Khan's squad could easily slip away when the time came.

Khan flicked her cheroot stub down over the edge of the tank onto the scorched ground. Despite being in the midst of a very loud, very visible battle force, it went against every Catachan instinct in her bones to leave any sort of trail. In the jungle, even a broken leaf could be tracked. Normally she'd have stubbed out her smoke and broken it down. But she wasn't about to extinguish a cheroot on a Baneblade's sacred chassis in front of a tech-adept. There were enough enemies ahead without making an additional one of their passenger. And perhaps, too, the old tank deserved better. It was a venerable relic that had been through hell and survived, something with which she felt a certain affinity.

Khan watched the little ember of light flicker away, the stub snuffed out under the boots of the marching soldiers, trodden down into the mud. There was no trace she'd been here, and soon perhaps there'd be no trace of humanity at all on Lazulai. She looked away into the darkness of the ravine. Only Him-on-Terra knew how it would end.

CHAPTER FOUR

It started with a sound like dead leaves. A whisper in the darkening gloom. The flood-lumens around Opal Bastion carved a hard lozenge of light from the darkness surrounding the small fortification. The pooled light was a small island of certainty, everything within normal and human. Outside, the unknown. And somewhere, the alien.

'Do you hear that, sir?' Sergeant Morton asked.

Anditz frowned and raised a noctis scope to his eye. He'd thought he'd heard something, but since the communications from the last spotter had gone dark, the vox had simply crackled out until it had broken down. The tension was so palpable the slightest sound or movement had the troops reaching for their weapons.

'Nothing on visual,' he replied.

Morton swallowed. 'Do you... feel something, sir? Something like back at Var Mine?'

Anditz stared out into the darkness. He knew what the sergeant meant. A dread hold that tightened around the heart, a fear beyond fear.

'Yes,' he said, gripping the edge of the bastion tower's battlements. He knew that they were out there, felt it. 'But until we have visual there's not much we can do.'

The whispering sound had grown louder, and was now undercut with a low drumming, almost below audibility.

'I don't like it, sir,' Morton muttered softly, so the patrolling soldiers wouldn't hear. 'If they've blocked the spotter, what's to say they can't interfere with visuals?'

'I don't think they blocked it so much as…' Anditz trailed off. He remembered the way the xenos had felt in the mine. The numbing horror at the cold, incomprehensible intelligence of something from beyond the void. The way that the Old Hand had moved through the air as if it were water, and how it had so easily directed his troops to die. Fear clenched at his hindbrain. A whisper from his subconscious reminded him, *We do not understand this enemy. We cannot even begin to understand the depths of our ignorance.* Anditz listened to the fear.

'Send up a starburst shell,' he ordered.

'Are you sure, lieutenant?' Sergeant Morton said, expression held respectfully neutral in response to his commanding officer's strange order. Ammunition was a precious commodity, and it was unthinkable to waste it for no apparent reason.

'Fire it north. And high. Set the fuse to detonate at the arc's zenith.' Anditz was acting on instinct. The pitch of the susurration had not changed, but something in the air was different. He felt it in his bones.

Whatever doubts the sergeant may have had, he carried out the order. They watched as the macrocannon growled round on its heavy metal turret. Anditz felt his heart thumping in his chest. With a mighty crump, the cannon fired a starburst shell high into the sky. He followed its path via the dim glow of heat and propellant on the shell casing. It arced into flurries of dimly flowing luminescent spores in the sky then exploded.

There was a burst of flame and a brief flash of white. Instead of illuminating simply empty plains and heaps of shingled tailings, the light flared into existence a flowing sea of living bone, a mass of horrors wrought of rictus jaws and osteoid carapaces so vast it stretched as far as the eye could see. It moved like a tide, one that would sweep over Opal Bastion as if it were a beetle in the path of a flood. The sight hit Anditz with a sickening lurch.

'Incoming!' he roared even as the shell's glow faded.

The Cadians moved as one, like a flesh-and-blood mirror of the bone and ichor surging towards them. They ran to their combat posts to defend the bastion's walls, readying ammunition and manning heavy bolter emplacements.

Something moved overhead, like a deathly pale, fluttering flag.

'Fire the macrocannon!' Anditz shouted.

CRACK!

Something hot struck Anditz in the cheek. He raised his hand to pull the shard of shrapnel from his face and felt cold shock at the sight of a splinter of bloodied bone in his hand. He turned to Sergeant Morton, but instead of the familiar features of his comrade, he was confronted with a mess of gristle atop his former soldier's shoulders. Morton's body still stood, hands gripped around the macrocannon's firing column.

Anditz felt as if the breath had been pulled from his lungs. The xenos had deployed some sort of projectile behind the macrocannon's gun shield. Numbly, Anditz dragged the corpse away from the gun chair and clambered in. Through the shield's vision slit he saw an incoming deluge of winged aliens.

'Aerial bombardment!' he shouted. He felt disassociated from his own voice, as if someone else had barked the warning.

The rustle of the aliens was pervasive. Why were they so silent? Why didn't they growl, or roar, or behave like any other animal? A felid or a grox broadcast its emotion. Even a damned kroot would probably exhibit something other than this unnerving abyss of self.

The cannon's autoloader rattled, burning through its ammunition. In a prolonged engagement, a full team of loaders would be ferrying fresh rounds so that the gun might fire without end. Those loaders were dead, or on the walls, struggling to get here. They had what they had, and Anditz had to hope it would be enough.

He rattled off a regular volley of starburst shells with a series of deep crumps. There was no visibility beyond the strip-lumens, but it didn't especially matter which direction he aimed in. He couldn't fail to hit the incoming rush of horrors which flew in like a blizzard. The shells lit a dazzle and flare in the darkness and once again momentarily illuminated the horde of xenos. The ground forces were much closer now. The undulating multitude of carapaces and livid connective tissue resembled a swarm of the dead, glittering with inscrutable eyes as dark as the void.

'Holy Terra,' muttered a Whiteshield standing next to Anditz. Anditz turned to look at him. He was young, very young. The colour had drained from his face, and he held his gun loosely.

Time seemed to slow, and Anditz experienced a moment of cold clarity. These soldiers were the best the Imperium had. They'd been drilled since childhood to face every possible eventuality and scenario that the enemy could devise. If the Cadians could not stand here, the Imperium itself could not stand. Even if nobody knew what had happened on Lazulai, this mattered. Even if they all died, they had to stand. Did the Emperor not see all of their actions?

Anditz knew that this was his purpose. What else was an officer for, if not this? What else, if not to make them believe?

He thumped the side of the macrocannon. 'We are Cadia!' he bellowed. 'This world is Cadia. The Imperium is Cadia. Cadia stands until not a single human soul remains!' He yelled over the incoming rattle of bone. 'Cadia stands!' *Thump.* 'Cadia stands!' *Thump.* 'Cadia stands!' *Thump.*

The troops took up the call. 'Cadia stands!' *Thump.* 'Cadia stands!' *Thump.* 'Cadia stands!' *Thump.* The staccato drumbeat of heavy bolters joined the chant, followed by the scream of lasguns as the aliens came into range. A few seconds later the wave hit.

At first, survival felt feasible. The hunched 'gaunts sprayed the bastion's defenders with a mixture of bone-shards and living, flesh-eating bullets, but the bastion's height and walls provided protection and the Cadians ground at them with lasgun fire. Anditz kept the macrocannon firing, a regular drumbeat thrum of recoil and explosion, eviscerating swathes of the airborne xenos still closing in. They kept coming. The bastion had become a small island of humanity in a sea of clicking and rushing bone. The erupting starburst shells provided a flicker-flash vision of the spread of horror. Death without end, as far as the eye could see, yet they were holding.

But something was happening. The aliens' behaviour was changing, as if it were being directed.

The 'gaunts threw themselves at the bastion wall in impossible numbers. Anditz watched in fascinated horror as they slammed into the wall beneath his feet and began to crush each other, climbing atop the growing heaps of chitin. The xenos below didn't attempt to struggle out from beneath their fellows, but merely remained lodged as the others continued to rush forward unthinkingly, higher and higher. The 'gaunts didn't attempt to evade the Cadians' fire either, and the corpses of those shot were crushed along with those of the living.

There was a sudden flurry of flighted xenos, each about the size of a human, with grinning skull faces. They clustered around the macrocannon and Anditz pulled his laspistol. But they didn't attack him – instead they began to force themselves into the barrel and air intakes of the emplacement.

'They're targeting the cannon!' Anditz yelled. He unleashed another starburst shell. It ruptured the aliens that had crawled into the gun, soaring into the sky with its momentum unslowed, exploding. It did not kill those that had already closed the distance, and more came, cracking their exoskeletons and shearing away their wings as they destroyed themselves to forcibly block the barrel.

A pair of soldiers were strafing them with las-fire, but the cannon was thick with too many crawling, fleshy bodies to clear.

By the time the giant weapon's autoloader had clanked another shell into place, the barrel was wedged solid. If Anditz shot again, he risked a lethal backfire that would take out half the bastion and do the tyranids' work for them. He clenched his fist in frustration. There were so many xenos now that it would be futile to even draw his laspistol. He looked out over the edge of the battlements. The 'gaunts were still flinging themselves into the wall. Then he had a sudden, terrible realisation. Each layer of dead tyranids was acting as a step for the next wave of the swarm. They were building a ramp.

'Fall back!' Anditz shouted. He pulled out his noctis scope. In the grainy darkness, something was walking towards them in a space where the swarm had parted. It was humanoid, but taller than a Dreadnought. It walked on backward-hinged legs and held four limbs outstretched, each terminating in a deadly sabre-sweep of bone. Vents on its back blossomed out shrouds of spores, which flowed behind it like a cloak of poison.

Anditz lowered his scope. It was close now, at the foot of the corpse-ramp. It moved with easy purpose, and it was near enough that he could see the barbs on its bone chestplate and the intelligence glittering in its terrible, unknowable eyes. Above the rictus grin, its snout swept upwards into a bladed horn.

This was something different. The realisation lodged in Anditz's heart. This monster could crush them as if they were insects.

The flighted tyranids swooped to flank it like a hideous mockery of a cardinal attended by cherubim, and the beast ascended the pile of bodies, now level with the bastion's wall. Lasgun fire seemed unable to harm it, and its attendant xenos acted as a living shield, flinging themselves in front of the heavy bolter fire.

The 'gaunts swarmed up the ramp before the bipedal xenos, firing borer beetles and chitin harpoons.

'Fall back!' Anditz yelled again. 'Get off the walls!'

Another hail of tyranids smashed into the ferrocrete walkway. Anditz pelted towards the parapet door and the soldier beside him was knocked to the ground by a falling flyer. Another trooper stopped to help her up and was disembowelled by the head-spike of a downed but still-living xenos.

'Keep moving!' Anditz shouted, shoving a pair of soldiers through the door ahead of him, before turning and peppering the nearest xenos with laspistol fire.

Two more soldiers fell as beetles bored through their skulls and out of their eye sockets. The massive leader tyranid advanced slowly, seemingly conducting the carnage that preceded it.

Anditz ducked into the corridor, holstering his pistol and barring the door behind him. He knew with cold certainty that there were wounded Cadians still alive out there, just as he knew that if the leader gained ingress to the bastion his remaining soldiers would die.

'Rank up!' he shouted.

'Sir, please!' Corporal Barette yelled, grabbing Anditz by the shoulder. You need to get down to the vaults!'

'What do you–'

'Captain Nkosi's orders, sir,' Barette said.

'Corporal Barette, I'm not abandoning my soldiers or my post.'

'No, sir,' Barette said, maintaining her grip on his shoulder. 'But your post is in the vaults now.'

There were screams and impacts outside.

'Brace for breach!' a soldier shouted.

'You have to go, now, lieutenant.'

Anditz looked around at the faces of his soldiers, flat with adrenaline and exhaustion. There were just half a dozen of them left now.

The corporal gripped his arm. 'Don't make me get Captain Nkosi, sir. She's stationed at the east-wall embrasure.'

'Stationed?' Last time he'd seen his commanding officer she was barely conscious.

'She made the medicae bring her up. She said you only need one arm to fire a bolt pistol.' Barette gave a hard smile.

'Collapse imminent!' the soldier shouted.

Anditz gestured. 'Fall back to the atrium.'

The atrium was at the centre of the bastion, above the vaults. Winged tyranids blocked the window slits now. Each aperture was far too small to accommodate one whole, but the pressure of their broodmates pushing them behind crushed those at the front through. The biting, spitting wrecks of bone and torn sinew that tumbled through were still a threat, dragging themselves forward on whatever unholy force animated them.

One snatched at a trooper's leg and fed her foot into its maw with cold precision. It took two soldiers to blast the alien horror off the ragged stump that remained.

Anditz took a final look around at the bastion. They had made their stand, the Emperor knew that.

'We'll all retreat to the vaults. The more of you I've got to keep these Catachans in check, the better. Watch that corridor,' he ordered. He wheeled the heavy vault door open. There were in fact two, each a foot and a half thick.

There was a smash behind them and the huge leader-beast erupted into the corridor. The doorway had crumbled where the thing had forced its bulk against the ferrocrete. It punched one sweeping sabre forward and impaled two troopers. There was perfect silence, but for the silky snick of the sabre entering their body cavities, then the sluicing of blood onto the floor.

The injured trooper opened fire. The monster's amethyst carapace deflected the lasgun fire as it struck it. The beast exposed its teeth, then bent and swept from side to side with its bladed horn as it moved forward through the corridor.

'Get into the vaults!' Anditz shouted. They didn't have the firepower to take something like this out.

The alien swiped out with its sword-like blade and cut three soldiers in half, their upper bodies falling cleanly away. The corridor was narrowing, and it was having problems advancing now. It rammed its bulky shoulder carapace into the walls, sending cracks running. It rammed again, and the walls began to crumble.

'Go! I'm coming!' shouted Corporal Barette, the only trooper remaining now. The whole squad, gone, in an instant.

Anditz stepped through the door and raised his gun as he turned to cover Barette.

'Cadia stands!' Barette screamed as she kicked the door shut on her commanding officer. He saw a final image of jaws and chitin and of Barette with a grenade in her hand.

The detonation blast rattled the steel door and Anditz was alone in the narrow descent. As he raised his hand to the wheel there was a sudden impact, and a fist-sized dent appeared in the door's metal.

Anditz turned and ran down the staircase to the lower door, slamming it shut. He paused for a few breathless seconds, listening. There was no sound. In a daze, he walked slowly down the remaining steps into the still vault.

Walled in vibrant green serpentine, the space was little more than ten feet square with cubby-holes for weapons and a niche for a brig. It had been built to withstand any collapse of the mines that surrounded it. He was alone, but for the cultist propagandist chained in the small brig alcove. She lay curled on one side, motionless. The only sound came from the hissing vox-caster, the signal indistinct.

Anditz moved in a daze to the small monitor stations, staring at the images displayed by the external vid-feeds, his face lit by their grainy green half-light. In the darkness of night, the sickly-pale vid-feed showed the remaining isolated troopers as simply white smears of light amongst a living wave of xenos. He leaned forward, gripping the monitor, trying to decipher the meaning of the confused images in front of him. A few of the feeds had winked out and hummed only with static.

'Report!' Anditz called over the vox. There was no reply. He pushed the vox-dial to maximum. In amongst the horrific chitter there were still screams and rattles of weapons discharge. He felt as if his head would burst. His eyes felt hot, his skin as if it was burning all over. He glanced at the metal door then back at the vid-feed. One of the inhuman shapes on the monitor tossed a human figure into the air as easily as if it was a las-pack.

He couldn't watch and do nothing. Whatever his orders, he had to do something. The leader-tyranid had likely moved on by now. Nkosi had been dying; she wouldn't last long, and then where would that leave the troops elsewhere in the bastion? Perhaps if he went out he could lead them, and order someone else down here to wait for these Catachans...

He was about to unbar the door when the prisoner spoke.

'You may as well let them in. They're going to kill us all anyway.'

It wasn't the strident voice of the Lamya DeShay he'd heard on the propaganda vids. Clipped vowels, like all of the wealthy here, but now hollow, the fire gone from her tone. He craned his neck to look at her. She sat with her arms around her knees, staring blankly at him with black-lined eyes. Dark curls of hair hung over her brow, the diamond and gold circlets around her wrists and neck glinting coldly under the strip-lumens. Her feet were bare, and she was chained to the wall by one ankle.

'That's what you want, is it?' Anditz said, pulling his hand back from the door's lever.

'No.' She shifted, eyes flicking uneasily to the vid-feed. 'But they will kill us. The angels are angry. Or maybe these aren't the angels. I don't know. I can't feel them.'

'Angels,' repeated Anditz, the word sour in his mouth. He was reminded of how close the enemy was. That was why sector command had issued the orders to recover the asset. Why he had to survive. The Imperial forces here needed anything they could get against the tyranids.

He took a step away from the door. Despite himself, he half winced at a distorted blast of agonised howling and desperate blasts of weapons fire.

'You could just turn it off,' Lamya said, eyes fixed on the flaring horrors unfolding on-screen. She rubbed her hands against each other anxiously.

'No,' snapped Anditz.

'I don't like the sound. It won't make a difference if you watch them die.' She pressed herself against the wall.

That brought on a sudden flood of grief. The propagandist was right. Nothing he did could make a difference now.

'I'm not going to leave them.'

Lamya sniffed. 'Do you have obscura here? Lho?' she tried in response to Anditz's expression. With only silence in reply, she put her hands over her ears and curled up again, facing the wall.

Anditz turned back to the vid-feed. The aliens were moving like terrible shoals of pale fish. There had to be thousands, perhaps hundreds of thousands. It was now almost impossible to discern one xenos from another. No human could survive that. And there were no human voices audible now. Just the sound of rushing bone as the tyranids flowed like a sea of death. The horror was mesmeric, the guilt greater than Anditz could process. The Cadian 82nd had been obliterated. Only he was left to carry out the final orders of his regiment.

The last vid-feed went out or was obscured, and he was alone.

He reached for something in his tunic pocket. The relic Captain Nkosi had ordered him to take from her trunk. A small, light tin. But heavy with the burden that he and it now carried.

The convoy had been moving for about an hour when Khan's vox crackled.

'Epsilon-rank officers. This is command. Opal Bastion has gone dark. Prepare for imminent contact.'

She glanced up and caught Haruto's eye. He was hunched, with one huge finger pressing the comm-bead in his ear. He'd heard the same message. The contact was earlier than command had anticipated, but just as Haruto had foreseen. He nodded. The tyranids were close.

'Squad, prepare to deploy,' Khan said over the vox. Speech wouldn't carry above the roar of the Baneblade her team currently rode on top of.

The flare of las-fire began to light up the darkness ahead.

Khan clambered down the side of the Baneblade and gave

Captain Thorne a crisp salute as he descended into the body of the tank to take up his station. Then she jumped down onto the hard ground. The rest of her team did the same, with Adair helping the tech-adept down. Khan had allocated her as Wrathe's escort detail. She caught a glint of an engraved cuirass under the robes as Wrathe dismounted the tank. It struck her that that might in fact actually *be* Wrathe herself. Just how human any of the Martians were under the robes, she would rather remain a mystery.

The squad checked their weapons. The tech-adept pulled out a stubby pistol with glowing rings where the chamber would normally have been.

'What's that? Plasma weapon?' asked Adair.

'Gamma.'

'Oh?' The bulky Catachan grinned, hefting her heavy flamer down from *Ofelia's Fist*. 'What's it do?'

'Pray to the Omnissiah you never see its savage spirit.'

'Now you've got me interested.'

'It'll cook the 'nids,' Haruto said.

'Fried xenos for breakfast? Can't beat the smell of toasted carapace, sir.'

'The sergeant is somewhat correct. Anything within a nearby radius will be immolated, at the discretion of the weapon's machine spirit.'

Adair whistled, then barked out a laugh. 'So, you aren't in charge of that gun then?'

Wrathe's vox-grille crackled in a way that Khan read as disapproving. 'I see you are mercifully untroubled by the burden of doctrinal knowledge.'

Adair shrugged her massive shoulders. 'Don't know about doctrinal, chief. Now, *lat*-rinal I can tell you something about.' She spread her hands. 'One time I was working operations back on Catachan. This wonk commissar set down one day. Here to manage us, he said. Never been in the jungle before and when he ate–'

'That's enough for now, trooper,' Haruto said, cradling his boltgun. 'We've got incoming filth already, we hardly need any more.'

'Form up around Tech-Adept Wrathe,' Khan growled. 'We stick with the convoy until we hit the canyon, then we'll break off and head east towards the objective. Understood?' She jerked her head. 'Ghost, eyes on flank.'

Ghost inclined his head and stepped back a few paces, gripping his long-las, keeping the squad where he could see them. The trooper could track a Catachan hawk on a cloudy day – there was no one better to keep watch.

'Adair, I want you up ahead with that heavy flamer.'

'Yessir.' Adair strode ahead, muscled back straining against the grox-leather strap of the weapon's heavy promethium tanks.

There was a crackle from the vox. 'Come in?' Khan said. The vox crackled again with a blurt of incomprehensible speech. The comms were going down. She felt a tingle across the back of her neck. Something made her look up.

The spore shoals that glittered in the sky were moving strangely. She frowned. Why would they be massing and eddying like that? Then cold realisation hit her like a gut-punch. The spores weren't moving. Something was moving *through* them.

'Lights up!' she yelled.

Her squad flipped their stab-lights upward, and the small cluster of beams played against something pale and flickering. Khan felt a terrible lurch in her stomach, like the inverse of being at sea and realising there are thousands of feet of cold, dark water beneath you teeming with strange, hostile life.

Here, the horrors were above.

'Lights up!' Khan bellowed, even more loudly. The other troops nearby turned their stab-lights to the sky to reveal a mass of bleached, fluttering flesh above them, a dread flock of silent ghouls. The visibility increased as soldiers noticed what their neighbours were doing and added their lights to the array. And as they were illuminated, the xenos suddenly screamed downwards.

'Contact!' Khan yelled, drawing her chainsword.

The winged things attacked in flurries, jinking and diving and clawing at the troops. Haruto's boltgun barked out and Adair's flamer screamed as the monsters rushed towards them.

The ones that survived being shot down were just as dangerous on the ground. One xenos, wings tattered by repeat las-fire, spiralled heavily to the ground into a cluster of soldiers. Adair ran forward, heavy flamer already spitting, but as the soldiers parted for her, she was stopped in her tracks. The downed monstrosity had attached itself to a Catachan soldier. The alien's body was about the size of a human torso and what remained of its wings were wrapped around the struggling trooper's face and upper body. Khan saw Adair throw aside her heavy flamer and try to cut the alien away with her knife.

Something lunged at Khan, and she spun around, the teeth of her chainsword screaming into hard chitin.

The hideous visage of one of the flying horrors grimaced mere inches from her face. Her chainsword had lodged into the launcher on its forelimb, blessedly impeding its ability to eject its insectoid projectiles, but leaving her without a weapon. She was so close she could smell the weird, corrosive stink of it, and saw the oesophageal-looking duct above its distended tongue start to contract.

With a grunt of effort, she ducked out of reach of its maw and barrelled her shoulder into its skeletal breastbone. She heard a hiss as it shot a jet of acid spray over her head while she tackled it to the ground, still gripping her chainsword. The teeth screamed as she tried to pull it free, but it was lodged firm in the monster's carapace. She pushed her knee into the thing's chest as it writhed on the ground, pinning it down while she drew her plasma pistol. Its barbed tail caught her a heavy blow in the back, half winding her.

Levelling her gun, she cored the abomination's head.

Haruto appeared from the melee and pulled Khan to her feet. 'We need to keep moving!' he shouted over the chaos of battle.

All around, clusters of combat were occurring, wherever one of the xenos had landed. *Ofelia's Fist* rolled on ahead through the fray, the sweep of the battle out to the left, the dark canyon dropping away twenty feet to their right.

Khan nodded and dislodged her weapon from the dead alien. 'Round up the squad!' she yelled. 'I want to keep pace with the tank. Where's the adept?'

'Ghost is minding her.'

'That's Adair's job.'

Haruto gestured with his weapon.

Khan turned. Adair was still trying to rescue the Guardsman. He was now on his knees, the thing clamped firmly over his face and upper body. She had given up trying to cut it away and was now attempting to prise it off with her hands.

'Jet!' Khan bellowed, striding towards her. 'Grant him the Emperor's Mercy.'

'He's still alive!' Adair shouted.

'It's going to spit,' Khan called.

Adair plunged her hand into the thing's maw, clamping the projectile tube shut with one massive fist. The alien began to thrash, but still remained locked to the Guardsman.

'Adair,' Khan warned. 'I'll put him out of his misery myself.'

Adair grimaced. She crushed the monster's oesophageal duct

tighter in her fist and with her other hand gripped its torso. Then she pulled. She roared with the effort, huge muscles straining in her arms as she slowly ripped the alien in two.

Black ichor sheeted out of the thing's body as Adair threw it to the ground and peeled the wings from the Guardsman's face. He fell forward on his hands and knees and retched, but he was still alive.

'Omnissiah's fuse,' Khan heard Wrathe say behind her.

Panting, Adair wiped her face and raised a fist into the air. The nearby Catachans cheered, punching her in celebration.

'Do that another couple of million times,' Haruto said, 'and we might just see the tyranids off.'

'Trooper,' Khan called.

Adair snapped to attention and hoisted her heavy flamer strap back over her shoulder, still panting with effort. 'Sir,' she said.

Khan nodded at her. 'Nicely done.' She could feel Haruto's disapproval. 'When you tear one in half, then you can complain,' she said to him.

He raised one heavy eyebrow but didn't have the chance to reply.

'There is something coming,' Wrathe called suddenly, her vox-grille projecting her voice. 'I sense many machine spirits convening on our position.'

'Navy's finally pulled their finger out then,' Haruto said.

Khan gestured. 'Get into *Ofelia*'s lee and keep marching. She'll be our shield. And keep in formation, Adair. From now on, those xenos bastards can chew up as many troopers as they want. Your only priority is this squad. Understand?'

The hulking woman nodded and led the squad single file, the towering Baneblade on their left side, and the emergent split of the canyon on the right.

'The canyon opens out rapidly from here,' Haruto said as he

marched behind Khan. 'Depending on the pace we can get up, I'd say we're only half an hour from the crossing point.'

'Good,' Khan said. 'And you're not right about Adair,' she added.

'I didn't say anything.'

'No. But I've known you long enough I could hear you thinking it.'

Haruto shrugged. 'First priority is to get over the crossing. Then we'll be clear of the xenos stampede and we can strike out ourselves to the excavation site. If the Navy can clear us a path, we can argue about Adair then.'

The tech-adept's senses had been correct. The distinctive roar of an incoming squadron of Lightning Strikes was soon audible even over the noise of *Ofelia's Fist*.

The skies were shrouded in smoke from weapons fire, dulling the foul, sickly glow of the tyranids' bioluminescence but making the night's visibility even worse. Khan watched through narrowed eyes. Any moment now, the vehicles below should call in targets for the planes. But they weren't. The pitch of the aircraft suddenly changed, and Khan saw mechanical shapes veering away.

Haruto realised what had happened first. 'The vox is down. Ground control can't transmit the targets,' he called.

Khan swore. Without vox or search-lumens the pilots didn't stand a chance in the darkness. Shoving aside soldiers and kicking aside dead tyranids, she ran to the back of *Ofelia's Fist* and scrabbled for the wired vox on the hull that would patch her through to the crew.

'Come in, *Ofelia's Fist*!' she yelled over the roar of the engine as she kept pace with the rolling leviathan. 'This is Tusk. Over.'

The vox-caster crackled, and she pressed it hard into her ear.

'Ofelia's Fist, *receiving*,' came Captain Thorne's voice.

'Air support unable to receive attack coordinates. Paint a target for them. Over.'

There were a few seconds of static. Had they heard her?

'*Ofelia's Fist?*' Khan shouted. 'Do you read me?'

Then a radiant beam of light shot skyward from the venerable tank, soft sporeglow visible at its edges. It lit up the underside of something massive cruising above the Imperial forces around which the smaller flying xenos shoaled. Something undeniably and disconcertingly organic, but with the bulk of a Thunder-hawk and the pale, cloud-camouflage stomach of a sky predator like the Catachan Shrike. Unlike her regiment's namesake, the keel of the monster was knitted with dense bone ribs running the length of its body.

'Holy Throne,' Khan muttered, grasping the aquila that hung at her neck.

There was a growl of skyborne engines as the Lightning Strike squadron returned, sweeping in to attack the monstrosity. The flash of their lascannons lit the sky with red fire. The great sky-tyranid spun lazily in the air like an impossible sea-serpent through whorls of sulphurous gun-smoke. The las-fire passed harmlessly under its wing. Through the gap its movement made in the smog, Khan saw the fighter squadron peel off and reposi-tion for the attack. They were fast, and the pilots skilled, but this thing *lived* in the air. They were fighting it in its element.

'Keep moving,' Khan called to her squad. Their comrades were buying them time they couldn't afford to waste. The smaller flying tyranids had backed off, and now thronged around the great alien.

The Lightning Strikes split into two groups, flanking the beast even as it dipped and dived with otherworldly grace. One fighter managed to clip the thing in its bone-ridged carapace with an explo-sive missile. The brood of smaller tyranids swirled furiously and mobbed the fighter that had struck their leader. The beleaguered plane bucked and listed.

'What are they doing?' Khan shouted to a grim-faced Haruto.

'Blocking the engine,' he called back.

Khan could see roiling whorls of black smoke issuing from the stricken fighter. 'Take cover!' she yelled as it veered noisily in their direction. As she dived behind *Ofelia's Fist* she glimpsed a last image of the Lightning Strike's canopy, smashed open and full of pale, writhing xenos. It screamed low over their heads with a stench of burning metal, spewing scalding promethium and scattering wreckage before crashing into the deep canyon beside them with a horrific boom.

The rest of the aerial battle had moved elsewhere although the clouds were visibly lit with the flash of weapons discharge.

'Status report,' Khan barked, clambering to her feet.

Adair had shielded Wrathe and now pulled the diminutive tech-adept to her feet. 'Still in one piece, sir,' she called.

Khan rolled her shoulder. It was stiff from where the alien had struck her previously. In her youth she'd have been able to shrug off a blow like that, but a life in service to the Emperor wasn't kind to ageing bodies.

'Twenty minutes to crossing,' Haruto reported.

Khan nodded.

'As long as the light show stays over there,' he added.

Khan turned to see a vast purple bioluminescent missile roar into the Imperial troops on the other side of the combat zone. The brightness momentarily lit up the distant, looming shapes of vast xenos Titans, slowly striding across the battlefield, spewing volleys of incandescent bio-acid and clouded with shrouds of spores. They had to be forty feet tall.

'Quick march,' Khan growled. 'Keep in the tank's cover.' The order stuck in her craw. It felt like running away from the fight.

Not that there was a fight any more, she reminded herself. This mission was all that mattered now. It mattered more than these troopers' lives, and certainly more than her pride.

Adair jogged ahead, blasting the occasional downed xenos with her heavy flamer. The tech-adept kept pace, striding ahead of Khan, back ramrod straight, red cloak billowing out behind her.

Khan felt someone grip her arm. Ghost was beside her, face drawn. It would be a strain for him to be in the presence of so many people. She suspected he'd rather be facing the tyranids alone.

He bent down to speak into her ear. 'Enemy infantry ahead. I'll take point on *Ofelia's Fist*.'

She nodded her agreement.

The xenos foot soldiers struck the left-hand side of the crusade force first. They were a variant that Khan had seen before. Hunched 'gaunts roughly the size of a human, variously armed with vicious talons or projectile weapons.

They barrelled their way into the centre of the crusade force, leaving the flanks relatively unbothered. Ghost picked off a couple of stragglers from his perch atop the mighty Baneblade as it ground across the battlefield.

Haruto examined his map, squinting with his ocular implant. 'Crossing's up here,' he said with a gesture.

Khan squinted. About fifteen hundred feet away in the flare of flood-lumens she could see the glint of a metal bridge.

'Looks like trees down there,' she said. She noted that the side of the canyon was covered in dark, scrubby undergrowth.

'Yes.' Haruto frowned. 'That wasn't on the intelligence picts.'

'General Kvelter did promise us a jungle.'

Haruto's frown deepened. 'Even on Catachan it doesn't grow that quickly.'

'You think it's the xenos?'

Haruto nodded. 'They've changed the climate. It's hotter and more humid.'

Khan pulled out a cheroot. 'But did they do it on purpose?' She shrugged.

Haruto shook his head. 'It has to be for a reason. To make it easier for the spores to grow?'

Khan took a long drag on her smoke. 'Well, let's see what kind of jungle they've made us.'

You couldn't talk to non-Catachans about the enemy like this, Khan thought as they marched on. It was anathema to even think about the aliens' motivations. She shared Haruto's frustration at the lack of intelligence handed down by command, or at least the redaction of almost all of it. She understood the need to keep that sort of thing away from regular citizens, but it seemed fairly futile to do so with a regiment up to their necks in xenos on a daily basis.

But the greater problem was that non-Catachan regiments didn't understand that when you hunted a predator, you entered into a relationship with it. Whether you wanted it to or not, it would learn about you. To not do the same was to give it the advantage.

If you didn't work that out pretty quickly on Catachan, you wouldn't survive long enough to worry about xenos corruption or anything else. Catachan was a planet of many different predators, each with the single objective of killing you. The tyranids were the same, and if Haruto was right, the bastards made every world their world. Khan didn't want to hang around long enough to see what that looked like.

A movement across the killing field drew her attention. Khan was veteran of enough battles to recognise disturbances in the movement of troops, even at a distance. Something was coming.

Not large enough to be entirely visible yet itself, although she saw the curve of its hunched back in the throng of soldiers and vehicles. And it was powerful enough to be carving a wake through infantry and – she squinted – vehicles by the looks of it. And it appeared to be heading directly for them.

Khan gestured to Ghost and Haruto, pointing in the direction of the disturbance then thumping a fist into the palm of her open hand. They understood immediately. They all knew what this was, had seen it before. A tank-killer was coming for them.

Khan ran back around to the Baneblade's wired vox. She'd seen these variants crumple Rhinos as if they were parchment, but whether a scuttle-basher could take out a super-heavy like *Ofelia's Fist*, she didn't know.

'*Ofelia's Fist*, come in!' she shouted over the engine's roar and battlefield din. There was no response. '*Ofelia's Fist*, come in! You have an incoming tank-killer!'

The vox crackled with white noise.

Khan swore and banged the vox-receiver back down. She could feel the ground thumping as the thing approached.

Ghost jumped down beside her. Khan grimly sheathed her chainsword and pulled out her plasma pistol.

The thumps were getting closer together as the thing built up speed and the ground was shaking. Khan ordered the squad to fall in behind her and led them out from behind the Baneblade. A tank was the last place you wanted to be with a scuttle-basher incoming. Time seemed to slow as the troops between Khan's squad and the incoming creature parted or were crushed before the xenos finally emerged, trampling the mass of soldiers ahead of it as if they were long grass. It was heading directly for the tank. This variant had some sense that drew them to armour, seemingly from miles away.

The tyranid was a massive, hunched thing, almost as tall as

the hulking Baneblade itself. A living battering ram. Its head was slung low beneath a domed carapace, its snout tipped with a blunt, human-sized horn. And it was charging forward at a terrible velocity, powerful legs pumping and sweeps of purple ridged armour plating positioned to ram into *Ofelia's Fist*.

'Keep clear!' Khan shouted.

Now the monster was in the tank's line of sight, the heavy bolters on the flank urgently barked out a defence and the main gun started to traverse. But it was too little, too late. Hackles of purple bone raised high, the monster would ram into the venerable war engine before it had the opportunity to defend itself.

The balls of fluorescent plasma from Khan's pistol barely singed the rampaging beast and the lasgun fire the surrounding troopers sprayed at the xenos seemed as effective as a handful of dirt thrown at a Catachan Devil.

Then two rapid shots with an unfamiliar cadence rang out. A cold, bright blue light crackled around the alien's flank, and it tripped as two of its near limbs were vaporised.

Khan glanced aside to see the tech-priest aiming her glowing gamma pistol at the enemy. Her eyes were narrowed and a binharic scream emitted from her vox-grille, amplifying her curses or prayers to audibility over the chaos.

Her shots had dealt the xenos a serious injury, but still it kept moving. The ruination of its nearside limbs had knocked it off trajectory, sweeping it away from a clean impact on the middle of the tank but hurtling it into the rear.

Its bone head-ram smashed into *Ofelia's Fist*, shearing away a sponson and gun turret and striking the ancient machine a terrific blow. The tank rocked violently backwards towards the canyon precipice but settled a few feet away from danger.

Khan's relief soured as she realised with growing horror that where the great thunderous heartbeat of *Ofelia's Fist* should have been, there was a terrible silence. The mighty Baneblade's engine was dead.

And into the quiet rushed the sounds of the xenos that the tank had been concealing. Papery wings and the clicking of bone on bone and the chitter of things from beyond the cold, hard vacuum of deep space. There were the usual human cries and battle sounds, but the tyranids were nightmarish in their silence. They didn't growl or scream or whimper – they simply kept on coming. Emotionless, expressionless, endless.

Khan hadn't realised how *Ofelia's Fist* had been shielding them from much more than just physical attack. She fought down the primal instinct to panic at the deep wrongness the aliens exuded. She forced herself to focus on the downed tyranid instead. The tech-adept's gamma weapon had melted a terrible hole in its side. Bone-like structures protruded from still-bubbling charred, livid tissue and it stank of chemicals and burning hair. Yet it was nowhere near dead. It had one scythe arm the length of two humans remaining, which it raised as it dragged itself towards the still and silent tank.

'Spirit of this machine, heed my will,' Tech-Adept Wrathe spoke, the vox-grille amplifying her voice across the battlefield, slightly distorted. Khan read cold fury into the toneless voice. To see the mighty machine laid low was a sacrilege for the Martian. This alien was doing no less than desecrating the altar at which she worshipped.

Wrathe raised her gamma pistol and advanced on the wounded tyranid. She loosed another shot from the radiative weapon. It blew away a chunk of flesh from its hunched back armour as easily as one might scoop a hot utensil through grox fat. But it still wasn't enough. Devastating as Wrathe's weapon might be, she was going to need to use it at closer range.

The xenos turned its massive head towards its attacker, its

entire face a carnassial sneer. Wrathe stalked closer, apparently unmoved by any concern for her own safety.

'Back her up!' Khan commanded, gesturing at the nearby troops, and moved forward with her own plasma pistol raised to flank the alien.

The soldiers ranked up to concentrate las-fire on the creature. It seemed to have no effect on the beast, but perhaps the density of fire could harm it.

There was a sudden movement, and the tank-killer lashed its tail towards the small, red-robed figure of the tech-adept. The tail-tip bone mace hurled towards her, but in response Wrathe moved with augmented speed, far faster than most humans would have been able to, screaming off a shot from her weapon. The tail-tip mass of knurled bone burst, sending shards of organic shrapnel shrieking outwards.

Wrathe had the beast's attention now. It shifted its bulk cumbersomely on its remaining limbs towards Wrathe's position at the front of the tank. Khan saw its throat bulge and distend like a lumpen goitre.

'It's going to spit!' Khan shouted, and burst off two more shots from her plasma pistol. They ruptured skull-sized holes in its flank, but it wasn't enough to stop it.

Wrathe levelled her gun and sent a blast into the thing's throat. A wet burst of acidic poison spattered across the troops as it retched. It shook its vast head, bile drooling from its fangs. Nearby soldiers screamed as the corrosive spray liquefied their bones.

'Hit it again!' Khan called. One more blast from the tech-adept's gamma pistol and the thing should be felled.

Wrathe shook her head and raised her gun. Khan saw that a small red light blinked on the weapon.

'Damn,' Khan growled. Her own plasma pistol was becoming

uncomfortably hot to the touch. She'd seen enough fatal over-heats to know when to stop firing. She stowed the gun and pulled out her chainsword.

Wrathe hadn't moved but was standing her ground as the fallen tyranid dragged itself forward with its remaining massive scythe. *She's drawing it towards the front of the tank*, Khan realised. But what for? The mighty Baneblade still stood silent, belying the frantic crew activity she knew would be happening inside.

With the tech-adept apparently no longer a threat, the tank-killer turned its attention back to *Ofelia's Fist*. It dug its horn under the front track, plunging its remaining limbs into the ground. It was going to try to flip the vehicle.

As soon as it was entrenched, Wrathe sprinted around to the rear of the Baneblade. She threw her hood back from her head. The slim mechadendrites that had been coiled around the locs of her hair unfurled themselves and rose up from her head like a living halo, sparking with electricity.

Wrathe's filigreed metal fingers moved across the surface of a hatch near the engine, which opened at her touch. She thrust her hands inside.

'Venerable spirit of *Ofelia's Fist*! Awake!' her voice boomed. 'Spirit of destruction, rise and heed the Omnissiah's call! The Motive Force compels you to take your vengeance! Wreak the power of the machine upon this abomination!'

A scream of incomprehensible binharic burst from her vox-grille. Khan winced. It was uncomfortable to organic ears.

Wrathe threw her head back and bright energies crackled around her. Steam rose from her shoulders, and she shook with effort as she gripped something within the guts of the ancient tank. As she did so, there came the sound of shearing metal as the alien tank-killer sought to prise apart the vehicle's armour plating.

But then there was another sound. It was just a rattle at first, within the tank. Then it became a snarl and rose to a stirring roar. The Baneblade lived! Clouds of incense-scented smoke gouted from *Ofelia's Fist* as she suddenly growled forward. The xenos was caught under the teeth of the vehicle's tracks as she rode roughshod over the alien, grinding its carapace into the ground and bursting its remaining organs under three hundred tons of furious, Martian-forged steel.

The monster was barely recognisable now, little more than pulp and gristle in a pool of foul ichor.

The tank's top hatch flipped open, and Captain Thorne emerged.

'Aren't you supposed to be escorting us?' Khan said, kicking her way across the pool of xenos viscera.

'Had a thing or two keeping us busy,' Thorne said with a grin.

'You still might if it wasn't for the Martian.'

Adair escorted Wrathe towards them. The tech-adept leaned heavily on the Catachan's arm. Khan noted that the metal of her hands was scorched.

'*Ofelia's Fist* lives,' Khan said. 'You've done us a great service.'

'Our debt of gratitude is to the Omnissiah and to this mighty engine. Her spirit is doughty, and she will fight on for more years than any of us will see.'

'Look after her, Thorne. You're on your own now.' Khan slapped the side of the tank and took a final look around. Despite the fighting they had already done, the troops were energetic and ready to continue the battle. The long months locked up were no good for any soldier, but worse for a Catachan. It was no way to die, cooped up indoors. And these soldiers were to die. She couldn't forget that fact. It was the destiny of all soldiers, she told herself. But a nagging voice told her that the difference was that they would die to protect her. To allow her to run away.

She gritted her teeth and locked away the guilt and betrayal she felt in her heart as she led her squad off the plain and down the track to the bridge. The sounds of the battle diminished as she walked into the dark of the new jungle that rose up to greet them.

CHAPTER FIVE

Anditz hadn't slept, but he hadn't been fully awake either. He didn't know if it was day or night from the grainy picture on the remaining vid-feed. All external movement and sound had stopped several hours ago, and the silence within the sickly mineral-green walls of the vault was overwhelming. The cultist slept fitfully, a frown on her face, cosmetics smeared down her cheeks.

The noise started quietly at first. So quietly that Anditz thought it might be an auditory hallucination, but it grew louder. It was a regular *thump, thump, thump.* Then he heard voices. Muffled, but definitely human. He frowned and drew his power sword with a crackle.

There was a sudden white flash and the acrid tang of a melta bomb. A head-sized hole sizzled into the door, dripping molten metal onto the ground.

'Piss,' someone said on the other side.

'You missed the lock,' someone else grunted in disgust.

'I can see that,' the first person snapped.

'Trooper Adair,' came the growl of a third voice, more distant than the first two. 'Is my guide in there?'

A woman's face appeared in the hole. 'Yes, major!' she shouted. She regarded Anditz. 'Stand back. Sir,' she added, noting his officer's insignia.

She withdrew, and there was a mighty thump as she kicked the door in. Then the huge woman swaggered into the vault, filling the doorway. She wore a ribbed vest and fatigues with a heavy flamer slung around her neck. Her arms were inscribed with kill-markings and a red bandana was knotted around one of her huge biceps. Her white-blonde hair was cropped short, and she grinned like a predator. She was the most Catachan thing that Anditz had ever seen.

'Just one Cadian to report, sir,' she called back up the stairs. 'All in one piece.'

'Unlike the rest of this place,' grunted the man who stood behind her. He had one bionic eye, and his face was clenched in what appeared to be a permanent scowl. His shock of dark hair was cropped at the front and tied long at the back. 'Sergeant Rutger Haruto,' he said, and saluted. 'Catachan Nine-Hundred-and-Third. This is Trooper Falke Adair.' He jerked his head towards the woman beside him.

'Lieutenant Kaede Anditz. Cadian Eighty-Second.'

The big man's heavy eyebrows knotted further, but he just nodded.

'I wasn't certain you were coming.'

'The route wasn't especially clear, sir,' Haruto replied. 'Although from the looks of this place I don't imagine I need to tell you why.'

Anditz nodded.

'You've been to this facility we're headed for, sir?'

'That's correct.'

'I've drawn up a suggested route, but I'd appreciate your eyes on it,' the Catachan said. 'We only had old information back at Cobalt.'

'Who's that?' Trooper Adair jerked her chin towards the figure of the prisoner.

'An enemy propagandist.'

'I have a name,' the prisoner spat, rising a little unsteadily to her feet and smoothing out the skirts of her dress.

'She looks familiar,' Trooper Adair said with a frown.

The prisoner raised her chin imperiously. 'I'm Lamya DeShay.'

Sergeant Haruto shrugged.

Lamya looked disdainful. 'Performer? Broadcaster?'

Realisation spread across Adair's face. 'Emperor wept. You did that song, didn't you? The one that was on all the frequencies?'

'Adair,' Sergeant Haruto said, gesturing impatience. 'It's not the time. Sir,' he addressed Anditz, 'Major Khan will see you now. Adair, bring the heretic.'

Anditz followed Haruto up the stairs. The sergeant didn't have Adair's bulk, but he was taller and broader than the majority of Cadians and filled the corridor.

Anditz emerged blinking into the light of what had been the bastion's atrium. It was no longer there. Neither was the rest of the building.

He stared around, momentarily disconcerted, the disappearance of the walls making the familiar place strange. Ferrocrete ribs cut upwards into the sky where the roof had fallen through. The sun was pale, filtered through a haze of dust and spores. Masonry dust coated everything, even the corpses of the xenos, which now appeared strangely powdered like the wigged dignitaries of a noble hive-spire. Here and there were bloodstains, crimson streaks in the white. The mounds of xenos corpses trailed out and down the broken bastion wall to the indistinct killing field beyond. The dead 'gaunts were so still now, little islands of spent death where they had flowed in a tide the night before. He could taste burning chemicals in the air.

Anditz cast around, but he couldn't see any human remains.

'We buried those of your dead we could find,' Haruto said. 'It wasn't many.'

Anditz glanced sidelong at him as they walked. The sergeant's gaze was fixed ahead. He halted and gestured for Anditz to continue past him.

A stocky, middle-aged Catachan sat on a chunk of crumbled masonry near to where the macrocannon had stood on the bastion's walls. Smoke twined behind her from the smouldering ruin of the emplacement, a final memorial to the last soldier desperate enough to have tried to fire a shell from the stricken weapon. She wore a battered pauldron over a combat vest and wore her red bandana around her arm. Her hair was cropped short, grey with the occasional streak of white. The Catachan took a drag on a cheroot and watched Anditz approach.

'Major Khan,' Anditz said, coming to a halt and saluting.

She had an aquiline nose and knowing eyes, and a calmness to her movements. She looked Anditz up and down as if to get the measure of him.

'So, you're our guide,' she said, her voice a deep husk.

'Sir,' he said, and nodded.

'You're going to take us to Magos Reiner Stuhl's excavation facility.'

'Those are my orders, sir.'

'You been inside the facility, lieutenant?'

'No, sir. The magos wouldn't admit any Astra Militarum forces. However, I'm familiar with the external layout.'

Khan grunted and rubbed out the end of her cheroot on the

masonry she was seated on. 'You survived. But the rest of your regiment is dead.'

She made the statement without accusation in her tone, but the words came like a knife to Anditz's heart.

'Yes, sir.'

'Why are you alive?'

A stab of shame. Anditz blinked. 'Orders, sir. My captain's last. Your mission was her priority.'

Khan scratched her head. 'Doesn't feel like enough of a reason, does it?'

He held her gaze. 'Sir. Do you question my honour?' he asked, barely able to suppress the emotion he felt.

'No,' she replied. 'Quite the opposite. If you were from any other regiment, perhaps. But Cadians always follow orders. You followed an order that had you locked in a box listening to your comrades die. That could send a good soldier half mad.' She regarded him with calm, hazel eyes. 'Has it?'

'Sir,' came a call from above before Anditz could reply. He turned to see a gaunt-faced Catachan with a lean, muscular frame folded into a crouch on one of the remaining outcrops of masonry. His long-las rested out towards the west. 'Cultists approaching.'

Anditz heard the distant growl of a vehicle.

Khan tilted her head. 'So they are. How many, Ghost?'

'Two. Tracked heavy industry, non-military.'

'Position for ambush,' Khan ordered.

'What shall I do with her?' Adair asked, gripping the prisoner's chain. Lamya stood defiant, the black silks of her fine dress rippling in the soft breath of the wind. But for the blotched cosmetics and hem-seep of sporedust, she looked as if she could have been about to attend a society affair.

Anditz was still discomfited by the major's words, uncertain of what to make of her. He forced himself to turn his attention to Lamya. If his new commanding officer was ever going to trust him, he'd have to establish his value.

'She's a cultist prisoner we took at Var Mine for interrogation, sir,' he explained. 'Their chief propagandist.'

'But the cult's been broken now?' Khan asked.

Anditz nodded. 'Perhaps. We've had no more organised activity reported.'

Khan shrugged. 'Then we've no use for her. Kill her.'

The cultist's face formed a mask of horror. Anditz suspected she'd considered herself too valuable to dispatch in such a way.

'Wait,' she said, stepping forward as far as the heavy chain would allow. The bravado had left her, and she folded her body into a pose of supplication. 'Please. Be merciful – I was coerced.'

Khan laughed.

Adair spat, disgust contorting her face.

Lamya extended her hands. 'I don't want to die,' she wheedled.

'Neither did any of the soldiers here,' Khan retorted.

'They controlled us. I didn't know what I was doing.'

'Would you like to shoot her before we head out east?' Khan asked Anditz, ignoring the woman.

A gesture of trust, Anditz thought. Albeit a characteristically Catachan one.

'You're heading east?' Lamya looked around, clearly desperate to seize a scrap of hope. 'You need to go to the eastern territories? Towards the capital?' She gestured dramatically. 'Full of cultists.'

'We killed your leader back at Var Mine,' Anditz said. 'You're not a threat any more.'

'Can you be sure?' She leaned forward, eyes wide. 'The route into Carnadine was ours. You don't know what you'll find, what traps we might have set. If you need to get through the capital, I can help.'

'They're nearly here,' Ghost called from his vantage point.

'They'll recognise me,' Lamya said. 'They'll think they're meeting an ally. You'll be able to kill them easily. Let me prove it.'

'We don't need your help,' Khan said.

'Wait. I-I can speak the cult's cant!'

'I would be curious to hear it,' came a toneless voice. A tech-adept stepped from behind a fallen tower in streaming red robes, a flash of colour in the powdered monotony of the smoking landscape. She wore a cuirass of fine, overlapping sheaves of metal. Her hair writhed in twists around the neural cables snaking into her skull and her eyes were clouded bone-white. 'Imperial intelligence has to date been unable to decipher the cult's code.'

Khan rolled her powerful shoulders into a shrug. 'It'll be easy enough to shoot her if she tries anything.'

The tech-adept's vox-grille crackled. 'My weapon is charged.'

The corner of Khan's mouth twitched into a smile, and she nodded. 'Troops, disperse.' The major gestured for Anditz to follow her.

He ducked down behind a blasted walkway next to Khan as the others positioned themselves in hiding places around the ruptured courtyard. Lamya, still in chains, sat in the centre of the ruined space as if left by captors.

The growl of engines stilled as the vehicles halted just outside the bastion. One sounded like a rockgrinder. Anditz winced at the memory of Var Mine, of the choking smog and thrashing offal in the lift shaft. He readied his laspistol behind the ledge of crumbled ferrocrete. Khan drew a battered plasma pistol.

'You a good shot, lieutenant?' Khan muttered.

'Yes, sir,' he replied in a whisper.

She nodded. 'Follow my lead.'

A dozen cultists moved into the opening, backlit by a stream of sunlit spores. They were variously armed with heavy picks and mining lasers and wore shabby overalls patched with the purple whorl that symbolised their profane kinship. They didn't bother to hide their mutations any more. Anditz observed things that had remained shrouded before. A distended cranium here, a third arm there.

Some were catatonic, led by the hands of their fellows. Others bore wounds that Anditz suspected had been self-inflicted. One individual had a swathe of dirty rags swaddled around his head, brown bloodstains crusted where his eyes should have been. Anditz was reminded of the cultists outside Var Mine who had pulled their own eyes out on the death of their leader. Throne only knew how far the death of the witch had rippled, and the precise nature of the insanity inflicted on the surviving heretics.

Lamya called out in a ululating language Anditz didn't recognise.

A tall man carrying a stub-handled mining axe lurched forward, responding in kind. He waved to his comrades to come forward.

'The enemy took our poet! But we have her back.' He turned to Lamya, hands outstretched. 'We have been wandering since the great silence fell.' His face contorted. 'The angels no longer speak to us. Our people are broken, scattered. What walks our world…' He choked. 'They are not as we thought. They cannot be the angels–'

'I know what happened,' Lamya said, raising a hand. 'Why the angels have forsaken us. It was the work of the accursed Imperium, a cruel trick by our former masters.' Then she dropped into cult cant and spoke urgently to the tall man, waving towards the quadrant of the courtyard where the squad was hidden.

Anditz stiffened. He should have known Lamya would betray them.

'Wait,' Khan whispered.

'Do you see what they've done?' Lamya said, speaking in Low Gothic now. 'You see how they have abused the angels?'

A gaggle of cultists moved to the broken bastion wall, from where the killing field was visible. Only then did they see the litter of xenos corpses on the ramparts and the spoil heaps beyond that Lamya had directed them to view.

The shock was palpable. Some threw down their weapons and wept openly, gesturing in a serpentine imitation of the Imperial aquila. Another struck his own head with all three of his arms, again and again in anguish. Another lay down beside one of the xenos corpses and tenderly cradled the monstrous visage as if it were the face of a waking lover.

Lamya watched them expressionlessly, hands folded in her lap.

'We must kill the enemy, as they killed the star children!' cried the tall man.

'Now,' Khan said, and surged forward.

The Catachans dropped onto the cultists like falling death. The rangy Catachan sniper killed a handful within seconds. Adair, the big thug, roared in with her heavy flamer. Anditz cracked off a series of precise centre-mass shots, felling the poorly trained rabble of cultists as they scrambled for their weapons. Khan's plasma pistol dispatched the final stragglers.

Khan walked over to the charred remains and rolled one of the bodies over with the toe of her boot. His head was overlarge and veinous, his skull visible through the purpled flesh as if it was a growing parasite. A hard, ridged plate grew in the centre of his forehead. Underneath one of his arms, a third lay curled and hidden, fingers terminating in nails that were closer to claws.

'Lieutenant,' Khan said, without turning away from the creature. 'You seen anything like this before?'

'Yes, sir. A lot of the cultists we get out here are twists like this.'

'It's worse than the 'nids somehow. Half human, half not.'

'And they've betrayed their own species,' Anditz said.

Khan nodded. 'Haruto, take Adair and clean up the vehicles. Make sure there are no more cultists alive and take anything of use.'

'You don't intend to requisition the vehicles, sir?' Anditz asked.

'No.'

'It would help us make up time,' the dour-faced sergeant said.

'I'm not going to make the same mistake as the squads Kvelter sent out before us. They were too visible. That's how they got wiped out. We move quiet.'

'But the swarm's passed,' Haruto replied.

'Viper,' Khan said, using what Anditz assumed was the sergeant's Catachan nickname, 'if we could predict what those bastards were going to do, we'd be winning the war. This isn't for discussion.'

Haruto shook his head. 'Then how are we going to make up time? It took us longer to get away from Cobalt Fortress than planned. From what we do know, things are going to get a lot worse on the planet, fast.'

Anditz watched the major closely, trying to control his own surprise at her sergeant's behaviour.

Khan spread her hands. 'Then *we'll* have to be a lot worse than the planet.' She shook her head. 'We're keeping this covert.'

To Anditz's amazement, Haruto looked as if he was about to argue more with the major, when there was the sudden snap of a long-las.

The group dropped.

Anditz turned, laspistol drawn, then stopped. Lamya cowered over the body of one of the dead cultists, a weapon steaming and ruined at her feet.

Ghost, the Catachan sniper, closed the distance to her, his long-las smoking from the recent discharge.

Khan lit up a cheroot and blew out a breath of pale smoke as she sauntered over to the cultist.

'I did what I promised,' Lamya said, trembling hands held over her head.

'And it was useful,' Khan said. 'Having you speak the cant. But you know what you don't need in order to be able to speak?'

Lamya stared.

'What you don't need are legs,' Khan said. 'Or arms.'

'She'd be lighter to carry without those, sir. Seems more efficient. Reckon our new Cadian officer'd approve of that,' Adair said with a grin.

'What do you think, lieutenant?' Khan said, turning to Anditz.

'It's your decision, sir. But I believe your first instinct was to shoot her in the head.'

Khan raised her eyebrows. 'So it was, thank you, lieutenant. I'll keep that option in reserve.' She fixed the cultist with an emotionless stare. 'Though what I'll do first if you try to run away again is cut your feet off. But I'll do it a slice at a time. Do you understand?'

The cultist averted her gaze and nodded.

'Can't get much of a fine slice off a chainsword, sir,' Adair said.

'Pity, that.' Khan shrugged. 'I suppose I'd have to take my time trying. Now, I need a moment with Lieutenant Anditz. Squad, search the vehicles for supplies.'

The troops dispersed.

'Walk with me,' Khan said to Anditz.

Anditz followed the stocky major out to what had been the bastion's walkway. The mass of dead 'gaunts that the nightmare leader-tyranid had ascended the previous night still lay against the wall, stark and dust-dredged. He followed Khan down a crumbled gully of dead masonry to the ground.

A mound of newly turned soil was heaped, darkly stark, outside the bastion's walls. A twisted piece of metal lay atop it, which Anditz recognised to be the remains of Captain Nkosi's bolt pistol.

'We did what we could for the dead we found while Adair was digging you out,' Khan said. 'I'm not familiar with your people's death traditions, or if there are any rites you need to perform before we leave.'

Anditz stared at the little patch of earth. All that remained of those lives. All that remained of the Cadian 82nd. He pulled the tin that Nkosi had left him from his pocket and stepped forward. He crouched down and carefully opened it, shielding the delicate contents from the wind. It was a precious relic, an irreplaceable treasure prized by his regiment. He took a pinch of the fine dust inside, and with his fingers pressed it into the mound that marked the place his regiment had died. Then he shut the tin and placed the container of Cadian earth back into his pocket.

Khan hadn't said anything. She just watched from a short distance.

'I should have died with them,' Anditz said, hoarse.

'Then the Cadian Eighty-Second would be dead,' Khan said. 'Is that what you really want? That there should be nobody left to carry their stories?' She took a drag on her cheroot. 'There's still work for you to do here, soldier. Work for the Eighty-Second to do.'

Anditz remained crouching and stared blankly at the mound. It seemed so small.

Khan came and squatted beside him. 'You know most Cata-chans never leave the planet?' she said conversationally. 'The world claims more than half of us before we're grown. Those who do leave are already survivors.'

'I didn't know that.'

'It's a hard world. We're proud to have been made by it. But the ones who didn't survive it are still Catachans. They had a different fight, but not a less worthy one. They're still part of us, part of our story.'

'This is different. I failed my soldiers,' Anditz said. He felt numb, as if the strange brightness of the day was pressing in on him.

'You'll fail them if you don't carry on. On Catachan we say that the jungle is coming for us all, sooner or later, lieutenant. Whatever world we're on, however far we are from home. It got them first, but you're still here. They'll continue to fight through you, if you let them. Keep fighting until the jungle comes for you.'

She got to her feet and extended a broad hand to Anditz. He took it and stood beside her.

'You have to fight the guilt, son. I know that.' She paused for a moment. 'I left the rest of my regiment to die yesterday. They were fighting to buy us time, to make sure this mission succeeded.'

'I'm sorry, sir.'

'Don't be sorry, son. Be angry,' she said. Then she cleared her throat. 'I assume you don't know why you're escorting us to Stuhl's excavation site?'

'No, sir.'

'A weapon,' Khan said, gazing out across the horizon. 'The Martians think Stuhl was digging up something that can take out tyranids. That he was trying to get it working when the excavation site went dark. And if we get it off-world, maybe the Imperium's got something they can fight these bastards with. I mean really fight 'em.' Khan gripped Anditz's arm and searched his eyes. 'Can I rely on you to help me do that, lieutenant?'

Something unfamiliar sparked in Anditz's heart. It felt like hope.

'To the end, sir.'

Khan nodded. 'Good. But we need to get to this damned excavation facility first. Let's frag us some xenos.'

There was a sudden explosion from behind them. Anditz and Khan ducked automatically, then, exchanging glances, ran towards the direction of the sound. They found the rest of the squad standing looking at the blasted wreckage of one of the cultists' vehicles. The wheels ruptured in the heat, screaming as they deflated.

'They'd booby-trapped 'em, sir,' Adair said by way of explanation.

'Anyone hurt?' Khan asked.

'No, sir,' Haruto said. 'But we would have been if it wasn't for her.' He gestured at the prisoner. 'She spotted some symbol. Told us there'd be an incendiary. Tech-Adept Wrathe was able to detonate it before it detonated itself.'

Khan nodded. 'You keep your feet another day, cultist,' she said to Lamya.

The woman's lip curled and she pulled at her hair, but she didn't say anything.

'Move out,' Khan said. 'Before trouble finds us.'

CHAPTER SIX

The squad had managed to salvage some powercells and rations from the cultists' remaining vehicle, and they had split the load between them. Now they marched south, with Opal Bastion disappearing into the distance behind them. The shale skittered underfoot as they walked down towards the winding ribbon of green that had grown up around the river.

Haruto walked ahead, eyeglass clamped in his organic eye, squinting at the map in his hand. The tech-priest walked stiffly alongside him and gestured with her hands at the route. Adair and Ghost marched at the rear with the cultist in their sights.

'There wasn't a forest when we pulled out of this region a few months ago,' Lieutenant Anditz remarked.

The Cadian strode beside her. He was small, his movements as precise as if he'd been born on a parade ground. He had dark, cropped hair, neat, fine features and the strange violet eyes peculiar to his people. He wore an antique power sword at his hip, no doubt a valuable relic from some gloried ancestor, Khan thought. Inherited, rather than earned. Cadian glory was passed down in the blood, they said, charted in family trees heavy with pyrrhic victories, as though having a particular second name might make you a better warrior.

'There's a jungle there now,' she said. 'We came through it on the way down from Cobalt Fortress. Haruto and the tech-adept reckon it's something the xenos are doing. They think it's following a flood basin or something.' She shrugged. 'Means there'll be more of it, anyhow. You ever fight in the jungle, soldier?'

'I've drilled for it, sir. Never been deployed in one.'

Khan grunted. 'This isn't going to be like anything you've drilled for.' She shifted her chainsword's strap. 'You ever heard the stories about the tyranid attack on Saint Capilene? A missionary world, like this. Supposedly they left it just a rock. No atmosphere, no nothing. Started with a cult, same as it did here.' She shook her head. 'How'd you go from this' – she gestured around – 'to a lifeless rock?' She thrust her jaw at the figures of Haruto and Wrathe ahead. 'The brains have been comparing the scraps they know, and they think the jungle is the next step in whatever the damned xenos are doing to consume this world.'

'If it's not too bold, sir, Sergeant Haruto isn't what I expected. Nor are any of you. Apart from…' He paused.

'Apart from Trooper Adair?' Khan grinned, guessing what he wanted to say. 'She's what everyone imagines we are. People are often surprised when they find we're all different. I'd say that's something we've got in common.'

'Sir?'

'Catachans and Cadians. People define us by what they think our worlds are. And of course, they're wrong most of the time. I don't know what it is to be Cadian, just as you don't know what it is to be Catachan. But your average Mordian thinks she's got the measure of us just because she's heard of our worlds.'

Anditz walked alongside her in silence for a few moments, brows knitted. 'I'd not thought of it like that before.'

'I don't encourage too much thinking in general, lieutenant. It's the enemy of action. Our job is to get into the facility and then we get the asset out.' Khan glanced at Haruto. The tech-priest was showing him something on her wrist hololith. 'Sergeant,' she called. 'We've a few hours to nightfall. Do you have a location for camp?'

'I thought we'd march on.'

'I want to rest the squad.'

'Are you sure? We need to make up time.'

'Reckon we've got enough distance between us and the swarm now. And do you remember Dank IV?' Khan raised an eyebrow. 'When you refused to stop and dry your feet and they half rotted off? I had to carry you back. This squad is the Imperium's most important asset on Lazulai. I'm going to take care of it.'

Haruto almost smiled, then nodded. 'Then we'll be in the jungle inside an hour or so. Recommend we make camp there.'

'No need to stop, sir. I could go all night,' Adair called jovially from the back.

'I know that, trooper. But then I'd have to listen to you gab all night,' Khan said.

Adair roared out a laugh.

As they entered the jungle, the sun was beginning to set, and the blood sky was washing down into the trees.

Not trees, Khan thought as they entered the foliage. Not all trees, anyway. There were indeed the trunks of Lazulai's indigenous flora, but made monstrous, thrusting up three times the size she had ever seen them. But there were other things too that had burgeoned like mushrooms, improbable and rapid with florid gills and voluptuous mouths and pendulously bellied pitchers. Their savage, spurred leaves and transpiring thorns marked them as not native to this world. The aliens' taint was in the purplish swell of their fleshy foliage, in the cruelty of the grass with fronded razor-teeth and the meaty stench of the blooms. And unlike any other jungle she'd been in, there was no other sound than the movement of plants. There was no chitter of insects or clatter of predators moving through foliage.

Despite this, the patterns of shade and damp heat were familiar, as was the way that the trees arched into a cathedral above their heads. Khan found her eyes adjusting to the silhouettes of the leaves and the smell of the soil.

'This one's moving,' Adair said. She had halted by a plant with a particularly large pitcher hanging from it.

Scowling, Haruto stormed back to where she'd stopped, slashing aside foliage with his Catachan Fang knife. He'd tied his red bandana around his forehead as a sweat rag.

'We don't have time to stop and smell the flowers.'

'You don't want to smell this, sir,' Adair said, wrinkling her nose.

Khan saw Haruto wince as he came level with Adair. The pitcher hung heavily from a broad, purple-barked tree. It was around the size of a person, garishly swollen with a fleshy lip around the rim. It stank like an abandoned charnel house.

'Curious,' the sergeant said, forgetting his anger as fascination took over. Without dropping his gaze from the unnatural sight, he fumbled out his eyeglass from his pocket and clamped it in. 'Recommend we cut it open, sir,' he said. 'I'd like to know what this is.'

'Make it quick,' Khan said, folding her arms.

'Adair,' Haruto ordered.

The cultist sat down. 'My feet hurt,' she muttered and fidgeted anxiously with her hands. Everyone ignored her.

Adair set down her heavy flamer and pulled out her Devil's Claw. At three feet long, the mercury-weighted knife was closer to a sword by the definition of most other regiments, but in Adair's huge hands it was as nimble as a combat knife.

She deftly slit the lurid pouch of the pitcher. An immediate rush of stinking, sickly-pink fluid spurted outwards. Adair hooked an arm around Haruto and yanked him backwards out of range. The liquid burned and sizzled whatever it touched, and the two Catachans backed up rapidly to avoid their boot soles being eaten away as the filthy secretion seeped towards them.

'Throne on Terra,' Lieutenant Anditz muttered as something slopped out of the split pitcher and slapped softly onto the moist forest floor.

A gelatinous mess of bones and offal and half-liquefied tissue heaped with a human skull pooled before them. Something metallic glittered amongst the remains. Adair trod forward cautiously and used her knife to prod at the corpse-gobbets, carefully lifting the relic out. It was a gold chain, with six tiny, clawed amethyst arms hanging from it.

'A cultist,' Khan said. That was a small blessing, if a foul one.

Lamya had stood up and was peering in horrified fascination at the fleshy remains. 'What happened to them?'

'What happened to this cultist was justice, heretic,' Haruto said. 'They got devoured by the horror they brought upon this world.'

Adair nodded agreement.

'We've stopped long enough. Move out,' Khan said. She was conscious of the sun moving overhead, of the time they had left trickling away.

'And nobody climb into any carnivorous plants,' Haruto added. 'As tempting as it apparently is to the chronically naive.'

'Wonder if that's how they got the cult to do all this,' Adair said, swinging her heavy flamer back over her shoulder.

'What? With plants?' Haruto raised an eyebrow.

Adair shook her head. 'By people being naive. Not thinking. Not realising what we did for 'em, that they had easy lives compared to yours and mine. Not realising that if you burn down your house, you'll have nowhere to live. And now they've gone and done it, they've lost their minds.'

'Don't think about the reasoning of heretics,' Khan said, turning to push her way through the foliage.

'Reasoning may not be the problem, major. We destroyed a witch at the cult's base,' the Cadian said. 'In Var Mine.'

'They're using witches?' A shiver ran down Khan's spine. The remains of the dead cultist held no fear for her, but the taint of the witch was something else. She'd wondered if the soldiers' tales about them had been exaggerated until she herself had served alongside a Wyrdvane unit. Something had gone wrong with one of the freaks during battle, and smoke started roiling from the top of his head. Half the troops nearby had fatal nosebleeds, and an unfortunate handful suddenly found their skulls inverted and their brains on the outside of their heads before a commissar terminated the witch.

'Yes. A twist. And...' Anditz paused. 'A tyranid.'

'A xenos witch?' Khan whistled. Heresy squared.

'We killed it.' Anditz stared ahead as if recollecting something. 'But I don't think it was the only one.'

The tech-adept appeared interested. She had thrown her hood back in the heat. Her cranial mechadendrites lay flat, and moisture beaded her brow. 'The cult had a centralised psychic control system?' she asked.

Anditz shook his head. 'We don't know. Something happened to a lot of the others when we killed those two. They went mad, pulled out their own eyes.' He gestured at Lamya. 'She passed out.'

Wrathe turned her attention to the former cultist. She had curled herself up at the base of a tree and was gently rocking back and forth, staring at a fixed point ahead.

'Do you recall it?' Wrathe asked, squatting down so she was at eye level. 'Could you hear the cult's witch? Did it speak to you?'

Lamya didn't answer, but turned her head away, muttering.

Khan banged the tree that Lamya leaned against. 'Answer the tech-adept.'

Lamya stopped muttering and glowered. 'No. I don't remember.'

'You are lying,' the tech-adept stated, metal hands resting on her knees. 'Is this due to your fear of us, or what your fellow heretics might do to you if you revealed their secrets?'

Wrathe watched the cultist's berry-dark eyes unblinkingly with her strange, milky-white ones. Khan wondered on which visual spectrum and with what acuity the Martian could see.

'I remind you at this juncture that you are in our company, not that of the cult. Perhaps this might inform a logical conclusion as to whom you ought to be most afraid of in this specific moment?' Wrathe's voice was as cold and toneless as it ever was.

Lamya's face twisted, and she glanced around as if she might be overheard. 'This isn't what they showed us,' she whispered. 'I don't think these are the angels. They were supposed to be coming to save us from the Imperium's Corpse-Lord.'

'Hear that?' Adair looked around. 'We've been worrying for nothing. The xenos are here to save us.'

'Not you,' Lamya spat. 'The people. The ones who cut the rocks and shape the gems and die of lung-rot in the mines and who the Imperium grinds to dust, the Imperium whose thirst will never be slaked.'

'Do you mean the people that you and your cult condemned to death?' Khan said coolly.

'Condemned to death?' Lamya hissed. 'What do you call life

under your Imperium? Endless toil in the grip of an iron fist, a miserable, choiceless existence solely to serve the endless hunger of your Corpse-Lord. You think it's any better? You think any of it is a choice?' she laughed, eyes wild. 'We're all being consumed by something. At least I had the agency to choose.'

Khan glimpsed Haruto kneeling to extract something from his pack.

'My only crime is to allow myself to be eaten by hope.' Her voice rose to a shriek. 'Yours is to perpetuate the dead hand of the Imperium and inflict a slow death on the billions condemned to be ground beneath it.'

Haruto slapped a vial of sedative into her arm.

Lamya jerked and clutched at the puncture point. 'You're all weak,' she spat. 'Mindless. If you only thought for yourselves, perhaps you'd deserve to live.' Her eyes rolled back into her head as the drugs took effect before she slumped down, unconscious.

The sergeant grunted. 'She talks even more crap than you, Adair. What do you want to do with her, sir?'

Khan sniffed. 'She's a liability. I'm inclined to leave her.' She noticed the Cadian shift slightly. 'Lieutenant Anditz, do you disagree?'

'We've not crossed the gem road yet. That's where any remaining cultists might be. It'd be a shame not to bring her a little further if she could be of use, sir.'

'Time is against us, lieutenant. She'll slow us down. Put the mission at risk. My Catachans can go at pace, but any outsiders put us at a speed disadvantage.'

'Sir.' The Cadian's brow was furrowed. He was either unaware of, or ignoring Khan's implication about his own pace. 'We've a long way to go to the excavation site. The success of this mission entirely depends on us getting there. I can lead us in the right direction, but the terrain has changed and the heretic is the only one of us with inside knowledge about the cult and the xenos. She's of value still.'

'I can carry her, sir,' Adair said. 'As long as she stays shut up.'

Khan gave Anditz a long look. His reasoning was sound. 'Fine. The heretic will live a little longer.' She looked up at the sky. It was beginning to wash out to an indistinct shade of indigo. 'We're losing the light for today, anyway. Sergeant, find us somewhere to camp down.'

They settled in a small clearing under pale starlight and the writhing xenos light of the aurora. They were surrounded by striated undergrowth and vast flowering stalks rising forty feet into the humid air. Ghost had managed to summon a fire despite the damp, and Khan, Adair and Anditz sat around it while the others took watch.

Khan smoked a cheroot and by the flicker of firelight watched Adair try to wind up the Cadian. She'd been briefing him on conducting jungle warfare while noisily eating a ration pack. In fairness to the lieutenant he seemed to be taking it fairly calmly. That was important. This was more than just banter, it was a test. If he couldn't integrate with the Catachans, he'd never earn their respect.

'Another thing you should know, sir' – Adair waved a massive finger inches away from Anditz's nose – 'is about grenades.' She rifled around the greasy bottom of the ration pack for any last crumbs.

'Believe it or not, Cadians are quite familiar with grenades, Trooper Adair.'

'You can call me Jet, sir,' she said, licking her fingers of the last starch dust. 'And the point is that you should never throw a grenade in the jungle.'

'No?' said Anditz. Khan detected a weariness in his tone.

'No,' the Catachan said emphatically. 'We had a Mordian com-missar once. Remember him, sir?' She winked at Khan. 'Very keen on punctuality. Anyway, we told him the same thing, but he didn't listen. Threw it anyway in dense trees. It bounces back and blinds him. He gets patched up, he comes back. Wants to show us he knows best, put us in our place. So, what does he do?' She grinned. 'He throws another grenade. And what happens?' She raised her eyebrows. 'That gave his position away, and he gets shot by a kroot. It didn't see me because I wasn't chuck-ing explosives. Killed it nice and clean, but it was too late for the commissar. He was always "late" after that.' She creased up.

Anditz sighed.

'Just trying to keep you safe, sir. You're a little more' – she ges-tured at him – 'delicate than we're used to. Now, me?' She gestured at herself. 'I was made in the jungle, sir. Reckon I could probably throw a grenade out there and be fine.'

'You could probably eat a grenade and be fine, trooper,' Anditz replied.

Adair grinned, then let out a belch. The Cadian was handling the garrulous trooper well, Khan thought.

'Would you be quiet?' came a hoarse voice from the other side of the fire. Khan glanced to see Lamya where they'd left her. The sedative was wearing off, which wouldn't be pleasant.

Adair raised her eyebrows. 'Hey!' she shouted. 'What do you call a cultist without a cult?'

'I don't know,' Lamya growled.

Adair paused. 'You,' she said, and laughed.

Anditz rubbed his eyes.

Khan leaned back so she was just outside the circle of fire-light and grinned.

'Tell me, heretic,' Adair said.

'What?' Lamya snapped, levering herself upright.

'Back at the bastion, that twist called you a poet. What did he mean?'

Lamya sat up, her poise returning. 'A brute like you wouldn't understand.' She tossed her hair with a touch of her old arrogance. 'I am a wordsmith, a creator of worlds and a weaver of dreams.'

'So, you make art, you write poetry.' Adair shrugged. 'That's nothing special. We do that too.'

'Catachan poetry?' Anditz said, eyebrows raised.

'Yes. It's not for outsiders. And certainly not for Cadians. You people have a stunted creative aesthetic,' Adair said loftily. 'No offence, sir,' she added.

Anditz's lip curled. 'How could anything like poetry come out of a death world like Catachan? You don't even have paper because of the damned humidity.'

Khan watched with interest. Why had this been the thing to break the Cadian's cool? she wondered. Perhaps it had been easier for him to dismiss Adair's jibes when he was able to imagine the Catachans as simple killers and nothing else. When he could imagine himself as superior.

Adair sat back with a grin and tapped the side of her head. Khan knew she'd smelled blood.

'We're storytellers. We keep the words here. Anyway,' she said with a slight smirk, 'I'd rather be from a death world than a dead world.'

'What did you say?' Anditz rose. Like hers, his skin didn't easily show a flush, but Khan could tell his blood was up. She took a swig from her canteen. She could bawl Adair out on Anditz's behalf, but it wouldn't help the Cadian gain the squad's respect.

There was a rustle from the trees. Adair was immediately on her feet with her knife in her hand.

Wrathe emerged into the clearing. 'My watch is complete,' she crackled through her vox-grille.

'I'm up,' Adair said brusquely, and disappeared into the trees.

Khan breathed a quiet sigh of relief as the tension dissipated. It could have been worse. Adair might be abrasive, but she was a bloody good soldier. If the lieutenant let his Cadian arrogance get in the way of seeing that, he would be as much of a liability as the cultist before long.

Anditz straightened his uniform. 'I should be relieving Trooper Hasan.'

'Ghost?' Khan said. 'He won't come back tonight. You may as well get some rest.'

Anditz frowned. 'Sir. I do not need to be coddled. I can fulfil my duty–'

'I need you rested, lieutenant,' Khan said. 'In order that you can fulfil that duty. I don't doubt your commitment, or your capability. But I need you sharp to keep us going in the right direction.'

He hesitated.

'If you can't sleep, you could maintain your weapons,' Khan suggested, recalling the proclivities of the Cadians under her command back at Cobalt Fortress. In times of stress, she'd observed the Cadian soldiery had seemed to take solace in ritual and protocol.

Anditz nodded and pulled out his laspistol to inspect. Khan got to her feet.

'Major,' the tech-adept said. 'With your consent I will undertake routine maintenance on your plasma pistol.'

Khan nodded. Without a tech-priest it was risky to attempt such a thing. She handed Wrathe the antique weapon. It had been by her side ever since she was voted in as an officer, and presented with the regimental relic.

The tech-adept took it gently. Khan noticed that the heat of the Baneblade's engine had tempered the metal of her hands with a rainbow sheen.

Something fluttered past Khan's face. She snatched her hand out to catch it. In her palm beat a tiny, white moth. She had seen such things when they had first deployed on the world many months ago, but they had become increasingly scarce as the climate had begun to change.

'You shouldn't kill moths,' said Lamya, still petulant. She was crouching with her arms wrapped around herself, watching Khan from beneath her shock of hair. 'It's bad luck.'

'You race the big ones here, don't you? Keep them as pets.'

'You've simplified the tradition, but yes.'

'I bet you've never seen the industrial moth farms on the southern continent, have you?' Khan said. 'Or smelled them.'

Lamya gestured dismissal. 'Why would I have?'

Khan regarded the cultist. 'We passed through there early in the deployment. Miles and miles of hangars. Thousands of workers in there, feet rotting off from trudging through ankle-deep rivers of moth shit all day, the wing-dust disintegrating their lungs.' Khan spat. 'One of them told me you're lucky if you last five years in the pens.'

'Why are you telling me this?'

'You said they were important to you, the workers.' Khan spread her hands. 'Don't you think you should know the price they paid for your traditions?'

Lamya wordlessly turned her back on Khan and hunched into a foetal position.

Khan looked down at the tiny moth in her hand. It was soft, furred and harmless – unlike anything from Catachan. It was also the first native creature she'd seen in Lazulai's jungle. There were no indigenous birds here, and few mammals, but still, there should have been insects. It was uncanny. The only sound was the crack of embers in the fire.

Khan opened her hand to let the little thing fly free, then

unsheathed her Catachan Fang and went out into the night to begin her watch.

Anditz rose early the next morning. He found Sergeant Haruto brewing something dark and bubbling over the fire.

'Lieutenant,' the bushy-haired Catachan greeted him. 'Recaff?' He gestured with a tin mug.

'Sergeant, that's the best offer I've had since we made planetfall.'

Haruto nodded. 'Adair getting on your nerves, sir?'

Anditz regarded Haruto, trying to read the dour Catachan. Was he trying to bait him into criticising Adair? He was wary after his outburst back at the fireside. Haruto had obviously heard it. The sergeant's face was an unintelligible mess of scars and scowls and the bionic eye didn't help in inferring his intent either.

As if reading his mind, Haruto shrugged. 'Nothing ulterior in the question. Just letting you know you're not the only one, sir. She's a pain in the arse, but the major likes her. And Throne knows she's pulled her weight on the mission so far.'

Anditz nodded. He'd known serving with the Catachans would be different, he'd just not anticipated quite how different.

'Would you care to have a look at the route, sir?' Haruto unfolded the map for Anditz to see. 'You were deployed on the eastern front?'

Anditz nodded. The terrain looked familiar, although the fauna had changed so much that it was difficult to relate their current position to the geographic features on the map. He squinted. 'We're just past the shale desert. On the way up to the coast road.' Anditz nodded. 'We'll reach the Tanzanite Cathedral soon.'

Haruto sat back. 'Do you know it, sir?'

'The cathedral? Yes. We used it as a base for a few weeks. It was a major pilgrimage site. Largest cathedral on the world, out in the middle of nowhere, looking out to sea.' Anditz shrugged. 'I don't know how they have so much space.'

'A lot of the workers live underground. Or did. We saw some of it when we were stationed out on the other continent.'

Anditz nodded. 'The cathedral's got a quartz wall around it holding the sea out. Must be more than a hundred feet high. Water up against it all the time. You can see things swimming in it on the other side.' He smiled at the memory. 'The troops didn't like it. My corporal said…'

He broke off as realisation curdled the recollection on his tongue. His corporal was dead. His captain was dead. His regiment was dead.

'What did your corporal say, sir?' Haruto asked. Anditz recognised something like care in the man's tone.

'She said that it looked like the ocean had been turned inside out.'

'Sounds nasty, sir. The people on this planet…' Haruto grimaced. 'Never been to a world so devoid of taste. Everything's so bloody gaudy.'

Anditz appreciated the opening the sergeant had given him to move the conversation on. 'You didn't see the cult's headquarters.'

Haruto winced. 'You'll notice that we don't wear metal jewellery. Perhaps some bone here, some wood there. Most of our weapons are dulled. On Catachan, if you make yourself noticed, you'll end up eaten.'

'Morning,' Khan said, emerging from the undergrowth. Haruto handed her a mug of recaff.

'The lieutenant is familiar with the terrain we're crossing next,' the sergeant said.

'We used Tanzanite Cathedral as a base, before,' Anditz said. 'There's a route we could take along the coast that might save even more time.'

Khan nodded. 'Good. Because things are going to get more inhospitable pretty quickly.'

'Sir?' Anditz frowned.

Khan took a sip of her recaff. 'The spores haven't cleared today. Every morning before now it'd start clear, then the air would start filling up with the stuff.'

Anditz glanced up. Khan was right. The sun was filtered through a shimmering haze. 'Do we have rebreathers?'

'No,' Khan said. 'We packed light. Didn't think we'd need them when we set out. Frankly, I didn't think we'd make it far enough to need much of anything.'

'Sir?'

Khan adjusted her grip on the scalding beaker of recaff. 'Ours was a mission of hope, lieutenant. Hope for this squad, and hope for the soldiers who went out to die as our cover that something might be salvaged from this world. That their deaths would be meaningful.' She blew on her drink. 'That they were still fighting for something that could make a difference.'

'And you don't believe that, sir?' Anditz asked, brow furrowed.

Khan's mouth quirked up at one corner. 'I believe what I'm ordered to believe. Nothing more, nothing less.' She took another sip of her recaff. 'Let's just say I'm pleasantly surprised by each dawn we see. From an old soldier to a young one, let me recommend that as an approach. Set your expectations low, and you avoid disappointment.'

Anditz nodded. 'Sir.'

'Anyway. We're still alive, so we're going to need rebreathers. Recommendations?'

'There was a supply cache at the cathedral,' Anditz said. 'We'll be passing near enough to scout it out. And if not, perhaps we can hold out until Carnadine City?'

Khan nodded. 'We have any sense as to how bad things are going to get and how quickly?'

Haruto frowned. 'Hard to say. Most of the intelligence about tyranid invasions is redacted. The Martian knows a little more.' He shrugged. 'From what I understand of it – perhaps a week?'

'To get to the excavation site?' Anditz said.

The sergeant raised an eyebrow. 'No. A week until there's nothing left. I couldn't even guarantee there'd be an atmosphere at that point.' He took a sip of his own recaff. 'Not that we really know what happens. For obvious reasons there are very few eyewitness accounts.'

Anditz felt the sergeant's words like a punch. Nothing left? How were they to save the world?

Khan slapped her knees as she stood. 'Then we'd best get moving if we're going to get off this rock in time.'

Anditz rose. 'There are still loyal forces on Lazulai, sir. If we're hunting down a weapon that could take out the tyranids on a planetary scale–'

Khan raised her hand. 'We're hunting down a device we're taking off-world. It's too late for Lazulai, lieutenant.'

Anditz felt his face burning. If that were true, the rest of the Cadian 82nd had died for nothing. The troopers that still fought were dying for nothing. He cleared his throat.

'With all due respect, sir. If we recover the device and it could turn the war...' He frowned. 'I think we're obliged to use it.'

'All right. If we make it to the excavation site...' She gestured at the filthy sky. 'And I reiterate my view that this seems unlikely given the conditions. But if we do make it, and if we find something that'll fix Lazulai, we'll use it. That, I promise.'

She tilted her head. Anditz knew she could tell he was unconvinced.

'Trust is everything to a Catachan. I mean it,' she said, and leaned back. 'But I'm assuming we won't, lieutenant. So just make sure you kill enough of the bastards on the road to make your peace.'

The march to Tanzanite Cathedral was hard. Anditz had reckoned with Haruto that it would take half a day, but they were still fighting through the jungle when the sun glowered over them at midday. Khan and Ghost scouted ahead whilst the rest of the group, slowed by Wrathe and the prisoner, doggedly pressed on. A persistent, mizzling rain had started, and showed no signs of abating. It was slightly acidic and made Anditz's skin itch. The Catachans seemed unaffected, but the cultist moaned and scratched welts into her flesh. Her flowing skirts clung to her legs and tripped her as they pushed through the undergrowth.

'Stop complaining,' Adair said. 'And while we're at it, walk a bit faster.'

'Stop tormenting me,' the cultist snapped. 'And to think, you see yourself as saviours.'

'No one's here to save you, traitor,' Haruto said.

'You think you deserve this planet. You think your Imperium deserves to win.'

'I think you deserve to be destroyed,' he said, deadpan.

She glowered. 'Such cruelty is the thing that will destroy you.'

Adair snorted. 'Like the cruelty that destroyed this world? Your cruelty? Spend a little time in Lazulai's mines and agri fields then tell me about cruelty.'

'So, we should all just keep living in moral filth?' Lamya pushed her hair out of her eyes. 'That's how your Imperium got like it is.'

'Trooper,' Anditz said. He didn't want the cultist becoming hysterical again.

'Maybe we like it dirty.' Adair leered, prodding Lamya in the back with the nozzle of her heavy flamer. 'You softworlders get big ideas then you make a mess like this and can't even follow it through. If you've grown up in grit like us, you're a bit tougher.'

'Leave her,' warned Anditz.

Lamya raised her head. 'This one at least has some manners.' She gestured at Anditz.

'They breed that into their officers on Cadia,' Adair said lightly. 'Don't they, sir?'

Anditz raised his eyebrows. 'What do you mean, trooper?' he said.

'Well, sir,' Adair said, stowing her flamer then pushing ahead of Lamya and slashing a path through a thick patch of foliage with her long Devil's Claw. 'On Catachan, we elect our officers. Like Major Khan. Catachans have to prove they have the right sort of qualities. Whereas, so I understand, on Cadia, it's more of a case of 'em just having the right sort of parent.'

'You nominate your officers?' Anditz said, keeping his face considered. 'Then when can we expect you to do something worthy of elevation, Trooper Adair?'

Haruto barked out a laugh. 'When the light of the Throne grows cold, lieutenant!'

Adair grinned good-naturedly at the slight, apparently impervious to insult. 'I'm young and handsome, sir. I've got the whole apocalypse ahead of me, sir. Plenty of time for a battlefield promotion should the sergeant not make it.'

Haruto half snorted. 'Who needs enemies when you've got comrades like these?'

'What did the major do to earn her promotion?' Anditz asked. It seemed like a safer topic of conversation.

'I've heard some of the stories,' Adair said. 'Sergeant was there to see some. Right, Viper?'

Haruto nodded. 'Some.'

'Tell him my favourite,' Adair called.

'I was there for this one,' Haruto said, his battle-scarred face twisting into a grin. 'We were a small squad, in enemy terrain. No chance of pickup for a month. Orks everywhere. Tusk' – he turned to Anditz – 'that's the major,' he said by way of explanation, 'she had us herding and baiting the xenos in circles. She knew what they're like, so she wound them up and set them off at each other.' He shook his head. 'Got the wretched things killing themselves. Just the half a dozen of us did the work of a small army with her smarts. By the time backup came, the stupid bastards had wiped each other out and we were sitting pretty.'

'That sounds…' Anditz paused for a moment. 'That sounds like a Cadian approach.'

Haruto gave a dry chuckle. 'Catachans are strategic too, lieutenant. How do you think our ancestors survived on a death world alone for so long? People think we just like fighting–'

'We do,' Adair interrupted.

'We do,' Haruto conceded, 'but we don't like waste. There's no room for that when everything is trying to kill you, so we take the straightest line to a thing. Sometimes that means thinking, sometimes if you can't solve a problem then you…' He gestured as he thought of an example.

'You tear it in half?' Anditz offered.

'You tear it in half,' Haruto agreed with a half grin.

'Now he's getting it.' Adair clapped a massive hand on Anditz's shoulder. 'Point is, the major is a thinker *and* a doer. Got a good sense for a fight, you know?'

'And she could sense you coming a mile off.'

Anditz started. A few feet away, Major Khan appeared from the undergrowth. She was leaning against a tree, smoking a cheroot and watching them. One moment she'd not been there, the next she was. She didn't appear to have moved, just hove into focus. She blew out a plume of smoke.

'Thought you were scouting ahead, sir,' Haruto said.

'Been and gone while you whelps were napping back here. We're about three miles out from the cathedral.'

'Told you she was good.' Adair jostled Anditz with her elbow.

'It's not good news.' Khan took another drag on her cheroot. 'There's a big xenos out there on the plain. Right on our route.'

'How big is it?' Anditz asked. The peninsula was small, an outcrop that bulged into the sea with the cathedral out on the headland. An enemy blockade that prevented them from taking the coast path would send them off-route up into the mountains.

'Titan size. Bigger than anything we've done without *Ofelia's Fist*.'

Adair shrugged. 'We can take it, sir.'

'Given time, I don't doubt that,' Khan said. 'But we don't have the time.'

'Agreed,' Anditz said.

Haruto pulled out the map. 'Where is it, sir?'

Khan pointed.

Anditz tilted his head. 'There's another way. If we cut through the cathedral, we can take one of the devotional coracles along the coast.' He glanced up to see the others' expressions. 'Small boats. They use them for festivals or dedications. There are hundreds in the vaults. Saw them when we were stationed there.'

Haruto shrugged. 'Seems sound to me.'

'March on, then,' said Khan.

The others forged ahead, but Anditz dropped back to walk level with the major. 'Quick reconnaissance, sir. Very quick.'

'Impressive, wasn't it?'

Anditz shot her a glance.

The major's eyes twinkled. 'Ghost went ahead and reported

back. No point both of us getting worn out. And' – she raised her eyebrows – 'my knees are getting too old for this.'

Anditz frowned. 'Why the facade?'

'Why?' Khan smiled. 'Son, ninety-nine per cent of leadership is belief. Your troops have got to believe you can do anything. Doesn't mean it's always a good idea to try and do it.' She pulled on her smoke. 'People remember how you make them feel. You make them feel like they're following someone who can win, they'll win. Doesn't matter how you made them feel that, only that you did.'

Anditz nodded slowly.

'Your captain,' Khan said, gesturing with her cheroot. 'She could do that, I'll bet. You'd have followed her to the ends of this world. And it wasn't just because of the chain of command, was it?'

'No,' Anditz agreed. 'It wasn't.'

'And you, lieutenant? How do you lead?' She gave him a sideways glance. Then Khan suddenly halted and stared keenly into the trees as if she was listening for something.

'Sir? What do you hear?' whispered Anditz.

'Someone trying to be quiet,' Khan muttered. She tapped her knife on the side of a tree. It was a tiny sound, but ahead Anditz saw the other Catachans halt and turn to look at their commander. Khan made a series of hand gestures to the group. Adair stepped quietly over to them and Khan indicated something in the undergrowth to her. Adair nodded and drew her Devil's Claw.

Anditz squinted at the leafy shrub Khan had indicated. Adair caught his gaze and plucked a leaf to show him. It had been bent, so that a hard white line bisected its midrib. She leaned down to whisper in his ear.

'Someone pushin' through the foliage. You'd be surprised

how many softworlders don't realise they're leaving a trail like this. A Catachan can read it like a book. Ain't any straight lines in nature,' she added.

And then she was gone, weaving her muscled bulk through the trees with noiseless grace. Anditz followed but kept his distance. He knew his tread was heavier than that of the Catachans, despite their size. The trees rose in a cloistral hush above, the hot air like rancid breath.

Anditz combed the ground for a trail, tree-blind until a smear of colour snagged his eye. Amidst the litter and groundspores was a crushed fungus, a bootmark-shaped bruise imprinted in its offal-coloured gills. Anditz gestured to Khan, who knelt to examine it. She grinned and gestured ahead. She and Adair ducked and crept forward.

Anditz could hear low voices nearby. He trod carefully, squinting through the trees. Then his foot hit something solid, and he heard a rising whine like an insect.

'Don't move,' called Adair.

Anditz heard shouts and saw Khan rushing forward with her plasma pistol raised. Then Adair barrelled hard into him. She gripped him under one arm and, holding him tightly, leaped like a diver into the trees.

Behind them, something exploded with a scream, and fire and shrapnel roared out after them. They landed face-first on the floor, flames licking out behind their heels. Adair stood, and wordlessly ran towards the sound of gunfire, weapon drawn.

Anditz swore. A mining charge – how could he have been so careless? He hadn't expected such a trap in this terrain. He got stiffly to his feet, pulled his laspistol and ran towards the fight. He burst into the clearing to find Khan picking through the pockets of three dead cultists and Adair cleaning her bloodied knife on a clump of foliage.

Khan nodded. 'We're done here.' She led the way back to the others.

'Recommend we bring Haruto next time, sir?' Adair said to Khan. Khan ignored her.

Anditz felt his face burn.

They made the rest of the march in silence.

As they broke out of the jungle the landscape opened up before them, bright and strange. The sky now roiled, curdled and vomitous, heaving an unnatural light over the open plains. To the right the sea shuddered, green and hard-looking. And inland, framed by the folded spine of a long mountain, was the monster tyranid Khan had reported. From this distance of so many miles it seemed to move slowly, a terrible serif of bristled bone the size of a building that propelled itself forward on great, spindled legs. Smaller winged tyranids were just visible fluttering in its awful orbit.

'Intriguing,' Wrathe said, her head on one side. 'What is its function?'

Haruto squinted, bionic eye whirring.

'We fought those before,' Anditz said. 'On the eastern front. They were the vanguard that swept through the cities, but they were always with an army. This looks more or less alone.'

'Perhaps its purpose is complete,' said Wrathe. 'Now that the cities are broken, it wanders without defined function.'

'Very intriguing,' Haruto agreed.

'I will record this,' Wrathe said to him.

Khan raised her eyebrows.

'We're keeping a record of the enemy,' Haruto explained. 'Their movements, tactics.' He gestured at the monster.

'We can move around it, sir,' Anditz said. 'As long as it stays in the centre of the peninsula we should be able to move out to the right along the headland and down to the cathedral.'

he'd not been so alone since he was locked in the
al Bastion listening to his regiment die. He'd rather
Adair's garrulous company than this solitude. All he
now was the roar of the sea as he swam towards the
carcass of the cathedral.

'The sea shouldn't be there,' Lamya interrupted.

The squad turned. There was a pause as everyone looked at the newly shimmering marsh ahead.

Anditz frowned. 'She's right. The agri fields have flooded.'

'It's ruined,' Lamya lamented. 'The tisane fields gone. Forever.'

'Tisane? I'm sure the miners would have preferred food was being grown,' Haruto said.

'Lazulai is a place of pilgrimage,' Lamya said. 'Of course it must be peaceful and the landscapes beautiful.' She waved at the flooded fields. 'The tisane is part of that.'

'Landscape? Beautiful?' Adair frowned. 'Landscape's just what's around you. Doesn't seem worth most people having to live underground for it.'

'You think hive city spires are any different?' Lamya shot back. 'Besides, the pilgrims came here for your Emperor. It's your mess.'

Anditz frowned. 'A lot of the Ecclesiarchy were in your cult.'

But Lamya wasn't listening. She had wrapped her arms around herself and was staring at the distant tyranid.

'You, cultist. Can you sense it?' Wrathe asked, curious.

'No.' She shuddered. 'It's so quiet. Now that I can't hear them.'

Wrathe's vox-grille crackled. 'And what do you feel when you behold it?'

'Fear,' Lamya whispered, tears welling in her eyes. 'I feel fear.'

'Lieutenant,' Khan said to Anditz. 'Lead us to the cathedral.'

They picked their way through ankle-deep water. It was warm, and like the rain felt slightly acidic. It soaked into their boots and made Anditz's feet itch.

'It's a fast ticket to foot-rot,' Adair said with a grimace, kicking through a slush of festering vegetation.

'Was it always this quiet here?' Haruto asked.

'No,' Anditz replied. 'When we moved through this area,

thousands of Ecclesiarchical workers and pilgrims were being evacuated. The cathedral was the biggest pilgrimage site on the world. You'll be able to see it in a moment.'

They rounded the corner and halted.

Adair cleared her throat. 'It doesn't look like the picts.'

The sea wall had broken, and the whole beach upon which the cathedral sat was now flooded. Only the top of the vast edifice was visible, the stranded mass of stone spires and nave appearing to float on the sea like a stolid, stone waterbird. Splintered teeth of quartz rose jagged around the marooned building, marking the place where the wall had held back the depths.

They walked to the edge of the cliff and the first colossal stone steps that led down to the cathedral's now submerged plaza. For arriving pilgrims, this is where they would have seen the infinite majesty of the Imperium and the infinite power of the ocean meet. The steps were two hundred feet wide, carved from the engineered minerals and precious stones that made up Lazu-lai's crust. They were formed of swirls of gems: green emeralds, purple amethysts, sun-bright citrine and flecks of night-black onyx polished smooth by the feet of worshippers over centuries. The steps descended into the sea flanked by drowned alabaster saints with dimmed rubies for eyes, mournful with water lapping at their chins.

Anditz eyed the far spires out in the water. The coracles had been stored on the other side of the great edifice, along with the cache of equipment.

'It's only a few thousand feet away.' He turned to the squad. 'We can get out there in fifteen minutes or so, get the rebreath-ers and get back on the coast road towards Carnadine City.'

'You've not noticed a problem with that plan?' Haruto asked.

Anditz looked at him blankly.

'The fact that half a mile of the sea is in the way?'

'We can swim there,' And[

'You can't swim?' he said,

'Within reason. But that d[
not, lieutenant, there's not muc[
want to drink, let alone swim in,[

'Or anywhere we're deployed,' add[

Anditz shook his head and sighed. He[
flak armour and empty his pockets.

'What are you doing, soldier?' Khan asked.

'Preparing to recover a coracle as per our pla[
said, setting down his laspistol.

'Solo?'

'Cadians train for this, major. Basic aquatic combat.'

'Done much battlefield swimming, sir?' Adair said.

'No, but you never know when you'll need to,' Anditz [
pulling his shirt off. 'That's the point. That's why we train[
every eventuality.'

'Fifteen minutes out, you say?' Khan said.

'Yes, sir.'

'Still faster than diverting round to the plain and engagin[
the tyranid out there.'

Haruto nodded agreement.

'Be careful, lieutenant,' Khan said as Anditz folded his fatig[
and laid them on the ground along with his power sword. [
provide what cover we can from here.'

Anditz nodded, then waded into the warm, slightly [
water of the sea. It slapped against him as it reache[
and he pushed off from the steps. He could just h[
of the Catachans on the shore fading out of ea[

'Why are Cadian-issue undershirts nicer tha[

'Shut up, Adair. Or you're going in after th[

Then their voices faded. As he moved i[

CHAPTER SEVEN

Anditz estimated it took him ten minutes to reach the cathedral. He swam on, under the ribs of flying buttresses that plunged into the water, and over the submerged basilicas and rotundas and chapels that had clustered around the main body of the cathedral. They shimmered far below in the distortion of the water as he passed over their darkness. Finally, he reached the most southerly point of the great building. To his relief, he saw that the water hadn't submerged the gallery windows.

He climbed up above the waterline and gripped a slender colonnette in one hand. Pulling out Khan's knife with the other, he smashed the hilt into one of the panes. He kicked as much glass away as he could then pulled himself inside, dropping down heavily onto the little gallery that ran around the inside of the roof, just above the water level. Fit as he was, he'd not trained in water for many months, and he felt his muscles protesting as he stood, dripping. He leaned on the handrail and stared around.

The vastness of the cathedral was made strange by the water filling it. The tide sloshed and sucked around the walls, reflecting strange ripples of light into the ribbed vaults overhead and magnifying the acoustics of its own echoing sluice. A strange, salty sea-damp permeated everything. The tide had carried as many things up to the surface as it had submerged, and around the walled sea bobbed dead servo-skulls and water-swollen prayer books and sodden parchment and scraps of fabric and incense vials. A half-rotten feral cyber-cherub hovered aimlessly, its eyes scabbed over, one hand scratching in the air with a long-lost quill.

And everywhere coloured light streamed in through the windows around the walls, depicting bright saints and martyrs and victories of the Imperium, painting a rainbow over the decay. The Blessed Master of Mankind watched the ruination from the immense rose window filling the apse, one hand a power claw raised in benediction, the other holding a flaming sword. The water slapped around the God-Emperor's knees, a briny sacrilege on the deity's person.

Then, like a blessing from Him-on-Terra, a boat bobbed into view. It was battered, a line drifting out wanly behind it where it had shrugged its mooring. Anditz clambered over the gallery rail and dropped into the water. He swam out to the boat and examined it. The engine of the powered launch seemed to be intact and started with a little persuasion. The flat boat would fit ten comfortably. This would transport them much faster than a coracle. Paper streamers of skulls and moths trailed, damp and distorted, in the bottom of the vessel, from whatever festival it had last served. A battered lantern hung on the prow, but it was otherwise empty save for the inbuilt flat benches. Fortune had been on his side, Anditz realised, for this boat to have floated up and into the cathedral. Now to recover the supplies. He steered the boat back to the gallery and looped the mooring rope over a leering skull-faced carving.

The supplies cache was above water, he reckoned. But the access to it wasn't. He could see the open flight of stairs beneath, down a level through the water. He would have to swim down, then along a broad corridor to the side-sacristy and back up to reach the cache. He considered the length of the dive. The depth looked to be twenty feet, then from his recollection it was about a hundred feet along the corridor and then twenty feet to ascend. As long as there were no major obstacles it would be comfortably within the distance he'd drilled for.

Anditz dived off the side of the boat and towards the sub-merged steps. His vision was immediately blurred, and he could see only with restricted clarity as he floated over the steps like a strange ghost. He pinched his nose and blew, equalising the pressure in his ears. He was aware of the darkness of the main space of the cathedral out to his right, but he focused on the route ahead. In less than a minute he was at the ascending steps and climbing out, panting, water sluicing from his body, his legs heavy. He looked around at the familiar space, made strange by the incursion of the water. This was the second cache Captain Nkosi had ordered them to make. The other, larger one was submerged far below the cathedral's vaults, now at a depth it would be unsafe to dive without equipment. The only reason this second cache existed, tucked into the eaves, was Nkosi's suspicion of the supposedly loyal Ecclesiarchy, who'd observed them making the first. She could never have foreseen the circumstances that had rendered it so advantageous.

Anditz recalled covertly stowing the supplies with Sergeant Morton over the course of a night. He half-smiled at the memory of Morton's suppressed incredulity that they were to spend hours climbing to the rafters of the cathedral. Then he had a flash of memory at the terrible way Morton had died, the way the soldier's face had ruptured and the way that he'd had to throw the body of his trooper from Opal Bastion's macrocannon as if it were refuse. As Anditz regarded the stack of cases in the dampness of the ruined cathedral, grief caught in his chest, and he fought down the flood of emotion threatening to break loose. He clenched his fists.

He would not break. He would not fail them. He would recover the anti-xenos weapon, whatever it took.

Anditz forced himself to focus and began to unpack the supplies. He picked out ammunition, food, medicine and rebreathers. He wrapped them tightly in tarpaulins across several packs to protect them from the water. He could do a few runs to load the boat. As an afterthought he pulled out a pair of tactical goggles and put them on. He may as well see where he was going for the loading trips.

He strapped the first package around his chest and, dragging another behind him, descended into the water once more.

This time, the goggles allowed him to see clearly underwater. He swam down the steps into the greenish light below and as he passed the long gallery view onto the cathedral floor, something caught his eye. He turned to follow the movement and looked out into the vast gloom of the sea-filled space. Against a backdrop of soaring pillars and statued niches and flags trailing through the water, moved tyranids. Forms he had previously seen on land swam nimbly, like eels, strange bioluminescence rippling along their bodies in coruscating patterns.

And deeper in the gloom was something else, something only half illuminated by the coloured rays of light shafting down from the devotional windows. On the cathedral floor rested a huge, terrible mass of corpses, stirred by the water into a foul agglomeration of thousands, waiting for their organs to bloat and carry them, buoyant, back to the light. And in amongst them, a dim horror squatted vastly, an obscene king ensconced in a decaying throne of flesh. At first Anditz thought the xenos might be wounded, as at its fore splayed a mass of livid tissue. But he quickly realised to his horror that the gaping mess was its maw, and it was thrusting whole bodies into itself to devour. The thing was upwards of twenty feet in size. Drifts of blood like skeins of gauze floated out in red tendrils from it. It shuddered as it crammed corpse after corpse into its swollen body, apparently unable to stop as steam vented forth from organic chimneys on its back. Dozens of small tyranids that seemed little more than mouths shoaled around it, devouring the chunks of flesh that floated from the giant monster's charnel feast.

Anditz fought the urge to retch, and twisted rapidly in the water to swim away as fast as he could. In amongst the flickering motes of coloured lights he'd caught sight of one of the bioluminescent tyranids drifting lazily in his direction.

Something shot past him, a splinter-bone-shard missile boiling a wake through the water. He felt a sharp pain in his leg, but he didn't look back. Anditz dropped the package of supplies he was carrying and swam for his life. The package strapped to his chest slowed him down, but there was no time to untie it now. His lungs felt as if they were burning, the effort of each desperate stroke powered by adrenaline. He felt his ears pop as he made the ascent to the surface.

Then his head broke water and he was gasping for breath. He hauled himself onto the little craft and with shaking hands started the engine. It growled into blessed life, and he turned the boat around. There was blood flowing from his leg, but he ignored it. Was he being followed? Were they coming? There was no time to look.

There was also no way out. He'd planned to consider his options once he returned with the supplies.

His heart thumped in his chest. He had to act quickly. What was it Haruto had said? That Catachans took the straightest line to a thing?

A manic, rictus grin fixed itself on his face. He thrust the boat forward as fast as it would go, piloting it directly at the half-submerged glassaic of the rose window. The Emperor loomed above, fifty feet high, written in light.

'Forgive me,' Anditz muttered, ducking down at the helm as the metal craft smashed into the antique glassaic, shattering the Master of Mankind into a terrible, vengeful shower of crystal spears.

It was a brief sprint to land under the dirty citrine sky.

Adair and Haruto waded in and caught the boat as he arrived back at the shore.

Khan smiled. 'Good work, lieutenant.'

'I may have been followed,' Anditz said.

'Cultists?' she asked.

He shook his head. 'Tyranids.'

Khan nodded. 'Get in,' she ordered the troops. 'I'll pilot.'

Anditz made his way to the back of the boat and slumped on one of the benches, eyes closed, water dripping from his body. Adair pushed her way past the others and crouched down beside him as Khan moved the craft out.

'You cleaned that yet, sir?' she asked.

Anditz opened his eyes to look at her. She was indicating the injury on his leg.

'It's just a scratch,' he said dismissively. Adair was the last person he wanted to deal with right now.

'No such thing as just a scratch on Catachan.'

'Because you know so much better than everyone else that you never get hurt?'

Adair chuckled. 'No, sir. Because even the air's trying to kill you there. You can't just leave something like that, or it'll fester. Let me have a look?'

He shrugged. 'Go ahead.'

She pulled out a battered medkit, rested his foot on her knee and examined the wound. The chitin weapon had carved a jagged arc into his calf, not deep enough to cut muscle, but deep enough to bleed a lot. Adair flushed it with a vial of counterseptic that made him wince, then carefully closed the injury with wound clips. Her normally insolent face was a mask of concentration as she hooked the tiny closures in place, her pale hair sweat-spiked as she bent over her work.

'Done.' She looked up with a grin when she'd finished.

'Thank you, trooper,' Anditz said.

She waved dismissal. 'Had enough rotten officers, sir, don't need you going the same way,' she said with a twinkle in her eye.

Anditz looked inland. The huge tyranid was drifting across the blighted fields beside the distant mountain, moving in the direction of the cathedral. He suppressed a shudder, imagining emerging from the glassaic window and finding that monstrosity blotting out the sky overhead.

'Just as well we moved out when we did,' Adair said, following his gaze. 'And got the boat.'

Anditz raised an eyebrow. 'Is that a roundabout way of giving me a compliment, trooper?'

She smiled evasively.

'Lieutenant,' called Haruto, making his way down the boat. 'Out the way, Adair, you need to watch the cultist. She's been acting even more oddly since that thing appeared.' He jerked his chin at the distant inland monster.

Adair rolled her eyes. 'It's like a shift back at the creche.'

'Yes. So, everyone takes a turn.'

Grumbling under her breath, the bulky Catachan made her way back towards the prow of the boat.

'Creche?' asked Anditz, pulling his uniform back on.

'Raising children on Catachan. Everyone does a rotation at a public creche.'

'Even you?' Anditz asked the scar-puckered giant.

Haruto frowned, his beetle brows bristling alarmingly over his bionic eye. 'Of course.'

'Well,' Anditz said, lacing up his final boot, 'everyone does things differently.'

'Manage to salvage anything?' Haruto asked, indicating the package beside Anditz.

He'd almost forgotten about it. The pack around his neck was the only thing he'd carried out of the nightmare cathedral. He unwrapped it. A couple of rebreathers, a dozen grenades and a handful of lasgun clips lay inside.

'Not much,' Anditz replied. 'I was forced to jettison the rest.'

A look must have passed over his face because Haruto leaned forward. 'What happened, sir?'

Anditz cleared his throat. 'Some...' He paused, trying to find words for the horror of what he'd seen. He gave up. 'New variants were down there.'

'Under the water?'

Anditz nodded. 'Yes. They were...' He rubbed his hair. 'Less aggressive?' Then he shook his head. That wasn't the right term. 'They were focused on devouring, not attacking.'

'A different function,' Haruto mused. 'What were they eating?'

'Drowned humans. I couldn't tell who they were. Probably whoever died when the cathedral flooded. Ecclesiarchy, workers, refugees.'

'Focused on consuming,' Haruto repeated. 'We haven't seen that before. I'll have to tell the tech-adept.'

'What for?' Anditz asked.

'She collects information,' Haruto said. 'She's trying to find patterns. Anything that might help' – he dropped his voice – 'when we get to the archeotech.'

'Has she told you anything more about it?'

Haruto shook his head. 'No. And I think we know everything she knows. The major's not convinced, but I don't see why Wrathe would be hiding anything.'

Anditz nodded. He'd not spoken much to Wrathe himself, and Martians were always hard to read. 'I'd never have figured a Catachan and a tech-adept would make a good partnership,' he remarked.

Haruto cracked a smile. 'Neither would I, lieutenant.'

The tone of the boat changed as Khan piloted it around the bay.

Anditz rubbed his eyes. They stung after immersion in the sea. The Catachans seemed less affected than he and the prisoner were by the rain, but then again, given their death world heritage they were probably more resistant to a lot of things.

The powered launch chugged to a slowdown as Khan glided it ashore. After the breeze at sea, the air suddenly felt stifling.

'It's got hotter. Again,' Anditz said as he disembarked.

'It is in fact three degrees hotter today than yesterday,' the tech-adept crackled through her vox-grille as she climbed from the boat, taking Haruto's arm to steady herself. She wore her hood down and her locs and mechadendrites coiled back against her neck. 'The humidity has also increased proportionately and continues to do so daily. I would speculate that the abnormal faunal growth and spore generation may be related.'

'The jungle's making it hotter?' Anditz asked.

'There is insufficient data to determine if the factors are causal or correlative. Possibly,' she added in response to Anditz's frown.

'Lieutenant,' Khan called. 'Directions, please.'

Haruto frowned at the map, which was increasingly dog-eared, and passed it to Anditz.

'We've come ashore here.' Anditz pointed. 'We're going to join the gem road and travel up to Carnadine City. From there, we'll cut across to the excavation site.'

'You're taking me to the capital?' asked Lamya.

'We're not taking you anywhere. You just happen to be going where we are,' Adair said.

'Finally.' The cultist ran her fingers through her dishevelled curls. 'Civilisation.'

Khan frowned. 'I don't like that we're travelling through a population centre.'

'The geography will add a few days otherwise,' Anditz said. 'Which I don't believe we have.'

Khan nodded. 'And you say you passed through Carnadine when you were stationed here before?'

'Yes, sir,' Anditz said. 'It's big. There had been looting when we redeployed, but we may still be able to acquire supplies.'

'If current pollutant escalation continues, rebreathers will be strongly advised within two days, and absolutely necessary within three,' Wrathe said.

'And we're three or four days from the excavation facility,' Haruto added.

'We only have two rebreathers at the moment,' Anditz said.

Khan nodded. 'Then we head for the city.'

CHAPTER EIGHT

Khan led the squad away from the waterlogged terrain of the coast and the dark horrors of the sea. They headed inland now onto the pale dust of the gem road, dirtied with smears of green slime, and away from the quivering cornucopia of xenos flora. The foliage was sparse here, scrubby scree rising either side of the sandy track. They were making progress towards the excavation site. More than she'd thought was possible given the circumstances. Perhaps Kvelter had been right to take the risk she had. But there was still a long way to go, and you didn't count your trophies until you'd killed the enemy.

The Cadian had done well to recover the boat, she thought, watching him march ahead. They'd spread the supplies he'd recovered between the squad, and now everyone was better armed. He had a skill that they were missing, and he'd deployed it effectively. Made the squad stronger because of it – she hoped he realised that. After what had happened to his regiment, he was wounded and prideful, and that could make for a toxic mix. It had hurt him to be rescued by Adair from that mine, she knew. But she also knew if she said anything directly to him it would backfire.

She sighed and pulled out a cheroot. She was down to her last few. This damned world had better end before she ran out of smokes, or she'd be the one to end it. She lit it, rolling it in the flame as she walked. It started to glow, and she clamped it between her teeth, then resumed her train of thought. The thing non-Catachan regiments often got wrong was that there wasn't shame in taking help. Oh, Catachans were proud all right. But there wasn't time to be *prideful* on Catachan. You gave and took whatever you could, because as sure as hell, if you didn't stand together the jungle would win. She exhaled a cloud of thick, white smoke. Only a coward was afraid to ask for help. If you put your pride before survival, everyone could wind up dead.

Khan walked steadily, holding up the rear of the squad and silently surveying her troops. Adair strode ahead, with Anditz keeping pace with her. She was gesticulating and no doubt recounting some lurid tale. Adair was the kind of soldier Khan liked. She was brash and fearless, but beneath the swagger she was straightforward, although she could wind up commissars and Catachans alike.

Her sergeant, Haruto, walked beside Wrathe. The red-robed tech-adept didn't even come up to the Catachan's shoulder, and he frequently bent to hear her speak. Khan took a drag on her cheroot. She wasn't sure what to make of Haruto's alliance with the Martian. Some instinct told her that Wrathe was holding something back. Haruto was stubborn, and he was loyal to ideas, not people. If he thought a thing was right, he'd follow it to the end of the world.

She glanced around to see where Ghost was. The quiet sharpshooter strode along behind the rest of the group. He didn't talk to the others unless necessary, but he listened to them and fought with them and was just as much a part of the squad as the rest.

Each of her squad represented a different facet of Catachan, she thought. A tiny fragment of home, a tiny fragment of the force that had fought on this world. So many were dead, so many lost. Her regiment gone. She sometimes thought she felt the drift of their ghosts walk alongside her, and wondered when she would feel the jungle calling her into its final embrace. Not yet, she thought. Not while she still had this squad to fight for.

There was a sudden howl.

Khan snapped from her reverie. The cultist had tripped and was rolling on the ground. She'd thrown Lieutenant Anditz off balance when she'd fallen, and he was now grimly pulling his boot off, aided by Adair.

Khan strode forward but was stopped by Ghost gripping her arm. He gestured at the ground. Amidst the scrub around the track were clusters of fungal boluses. They ranged from the size of a thumbnail up to a clenched fist and blushed bilious in lurid shades of chartreuse. Around the cultist the spheres had burst open like filthy stars, erupting their caustic spores into the air. Khan stepped carefully around the gravid orbs, glancing at the wailing heretic, whose skin had blistered into pustulous sores. Another hazard they would have to avoid, she thought.

'All right, soldier?' she asked Anditz. The cultist's clumsy tread had scattered spores onto his boots, and although Adair had emptied a canteen of water onto his feet, they were reddened and swollen.

'Fine,' he said with a grimace.

'Your boots aren't,' Haruto said, peering at the soles. 'It's eaten right through.'

'Intriguing,' came the flat voice of the tech-priest. She was looking down at one of the burst spore-bombs.

Haruto joined her, his curiosity piqued. 'Looks like a tiny tree inside.' He frowned, craning over the imploded sphere.

'Maintain caution,' Wrathe said sharply.

Haruto nodded. 'This is where the jungle will spread next. How long until it's fully grown, I wonder?'

'It is unnecessary to wonder,' Wrathe said. 'I am in fact able to perceive measurable increments of its growth. Within the last minute it has increased in size by nought point two inches. I would estimate that it will reach the height of the trees we passed within two days.'

'That's a neat trick,' Haruto said.

'A calculated enhancement rather than a trick,' the tech-adept retorted.

Something that might have been a smile moved across Haruto's scarred face.

'I would speculate that these are floral hybrids. Lazulaian plants parasitised by xenos to serve some function. Likely the generation of more spores,' the adept continued.

'Just what we need,' Adair said.

'Can you walk, lieutenant?' Khan asked the Cadian.

Anditz nodded, but winced as he levered himself to his feet. He was clearly in pain.

'How far to Carnadine City?'

Haruto sniffed. 'Half a day. Perhaps longer,' he added, glancing at Anditz.

'Something's coming,' said Ghost. Everyone turned at the unfamiliar sound of the Catachan's speech. He was pointing down the gem road at a rising cloud of dust. 'A vehicle.'

'We'd make up time if we had one of those,' Haruto said.

Khan raised an eyebrow. 'We've discussed this before. We're on foot for a reason, sergeant. So that we don't attract attention.'

Haruto nodded. 'Yes, but given the increase in spore load the situation has changed, sir.' He turned to scan the horizon. 'The Titan xenos out near the sea looks to be ignoring it, so I'd judge that danger has likely passed. It's worth the risk, sir. We don't know how long this planet is going to hold out.'

Lieutenant Anditz looked through his magnoculars. 'It's covered in heretic insignia.'

Khan squinted. The huge alien had indeed slowly moved off into the distance. There was a heavy hauler visible now, coming towards them. It had emerged out of the jungle into the scrub-land from back the way they had come. Still minutes away, but not many.

'What are you thinking, Haruto?'

'They won't have seen us yet from this distance. We ambush them from over there,' he said, gesturing. 'There's a dip on the other side of the road we can hide in until they're close by.'

'How are you getting them to stop?'

'We pretend to be heretics. We've got her...' He nodded at Lamya. 'Those other cultists were pleased enough to see her before.'

'I won't help you.' Lamya was clutching at her blistered legs.

'You are still loyal to the cult?' enquired Wrathe.

'No,' she moaned. 'None of it was real.' Khan couldn't tell if the woman was weeping from pain or distress. 'All of it lies. Everything we believed.' She took a series of choking breaths.

'So, help us,' Haruto said.

'Look at me,' she screamed, eyes wild, holding out her pus-covered hands. 'Look at what you've done to me! You disgusting, reeking bastards!'

Khan crouched down beside the cultist. 'Adair, get the medkit out,' she ordered. 'Now,' she said, addressing Lamya. 'We can make the pain go away, but we'll need you to help us.' Adair passed her a vial. Khan shook it. 'If you don't help us, we'll tie you up and leave you here.' She glanced around. 'Perhaps on top of one of these tree spikes. I'm sure our tech-adept colleague could calculate how long it would take for it to puncture your flesh. She might even know how long you'd stay alive while it slowly punched up through your guts.' Khan sniffed. 'Or, you could help us stop this hauler.'

Lamya eyed the vial and licked her cracked lips. 'I'll help.'

At Khan's nod, Adair punched the vial into the cultist's arm. She relaxed almost immediately, her shoulders shuddering in relief.

'I want someone to go with her,' Khan said.

'I'll do it,' Haruto volunteered.

'Hah,' Lamya said, woozy. 'They'll know you're not Lazulaian from a mile off. You're two feet taller than most of us.'

'We all are...' Haruto broke off, and along with the whole squad, he turned to look at Anditz.

The Cadian sighed. 'Fine. But I am in uniform.'

Wrathe took off her red cloak and handed it over. 'You may use this.'

Anditz swung it around his shoulders and gripped Lamya firmly by the arm.

'Positions, squad,' Haruto said, and the Catachans retreated to their hiding place on the other side of the road.

Anditz watched as the great mining hauler approached. It had been augmented with the cannibalised remains of other vehicles. It had a broad, blunt face with metal jaws and a digger rig on top. Someone had taken the laud hailer from an Ecclesiarchical vehicle and strapped it onto one side. As it approached, he could hear a low dirge in the cult's cant bleakly blaring out into the desert.

He adjusted his grip on Lamya's arm as the vehicle ground

to a halt in a cloud of dust beside them. He could see a dozen heretics riding it. Their appearance was outlandish, mining overalls and jackets embellished with broken glass with scraps of silk and swags of stolen uniforms, some even sporting the brocade of Lazulai's own disgraced Astra Militarum regiment. Their faces were daubed with ground amethyst pigment, purple whorls of the cult's symbol on their foreheads, and dark thumb-smears beneath their eyes to flatten the sun's glare.

'What have we here?' said a woman, dropping down onto the sand in a flutter of brocade. She wore looted gold pauldrons with purple streamers of silk that blew out behind her in the hot wind. She regarded them imperiously. Her comrades watched from various positions on the vehicle, each armed, each regarding Anditz and Lamya with blank, shuttered faces.

'Sister,' Lamya said. Anditz detected anxiety in her tone. This was not the warm welcome she had apparently envisaged. 'You may not recognise me' – she gave an apologetic laugh and indicated her tattered dress – 'but I'm Lamya DeShay.'

The woman raised her painted eyebrows. 'Do you hear that?' She turned back to the hauler. 'We've been blessed with the presence of Lamya DeShay!' When the woman turned back, there was an unpleasant smirk on her face. 'Lamya DeShay, the dirty little propagandist, husk of the old order.'

There were a few grins among the watching cultists. Unpleasant ones.

'This is indeed a blessing,' the woman continued, 'because we're on a mission for the angels. The true angels who have come from the skies and from the earth to purge the unworthy from this world. We fight for them, not your old gods,' she laughed, pointing at Lamya. 'We have seen our angels eat your gods.'

The woman's eyes were wide and reddened. Any sanity she

may once have possessed had long been lost, Anditz thought. Anyone at this point who thought the tyranids were doing anything other than simply devouring Lazulai whole was dangerously separated from reality. Anditz felt the cultist squirm beside him.

The gold-pauldroned woman walked closer. Anditz could smell a strange musk from her, something alien.

'You are the most prominent member of the old gods' court we have come across,' she said to Lamya. 'You will be taken to a reader of entrails, who will pull out your gizzards while you still live to divine the desires of the angels. And you...' She turned to Anditz. 'You will make a pretty trophy. Look at your eyes!' She smiled, revealing sharpened teeth. 'Purple, like our beautiful masters. Exquisite.'

Anditz was aware of the weapons trained on them. If he pulled his laspistol now, he and Lamya were both dead.

'Load them.' The woman snapped her fingers. 'We need to be back at the settlement by nightfall.'

Two bulky mutants dropped down. Lamya wrenched her arm free from Anditz and ran, pelting away from the hauler.

'Get her!' the woman shouted. 'I want her alive!'

Anditz moved quickly behind the hauler as the cultists rushed forward in a rabble. Out of sight, he unholstered his laspistol and pressed his back up against the vehicle. The Catachans must have seen what was happening. If he could signal across the scree on the other side of the vehicle–

'Drop it.' A bulky woman with an amethyst flush to her skin had a mining laser trained on him. She'd emerged from behind the hauler and was flanked by two mutant heavies with ridged cranial deformities and talons bursting from their fists.

Anditz placed his weapon on the ground.

'That's Militarum-issue,' the woman said, looking at the

weapon, her eyes narrowed. 'Is that a uniform you're wearing under there? Take off that robe.'

'I defected,' he said.

'We'll decide that. Take the robe off.'

Anditz hesitated. He'd glimpsed a movement. Someone was climbing across the truck towards them.

'Or we'll take it off for you,' one of the heavies growled.

'Come on then,' Anditz said, playing for time. 'Do it.'

One of the heavies laughed. 'He wants to fight us.'

'Shall I just shoot him?' the other asked.

'No, Blazda,' snapped the purple-skinned woman. 'Faustyna wanted to keep him. Search him. If he's a soldier, then you can kill him.'

The first heavy moved forward.

'You're going to get knocked out,' Anditz warned.

The heavy grinned. 'You think you can take me?'

'No,' Anditz said. 'But she can.'

Adair dropped down into the sand behind the cultists, six foot seven inches of pure muscle and belligerence.

There was a brief moment of silence as the cultists began to turn, but Adair had already lunged to smash the skull of the one holding the mining laser and was whipping her fist round to strike at the nearest heavy before he'd even realised what was happening.

Anditz grinned, sliding across the ground to recover his laspistol.

The second mutant was more resilient, and Adair snarled as she repeatedly smashed her massive fist into its purple-ridged cranium, gripping her opponent's mining overalls in her other hand. The cultist choked on their own blood as Adair caved in their orbital bones and threw them to the ground.

The heavy that had been descending on Anditz had turned to charge Adair. Anditz raised his weapon as the Catachan spun nimbly away from her attacker, drawing her enormous knife as she moved. She turned and thrust it deep into the guts of the oncoming enemy, impaling them on the force of their own charge. As they toppled to the floor, Adair pulled her knife out of the corpse in one fluid motion.

As Anditz was marvelling at the Catachan's skill, there was a sudden growl as the hauler's engine started. 'Look out!' he yelled, and Adair dodged out of the path of the crushing wheels.

The hauler was moving slowly and cultists on board were returning fire into the scree from where the Catachans had attacked.

Anditz and Adair jogged along in the lee of the vehicle to stay out of the exchange of fire. Anditz saw that one of the cultists had caught Lamya and had her in a headlock. There was the familiar whip-crack sound of a long-las before the captor's head burst, and Lamya struggled free from his dead weight.

'Hah! That'll be Ghost's work,' Adair said.

There was a sudden rushing sound and Adair was enveloped in a net. It happened so fast Anditz barely had time to register her look of surprise before she was slammed forward onto her face. One of the cultists had fired a netgun from atop the moving vehicle, and the squirming Adair was now being dragged along behind it. The hauler skidded around, whipping Adair from side to side. Anditz realised they were lining something up on top of the vehicle. Concealed under a tarpaulin they were removing was an enormous plasma cannon. The weapon had been torn from a tank, with remnant pieces of armour plating still welded to it.

Anditz swore under his breath. If they had the chance to use it, they'd be firing a small sun right into the Catachans' position. That was if it didn't overload – he wasn't surprised they'd kept the mighty weapon in reserve given the danger of deploying it in such a haphazard way. Whatever happened, he couldn't see a way of freeing Adair before they drove off. Anditz could see only one course of action open to him, although it would put Adair at risk. He pulled a grenade out of his webbing pouch, assessed the distance to the plasma cannon atop the hauler, then armed and threw it.

He dived down into the sand and covered his head.

The blast shook the ground as the grenade ruptured the plasma cannon's fuel tanks and blew the hauler in two.

Anditz got to his feet and ran to the back of the vehicle, dodging debris and dying cultists. 'Trooper!' he shouted, desperately searching for Adair.

'Here, sir!' he heard her yell in reply.

Relief surged through him. She was half buried beneath a pile of sand and still tightly tied in the net, but otherwise unharmed. Anditz freed her, and she stretched out her arms.

'Lucky hit there, sir,' she said.

Anditz nodded, although the tension was still leaving him.

'Think it'll still drive?' she said, grinning, as the rest of the squad made their way across the road.

Anditz regarded the smoking wreckage. The gold-pauldroned leader lay dead among the twisted scrap. 'I think it best to assume we'll be walking, trooper.'

CHAPTER NINE

Carnadine City was not only the capital of Lazulai, but also marked the final leg of their journey. They were getting closer to the excavation site, almost on the open run out to the east. Anditz felt frustrated impatience. They were so close, but success was not yet guaranteed.

The approach to the city was unlike anything Anditz had ever seen. The spectacle still retained the shock it had held for him the first time he was posted there with the Cadian 82nd.

On every other world he'd been to, cities were built with a function. In most places, hives grew upward, maximising the space available to them. Even on agri worlds with low population densities, the habs rose high. On Cadia, the kasrs had been crafted to provide maximum siege defensibility, the streets of the fortified cities woven in geometric knots of endless defence lines and slab-sided bunkers.

In contrast, the builders of Carnadine had been unconcerned with function and apparently only interested in form.

There were no outer walls, rather terraces of flowers and wide topaz boulevards radiating out from the centre. There were no habs above ground; instead, tall palaces of carved ruby and rough-hewn jade rose between crystal waterways from which the many heretics among the Ecclesiarchy had planned the surrender of the world to the xenos. Unlike on Cadia, the streets and buildings had not been designed around protection, but with the intent of ushering the light of the sun to illuminate select shrines and statues.

This decadence was one of the reasons that it had been so difficult to protect the city from the xenos when they came. The bitter blood of the Astra Militarum had washed the boulevards, loyal soldiers paying with their lives for the hubris of a people who had thought themselves above war.

'This place must have been hit hard. What happened to the defences?' Adair remarked as they approached Carnadine. The Catachan padded softly beside him, her footfalls silent despite her bulk.

'There never were any,' Anditz said.

Adair made a face. 'No walls?'

'Didn't think they needed them,' Anditz replied with a shrug. 'Or thought it looked better without them. Or perhaps they even designed the city to fall from the start. Throne knows how long the xenos have been corrupting this place.'

'That would wind up a Cadian,' Adair grunted.

'What, xenos?'

Adair laughed. 'Clearly that. But I mean doing something just for the look of it.'

'True enough. It's wasteful,' Anditz said. 'Naive.'

Adair's mouth curved into something more like a smile than her usual smirk.

'What?' Anditz asked.

She shrugged, her massive shoulders rolling like a pair of boulders. 'Nothing.'

'Soldier,' Anditz said, mock-serious. 'Don't make me order you to tell me.'

Adair barked out a laugh. 'Just thinking it's funny how people would think Catachans are more boorish than Cadians, sir.'

'Of course,' Anditz said. 'Because your world is so well known for its rarefied cultural output.'

Adair grinned. 'Just because people don't know about it, doesn't mean it's not there.'

Anditz rolled his eyes. 'Trooper, you're not going to convince me Catachan poetry is real.'

'It is!' Adair protested. 'Ask the others.'

'No,' Anditz said. 'And I need you to scout forward with Ghost now. We're coming up on the Carnelian Gate.'

He pointed, indicating the landmark. It was a tall, isolated crystalline structure, the symbolic gateway to this side of the city. It stood alone, two mighty pillars with a sweeping lintel across the top.

'When we were fighting here, the cultists used to mount ambushes from the gate. We should proceed with caution, in case they've returned to the area since Astra Militarum forces withdrew.'

Adair saluted and strode ahead, throwing a wink over her shoulder as she went.

Anditz fell back to where Major Khan and Sergeant Haruto walked. 'Sir, we'll need to be on alert for potential cultist attacks here.'

'Doesn't look like there's much of the city left. Reckon the xenos-worshippers are still hanging around?' Khan said.

'Even if they aren't, they might have left traps.'

Khan nodded. 'We go in, we get out. I don't like the looks of this place, lieutenant.'

Anditz raised his scope. Carnadine had suffered since he was last here. The fine spires and towers were crumbled, and smoke rose from the blackened window-eyes of dead buildings.

'No walls.' Khan made a tutting sound. 'It's as if they had a death wish.'

'Perhaps they did,' Haruto said. 'They may not even have realised it.'

'What do you mean?' Anditz asked.

'On Catachan, there are types of parasites that make the host behave differently. Even do things that endanger the host's own life but enable the parasite to spread. Looks to me like what's happened here. This whole world is being eaten alive now and the xenos will just move on when it's dead.'

Not if we can help it, Anditz thought. But he didn't voice this sentiment aloud.

'You can say what you like,' Lamya said. 'You're about to see what civilisation really looks like.'

'I doubt that,' Haruto muttered.

'Our builders are finer than any others, the work of our gem-masons more exquisite.' The cultist raised her head haughtily. She had torn away strips of silk from the bottom of her gown and tied them around the suppurating sores on her legs. Whatever Haruto had given her must have numbed all sensation because she now walked barefoot across the rough scrub and road. She inhaled with importance, then intoned two lines of poetry.

'Come to the crystal city on the sea, a wound of light wrought by hand,

Where blossom bleeds perfume sublime, and the gem-wright's roses stand.'

She looked at the others expectantly. 'Well?'

To Anditz's surprise the Catachans had listened to the verse silently but regarded her blankly.

'The bard Aguen's *Ode to Carnadine*?' Lamya said, eyebrows raised in disbelief.

'Not to my taste,' Khan said.

'Not to your taste?' Lamya scoffed. 'I'm sure that anything that isn't a gun or a knife falls into that category.'

Khan shrugged. 'Words are all you've got left of this place now, heretic.'

'What do you mean?'

'Keep walking and you'll see,' Haruto said.

Lamya hastened her step, rushing ahead of the others, a dark, ragged figure in the bleak landscape. Overhead the sky roiled, greasy clouds squirming and curdling with a carrion tinge. Rain the colour of bloodied saliva began to spit down on them. Anditz slapped his hand against his arm. It felt as if he were being bitten by insects where the water touched him. This time the Catachans too were vulnerable to whatever it was.

Khan grunted and rubbed at her skin. 'Something's in the rain.'

Only Wrathe was unbothered, the tech-adept's lack of exposed flesh rendering her apparently immune. She had recovered her cloak, and it hung limply from her slight shoulders in the damp. 'Let me see,' she said, reaching for Haruto's arm. She bent low over his wrist where a droplet of the stained water lay on his skin. 'Remain still,' she scolded softly.

Anditz didn't know how the big Catachan wasn't itching and cursing at the painful stinging, but he remained motionless while Wrathe examined him. After a few moments she brushed the water from his arm with her metal fingers.

'It appears that the droplets contain xenoforms.'

'What?' Khan frowned.

Wrathe's vox-grille crackled. 'Microscopic ones. Visible only under strong magnification. Similar to microbial life.'

Haruto wrinkled his nose. 'Why?'

'Like the spores, perhaps they are part of the consumption process.'

'So, they're eating us alive?' Haruto asked.

'Perhaps, similar to digestive fluids. I cannot say with any certainty.'

Khan swore.

'We need to find a way of making up time,' Haruto said.

'I don't want to hang around any longer than necessary either, sergeant,' Khan said.

'There are maglev tracks,' Haruto said, gesturing ahead. 'Any chance of getting a ride?'

'That went so well last time,' Khan said drily.

'There was a cargo shunt and a passenger carriage that passed through Carnadine on the way up to the north-east. Whether it's intact now, I don't know,' Anditz said.

There was a sudden cry ahead. The cultist had stopped in her tracks as if she'd been winded.

'Has she suddenly worked out that the buildings shouldn't be smoking quite so much?' Haruto said.

Adair hove back into view, jogging across the scrubland and past the stricken cultist, heavy flamer bouncing in her arms. 'Clear to proceed, sir, no sign of traps on the track. Ghost is covering us up ahead. Suggest we loop around to the right, there's more of those spore cannons coming up if we go direct, and' – she wrinkled her nose – 'some kind of pool.'

'Pool?' Anditz said, raising an eyebrow.

'You don't want to swim in this one, sir, trust me,' Adair said, shaking her head. 'Saw what was left of some people who tried. It's like...' She scrunched up her face. 'Like an ulcer in the soil.'

'I believe Trooper Adair is referring to an acid sink,' Wrathe said. 'I have read accounts of this phenomenon. The surrounding terrain is likely to be unstable.'

'We'll go round,' Khan said. 'Any signs of cultist activity at all?'

'No. Saw a few people milling about, but they looked like civilians. All pretty rough. No organised defence that we could see.'

The Carnelian Gate was somehow still intact when they reached it. It was impressive, an inverted 'U' shape intricately carved from a single, huge slab of mineral the height of three people. It served no practical purpose, but a symbolic one. Beyond the threshold, on either side, the remnants of the pleasure gardens that had lined this entrance lay fallen and rotting. The rare cultivated flowers had decomposed into a filthy, stinking slush, and up through their decomposing mass thrust spikes of the alien growth.

Anditz and the others walked through the gate past stagnant and stinking ponds and once-beautiful fountains in which corpses lay, half in, half out of the scummy water.

'Where are we going here, lieutenant?' Khan asked. 'I want us in and out as quickly as possible.'

Anditz nodded. 'I agree, sir. Recommend we carry on up to Carnelian Square. From there we can try the Bishop's Palace or the garrison. We'll come out on the other side of the city and can continue on to the excavation site that way.'

Khan nodded. 'Stay alert, squad. There's a lot of cover here, and we likely won't be the only ones using it.'

They walked through streets turned charnel houses, where defenders and civilians alike had been cut down by roving bands of xenos. Buildings were ruined, torn apart, alternatingly by conventional weaponry and the claws of monsters. Elaborate murals, artworks dedicated to heroes of the city's past, turned to dust and blood spatter. Lamya dragged behind, as if in a daze, struck silent seeing the state of the city. The xenos flora had begun to crawl over the ruins already, veiling fallen pillars in shrouds of fleshy purple and pink, trailing pendulous fruiting bodies behind them.

Anditz led the way through the familiar streets made so strange. He'd patrolled here with his regiment what felt like a lifetime ago. Now the place and regiment were destroyed alike. Although not completely, he reminded himself. He still remained of the Cadian 82nd, still had hands to do their work. And elsewhere on the world, Cadians would still be fighting. It was for them that this mission must succeed.

There was a sudden babble of voices ahead and Anditz signalled for the rest of the squad to halt. There was a square before them, paved in white quartz with Ecclesiarchical buildings rising around it, chief of which was a beautiful but heavily damaged cathedral.

In the centre of the square proceeded a hideous cavalcade of grotesques. All looked as if they had once been human dignitaries. At their head was a spry old man with pouched eyes and a fringe of wild hair, wearing what had once been fine vestments. He carried a heavy gold processional aquila and behind him trailed all manner of ragged people with penance-play puppets and bundles of belongings, who clanged utensils as they went.

'Atone! Atone for the Emperor!' the old man called out as he shuffled towards the Carnadine Cathedral, which rose up over the east side of the square.

'They loyal?' Adair asked.

'Let's find out,' Khan said, drawing her plasma pistol.

As she strode out into the square the crowd cowered and the old man turned, brandishing the aquila before him.

'Halt,' he cried. 'We are the Emperor's guard!'

'Which Emperor?' Khan asked.

'The right one!' he said brightly.

Khan levelled her weapon at him.

'Ah,' he said. 'He who sits on His Golden Throne, for whom humanity was made to serve and die!'

'Where are the xenos-cultists?'

The old man's face crumpled into a scowl. 'Dead!' he exclaimed. 'Dead and in the water. We put them there so their foul crab-lords take them back.'

'Please, confessor. I must speak with our guests.' A suave, smartly dressed man strolled down the cathedral steps. He looked at Khan. 'You have me at an advantage... Major?' he added, looking at her insignia.

'Major Wulf Khan, Catachan Nine-Hundred-and-Third.'

The man extended a hand, which Khan shook. 'Binar Rouffe. Administrator Primus and overseer at Carnadine,' he said. 'It's a relief to see the forces of the Imperium again. We were beginning to feel quite abandoned.'

'Do you know my lieutenant, Kaede Anditz of the Cadian Eighty-Second?' Khan asked.

'No, major. But I regret that our hospitality has not been as it once was this past year or so.'

'Administrator Rouffe.' Anditz stepped forward. 'We are on a vital mission, and in need of resupply. Whatever you have not spent in defence of the city could increase our chances of defeating the enemy.'

'What do you require, lieutenant?'

'Anything you can spare. But chiefly, ammunition and rebreathers.'

Rouffe nodded. 'Everything you need is inside. Please, follow me.' He turned to ascend the cathedral steps, stepping over the debris.

Khan gestured for Adair and Anditz to follow her whilst the others stood guard outside.

Adair jabbed Anditz in the ribs and made a mock-haughty

face. Anditz ignored her. Rarefied the administrator might be, but thank Creed there was at least a single sane soul left in this place. When his regiment was stationed here, the cracks had been apparent in civilians and soldiers alike, but now it seemed as if the whole damned place had fractured under the pressure of the invasion.

He blinked as they entered the building. Half of the roof had caved in, but it was still majestic, built from a rainbow of tourmaline panes thin enough for the sun to shine through and light the cathedral with a bright, multicoloured glow. A world away from the sodden, shadowy nightmare of the last holy building he'd entered, he thought. He noticed Adair bow her head as they entered and make the sign of the aquila, the harlequin lights illuminating the paleness of her hair and the strong contours of her arms.

'Now, if you'll follow me. I pride myself on the fact that we have everything here.' The administrator shooed a filthy man with matted hair and a bucket of jewels out of their path.

'What's that?' Adair muttered to Anditz.

He squinted. At the other end of the nave something was piled up around the altar.

'I don't know,' he replied.

'It stinks,' Adair said.

She was right. A terrible stench of marine decay emanated from the far end of the building. For a moment Anditz was transported back to the submerged cathedral, and the terrible xenos devouring flesh at the bottom of the sea. He shook himself.

'What is this?' Khan growled as they approached the altar. They were close enough now to see that it was covered in a terrible mass of dead crustaceans that were spoiling fast in the humid air.

'You arrived here looking for something. This must be it.' The administrator nodded and folded his hands in front of him.

'This is what you've done,' Khan said flatly.

Rouffe nodded. 'Of course. We had to do something. When the rations ran out and the soldiers left and there was nothing remaining.' His eye twitched. 'These people were my responsibility. They looked to me. Through the long months. Through the death.'

For a moment, Anditz saw a flash of something on the administrator's face. A tiny window of sanity that was shuttered just as quickly as it had opened, lest reality get in.

Rouffe turned back to the altar. 'It has been a challenge to keep people from eating them,' he said. 'But if Him-on-Terra is to know of our predicament we must convey to Him the nature of our foe.'

'Heresy!' The man with the processional aquila was storming towards them, illuminated by the kaleidoscope of light thrown down by the cathedral's walls. The man came up to the administrator and thrust a finger to his face. 'You should know better than to discuss such sensitive things!'

'I don't see that it matters. As agreed, and to accommodate the variant views on this matter, we shall give all of the representative offerings to the Emperor so He has the information required about what the aliens might be and therefore how to destroy them. You've brought yours, I'll imagine mine.'

Khan jerked her head at Anditz and Adair. They followed her out, leaving the ragtag group bickering behind them.

Outside they found Lamya sitting with her head on her knees, lank hair covering her face.

'Get what you wanted?' she asked. 'Was it worth it?'

Khan shook her head.

Anditz turned to regard the square. The gaggle of people who'd formed the procession were gathered around a man lying prone on the ground with a distended stomach. The man with the matted hair from inside the cathedral sat cross-legged beside him, feeding him gems from the bucket. The man lying down moaned but pushed the sharp stones into his cracked lips, past ruined teeth, and swallowed them painfully.

'Throne,' Adair muttered.

On the other side of the square, it became apparent that one of the watching civilians had died where he sat. Half-starved people jostled to tear into the deceased's meagre belongings, fighting for the rags and trinkets and scraps of anything edible that might have been on his person.

'Do you wish to take the gem penance, sir?' A scabrous woman genuflected her way over to Adair.

'No,' Adair said.

'Prove your faith to Him-on-Terra?' she wheedled to Anditz, and weighed a handful of emeralds under his nose. He ignored her and she moved on, coughing loudly as she went, and spitting up something that looked like a lump of lung onto the ground.

'Lieutenant,' Khan asked, 'where are we going to pick up these damned rebreathers?'

'Suggest we split up, sir,' Anditz said. 'The Bishop's Palace is twenty minutes that way.' He indicated down a wide boulevard. 'Adair and I can run recon out there if you take the rest of the squad to check the garrison. That's five minutes down the avenue past the cathedral. It's the green building with gold columns. Suggest we liaise outside there within an hour and a half?'

'Agreed,' said Khan. 'Let's go.'

Anditz led Adair through the streets. He'd been stationed in one of the other octants, but each of the eight slices of the city were laid out the same, with mirrored boulevards and cathedrals and palaces, each presided over by a bishop who controlled a corresponding eighth of Lazulai's wealth. The place had been thronged with people only months ago, multiple Astra Militarum regiments operating defence for the region from this city base. Until the xenos had come in a tide, washing everything away.

Unheeded, Anditz's mind presented him with a flicker-flash remembrance of the terrible swarming of chitin around Opal Bastion, the unthinking death that had consumed his regiment. Each alien they shot down replaced by three more, bone scythes and talons pulling defenders from the walls and devouring them–

'All right, sir?' Adair said.

'Yes.' He shook himself.

Here and there people drifted past them like ghosts, faces shuttered up with grief, or horror, or despair. The dust of tumbled masonry lent a strange blankness to the banquet that ruination was making of the city's bones.

He and Adair walked through the crushed remains of civilian habitations, small and poorly built and hidden away. Far more space had been given to the pleasure gardens that had run through the city, now reduced to broken stumps and stems where occasional civilians sat or lay with bundles of belongings or with children or the wounded. They appeared to have halted wherever they had run out of impetus and simply stopped. If the activity around the cathedral was a form of madness, then this inactivity was a form of cold sanity in the face of sheer despair. The world was ending, there was nothing more to be done. Any living thing could feel it – in the rising heat, the spores, the nightmares coming to devour them all. Time was slipping away from Lazulai, and these people's indolence was a logical response to impending mortality.

He understood the despair in the drawn faces. If there was truly nothing that could be done, perhaps he might feel the same. As far as these people knew, their world was doomed, and they had no reason to fight. But he knew that there was a way. He slipped his hand into his jacket to grip his regiment's treasure, the tin of precious soil from Cadia. It linked all of the Cadian dead to their home world, bound his regiment with the planet that had made them. And when he found the weapon that would destroy the tyranids, he would lay some there too, so that the 82nd might yet join the final fight. He pulled it out of his pocket for a moment. It was something solid, something real. Something to fight for. He slipped the tin away quickly as he heard Adair closing in behind him.

The spores hazed around the crumbled towers of the once-great city like a quiet shroud. The melancholy of it seeped into your bones, the sorrow of a whole world that knew it was dying.

The mournful silence was broken by Adair, who had started whistling.

Anditz turned and looked up at her, disbelieving. She gave him a jaunty grin and kept up the tune as she strode alongside him.

'What are you doing, Trooper Adair?'

'Whistling, sir.' She shot him a sidelong look. 'Reckoned you were going into your thoughts too deep.'

Anditz was taken aback. He'd not credited her with that much insight. 'I'd wager you've never had that problem, Trooper Adair?'

She grinned. 'Not me, sir. Blessed with linear thoughts, thank Him-on-Terra.'

Despite himself, Anditz smiled. 'What's the tune? Another masterpiece of Catachan culture?'

'That's right, sir. And it's dirty. It goes–'

Anditz caught a glint out of the corner of his eye. 'Down!' He shoved Adair as las-fire blasted past them. As he dived, he had a brief glimpse of an angry yellow beam cracking into a statue opposite and boiling its upper body into nothingness.

Even as he came out of the roll, Anditz was pulling his pistol out and returning fire. From behind the cover of a fallen pillar he saw their attacker, standing astride a heap of rubble on a slope above them. It was a xenos-cultist with a swollen back and a bulbous head. In its three arms it cradled a hefty mining laser.

'I'll flank it, sir,' Adair said.

'No,' Anditz barked. 'Stay in cover.' Adair wouldn't be able to get close enough with her weapon without getting dangerously exposed.

Anditz fired his laspistol again and the xenos-mutant sagged, a fistful of bone bursting from the knee of its mining overalls. It roared and blasted the mining laser towards them again.

This time Anditz rolled aside as the laser fire ruptured his cover. This was good, he thought. The more he could bait the mutant into firing, the greater the chance of the weapon overloading. He was fast, and its reactions were slow. He just had to stay faster.

He turned to see that Adair had drawn her Devil's Claw and was standing, brows furrowed.

'Trooper!' Anditz shouted. 'Get down!'

Ignoring him, Adair weighed the enormous blade in one hand then hefted it like a javelin towards their attacker. It speared the mutant through the chest, throwing it backward. It dropped the mining laser, the beam jammed and blasting skyward from where it had fallen. An injury like that would have killed a normal human instantly, but the freak still lived and was growling with effort as it rose, the blade jutting from its sternum.

Eyes sparkling, Adair vaulted onto the scree slope. The mutant was almost as tall as her, and somehow even broader. It pulled out a knife and slashed at her. Fists raised, Adair danced out of range exuberantly before darting in and slamming a punch into the mutant's face. It shook its head and lunged for her again, but she spun away, skittering broken glass and ground jewels as she dodged the mining laser's still-active beam.

Grinning horribly, Adair lashed out at the monster's wounded leg. Her boot made contact with a crunch, and it collapsed. Then she was on the mutant, pummelling its bony head with her massive fists. Blood drooled from the corner of its mouth, and Anditz thought she'd finished it.

Even as Adair was pulling her knife out of its chest, the creature suddenly stabbed out with its third arm. Something glinted in the long-fingered hand and slashed against Adair's thigh. She fell back with a curse and gripped her leg.

The mutant launched itself at her, leaving little time for Anditz to take a clean shot before it had her. He cracked off two bursts from his laspistol. One hit the thing in the shoulder, but the other clipped its neck, bursting an artery. Gouts of blood arced outwards, spitting and crackling as they were evaporated by the mining laser's beam. The mutant teetered, eyes rolling back in its head. It had clamped its purpled hands about its throat in a futile attempt to stop the blood gushing out of it. Its foot caught a piece of broken masonry, and it stumbled forward into the still-streaming yellow beam of the mining laser. The terrible force of the industrial laser immediately evaporated its neck and shoulders, and the charred head and feet rolled away, unrecognisable remnants of what had been a living creature a moment before.

The las-beam shimmered in the air and Anditz detected the stench of overheating metal. It had been active for too long and an overload was imminent.

'It's going to blow, soldier!' he shouted as Adair scrambled to recover her weapon from where it had fallen. She plucked the Devil's Claw from the ruins before scrambling back down to the boulevard next to Anditz.

He slapped her on the back urgently. 'Run!' he yelled, and they pelted away, the rising whine of the overheating laser behind them.

There was a blast and shriek of shrapnel, then small pieces of xenos-mutant and crystal began to rain down around them. Adair laughed aloud.

'What?' Anditz snapped.

'Nothing like not being dead to make you feel alive,' she said, and grinned.

Anditz shook his head in exasperation. 'How's your leg?'

Adair examined the injury. 'Just a slash. Bastard picked up a piece of glass and cut me.' She leaned her weight against a broken pillar and pulled out her battered medkit. 'One moment, sir, while I see to this.'

'Do you need assistance?' Anditz asked, eyeing the jagged injury.

'You're all right, sir. Cheers anyway,' Adair said, biting open an ampule of counterseptic. 'So, this palace,' she said conversationally as she flushed the wound. 'There's going to be some good stuff in there?'

'There was,' Anditz said, noting that the Catachan didn't so much as flinch as she doused the caustic fluid over her injury. 'When we were stationed here before. The bishops liked to look after themselves.'

'Were all of 'em rotten?'

'Seems that way.'

Adair shook her head. 'How'd it happen? On a world like this? For things to go so bad?'

'That's above my rank to worry about, and yours, trooper.'

Adair sniffed and began to apply a wound clip. 'Yeah. But don't you ever wonder?'

'Wondering's where the trouble tends to start, trooper.'

'Could be, sir, could be.' She stood and tested her leg.

'Can you walk?'

'Yessir. Lead on.'

They walked for some time without seeing anybody. The over-loading laser had probably been enough to send any remaining civilians underground. There were no signs of cult activity or sigils and Anditz wondered if the mutant they'd seen had been the only one left. They clambered through the stinking ruins of what had been a hanging orchid garden, then rounded a corner, coming out onto a large square.

Anditz halted.

'Hmm,' Adair said, surveying the scene ahead. 'Was that it?'

'Yes,' Anditz said, looking at the mess of rubble that ran down to where the entrance of the Bishop's Palace used to be. The once-familiar halls where he'd been stationed were no more. A huge statue of a robed saint had fallen face-first into the centre of the pink marble confection, smashing through pinnacles and chapter houses. The council chambers were crushed beneath its belly, the bishop's apartment had been obliterated by a shoulder, and a side chapel that had been wondrously spangled with opals lay ruined beneath one vast knee.

'We can get around.' Anditz frowned. 'There's a way through the Halls of Court.' He indicated the comparatively austere, carnelian-faced facade beside the destroyed palace.

Clouds of pink dust still hung in the air as they skittered down towards the entrance to the halls over the broken bones of a chapter house.

'Must have come down recently,' Adair remarked.

Anditz nodded. 'Tread carefully. We don't want to dislodge anything else.' He suddenly became aware that Adair had frozen beside him, facing the opposite direction.

'Oh, Throne,' she muttered.

Something in her tone sent a fear prickle up the back of Anditz's neck. He turned, and animal panic clenched his stomach at the sight before him.

It hovered motionless in the air several hundred feet away, facing them. Its huge, bony head was plated in sweeping chitin, with a rictus grin nestled beneath. Its skull appeared eyeless, but Anditz's skin crawled as if it stared directly at him. A thin, atrophied body hung impossibly from the swollen cranium, little claw-like limbs folded against the ridged sternum like the humbled hands of a devout penitent. Every now and then a little flicker of electricity played over the thing's pallid surface, and some sort of rolling mist sublimated across its black-amethyst skin. Its weird form was so preposterous that it should have been comical, but it wasn't. It was petrifying.

Like the nightmare sabre-wielding leader-xenos Anditz had encountered that fateful night at Opal Bastion, this alien seemed sentient in a way the masses had not. It was observing them. Anditz felt trapped, frozen with cold, sickening panic. Even immobile, the xenos was nightmarish. Despite the oppressive humidity, cold sweat prickled his skin.

'Sir.' Adair laid a hand on his shoulder and spoke quietly. 'Walk backwards, slowly. It hasn't attacked yet, so I reckon something's holding it back. If we take it slow and don't give it a reason to chase, it might just ignore us.'

They started to fall back cautiously, stepping with great care over the rubble. Each skittering stone jangled at Anditz's nerves, but every step further from the unnatural creature brought a little more relief.

'You don't think we should try to take it out?' Anditz said.

'Them, sir. Not just it. Another two are coming in.'

Anditz grimaced. 'Then we continue to fall back.'

'Agreed, sir.'

By the time they reached the huge double doors of the Halls of Court, two more of the xenos had drifted to flank the other, all three now facing the building like silent ghouls.

One of the great doors hung from the hinges, scratched with cultist graffiti and over-marked with Astra Militarum signs the occupying forces had left. Even though the building offered little protection, simply being out of the line of sight of the monsters was a relief.

'What do you reckon they're doing?' Adair frowned, leaning against the ruins of a once-grand frieze.

'Other than planning to kill us? I don't see that it matters.'

'They're aware of us, sir. Watching us. You see a predator watching you, you better start thinking about why.'

'It didn't look built for physical combat.'

'Didn't look like it was built for anything. With a head like that, its neck should have snapped under its own weight. Has to do something bad though, they all do.'

'Let's not wait to find out what.'

Anditz had only been through the building once. During the campaign for the region, the senior staff had set up base in what had been the Carnadine Bishop's conference hall. At that time, General Kvelter had called Anditz through to report to several dozen tired-looking military leaders.

Shortly before this the traitor bishop herself had been eviscerated, and her remains divided and draped luridly at the front of his palace, a gruesome reminder to any of the local Lazulaians of where their loyalties should lie. The Cadian 82nd hadn't been present for the taking of the city, and by the time they arrived the vestments and jewels of the heretic clergy had been burned or taken as souvenirs with only their decomposing, organic remains left behind.

Anditz led Adair through echoing halls and corridors, stripped of their wall hangings and fine furnishings. This had been a public building once, a site of ceremonies and meetings and the workplace of high-ranking Administratum workers. The faces of the statues were defaced, scratched away in the months after the uprising. In the face of planetary annihilation, what people had thought they would do with the stolen jewels that the statues had worn, Anditz didn't know.

They trekked over rubble and broken glass to the back of the building, past scalloped alcoves and statued fountains overgrown with filthy pinkish xenos algae, to the series of chambers connecting the Halls of Court to the Bishop's Palace itself.

He rattled the gold-handled double doors. 'It's locked.'

'If you'll allow me, sir?' Adair said.

Anditz gestured assent and readied his laspistol as Adair kicked down the doors. The room behind them was dark, and Adair pulled Anditz's stab-light from his belt and shone the narrow beam into the space ahead. The beam illuminated something glittering in the black, and there was a sense of a large, silent chamber beyond.

Anditz and Adair trod softly into the darkness, when there was a click, and suddenly a series of low-hanging, elaborate chandeliers lit themselves one by one along the vast hall they found themselves in. The floor was tiled in marble and gold, and the walls rose up in a dazzling confection of gilded alabaster statuary. The high ceiling was painted blue with white clouds billowing across it. It was so beautifully wrought that you could almost ignore the nightmare sight of Lazulai's real, roiling sky visible through the hole in the roof at the hall's opposite end.

'What is this?' Adair asked, turning to stare around.

'I think it's a ballroom,' Anditz said. 'Or was. A place to dance.'

A servo-skull descended, creaking on an ancient motor. Its

features were picked out in jade and carnelian, including a sweeping moustache.

'What would you like played?' it croaked from a tired vox-grille.

'I don't know,' Adair said.

Its eyes flickered for a moment. 'Conductor's choice,' it said, and drifted backward.

A pair of curtains creaked apart on one side of the wall to reveal an orchestra of delicately crafted automatons, each holding an instrument and suited in red with fine brass braid. There was a wheeze, then lilting music started to play, with the artificial musicians jolting just out of time to the tune.

Adair laughed in confused amusement. 'People would dance here?'

'I suppose,' Anditz said. 'Wasteful idiocy. The luxury here, when the city lay undefended.'

Adair's lips quirked upward mischievously. 'Come on, sir. The xenos don't dance. Only humans dance. And if the bastards stop us being human, haven't they won?'

Anditz shook his head. 'You're a philosopher now too?'

Adair twirled up to him in a mock dance-step.

There was something infectious about her grin. He didn't really know why he did it, but Anditz laughed. For a moment, when she moved close the smile she returned wasn't a smirk. He noticed that a fine scar ran from her chin over her lower lip up to her nose.

And then the moment of levity was over as the sound of gunshots cracked out.

Adair flung Anditz down, shielding him from the attack.

He crashed into the marble floor, head turned to one side as the Catachan landed on top of him. He saw the shots shred the delicate fabric clothes and paper drumskins of the auto-maton orchestra, their faces shattered into messes of paste and parchment. Brass horns and silver pipes buckled and twisted under the onslaught as the music blared to a distorted crescendo then ground to a halt.

Adair growled and rolled for her heavy flamer.

His arms freed, Anditz raised his laspistol and fired in the direction of the attack. At the far end of the ballroom were a gaggle of civilians armed with autoguns. One of them fell, clutching his gut where Anditz's laspistol had struck him, and his comrades scattered.

Adair roared her heavy flamer to life, face twisted into an angry snarl.

'Wait!' Anditz said. 'They're not cultists!' He gestured for Adair to duck back. 'Are you Carnadine Militia?' he yelled.

'Yes,' a voice called back from outside the ballroom door.

Anditz shook his head. 'We're Astra Militarum. I'm Lieutenant Anditz of the Cadian Eighty-Second.' Adair caught his eye. 'I was stationed here a few months ago.'

'We remember,' came the reply. 'Thought you were xenos. There's three of the bastards outside.'

'We're not xenos,' Anditz said.

'You're not. What about the brute?'

Adair raised her eyebrows and gave Anditz an incredulous glance.

'She's Catachan,' Anditz said, carefully keeping his face straight.

'I'm putting down my weapon.' A man emerged, hands raised. He was wearing a ragged tabard over loose trousers. His face was pinched and tired-looking. 'You killed Czara,' he said, apparently emotionless.

'I'm sorry about that,' Anditz said.

The man nodded. It was as if he'd been given slightly disappointing news about a ration allowance.

'How many are there left of you?' Anditz asked.

'Five of us here,' the man replied. 'Don't know about the rest. Not heard from anyone else for a long time.'

Anditz was taken aback. The militia had numbered thousands before.

'You here to help us? Gotta kill those aliens out front.'

'We can't help, sorry. We're on a mission.'

The man took the news as indifferently as he had the death of his comrade and turned away.

'Wait,' Anditz said. 'We need supplies. Is the bishop's storeroom still intact?'

'No. Ammo's all gone.'

'Rebreathers?'

The man considered and gave a sideways nod. 'Could be. Nobody was thinking of much beyond weapons when the xenos came.'

Anditz nodded. 'Thank you.'

The man gestured, and the remaining fighters followed him across the ballroom, towards the entrance and the waiting xenos. They all had hollow eyes, sallow skin and ragged clothes, and not one spared a glance for their fallen comrade, or for Anditz and Adair.

'Throne,' muttered Adair, stepping over the dead militia fighter, whose blood had pooled into a ruby meniscus that dimly reflected the glittering lights above. 'Sorry bastards may as well already be dead.'

'You don't think their struggle noble?' Anditz asked as he led Adair forward into the Bishop's Palace. 'Seems like a pretty Catachan thing to do, going up against unknown odds like that.'

Adair laughed. 'Now that's a common misunderstanding, sir.'

Anditz checked at a corner that the route was clear before leading them on. 'Am I about to be treated to a lecture?'

'Don't need one. It's simple. People think we try to do

impossible things, but we don't. The odds might be impossible for other regiments, but they're not Catachans. We're bloody hard so we know we can do it.' She shrugged massively. 'You've got to know what you can do. Nobody gets very far on a death world without knowing what's in their hand and how to play it.'

'You're full of surprises, trooper,' Anditz said, advancing down a corridor, laspistol raised. 'Here,' he said, indicating a heavy metal door.

Adair heaved it open to reveal a narrow strongroom of mostly empty shelves and crates.

'Keep an eye on the door,' Anditz ordered. Adair took up sentinel duty while he searched.

As the militiaman had reported, the ammo had gone. There were a few scant medical supplies and ends of rations. In a crate at the back, Anditz found half a case of rebreathers. They were high-quality manufacture, not standard Munitorum issue. They'd presumably been intended for the bishop and key members of her household in the event of a chemical attack on Lazulai. They should do. He stuffed them into a satchel and slung them over his shoulder.

'Sir,' called Adair. 'Your mates have started fighting those flying worms outside.'

There was a sonic boom and the sound of glass shattering back in the ballroom.

The sharp noise sent jitters of discomfort up Anditz's neck. 'Follow me,' he said, moving briskly towards the servants' stairs. 'Worms?' he said after a moment.

'Yeah. The flying ones out front.'

'They don't look like any worm I've ever seen...' He paused and sighed. 'Catachan worms, right?'

'That's right, sir. Bony and 'orrible, just like at home.'

There was the sound of another blast and a greasy stink of

ozone filled the corridor behind them, followed by a swirl of masonry dust. A familiar chill and a sense of creeping horror began to play at the corners of Anditz's mind.

'Feel that, sir?' Adair frowned. 'Feels like someone's walking on my grave.'

'And mine,' Anditz said. He hesitated. 'I felt something like this the night that swarm killed my regiment.'

'Reckon there's another swarm coming then?'

'We can't assume anything,' Anditz replied. 'But I'd say we need to get back to the squad as quickly as we can.' He held Adair's gaze for a moment, and something unspoken passed between them. They'd seen enough stationed on this hellworld to know what was likely descending on them.

Adair nodded. 'Lead the way, sir. I've got your back.'

CHAPTER TEN

Khan had found no supplies on her search of the garrison. The green and gold columns Lieutenant Anditz had described were splintered and smashed, and the interior had been picked clean. A few civilians had clearly been living in the bare building and fled at the sight of the soldiers. After the local regiment had turned traitor, the population had learned it was simply safer to avoid anyone with a gun during times of starvation.

'Anything at your end?' she asked Haruto as he re-emerged into the exposed atrium.

'Just dust and bones,' he said.

Khan nodded and scratched her arm. The spores were beginning to irritate her, getting into wounds and scratches. Bruises were taking longer to heal too, she noticed. 'Let's hope the lieutenant has better luck.'

'I have discovered something,' the tech-adept said, stepping into the atrium, robe hanging limply around her ankles in the damp heat.

'Supplies?' Haruto asked.

'Communications,' she replied. 'Hidden behind a wall. I am able to feel the vox-waves.'

'Where?' Khan asked.

They found the vox walled up in what looked to have been an officer's room, although the shelves were bare and the room had been stripped like the rest of the building. Khan detected a palimpsest of an orderly spirit. Perhaps a Cadian had once been stationed here.

Ghost and Haruto had pulled apart the wall to reveal a recess with the vox-caster hidden inside. Nothing else. Just a small cache of hope that a soldier had left, and never returned to.

Khan brushed mortar dust from the top of the device.

'May I?' the tech-adept asked.

Khan nodded. 'Please.' Anxiety clustered in her throat. She knew logically that her squad was likely all that remained of the Astra Militarum forces on this world. But she had not had to confront that reality until now, had been able to continue in wilful ignorance with a small grain of hope. 'Look for any Astra Militarum signals. As far as you can reach.'

'I believe I will be able to extend the range,' Wrathe said. 'One moment.'

There was a crackle as the vox-caster started to scan through frequencies. As Wrathe slowly turned the dial, there was only the sound of dead static.

Stupid, Khan thought to herself. Weak, to have hoped for anything else.

'Was that something?' Haruto said suddenly.

'No,' Wrathe said.

Khan exhaled. 'It was worth a try.'

Then there was a blare of sound.

'What was that?' Khan asked. Her speech came out more rapidly than she'd intended.

'Wait,' Wrathe said, adjusting the wavelength.

The crackle resolved into a voice. *This is Jasper Fortress. Broadcasting on all Astra Militarum frequencies. Rally to our coordinates. We are holding Jasper Fortress. I repeat, rally to Jasper Fortress.*

'The crusade force?' Ghost looked up, disbelieving.

Khan shook her head. 'We can't assume anything,' she said. 'Patch me through. Now,' she told Wrathe.

The seconds felt like agonising eternities as Wrathe adjusted the transceiver. Light slanted into the ruined office, filtering through the fleshy xenos vines that scrambled overhead and tinted the room pink.

Wrathe turned to Khan. 'The line to Jasper Fortress is open.' She gestured at the vox-unit.

Khan stepped close to the vox-thief, fists clenched.

'Jasper Fortress, come in. This is Cobalt Fortress Special Operations squad.'

There was a hum of static, then a faint crackle.

'Cobalt Squad, this is Captain Thorne of the Catachan Night Shrikes. Confirm your identity.'

Khan laughed aloud and passed her hand over her face. Haruto's taciturn face had split into a grin and Ghost slapped the sergeant on the back with a matching smile.

'Thorne, you officious bastard. This is Tusk.' Khan smiled.

'Him-on-Terra!' Thorne exclaimed. *'You're harder to kill than Marbo, major. We thought we'd lost you.'*

'Coming from you?' Khan exclaimed. 'You survived the swarm.'

There was a pause. *'Ofelia's Fist made it, sir. Not much else from Cobalt. A couple dozen of us in total. We've had a few more survivors, trickling in. We're rallying any remaining Astra Militarum here. Reckon Jasper's the last fortress standing.'*

Khan swallowed. 'Kvelter?'

'*Gone, sir. She went down taking out a city-killer. It was a good death.*'

Khan's heart sank. It had been too much to hope that Kvelter had survived, but if anyone could have, it would have been the tough old Cadian general. At least she had met the end she wanted, going down fighting, taking the bastards with her. Khan cleared her throat. 'And you're holding Jasper Fortress?'

'*Yes, sir. Just.*'

'We're at the capital. Not for much longer. We need to move faster.'

'*You're at Carnadine City, sir?*'

'Correct.'

There was a rustle at the other end of the line. '*Don't know if it's any use, but one of the other regiments came in with some intelligence on caches. During the uprising, the cult mine workers held shunts over in-service pits. A bunch of Mordians rode in on one they'd dug up a few days ago. According to the information they handed over, there's one near you. About an hour west.*'

'Thank you, Thorne. But if we can't verify it's still there, that's a risk too far with the speed that the world's declining.' Khan saw that Haruto was already getting the map out, Wrathe craning to see it.

'*Fair enough, major. I'd best not delay you further.*'

'Stay well, Thorne. And tell the troops I'm coming for them. We're getting off this bloody rock one way or another.'

'*Understood, sir. We'll keep the bastards at bay until then.*'

Khan closed the line, almost unable to contain the gladness in her heart.

After Khan had spoken with Thorne, the squad waited outside in the garrison's courtyard.

At one time the rows of trees might have shaded the sanded

parade ground, but now they stood denuded, blackened stumps under an ochre sky smeared with urine-coloured clouds. The light was at once bright and dim, tinting everything pale ochre. It reminded Khan of a storm brewing on a desert world. But no desert was this humid. There had been a long ornamental pond running the length of the courtyard. It stank in the heat and was choked with coiling strands of alien algae in venous mauve.

'Something's on the wind,' Khan remarked.

'I feel it,' Haruto said.

'The other two aren't due back for a while. I'd like to get a lookout, scout the route ahead.'

Haruto nodded. 'If there's any high ground left in the city, we can see what we can see.'

Khan cast around. Visibility was poor with the spore-haze and fallen towers. 'You, heretic,' she said.

'What?' Lamya said. She had been combing her hair through with her fingers, looking at her reflection in one of the few surviving pieces of glass.

'You're to make yourself useful,' Khan ordered.

Lamya gave her a blank glance.

The heretic was retreating further into herself, Khan thought. If she didn't snap out of it soon, she'd cease to be worth retaining.

'What's that building?' Khan pointed at a tall, green tower.

Lamya glanced up. 'The Serpentine Pavilion. Obviously.'

'What was it for?'

Lamya shrugged. 'Entertainment. Gaming. I sang there once.'

Khan nodded. Not a military installation then. 'Ghost?' she said. The wiry Catachan dropped from a jasper portico, long-las over his shoulder. 'Did you catch that?'

He nodded.

'Good. Get as high as you can and have a look. I can feel something in my bones.'

Ghost left without saying a word.

'Why doesn't he talk? Have you done something to him?' Lamya asked.

Khan ignored her.

'I like him best because he doesn't say anything. Where's the big rude one, and the small stuffy one?'

Khan and Haruto exchanged glances and turned their backs on the cultist.

'That's not a bad question,' Haruto said. 'Time's against us.'

'We go as soon as they're back,' Khan muttered. She glanced over to where Wrathe sat on the garrison steps. A couple of children were daring each other to scurry up to her, then running away with frightened laughter. They grew bolder and came closer. The tech-adept pushed her hood back and extended a hand. Curious, the children approached to see. Wrathe twisted a cuff at her wrist and a weak hololith flickered to life in the palm of her hand, the rotating image of some fluttering avian, a tiny miracle wrought in light. The children gasped.

'They don't have birds here. She's showing them something they've never seen.' Haruto's face twisted into a half grin.

'Something they'll never live to see,' Khan said.

Haruto's expression dropped back to its usual glower.

Khan felt a pang of guilt. She pulled out a cheroot and lit it. The civilians left on this world were like shadowy parchment cut-outs to her, immaterial, already dead. Within days, everything here would be gone. All people, all life. There was no point caring about any of it. The only ones she could do anything about were her soldiers. If she let herself forget that, they wouldn't stand a chance.

She blew out a plume of smoke as she watched a parent call the children back.

Wrathe straightened her robes and stood. 'Major,' she said as she approached. 'Sergeant.' She nodded at Haruto. 'We must move soon. Atmospheric acidity has increased significantly since our arrival in the city.'

'What does that mean?'

'Uncertain. However, conditions have now moved beyond sub-optimal for both non-organic and organic matter. It will not be long before the climate is fully non-conducive to life.'

Khan looked up at the sky. It was sickly and curdled, the heavy clouds dark and gravid-looking. 'As soon as the others are back.'

'Respectfully, the shunt would move us faster than our feet can, major,' the Martian said.

'The shunt we cannot confirm is there, and that going to investigate will lead us away from our objective? That's not just an unacceptable delay, Tech-Adept Wrathe, but most likely a fatal one.'

'I do not believe you have fully considered the variables, major.' Wrathe's vox-grille crackled, and her strange, blank eyes bored into Khan. 'With our current pace and the escalation of atmospheric conditions, there is no guarantee that progressing as we are will achieve results.'

Khan took a drag on her cheroot. 'Even if the damned thing is there, there's no guarantee it will work, or the track beyond the city is viable. And don't forget – the intelligence about the location came from the cult. You think they can be trusted? The Mordians got lucky. No guarantee that we will.'

Ghost arrived back onto the street at a run, his face twisted into a grimace.

'Report,' Khan barked.

'A swarm,' he said. 'Hundreds of thousands of xenos, moving up from the south sea.'

Khan felt a flare of adrenaline. 'How far off?'

'Thirty minutes. Maybe less.'

Khan swore. 'Prepare to move out,' she said.

'Sir,' came a shout. Adair ambled around a corner with Anditz marching beside her.

Khan felt a flood of relief. She wouldn't have to decide whether she could afford to wait for them or evacuate the rest of the squad. 'Swarm incoming,' she said. 'We need to get out now.'

'Understood,' Anditz said. A fine dust speckled his dark hair. 'We encountered a new xenos form that appears to act as a controller. But we recovered the rebreathers.'

'Good.' Khan nodded, taking a final drag on her cheroot. 'The garrison was cleared out, but we made contact with Jasper Fortress. We've got Cobalt survivors to extract.'

The lieutenant's eyebrows rose in astonishment.

'Thorne's alive?' Adair said.

Khan grinned. 'Yes.'

'General Kvelter?' Anditz asked.

'I'm sorry, son, no.' Khan placed a hand on his shoulder. 'But she died a hero's death. I'll tell you what I know on the road, but we need to move now. We're heading east,' she called to the squad.

'Wait, sir,' Haruto said. 'We still need to consider recovering the shunt instead of proceeding on foot.'

'No,' Khan said. 'We leave now, and we leave on foot. There's no time for this discussion.'

Rain started to spit out of the sky. It fell like clots of old blood, dark like rusted rubies.

'Major, I still believe locating the shunt would be the best option,' the tech-adept said.

'What's this, sir?' Adair asked.

Khan sighed. 'We've had some intelligence that there might be a hidden cargo shunt an hour that way.' She pointed. '*Might* be. In the opposite direction we want to be going. Swarm's coming up from the south, I don't want to risk it cutting us off.'

'We have lost enough time that I am uncertain we will otherwise reach the excavation site in time,' Wrathe said. 'The archeotech is at risk every moment it is left unattended. I cannot allow that.'

'It's my job to get you there,' Khan said, brow furrowed. 'I decide how we do that.'

'And yet we are still not there,' Wrathe replied. 'I am obligated to remind you that this is significantly more important than your pride.'

'Pride?' Khan glowered, drawing herself up to her full height and closing the distance to Wrathe. 'This isn't about pride.'

'Then you will be satisfied if I make my own way to the cargo shunt,' Wrathe said, impassive. 'You may continue as you think best.'

'I'm going with her,' Haruto said.

His words hit Khan like a gut punch. 'What?' she said, turning to look at her sergeant.

'She can't go alone,' Haruto said, squaring his shoulders. 'And I think she's right. We don't have time to do things your way, and the mission's too important to fail. I'm sorry, Tusk.'

Khan felt her fists clench, and stared at her old friend. Haruto held her gaze. He wasn't going to back down, she could tell. Just as she'd found out more of her troops were alive, she was losing her sergeant. It felt like a bitter betrayal. For a moment, she couldn't find the words, but then a cold bloom of fury froze her heart and compelled her to speak.

'So that's how it is?' She spat into the dust. 'Good. If you don't trust my decisions, I can't trust you.' Khan stepped back, and turned to the rest of the squad. 'If anyone else doubts my leadership, feel free to desert the squad now. I don't fight with turncoats.'

Adair, Ghost and the Cadian stood silent. The red rain fell harder, washing the desolate ruins of the city with what looked like blood.

'Sorry, sir,' Haruto said, shouldering his pack.

'You're not,' Khan said. 'You've made your choice.'

He regarded her, stony-faced.

'Here,' Lieutenant Anditz said awkwardly, handing across a pair of rebreathers to the sergeant. Khan realised how this must look to the Cadian, for whom insubordination would normally be met with a bullet.

There was a scream from a civilian on the other side of the square. Overhead, a small, winged tyranid flew, turning in a lazy spiral like a hunting bird. The vanguard was arriving, Khan thought.

'May the best survive,' Haruto said. 'And I hope that's all of us.'

Khan didn't reply. She had nothing else to say. Then Haruto turned and walked away with the tech-adept at his side. Neither looked back. Khan watched them. She burned with rage, and with hurt.

Haruto disappeared around the corner of the square.

'Ghost,' she said after a moment. 'Go keep those daft bastards safe.'

He nodded, and ran swiftly after the departing group.

Khan stared blankly after him. She prayed to Him-on-Terra that they would return.

'Recommend we take the cisterns north, sir,' Anditz said, clearing his throat. 'There's likely less damage underground so we should be able to move faster, and we'll be protected from the aerial vanguard. We'll come out near the bridge across the Malachite Gorge.'

'I don't use the bridge,' Lamya spat.

'What?'

'When I'm going to the opera, I take the footway,' she said haughtily.

Khan and Anditz exchanged glances. The cultist's grip on reality was becoming even more slippery.

'Where's this footway?' Anditz asked.

'Near the Garnet Court,' Lamya said. 'But it's not for commoners.'

'I expect you need to have special access,' Anditz said conspiratorially.

She smiled smugly. 'I do.' She flashed her wrist at them.

'Reactive implant?' Khan muttered quietly to Anditz, although the cultist was ignoring them now.

'Looks like it. Worth a go, sir. We'll be passing the Garnet Court anyway. It's before the bridge.'

Khan nodded. 'Let's move.'

Anditz led the remainder of the squad towards the plaza ahead, the closest entry point to the cisterns. He was unsettled and could feel that Adair was too. Even the cultist, Lamya, had shut up. Khan hadn't spoken a word. He didn't know why she hadn't prevented Haruto from leaving. She'd not ordered him to comply or threatened him with penalties for desertion or mutiny. Maybe it wasn't how Catachans did things, but it had left them in a bad position, especially now they were without the sniper, Ghost. Now they were a skeleton force with an incoming horde of xenos, trying to recover archeotech without a tech-adept. But he wasn't about to abandon the major. She deserved better.

Anditz saw a glimpse of the open square ahead. 'We're approaching the court now,' he called ahead to Khan.

'There going to be cultists down there, sir?' Adair asked beside him. Her voice was as jocular as usual, but there was something uneasy in the set of her shoulders.

'I don't know,' Anditz replied. 'But we don't have much choice.'

'Damned well hope there are, sir. I'll keep Little Marbo ready,' she said, patting the side of her heavy flamer. 'Gonna cook us some heretics for lunch. Eat their extra arms.'

Anditz grimaced. 'Are you all right, trooper?'

'You know me, sir. Always top-notch. A-okay. Better than everyone else, I reckon.'

Anditz gave her a sideways glance. The trooper grinned, but there was no laughter in her eyes.

He looked away, then patted one of her huge arms. 'It's not called that.'

'What, sir?'

'Your flamer. It's not called Little Marbo.'

'No.'

'So, why did you say it?'

'Thought it might get a laugh.' She shrugged massively and let out a sigh. 'Xenos, no problem. But seeing the major like this? Puts the wind up me.'

Anditz nodded. Adair might be the brashest, cockiest knuckle-head he'd had the misfortune of serving with, but she was loyal to a fault. That mattered. If she hadn't been unsettled by the squad's split, that would have been more cause for concern.

There was a rising whine then a blast from behind them. They turned to witness Khan striding over, grim-faced, plasma pistol raised to the sky. She didn't even turn as the smoking corpse of a flying tyranid she'd shot hit the ground next to her.

'Move,' she barked. 'And stay alert. That bastard was nearly on you.'

'Yessir,' Adair said.

'We're almost there,' Anditz said. At least he hoped they were. It had been months since he was here last, and the city's geographies had been blasted into strange new forms. And not just by the attacking tyranids. They passed a wall imprinted with the organic silhouettes of some unfortunates obliterated by an Imperial energy weapon. Perhaps not unfortunates, perhaps they'd been cultists, Anditz told himself.

'The state of some of these buildings,' Adair said as she jogged, disdainfully gesturing at a collapsed gilt facade. 'Wealth can't buy you taste.'

'That an old Catachan proverb?' Anditz said. He didn't feel like talking but knew that Adair needed the distraction.

'Ha,' Adair said. 'Very funny, sir. Reckon they look better as ruins.'

'This city is greater than anything your people have ever built,' Lamya said, her tone flat.

'That so?' Adair laughed, eyeing the blast-marked ruins around them.

'You have no idea of the heritage, the weight of history,' the cultist said, staring unblinkingly into the distance. 'Here, in this place where the founders came from the stars and built something brighter than the Imperium could ever hope to surpass.'

There was something odd about the way the cultist spoke, Anditz noted. Detached. When they'd first picked her up she'd been angry. But now she seemed to be drifting.

Something flickered overhead.

'Incoming,' Anditz called and raised his pistol. He saw Khan do the same at the rear. A shoal of flying horrors passed above them, but quickly flapped away. Anditz lowered his weapon with a frown, then saw what had made them move. Something large was descending slowly through the lower atmosphere. It was hideously veined and bloated and there was a perverse dignity to its slow descent. As it drew closer, Anditz realised just how big it was. It had to be almost thirty feet across.

It disappeared over the city, and a few moments later a spiral of purple spores rose into the air.

'I don't like the look of that,' Adair said.

'No,' Anditz said, glancing up at the sky. 'And there's more coming down. This way.' He sped into a run, the others following behind.

They were moving down the shaded narrow street that had been the Boulevard of Makers. The old, shuttered manufactoria were smashed and ruined, the perfumed trees dead or uprooted. When Anditz had been stationed here most of the craftspeople had already gone, along with their miraculous trinkets and jewellery, but he'd still seen a tiny ruby effigy of the Emperor carved into a nutshell the size of his thumbnail, and gold cloth spun so fine the sun glowed through it. All obliterated now, all gone. Like the hands that had made those things.

They burst out of the narrow alley and into the sulphurous glow of daylight again.

'There!' Anditz shouted back to Khan.

On the other side of the Moonstone Court, the tall, arched gate to the cisterns hung open on one hinge. The entrance stood between two pale buildings carved of opalescent stone with rivers of sapphire flowing along their facades.

The cistern gate hadn't been hidden away with the rest of the settlement's infrastructure; rather, it had been seen as a curiosity. It was older than the city itself, and the more flamboyant wealthy had hosted decadent parties in its depths, quaffing priceless amasec among the vast, screaming heads of statues upturned in the echoing, watery caverns.

Anditz flinched at the sound of a crushing impact behind him. He kept running and something sharp shot past his ear. He heard Adair swear close by.

'Keep going, sir!' she shouted. 'This one's full of the bastards!'

'What?' He glanced behind him in alarm.

Something shaped like the spore bag that had descended across the city had impacted on the other side of the square. This fleshy capsule had burst on impact, and xenos armed with projectiles were pouring forth from it across the ruins and out into the city.

Anditz skidded to a halt by the entrance. Symbols had been daubed there in the cult cant. He swore.

'Is it trapped?' Adair halted beside him.

'I don't know. I can't read it. Where's the heretic?'

They turned. Khan was blasting off shots at the skittering nightmares.

'There,' Adair called.

Lamya was running on swift feet up the spiral stone steps of a crumbled tower, the winding stairs exposed where one wall was blasted away.

'Leave her,' growled Khan.

'There's cultist scrawl on the entrance, sir. She'll be able to tell us if it's a trap.'

Khan nodded. 'Then bring her back. Adair, watch his back, I'll cover you both.'

Anditz ran, dodging debris shed by more descending tyranid transport pods. Behind him Adair snarled, heavy flamer belching out fire as bleached-bone horrors snapped at her.

Anditz took the steps of the tower two at a time, putting an arm against the curve of the wall as he ascended. This building was old. The walls were three feet thick, crudely assembled with blocks of quartz rather than poured ferrocrete, the construction now visible where missiles had punched through. Anditz shouldered open the small door at the top of the stairs and came to a sudden halt. Adair nearly ran into the back of him.

The room at the top of the tower was circular, ringed with small arched windows. Above each, on the inside, was a small shelf with a black plaque inscribed with gold antique lettering.

On the floor sat a wizened old man dressed in tattered velvet robes, clutching something to his chest. Lamya knelt beside him, her skirts spread behind her in a pool of black silk.

'You need to come now,' Anditz ordered.

She turned to look at him incredulously. 'The opera is about to begin. I can hear the overture. What would the gentry say if I arrived like this?' Her lip curled. 'Dressed this way? Without an entourage? Without my ritual moths?'

The old man shifted, and the things in his arms moved.

'What in the hell is she on about?' muttered Adair.

Anditz saw that the old man was holding a pair of enormous moths. Each was about the size of a battle-cannon shell, fat-bodied and softly furred dark brown, with anxiously twitching antennae.

'Come on,' Anditz said.

Lamya gave him an imperious look. 'It is not for the likes of you to rush the court lepidoptera.'

She's gone mad, Anditz realised, looking at the woman's shining eyes. *She is standing in a ruin and there are aliens falling from the sky that she's ignoring and there's music playing in her head that nobody will ever hear again or remember, because all of the musicians are dead and the world is dying and before long, there will be nobody left who remembers Lazulai.*

There was an inhuman scream from outside the tower.

Anditz gripped the cultist by the elbow. She glowered, but didn't resist. 'You'd best leave,' he said to the old man, 'it's about to be overrun.'

'No, sir,' the old man said. 'These are the last two.' He choked at this. 'The founder, she trained and flew their ancestors, sir. They're as much Lazulai as the city was.'

Anditz turned away, steering Lamya back down the tower's twisting steps. She cried openly, her hands over her face. Whether it was distress at her illusion being shattered, or she was frustrated at not getting her own way, he didn't know.

Halfway down, Adair sighed heavily, and put a hand on Anditz's shoulder. 'I'll see you at the bottom.' She jogged back up the stairs and a moment later, Anditz heard three shots crack out. The cultist was too lost in grief to realise what had happened.

Adair emerged at the bottom of the staircase, grim-faced.

'Come on!' Khan shouted.

To Anditz's horror, one of the grotesque floating xenos hung motionless on the opposite side of the square. He felt the chill of its presence through the city's heat. It slowly rotated to face them and 'gaunts skittered up behind it, streaming towards their position. It was hard not to believe the malign intelligence radiating from the monster was being directed specifically at them.

Khan fired her plasma pistol at the alien. The ball of energy stopped several feet from the monster, appearing to smash onto an invisible barrier, flattening and evaporating. Khan swore and fired again. The same thing happened.

'Run!' she shouted grimly.

They ran to the cistern entrance and slammed the heavy gate closed. Anditz and Adair shoved a few chunks of broken masonry in front of it. Anditz kept his eyes down, not wanting to see the silent, floating horror across the square. There was a wet, organic sound as another capsule landed beside the tower they had just left. As the scuttling horrors burst forth, the squad turned and ran into the damp, echoing darkness of the tunnels.

CHAPTER ELEVEN

Haruto ran, the tech-adept keeping pace at his side. A filthy blood-rain plastered his shock of dark hair to his forehead. They were back in the open, pounding across the dead fields they'd crossed before, following the maglev tracks away from the city. The shunt was somewhere along the line. Had to be.

Just after they had left Carnadine, they had seen xenos projectiles slamming into the city behind them. Whether the rest of the squad had survived, he did not know, but it seemed unlikely.

That had been almost an hour ago, and conditions were worsening. It wasn't just the rain. The embryonic trees they had seen before were growing, even faster than Wrathe had predicted. The dead tisane fields were now littered with fanged pumps, grotesque organic vessels that vomited spores into the air.

They had seen something like them before, back at Cobalt Fortress. Their first appearance had heralded Lazulai's terminal decline towards inhabitability. At first, they'd tried to blast the alien constructs as they appeared. Not only did their spined claws provide a surprisingly effective shield, but if struck, the puckered maw at the centre would violently disgorge a lethal cloud of spores. They had grown faster than they could be stopped, like the xenos-hybrid jungle growth that had erupted from Lazulai's carcass and now stood ahead of them. Haruto pulled out his Catachan Fang, ready to slash a path through the fleshy wall of leaves ahead.

'Look,' Wrathe crackled through her vox-grille. 'A new form.' She pointed.

Haruto wiped the filthy rain from his eyes and squinted. 'What on Terra is that?'

A vast tower of ridged chitin shot upwards into the sky. Its base must have been thirty feet across, the top disappearing into the dark, yellowed clouds. The vegetation around the base appeared to have liquefied, the surrounding ground broken and crusted like a weeping sore around it.

'The current pollution makes it hard to determine, but it appears to reach into the lower atmosphere.' She frowned. 'Its configuration is suggestive of an orbital spire.'

'You think it's some kind of transport? For more forces?'

'I do not know.'

Wrathe made a gesture. Haruto noticed the tech-priest's hand as she moved. The fine filigree was pitted with rust, the joints thickened and stiff.

'What happened?' he said, stepping forward to lift her fingers to his eye.

'I believe an interaction between the humidity and the spores. The initial superficial damage appears to have accelerated in the current conditions.'

Haruto frowned. 'We're being eaten alive, aren't we?'

'Broadly speaking, that is a reasonable assessment of the situation.'

'Does it hurt?'

She blinked, her white eyes expressionless. 'Yes,' she admitted after a moment.

'This one looks worse,' Haruto said, comparing her hands. 'Here,' he said, untying his bandana. 'This will keep the worst off.' He wrapped the tech-priest's fingers in the red fabric.

'Are you certain? I believe this is an important Catachan cultural artefact.'

Haruto shrugged. 'My hair can't look any worse.'

There was a burst of static from Wrathe's vox-grille that might have been a laugh.

Haruto grunted. 'How close do you think we are to the cargo shunt?'

She stood and turned to face the bristling jungle. 'Not far, I believe. Although the terrain is altered.'

There was a rushing sound like parchment over bone, and a flying tyranid swept past overhead. Haruto swore as the vast monster disappeared in the direction of the city.

They carried on along the tracks.

'How long will it take to get the shunt running?' Haruto asked.

'Impossible to say. It depends greatly on the condition and inclination of the machine spirit.'

Haruto slashed aside a fleshy, crimson-veined shrub in his path. 'Look.' He gestured to where the maglev tracks beneath their feet sank into the ground. 'How do we get in?'

Wrathe crouched down, her red robes trailing in the filth of the forest floor. She reached her delicate hands into the red mire, following the maglev tracks. There was a cracking sound and she stepped back quickly. The forest floor appeared to be rising, splitting apart. The xenos flora had thin, matted roots like fungus and slipped easily away, uprooted by the two trap-doors that had fully opened to reveal the nose of a large cargo shunt underground. The glow of strip-lumens was strange to see after so long in the wilderness.

'There's a shunt all right,' Haruto acknowledged.

The tech-adept had already stepped down into the storage shed. She ran her hands along the surface of the cabin. 'It lives,' she said, and pulled open the cabin door. 'I will examine the machine spirit more closely.'

'I'll stand watch,' Haruto said as she climbed inside. Something was itching at the back of his brain. Some instinct was telling him he should be ready.

Their journey so far through Lazulai's new jungle had been peculiar because it had been silent, the opposite of the constant chitters and rustle of Catachan. It had taken a while to get used to. But something had changed. He'd not heard a noise, but he sensed something at the edge of audibility, some difference in the texture of the sound.

He strained his ears to hear as the thick, red rain spattered on the sodden ground. He padded softly around the edge of the sunken service-shed mouth. Behind the rise concealing the opening, the ground sloped down into what was rapidly becoming a shallow pool of filthy, spore-tainted water. Visibility was poor in the downpour, and he squinted to see through the haze of water.

The liquid on the ground ahead bubbled. Could it be the thick texture of the rain? Haruto thought. He frowned. No, something else was moving.

His vision suddenly resolved the indistinct morass ahead into clusters of pits, ridged and stomatic, sunk into the ground, reminiscent of the nurseries of hive insects. There were hundreds of them, each the size of a Baneblade's hatch, the nearest a mere twenty feet downslope. And within them… He watched in horrified fascination as a single scythe burst forth from the viscous membrane that had been covering the nearest pit. He barked off a series of shots. A hideous figure, pale and glistening with natal detritus, burst from the birthing pool, venting ichor where the boltgun rounds had shattered its chitin. Haruto recognised it as some sort of 'gaunt. Hunched, human-sized and fast. Individually not a concern, but in their hundreds? Even newly emergent it was as hostile as the hordes they'd faced back at Cobalt Fortress.

Haruto snarled as he peppered it with fire. Even once he'd shattered its lower limbs, it kept dragging itself forward towards him as if propelled by some unnatural force. And all around it hundreds more were stirring in their foul recesses. Haruto swore and turned to run.

'Nefeli!' he bellowed. The only chance they stood of getting away was if the tech-adept could bring the shunt to life.

Something hit him hard in the side and sent him skidding into the sodden ground. He coiled to leap to his feet and found he couldn't. His left leg was unresponsive. And whatever had struck him was now leaping at him out of the deluge. He pulled his knife and thrust it upward with a prayer as the 'gaunt descended on him.

It was too damp in the cisterns for Khan to be able to light up a cheroot. She ground her teeth and strode on through the humid darkness, following Adair and Anditz, who led the way with a stab-light. Khan's fingers itched for a smoke. She needed to do something to distract her from Haruto's fate. The damned idiot. He'd always been stubborn, and that streak had served her well over the years. Maybe the Martian had been right and the maglev shunt could have taken them to the excavation site quicker, but there was no way they could have survived the aerial bombardment of xenos the city had just experienced.

Another good soldier, gone. And a friend. And Ghost too, although she had nobody to blame for his loss but herself. She should never have split the squad further. It was a fool's game, born of a sentimentality Khan hadn't realised she still possessed. The tyranids would devour this world whatever they did. All she could do now was get her remaining soldiers to the target and try to get them off this world. That way, at least something of the Catachan 903rd and the Cadian 82nd would survive. That mattered to her as much as the archeotech did.

'Hurry up,' she snapped at the heretic. Lamya was lagging behind. Whatever had happened when she'd run off back at the square had struck her silent. She'd read the cult-marks when instructed – they'd dodged a mine thanks to her translation – but she was closed-off and pensive.

That didn't matter, though, as long as they got out. Khan's fingers brushed her cheroot case. She admonished herself for the unconscious movement. She had to stay sharp.

The walkways through the cisterns were semi-flooded. Water sluiced coldly over their ankles in some places and the mournful, carved faces of ancient heretic gods or city founders rose above them, half shadowed in the dank, columned depths. It was cooler here than the surface and sweat chilled on her flesh.

'How much further, lieutenant?' she asked.

The Cadian turned, the flare of the stab-light lending his face hard lines. 'The cisterns are built on the city plan, sir. I'm fairly certain we're about to reach the Jasper bisection. From there, we turn out left towards the east and continue for a mile or two.'

Khan grunted. Whether it was enough distance between them and the swarm remained to be seen. They had to move faster if they were going to get to the excavation site in time.

'What in the hell is that?' Adair said. 'Light up the water here, lieutenant.'

Anditz swung his beam in her direction. Something foul floated in the water alongside them. It looked as if it belonged inside something living. Ribbons of livid tissue dredged out in the water behind it and Khan thought she saw it moving.

'It's a xenos explosive,' Khan said. She'd seen such things shatter through tanks.

'There are more coming downstream,' the Cadian said, squinting at them in the stab-light beam.

'Go. Carefully and quickly.'

The squad moved swiftly down to the junction until Adair halted.

'Way's blocked, sir. Looks like there's been a collapse.'

Khan inspected the blockage. Rubble rose high into the vaulted ceiling. 'Rest of that passage looks to have gone,' she said. 'What options have you got for me, lieutenant?'

The Cadian frowned. 'A long detour I'm sure of, or a side route I'm not.' He pointed. 'If we go back that way, we can drop down into the understructure. We're only a mile or so from the exit and there'll be a way out, but it's a warren down there. If we go on it's a straight line, but it'll be another four or five miles before we can turn east again.'

'I vote the quick way,' Adair said.

Khan nodded. 'Take us to the understructure, lieutenant.'

The warren of ventilation shafts smelled worse than Anditz had remembered from the cursory inspection they'd made on securing the city. The heat likely wouldn't have helped, he thought. The ceiling was low, and Adair grumbled about having to hunch over. Khan moved ahead, the ceiling brushing against her buzz-cut head. The passages branched and forked apparently at random, and they had found themselves coming back out into the same corridor after a circular detour more than once.

Anditz could tell that Khan was becoming impatient. He was fairly certain he could lead them back to the main walkway, but they had lost time they could ill afford.

'I think we're going east, now,' Anditz said. Instruments like compasses had long since stopped working, the mechanisms gummed with spores. They were going on instinct alone, something which he didn't like.

He stepped over a puddle then paused. Something bright caught his eye, floating in the water below his feet. He bent and picked it up. It was a scrap of a ration pack.

'Sir,' he said quietly, turning to Khan to show her. 'This looks as if it's just been dropped.'

Khan took it and turned it over in her fingers. 'Weapons ready.'

'Look at this,' Adair said from behind them. She'd pressed her fingers against the wall, feeling the shape of the markings scrawled there.

'Cult signs,' Anditz said.

'What does it say?' Khan whispered in Lamya's direction.

Lamya either ignored her or didn't hear.

'Hey,' Khan hissed.

'Can you read this?' Anditz asked, steering the blank-faced cultist to the wall.

Her eyes focused ahead. 'Yes.'

'What does it say?'

She shrugged. 'Holy texts. Mantras.'

'Looks like someone was living here,' Anditz said, examining the detritus in the corridor ahead.

'Then they'll know how to get out,' Khan said.

There was a sound from somewhere above them. Anditz turned up his stab-light. They had a brief glimpse of a pale face before it disappeared into the hole it had come from.

The squad aimed their weapons.

'Hold,' Khan said.

'Call him back,' Anditz ordered Lamya. 'In the cant. He might trust you.'

Lamya sighed then cleared her throat. A ribbon of ululating speech echoed around the corridors. After a moment, the face reappeared in the hole. Cautious and grimy, it appeared to belong to an old man. He trilled back to Lamya in the cult tongue, and she replied.

'What's he saying?' Anditz asked.

'He says he's alone,' Lamya said. 'And that he didn't know about the angels arriving. He's been down here since before the ascension day.'

At that moment the old man crept out of the hole and dropped down into the corridor.

Adair stepped forward and gripped the ragged figure on one bony arm. 'Got you, you little bastard.' She grimaced. 'Eugh! He stinks, sir.'

'Silence, brute!' the old man spat in Low Gothic. 'How dare you speak to one of the star children this way!' His reedy voice trembled with fury.

'He doesn't look like a mutant,' Adair said. She frowned, examining the noisome figure.

'IIa!' the old man snorted contemptuously. 'Witness my gods-given talons.' He stamped down hard on the sludgy ground.

Adair squinted down at his filthy, shoeless feet. 'They just look like long toenails to me.'

Khan leaned forward and gripped the tiny man's collar, leaning forward so her face nearly met his. 'Which way is out?'

He squirmed under the brightness of Anditz's stab-light, but didn't reply.

'We need to exit to the east,' Anditz said.

'Tell us, and we'll leave you here,' Khan said.

The old man shook his head.

'You're going to tell us where the eastern exit is, or I'm going to cut your damned feet off,' Khan snarled. 'Do you understand? Lieutenant, pull my chainsword.'

The old man spluttered. 'You're going the right way,' he said. 'Keep to the left and you'll find the way out.'

Khan dropped him, and the aged heretic smoothed his rags indignantly. As he turned to re-enter his cubby-hole, Khan moved after him, knife in her hand. Swiftly and smoothly, she gripped the top of his head and before he realised what was happening, she pushed her blade up through the base of his skull.

The old man gasped – whether in shock or pain, Anditz did not know – then slumped, lifeless, to the ground. Khan rolled him aside with the toe of her boot.

'Let's move,' she growled.

Anditz blinked, taken aback by the speed with which she had dispatched him. 'I don't think he was actually a mutant, sir.'

'No. But he knew where we were going,' Khan said. 'If he was telling the truth, it looks like you had us on the right route, lieutenant. Lead on.'

It took less than half an hour for them to get to the exit. They continued in the same direction, keeping to the leftmost pathways. The dirty, spore-filtered light that struck them when they exited the cisterns was murky, barely distinguishable from dusk. Although, perhaps it was dusk. Anditz glanced at his wrist-chrono and frowned. It was misted as if with breath, the numerals unreadable.

'Spores're breaking down everything mechanical,' Adair said.

'I wonder how the tech-priest is faring,' Anditz said. 'If she's still alive,' he added.

'The sergeant's a tough old bird. He'll get them through,' Adair said.

Anditz nodded. Now she'd had a little more time to reflect on it, he'd been wondering what Adair thought about the squad's split. Had Haruto been Cadian he'd likely have been executed on the spot, but Catachans apparently did things differently.

'Directions,' Khan ordered.

Anditz nodded, looking around. They were outside the city boundary. His regiment had remained here holding the eastern frontier as the other forces had redeployed elsewhere.

'South, along the city's edge. We can follow the maglev tracks out over the bridge towards the excavation site.'

'Terrain?'

'The city's necropolis sits on the border. And beyond that there are more tisane fields running up to where the maglev bridge spans the Malachite Gorge. The bridge will take us on the most direct route, unless the cultist's footway gets us there faster.'

Khan nodded. 'Take us there, lieutenant.'

Haruto had a brief impression of a rictus grin through a wall of blood-rain as he rolled, and a scythe slammed down by his left ear.

In its fury, the xenos impaled itself on his knife, the Catachan Fang cracking through the chitin up to the hilt. With a roar, Haruto pushed upwards, rolling the alien off him. It lashed out with its razor scythes, but one suddenly burst in a spray of bone that slashed Haruto's cheek. Another shot exploded into the monster's side, and it writhed away from Haruto, wrenching his knife out of his hand as it leapt off him, weapon still embedded in its fused ribcage.

Haruto sat up and pulled his boltgun. His nose was full of the terrible, natal stench of the wounded alien, which was now pounding towards a figure in the trees. Another shot rang out and the alien tumbled. Haruto almost laughed in relief. Through the darkness he'd seen the flash of a long-las.

'Ghost!' he shouted as his comrade ran towards him.

'Sir.' The rangy Catachan gave him a nod of greeting, slinging his weapon strap over his shoulder and extending a hand.

Haruto struggled up out of the mud. His left leg was numb, and he couldn't put any weight on it, but it was too plastered in filth to see any injury.

'Can you walk?' Ghost asked.

'Not well,' Haruto said, leaning heavily on his comrade. All around them, innumerable pits sucked and squelched with movement.

'If you take the thousand on the left and I take the thousand on the right, we might just get through this,' Ghost said as they moved back towards the shed.

Haruto barked out a laugh. Pain flared through his ribs from where the alien had landed on him. Then there came a sound sweeter than any psalm: the sputter of an engine rolling up to a resonant growl.

'Ha!' Haruto grinned. 'Throne bless her. She's done it!'

'How fast do you think it'll go, sir?'

'Pray the answer to that is "very",' Haruto replied as he limped down into the shed.

Haruto had been fairly certain that they would die. The odds certainly suggested it. Most people might be surprised that a Catachan would make such an assumption, but most people didn't realise that Catachans were some of the most pragmatic citizens the Imperium had. It might look as if they were being cocky when they stated that you could send a single Catachan in the place of ten Mordians, but they were just making a logical assessment of the situation. The reason they assumed they were better than other regiments was because they *were*. Not better, Haruto corrected himself. But simply better at the things they were truly good at.

He grimaced and hauled himself half out of the window of the moving cargo shunt, his injured leg dragging uselessly behind him. He hung by one hand from a ceiling grip. With the other, he took aim with his boltgun. He thumped out a couple of shots, bursting a pair of 'gaunts running alongside that had got too close. He pictured the horrors still emerging from the ichor-filled birthing pits back down-track. The tyranids pursuing them were already innumerable, but he didn't doubt there would be more yet. The swarm grew, stretching back into the distance and eating up the terrain like some chitinous optical illusion.

The shunt was moving, but it was still travelling too slowly despite Wrathe's frantic work in the engine chamber.

Haruto glanced back inside the carriage. Ghost leaned out of the window on the other side, his long-las hissing instant death into the chitin skulls of the xenos he struck.

The blood-rain sheeted down, reducing visibility to a pink-red blur. Haruto squinted, trying to identify another target. Thank Him-on-Terra for the sharp-eyed sniper.

There was a sudden flash of teeth to his left and Haruto swung himself back into the carriage. The 'gaunts were getting too close now, making moves towards boarding.

Bracing himself, he slid the nearest external carriage door open. An undulating swarm of xenos raced alongside like the foam on some terrible wave crest. They moved in unison, giving an impression of solidity, as if one might be able to step out onto the chitin tide and ride its serpentine motion. Hundreds of void-black eyes flicked to regard him. Haruto grasped the grip-rail and swung his good leg out to kick the nearest xenos right in its rictus grin. His boot made contact with a sickening crunch and threw the alien under its fellows. The tide barely stumbled, rippling emotionlessly over their fallen comrade. Haruto barked off a couple of rounds from his boltgun, sending splinters of bone bursting from the swarming aliens. But it was futile. Their numbers were too great to make any meaningful difference.

'Sergeant,' Ghost called. 'We're coming up to a bridge over a mineshaft. Single track, that'll slow them down.'

Wincing at the pain in his leg, Haruto turned to look. Sure enough, he could see that the track curved around over the vast crater of a mine, rising hundreds of feet high on metal struts over the vertiginous drop. It would slow the tyranids, but it wouldn't stop them. Haruto pictured them flowing across the thin line of track, almost like a liquid, before regrouping on the other side and ultimately overwhelming the maglev.

Haruto frowned, carrying out some quick calculations in his head. 'How many grenades have you got left?' he asked the sniper.

'Four,' Ghost replied, picking off a 'gaunt that had crawled up onto the side of the maglev.

'Give them to me,' Haruto said, holding out a massive hand. He limped down the carriage, his lips moving as he considered how far across the bridge they'd have to be before he could safely blow the back carriage. These things were always as much an art as a science, but there was going to be little room for error.

He moved into the next carriage, ducking as a 'gaunt smashed through the window. His injury was slowing him down and the cadaverous thing got far closer than it should have before he was able to shoot it.

Most of the carriages were empty, ready to be filled with gems to be taken for processing by artisanal workers, but the next car was loaded with supplies ready to service the mines. The cult's stash, Haruto thought. There wasn't much in the way of weaponry, but a few barrels of promethium were all he needed. He jammed the wide hatch to the next carriage open and rolled the barrels through. He was aware of scritching sounds at the plasteel hull of the shunt as he did so – like the rougher parts of some warp journeys, he thought.

There was a jolt, and the vehicle started to pick up speed.

Cold sweat beaded on his forehead as he manoeuvred the bulky barrels into place. His leg wound still oozed. It should have clotted by now, he thought. He'd seen xenos injuries become infected before, and it rarely ended well. Not that there was time to worry about it now. If this didn't work, the swarm would kill him a lot quicker than bad blood.

There was sudden silence as the maglev shot out across the high tracks, and the swarm was reduced to a single stream behind the vehicle.

They were moving faster now, and he'd have to act quickly. He slid open the external door and was met with a blast of humid air. It was dark outside, the spoil-heaps vanishingly far below, glittering like sand from this distance. Behind them curled the track, the racing tide of xenos narrowed temporarily to a stream. Frowning in concentration, Haruto levered himself out over the treadplate, looking for the cut lever to uncouple the carriage.

Once it was in his grip, he jerked it upwards and felt the shunt shudder. He pulled himself back in and checked he had a clear shot into the next carriage. Then he initiated the uncoupling.

There was a strange rush of air and an instant of visually unsettling movement as the carriages pulled away from each other. Haruto drew his boltgun and aimed it at the promethium barrels in the disconnected carriage. The 'gaunts were already swarming up and into it. Haruto counted down the seconds as the barrels were lost beneath a writhing mass of xenos flesh.

'One, two, three!'

He fired. The boltgun barked, and the disconnected carriage erupted in a blossoming tower of fire. Haruto flung himself away from the open door as the blast wave roared outwards. As the last shards of shrapnel shattered away, Haruto looked up to see the slim struts of the bridge folding and falling away into the yawning mine hole along with hundreds of 'gaunts, tumbling down like snow.

He felt a lurch in his stomach as the shunt lifted, and he wondered if his calculations had gone awry. Then the landscape shooting past suddenly changed, from low, reddish scrub to undulating cliffs of malachite, and they were rattling by on solid ground again. They had cleared the bridge.

Haruto nodded and made his way back down the maglev. He rifled through the storage racks but found only supplies for vehicular repair, not human.

He limped to the front of the vehicle.

'Sir,' Ghost said as he re-entered the forward carriage. 'We've lost the 'gaunts, but there's a couple of airborne incoming.'

'Type?'

'Human-sized. Like when we were moving out from Cobalt Fortress.'

Haruto slid aside the door to the engine cabin. No need to give Ghost orders, he knew to shoot the bastards as soon as they were close enough.

The tech-priest turned, her filigree metal fingers pausing their deft work among coiled cables. Sweat beaded her forehead, and delicate mechadendrites rose from her locs, sparking with static. She'd shrugged off her red robe in proximity to the heat of the engine. He could see that her upper body was comprised of an engraved silver cuirass of the same design as her hands and lower arms. Aside from her face, the dark brown skin of her slim upper arms was the only apparent reminder of her organic origins.

'You bloody well did it,' Haruto said. 'You got her moving. We just dropped a couple of hundred 'stealers into a mineshaft.'

The corners of Wrathe's eyes creased pleasantly and a crackle came from her vox-grille that he read as laughter.

'A relief indeed,' she said. 'Give thanks to the Omnissiah. It is they who have looked kindly upon us.'

Despite himself, Haruto found his mouth curving into an unfamiliar smile. 'I'm fairly sure you deserve some of the credit.'

The tech-adept tilted her head to one side and frowned, looking at his leg. 'You are damaged.'

'Unfortunately.'

'How seriously?'

'I've not looked.'

'I'm afraid I am of little service with organic repairs.' She paused for a moment. 'Trooper Adair would have been able to help.'

'She was handy with a wound clip,' he acknowledged, then barked out a laugh. 'You'd have to be when you got into as many fights as she did.'

It was the first time he had spoken about the squad in the past tense. A sudden weight fell over the carriage.

'I am sorry for their loss,' Wrathe said. 'Although it demonstrates the necessity of the choice you made to recover this engine. To remain in the city would have meant death.'

'It was the logical decision for the mission,' Haruto said.

'Yes. But not, I think, an easy one.' She reached out and placed her hand on his arm. Her metal fingers were warm, almost as if they were flesh, the joints gently articulated.

There was a sudden lurch, and a shout from Ghost. It sounded like trouble was on the way.

'What did he say?' Wrathe asked.

'He said there's a big one coming,' Haruto relayed, pulling his boltgun and dragging himself back through to the other carriage.

'Omnissiah protect you.' Wrathe interlinked her fingers and made a circular gesture.

As Haruto passed through into the next carriage there was an impact that threw him hard against the wall. He gripped his gun with one hand and steadied himself with the other.

There was a dent on the carriage roof which crumpled the metal as if a giant fist had punched down on it from above. The windows had been obscured with some sort of venous membrane, the light inside now filtered an unpleasant fleshy pink. Haruto had the momentary impression that they had driven into the interior of something living, but then whatever was obscuring the windows moved. Vicious carpal spurs gouged the plex-glass as the membrane withdrew. He grunted, feeling a surge of adrenaline rush through his body in response to the horrific sight. So, a flighted xenos had landed on the roof. Xenos of this size that he'd seen before tended to be armed with projectiles – that was going to be a problem in close quarters.

There was a sudden blare of sound, the violence of which felt like an assault. Haruto gritted his teeth. His ears rang as noise blasted across every audible frequency, from a bass rumble that shook his bones up to a piercing scream that felt as if it was drilling into his skull. Ghost had doubled over, hands over his ears. Then the noise suddenly stopped. The relief was brief, as it was replaced with a rising whine. Something in the tone struck concern into Haruto.

'Get back,' he called to Ghost. He could barely hear his own voice through the fug of his damaged eardrums.

At the other end of the carriage there was a sudden blast, and a section of the roof ripped off. Bleak daylight streamed in along with filthy red drizzle.

Fist-sized projectiles trailing barbed flails smashed through the open aperture. They burst on contact with the walls or floor, violently ripping themselves inside out, the barbs tearing aside metal plating as if it were flesh. Haruto watched in dismay as they ripped through the floor of the shunt, revealing the tracks below. Another hit and this carriage would likely split.

The maglev lurched as their attacker's weight shifted. There were loud impacts on the roof as the xenos made its way along the carriage above them, buckled dents bursting through the metal as it moved. Then an armoured head thrust through the hole. It was a heavy, living skull plated in purple: teeth bared, stiff tongue protruding and suppurating with unknown venoms. A barbed horn swept up from its head and its tiny eyes glittered unreadably.

The sight of it sent a chill down Haruto's spine.

'Coming up to a cliffside tunnel, sir!' Ghost shouted. His voice sounded strange, as if he was underwater. 'If we can keep its attention long enough, it'll smash itself against the rock.'

As long as it doesn't embed its talons any further into the maglev, Haruto thought. If it was too firmly entrenched the impact would derail them.

'I'll distract it, you draw it off!' Haruto shouted. He barked off a shot from his boltgun. The xenos swivelled to reposition itself over the aperture at an unnerving speed and he suddenly found himself facing down the barrels of two organic missile launchers that bulged and distended.

'Now!' Haruto yelled. They had to keep it moving, else they risked it ripping the shunt away with it when it struck the rock.

His damaged eardrums didn't register the crack of Ghost's lasrifle, but he saw the beam scream into the side of the alien's head and cook one of its eyes. It pivoted and explosively birthed a live missile in Ghost's direction.

Haruto swore and dodged, covering his face as the biological weapon erupted through the carriage. At the moment the xenos turned its attention back to him, there was a sudden change in pressure and a terrible crack, as if the Emperor himself had split the mountainside.

The alien vanished, as if it had been plucked from the maglev's roof, and there was darkness outside as they plunged into a tunnel.

In the cold light of the strip-lumens Haruto limped towards the adjacent carriage. It was heavily damaged from the tyranid's missile, but still mercifully attached to the rest of the shunt.

There was no sign of Ghost. Haruto's heart felt flat. He paused in the doorway to survey the ruin, steadying himself against the buckled frame. The second blast from the xenos had burst a human-sized hole through the wall of the carriage. The stone of the tunnel wall rushed past, a lurid kaleidoscope of Lazulai's unnatural strata. A mercy that Ghost had drawn the fire away from the floor of the train. With his last action, he had undoubtedly saved them.

Haruto clenched the doorframe, his knuckles white around the metal. Another Catachan dead. Another of the squad gone. Was he the last Catachan on this world now? Fury clenched his stomach, along with a flare of shame. Would this have happened if Khan was in command?

There was a movement behind him, and Ghost dropped from the ceiling where he had secreted himself away from the blast.

Haruto barked out a laugh and clapped his comrade on the shoulder. 'I thought we'd lost you!'

Ghost gave him a sideways smile. 'You'll have to try harder than that, sir.'

The maglev was filled with greasy light as they shot out of the tunnel and back into the open. The vehicle was moving along at speed now over a selection of elevated track.

'Throne,' Ghost said, staring out of a ragged gap in the side of the carriage. Haruto moved to join him.

The landscape no longer looked as if it belonged to a human world. Bathed in the reddish glow of a terminal sunrise sprawled a nightmare diorama of barbs and spines and organic towers. Pockets of blue fire burned where the ground had split in the gas-rich air. Far beyond, the sea boiled, black and juddering. How could a human victory be pulled from this? Haruto wondered. How could they snatch victory from the jaws of a monster that was a whole world?

Vertiginous constructs wormed their way into the roiling clouds, where vast shadows moved like deep-sea predators. Stomatic apertures glistened at the end of tubules dangling from unseen things moving in lower orbit. The ground had split in several places, forming great shallow craters like crusted sores, filled with some purplish excretion. There was an occasional building or vehicle marooned in these pools, but more dreadful was the parade of xenos horrors that marched into the liquid, throwing themselves into the foul ichor. It sloughed away chitin on contact, revealing the dreadful architectures of life that powered the still-living xenos armatures. Haruto had the disturbing feeling that he was watching the deliberate and systematic unmaking of something for a purpose he didn't understand.

As the maglev rattled past the vista of ruination, a great abscess in the ground opened up, tipping an agri building into the sizzling filth that pooled from below. Coils of greasy smoke rose as the liquid started to degrade the ferrocrete construction.

Haruto wondered if it was because of the blood-rain that had been falling. Perhaps the water table of the planet had been so deluged with the genetic material of the tyranids that it was only a matter of time before the whole surface was subsumed.

The entire world had been turned to the use of the xenos – even the plants had been rewritten in a template of their own design. And it had happened in a matter of months. Even on Catachan the jungle didn't move that fast. Haruto spat. This world and its infestation needed to be burned entire.

There was a flurry of movement, and Haruto watched as a mass of tiny flying tyranids shoaled across the sky in a foul murmuration. There were thousands of the creatures, each little more than huge rictus jaws with wings. They moved in perfect synchronicity, sweeping low over the mottled-flesh canopy of the tyranid jungle, stripping the pseudo-trees of foliage then dropping into the acrid pools to be subsumed.

Their flowing movement reminded him of the shoals of carnivorous fish in Catachan's waters. He felt a sudden, painful rush of yearning for his home planet. It was a feeling that lived in the hearts of all Catachans, for the living smell of the soil and the green, filtered light of their jungle. There wasn't a word in Low Gothic for it, but all Catachans felt it, in the quiet grime of hive cities or transit ships, or in the damp cold of deep trenches. It may have been constantly trying to kill them, but it had *made* them. Lazulai may be a death world and may now have a jungle, but Haruto had never felt further from home.

Shadows moved across the land, cast down by the monstrosities that roved in the heavens, fading and re-forming as the planet was twisted into something as far as could be imagined from anything a human could call home.

And then something unnatural even in the context of this spore-mottled hellscape hove into view. The scale was hard to determine at first in a landscape so stripped of comprehensible reference points, but the speed and trajectory suggested it was colossal, coming up fast behind the maglev. It moved on spindled limbs like an arachnid, the appendages stabbing into the ground with each scuttling stride in precise, powerful movements. It had hideous jaws slung low beneath a ridged, undulating spine, and looked like the vast, drifting bioform they had seen on the approach to Carnadine City.

'Brace!' Haruto yelled.

The monster must have been over sixty feet high, covering huge swathes of ground with each stride. And it was set to impact the maglev within seconds. There was nothing they could do, other than pray to Him-on-Terra. Ghost stationed himself at the end of the carriage, arms braced in the metal doorway, the place most likely to withstand impact from above.

Haruto wrenched open the door to the engine cabin. The tech-adept turned, alarmed.

'Come here,' he called.

As she stood, he pulled her into his arms then threw them both into the near doorway as the impact struck. Haruto briefly experienced a flash of light, the sensation of pain and a taste of metal in his mouth. Then he knew nothing more.

CHAPTER TWELVE

The City of the Dead ran parallel to the eastern side of Carnadine, a warren of black obsidian tombs and mausoleums with decorative skulls and the names of wealthy Lazulaians worked in gold and opal. Jet domes and intricate gates glittered, even in the murky light. The mortuary complex bordered Carnadine in a long strip, with the city of the living rising up to the right, and the tisane fields extending away to the left. Anditz reasoned that it would be safer and quicker to get to the bridge over the gorge if they cut through the tombs than work their way back into the city. This way they also had a clear exit to the left if needed.

Displaced people had been squatting among the houses of the dead when Anditz had passed through with his regiment before. The place was abandoned now, eerie. The offerings had disappeared too. The few living who remained no longer had time to leave flowers or food for the dead. Things that would have been looted on other worlds had been left here – long-cold jade censers and silver salvers were untouched outside the tombs – but the mouldering victuals that they'd held were gone.

They were halfway to the bridge when they picked up the vox-signal.

Khan had stopped and pressed her comm-bead to her ear, eyes darting as she listened.

'Do you hear that?' she asked.

'Sounds like ghost chatter, sir,' Anditz said, listening to the static.

'It's Astra Militarum,' Khan said, her craggy brow furrowed. 'Come on, pick up the pace. If we've got survivors, I want them with us.'

Despite the sun's shroud of atmospheric filth, Lazulai was growing even hotter. The miles of obsidian funerary buildings trapped the heat in their black walls and galleries. It was a suffocating wet heat, and Anditz felt his breath clammy in his lungs. He coughed to clear his throat.

'This what it's like on Catachan?' he remarked to Adair.

She sniffed. 'No, sir. You've got the canopy on Catachan. Keeps things shaded. And it never gets hotter than it gets, if you catch my meaning.'

Anditz nodded.

'This bloody planet's going to keep boiling until we're cooked.'

Anditz raised his eyebrows. 'Another incentive to complete the mission, trooper.'

'They just keep piling up, sir.' She paused. 'It'd be a shame if that was it, sir,' she added. 'If we didn't make it because of something as stupid as the heat. After everyone that's paid for us to get here.'

Anditz shot her a sideways glance. Adair's face was expressionless for a moment, then she shifted the strap of her heavy flamer.

'I'm so sweaty I think I'm permanently stuck to this damned thing.'

Just as the trooper seemed to be approaching something like solemnity she had to ruin it, Anditz thought.

'And this isn't healing.' She frowned, indicating the injury on her leg where the mutant had slashed her. A little trickle of blood ran from it.

'It hasn't been long.'

'Catachans heal fast, sir,' she said. 'Something's not right.' Adair sniffed, then frowned. 'Can you smell that? Something's rotting. More than normal on this damned planet, I mean.'

Anditz raised his head. There was something in the air all right. A heavy, sickly scent. He was about to reply when he saw Khan come to an abrupt stop ahead, at the crest of the hill that marked the end of the necropolis. She stood motionless for a few seconds, then turned slowly back towards them. The sun behind her was blood-red like a wound, lighting her in silhouette through a haze of spores. He caught a glimpse of her aquiline profile as she moved, then she faced them, her features cast in darkness.

'Lieutenant Anditz,' she called, voice flat. 'Come here.'

Anxiety thrummed in Anditz's stomach. The major sounded unsettled. He jogged towards her, leaving Adair and Lamya following behind.

He drew close enough to Khan to see her face, which was strangely expressionless, although her eyes looked wet. She had shut off the white-noise drone of the open vox-channel.

'Soldier,' she said. 'We've found the source of the vox-signal.' She paused. 'I don't have the words to tell you what's out there, so you're just going to need to look.'

Heart thudding in his chest, Anditz moved rapidly past her, up the incline to where he could see downslope onto the plains. For a moment, his brain failed to comprehend the appalling truth. He blinked, trying to understand the reality of what was spread out before him on what had once been tisane fields.

The growing leaves on this side of the city had been crushed months ago under the boots of the troops stationed there, but something else now filled the low plain that, at first glance, had looked like a strange parade running on as far as the eye could see.

Horror rose up through Anditz, impaling him as painfully as if it were a blade. Before him were hundreds of Cadians. They stood frozen, trapped upright in a foul pink swamp that now filled the plains, only their torsos protruding at odd, skewered angles. Some were buried to the hip, others to the chest, their faces contorted into grim rictuses. Turned vehicles peppered the morass, looking like toys that had been dropped by a child who had been carelessly playing at soldiers.

Rigid, flanged towers of tyranid matter thrust out of the flooded plains in the distance with moist, semi-translucent cauls hanging from them.

Unthinkingly, Anditz's legs carried him closer, down the slope towards the unctuous charnel tide that slapped wetly against the road. The acrid, intestinal stench was now almost unbearable.

He stumbled forward until he reached the shoreline. Pink scum floated on the hot breath of the wind where the effluence slapped against the land. The nearest body was submerged to the waist, its face bloated and almost unrecognisable as human, although the insignia of the Cadian Gate on its shoulder pauldron remained pristine.

Anditz stared, unable to process the horror ahead of him. All this time, he had believed that there were other Cadians on this world, still fighting. Surviving, like he was. He saw now, confronted with this field of the dead, the futility of this hope. There was only death here. Death was all this world had left.

A sudden moan escaped the body nearest to him. Anditz

swore in shock and rushed desperately towards it. Half aware of Khan shouting a warning from behind him, he gripped the Cadian under the arms and pulled them free from the liquid.

He realised as he was falling backwards that the soldier was strangely light. Too light.

Anditz found himself on the ground gripping only a torso. The soldier hadn't been half submerged, rather only half there. He rolled aside, leaping up. The remains of the Cadian lay on the ground, face unmoving. It was as if someone had sliced the body at the hips, leaving only a pink seam where the legs had been, an obscene mess of congealed meat and bone slime as the soldier had slowly melted from the feet up.

Anditz buried his face in his hands and wept in shame and anger at the horror he felt at the body in front of him. So many dead, so much wasted. Like his regiment, so many of Cadia's sons and daughters made carrion.

He felt a firm grip on his shoulders, then Adair pulled him into a bear hug, wrapping her powerful arms around him and for a moment blocking out the horrors of the dead regiment. When she pulled back, he saw Khan standing close by, face set in a grimace and wet with angry tears.

Another groan emanated from the half-body on the ground. Wordlessly, Khan shot the soldier in the head. It burst, the skull soft and pulpy.

'They're still alive,' Anditz cried.

'No, lieutenant,' Khan said. 'They can't be. Half a soldier can't live, or feel.'

Anditz looked out over the field of Cadians. He pushed one trembling hand into his jacket to touch the tin of Cadian soil he carried there. 'But if they are...'

'They're dead,' Khan said. 'But corpses are strange things. They can make noises. Sometimes they move. You've been on a battlefield, soldier, you know that. You know that in war there's rarely such a thing as a quiet death.'

'We need to give them the Mercy, sir. We can't leave them.'

'The dead need no mercy, soldier.'

Anditz turned his gaze to her, eyes burning. 'Please. These are my people.'

Khan's posture changed. 'We can't do anything for them, son. This goes on for miles. We don't have the time, and we can't spare the ammo.'

'But—'

'And you can't get out to them. You've seen what that stuff has done to tanks. What do you think it's going to do to your legs?'

Anditz made as if to speak.

'Lieutenant,' Khan said firmly. 'General Kvelter tasked us with our duty. These were her last orders. We have to keep going. Understand?' She searched his lilac eyes. 'You are going to make peace with your dead, then I am going to order you to take us on a route where we can get past this. Understand?'

Anditz nodded blankly.

Khan and Adair stepped back, leaving him at the shore.

Anditz gazed out at the army of corpse-soldiers. So many Cadians dead, so many wasted, when there were so few left. They looked almost comical, as if emerging from parade in a lake. A waste, and an insult to the planet that had forged them.

Anditz felt himself come apart, his sense of who he was pulling away like a strip of flesh. Numbly, he felt in his pocket for the tin of Cadian soil. He opened it, and tipped it all onto the ground, dropping the battered tin onto the small mound of earth. It no longer mattered.

Haruto didn't know where he was. In front of him were fluctuating cogs and streamers of redness and there was the stench of burning. He was lying on something uncomfortable that was pressing hard into his head. He moved. His head still hurt. He became aware of a rhythmic scraping sound nearby. Then something punched into his leg. His system flooded with the familiar rush of stimms, and his consciousness floated up out of the haze it had been bobbing in. He realised his eyes had been closed, and he opened them, banishing the hallucinations that had been playing out in his mind's eye. The edges of his vision were blurred and flickering, but after a few blinks the scene in front of him started to resolve into something solid. He was lying on the floor of the carriage, half of which was missing. There was smoke everywhere.

Ghost was kneeling beside him. He couldn't see the tech-adept.

'Where is she?' he said.

'Trying to rouse the machine spirit,' Ghost replied.

'What happened?'

'Catastrophic stop. We're grounded. The tyranid punctured the maglev in a few places.'

'Where is it?'

Ghost shrugged. 'Moved off,' he said. 'Stabbed us, then took off pretty fast towards the city.'

Haruto coughed, then spat blood. A wave of nausea swept over him.

'You cracked your head on the steel door when the talon pierced us,' Ghost added. 'You stopped the same thing happening to the tech-adept.'

'I don't remember,' Haruto groaned. 'But I don't think Wrathe would have fared as well as I did. And I feel like grox-shit.'

Ghost nodded. 'Rather you took the blow than she did. Swarm's coming and she's the only one who can get this started.'

Haruto winced and rubbed at his temple. His fingers came away wet with blood.

'Does she need help?'

There was a furious scream and the stench of ozone from behind the door of the engine cabin. The Catachans exchanged glances.

'She said she didn't,' Ghost said.

Haruto tried to sit up. The carriage was spinning.

'Leave it a while, sir. Filled you up with counterseptic and stimms, but we need to splint that leg.' He sniffed and pulled out a syrette that looked tiny in his hands. 'Reckon this is all the obscurine we've got, but I'll give it to you before I start. I'm no chirurgeon,' he said apologetically, cracking the syrette's cap and shaking the vial, 'so I'm giving you everything we've got.' He stabbed the drug into Haruto's upper arm.

The flood of painkillers hit almost immediately, rushing through Haruto's broken limbs and dimming the agony. A hazy numbness settled over him. 'Do what you need to do,' he said, and gritted his teeth.

The splinting took longer than was comfortable. Ghost worked slowly and kept stopping to check the progress of the approaching swarm.

'How close are they?' Haruto asked.

'Pretty close, but I've got a clear view out over the plains from here. They're not going to surprise us. Wrathe has a little longer to get the machine going.' He sat back and glanced at Haruto's leg. 'You feeling up to running yet?'

Haruto laughed, then frowned. 'You need to go on without me. Take Wrathe with you.'

'Even if we did, we couldn't outrun them,' Ghost said with a half-smile. 'We survive together, or we die together. It'll be as the Emperor wills it.' He tied the final knot on Haruto's splint.

Haruto tried to lever himself up again. He managed to sit

this time. He felt as if his senses were kicking back in gradually. There were still blurry edges to his vision and his depth perception was off, but he could feel himself recovering.

Ghost picked up his long-las and took up a post by what remained of the left-hand side of the carriage wall. Haruto could see the horde now. A rush of chitinous horrors moving towards them. The sheer scale and inevitability of their arrival somehow robbed them of their terror. It was impossible to comprehend. A single xenos was a nightmare beyond imagining, but a hundred thousand were impossible to process. Or perhaps that was the obscurine talking.

Arms shaking with effort, Haruto levered himself upright.

'Sir?' Ghost said.

'I'm not going to die lying down,' he said, pulling himself into a standing position. 'Get my gun, trooper.'

There was a mechanical splutter and a jerk, and the maglev's engine roared into life. Very slowly, the vehicle rose and began to move.

Haruto grinned and thumped on the door of the engine cabin. 'Well done!' he called. There was the sound of furious chanting from inside, and the occasional blast of binharic as the tech-adept fought with the engine.

Wordlessly, Haruto and Ghost took up post on each side of the carriage, aiming their weapons down the track, where the first wave of the oncoming horde scrabbled over one another to close the distance. The cargo shunt wasn't moving quickly enough, and they didn't have enough bullets. But it didn't matter. They both knew their duty.

'What are the odds we can outrun them, do you think, trooper?' Haruto asked. The vehicle was drifting along at walking speed.

Ghost smiled. 'I don't gamble, sir.'

'Just as well.'

CHAPTER THIRTEEN

Khan strode through the sheeting rain that had begun falling on them. It was rust-red and stank of iron and something more alien. You could see tiny flagellant things moving in it when it hit the ground or your flesh.

The lieutenant was in a bad way after seeing the half-devoured Cadian regiment, but he'd continued to provide directions. Khan hadn't been sure that he'd remain functional after what he'd witnessed, but he kept his eyes on the mission. She was impressed. Not many would have been able to do the same.

The flesh morass that was absorbing the Cadian regiment went on for miles and stank like the acrid inside of a carnivore's guts. The damned planet was eating them alive. She'd sworn to the lieutenant they were all dead already, but between her and the Emperor, she couldn't be sure. She'd wanted to get the lieutenant away from it, but their route took them right past it.

There were things on Catachan that could inject you with toxins that kept you just far enough away from death to ensure your meat stayed fresh while they ate you alive. She grimaced. An appalling way to die, robbed of the ability to fight. If that was to be their fate, the Adeptus Mechanicus could go to hell. Whatever machine they wanted wasn't worth more than flesh and blood. She would carry her troopers off this bastard world if she had to.

She pulled out a cheroot and clamped it between her teeth, noting that it was her second to last.

They swung around a corner, and a strange vista opened up. The City of the Dead stretched out before them. It terminated abruptly in the distance, a long ribbon of obsidian cupolas and sepulchres that had unfolded itself alongside Carnadine year by year.

To the right, the city of the living crawled with xenos horrors and burned with thick smoke. To the left was the end of the digestive sea, and beyond, a sweep of rotten tisane fields, on which huge, swollen feeder-beasts grazed like profane ruminants.

And ahead of them, incongruous in the chaos, was a bright sweep of metal, pocked with the beginnings of xenos corrosion.

Anditz pointed at it. 'That's the maglev bridge.' The construction rose more than fifty feet above ground, sweeping high across the feeding xenos.

'Can we cross it?' Adair asked.

'Perhaps not,' Anditz said, squinting through his magnoculars. In the distance, moving slowly alongside the rails, was one of the vast tyranids, the city-killers. Its back rose forty feet high, bristling with spore chimneys wafting out clouds of sickly purple smoke. It moved forward precisely on spike-spindled legs, its head low to the ground, jaws a mess of pincers and fangs.

Khan grunted. 'So, we take the cultist's route.'

'Sir. Providential that we have an alternative.'

'Indeed,' Khan said. 'Knew there was a reason for dragging the damned heretic with us all this way.'

'There's a reason for it. There must be,' Khan heard the cultist say calmly behind her.

'I don't want to hear anything else about those monsters,' Adair snapped.

'They're not monsters,' Lamya said, suddenly animated. 'I understand it now,' she continued, as if having a sudden realisation. 'Things went wrong when you arrived. They are here to remonstrate for your sins. You did this. You took our paradise, you killed those soldiers.'

There was a sudden gasp. Khan turned to see Adair gripping Lamya at the throat. Her massive fist encircled the cultist's slender neck easily, and the Catachan pulled the woman close to her face. 'Shut up, or I'll shut you up,' she snarled.

'Put her down,' Khan ordered. Lamya was red-faced and spluttering for her breath, her feet brushing the floor as Adair held her up. The Catachan didn't respond. 'Trooper,' Khan growled. 'Drop her.'

Adair released her grip on Lamya. The cultist stumbled to the ground, gasping and coughing.

'We need her to find this footway,' Khan growled. 'Have you seen what's guarding the bloody bridge, trooper?'

Adair nodded, sullen.

'We're too close to let emotions trip us up. You put this mission in jeopardy now, you'll find yourself swimming through that damned river. Do you understand, trooper?'

'Yessir.'

Khan took a drag on her cheroot. 'I'm about to run out of smokes, soldier. Now is not the time to start pushing me. Do you really understand?'

Adair grimaced. 'Yes. But you heard what she said, sir.'

'I heard. And I was ignoring it, just like you ignore everything that comes out of a heretic's mouth. You too much of a meathead to be able to ignore a heretic, Trooper Adair?'

'No, sir.'

'Good.' Khan turned to the Cadian. He was silent, staring ahead. 'You're not about to kill the heretic, lieutenant?'

'I'm going to kill them all, sir,' he said flatly.

Khan scratched the back of her neck. 'Fine,' she said after a while. 'On the condition we get to the excavation site first.'

'Sir,' he said, noncommittal.

Khan motioned for Adair to give her some space. 'Do you remember when we first met, lieutenant?' she said.

'Yes, sir.'

'I told you we have a saying on Catachan. It's that the jungle is coming for us all, sooner or later.' She paused, and the Cadian held her gaze. 'Sometimes that's a jungle of our own making. Don't lose yourself in there, son.'

He nodded.

'Remember why we're doing this. Remember what's at the facility.'

'The weapon,' he said.

'That's right,' Khan said.

'I promised you I'd fight with you to the end, sir. And that's what I'll do.'

Khan nodded, satisfied. Something had lit up in the Cadian's eyes. 'Trooper Adair,' she said. 'You're going to take point whilst Lieutenant Anditz escorts the cultist. We can't find this footway without her, and I don't trust you not to cave her head in.'

Adair made a show of grumbling, but Khan knew she could tell what she was doing. Cadians did better if you gave them something to do, and right now, the lieutenant needed something to focus on like she needed more smokes.

Anditz felt as if everything had become very clear. He was probably now the only Cadian left on this world. He carried the weight of every Cadian soul spent on Lazulai with him, and it was for him to make their deaths mean something. His singular imperative was to destroy the enemy, whatever the cost. Whatever he as an individual wanted or felt was unimportant now. The Catachans were right in venerating as their most famous kinsman a soldier who worked alone. Without complications, without attachments.

'What in the hell was that?' A shout from Adair dragged him back to the present moment. He drew his laspistol.

'What did you see?' Khan shouted.

'Not sure, sir. Something quick. Running up the side of the tombs.'

'Xenos?'

'Had to be.'

Anditz scanned the terrain. The mausoleums they were walking through now rose high above the rest on a raised terrace. Spread out below were the pillared resting places of lower-level functionaries and church dignitaries. Here, however, the balustrades and columns rose higher and grander, and some withered flowers still remained. Even amidst the death throes of their world, the people of Lazulai apparently retained some sense of hierarchy and had not dared to damage or shelter amongst the charnel houses of their most vaunted luminaries.

'It was on the city side.' Adair gestured, gripping her heavy flamer. Anditz turned to look. In the distance what had been the living city rose, spires now wreathed with spores and flying horrors.

Then something scrambled out from behind a far tomb.

'Hold fire,' Khan growled.

Anditz squinted. It looked like a genestealer, lithe and chitinous. Something massive was charging behind it, seemingly in pursuit. Anditz recognised it immediately, although last time he'd seen such a monstrosity it had been at the bottom of the flooded cathedral gorging on corpses. Without the distortion of distance, it seemed even larger, the raw, splayed maw of flesh making it seem as if the alien's face had been peeled back over its body, the better to expose its digestive facilities to consumption. It staggered forward on swollen legs that terminated in hoof claws. Complex mouthparts chittered like a meat-grinder. As it passed a curtain of pink, fleshy plant growths, something lashed out from inside the creature and pulled the organic matter into itself. Steam vented from the fluted organic chimneys on its back.

'It's chasing the 'stealer,' Khan observed, curious.

She was right. The feeder-beast lunged out with a claw the size of a human, slashing at the smaller xenos, but missing. The genestealer leapt away, ichor spattering from a wound.

'It was already injured,' Khan said.

'Betrayal! The angels' tools have turned on it,' Lamya cried.

The 'stealer scrambled up the side of a small temple. The huge beast rammed into the side of it, cracking the ebon pediments and sending the xenos atop skittering in a leap to a nearby shrine. With the genestealer out of its line of sight, the vast, offal-faced beast swung its head back and forth. It seemed to scent the humans and started moving in their direction.

'Move!' Khan bellowed.

They started to run, when the 'stealer scurried down the building and dashed past the feeder-beast. It moved with some of the lithe, otherworldly elegance Anditz had observed before and it slashed at the hocks of the huge xenos as it passed. The heavy-set creature listed to one side, whatever organic armature powering its propulsion having been damaged.

Pain wouldn't stop it, though, Anditz thought, recalling the appalling sight of its undersea counterpart stuffing itself with corpses to the point of rupture. And it didn't. The thing continued to drag itself forward on folded and flapping forelimbs, maw quivering with frantic wetness as it sought to devour.

'The angel saved us,' Lamya said, voice quivering, even as Anditz dragged her up onto an ornate ossuary.

'Marbo's tits,' Adair swore as she looked around.

There were about a hundred of the feeder-creatures descending on their position from the direction of the city. Most of them moved awkwardly, their bulk dragging on the floor, flesh distended and mottled.

The largest and most cumbersome of the beasts were doggedly moving towards the deathly ocean. As they passed by beneath the ossuary, Anditz noticed with disgust that the flesh around their bellies had begun to split, the thin wounds revealing guts full of roiling meat. He watched as one engorged xenos snagged its hanging stomach on some sharp debris, tugging open an existing wound in its stretched, purple skin. Offal tumbled softly out, hitting the ground with a wet sound. Anditz felt something rise in his gorge. One of the undigested fragments that dropped out was a human hand complete with fingernails and a ring on one finger. The creature it had fallen out of waddled on, apparently oblivious to the terrible hole in its side, but the xenos behind it lunged forward greedily and snorted the remnant appendage into its foul gullet.

'What are they doing?' Adair asked, gesturing. Some of the vast xenos had reached the sea of digestive fluid and were wading into it. They lay down and steam hissed as the acidic liquid began to eat away at their flesh. They didn't thrash, or move, but lay still as they allowed themselves to be slowly consumed as the Cadian regiment had been.

Adair spat. 'Sick bastards.'

'Stay alert!' Khan said, drawing her chainsword. Some of the more active feeder-beasts had not headed into the swamp with

their kin but had diverted off the main route around the courtyard where the squad were. Some xenos were snuffling around
the base of the ossuary and ramming into it, seemingly aware
at some level that there was matter to devour nearby.

'Put some heat on them, trooper!' Khan called.

Adair swung her heavy flamer down over the edge of the ossuary
and doused the aliens with burning promethium. The white-
hot flames licked the fleshy mouthparts, and Anditz saw the
livid skin pucker and singe, but the creatures seemed impervious to pain.

Grunting in frustration, Khan levelled a shot with her plasma
pistol. It roared a skull-sized hole in the nearest monstrosity,
but it didn't stop the creature. They were starting to clamber
atop each other as they had at Opal Bastion, Anditz realised
with a chill of horror. Before long they would be able to reach
the squad.

More and more of the huge xenos were crowding down into
the courtyard from the city of the living on the right and clus-
tering around the tombs, tiny eyes hidden up in the folds of
their unholy faces.

From their vantage point, Anditz could see the walkway they
needed to be on. It ran dead ahead, just down to the left of the
necropolis, alongside the iron fence that marked the border where
the City of the Dead ended and opened out onto the plains. It
would have been easy to cut between the charnel buildings and
out onto the pathway, had it not been teeming with xenos.

Suddenly the 'stealer that had been crouching out of reach of
its fellow aliens bounded from the opposite tomb-top onto the
squad's ossuary. Its carapace was a purple so dark it was almost
black. It moved with liquid grace onto the dome above the
ossuary then skittered down the opposite side away from the
oncoming horrors.

Anditz winged it with a couple of shots of his laspistol. Lamya cried out as the bolts sizzled into one of its hindlimbs, but the creature didn't retaliate.

'Adair, take that side, I'll defend this edge,' Khan barked. 'Lieutenant, watch the rear and guard the cultist. We need to get to that footway.' She roared off another shot towards the feeder-beasts from her plasma pistol. 'Let's beat them back, then cut a path and make a run for it.'

'Sir,' Adair acknowledged, moving into position as instructed.

Anditz knew he could be of no help with a laspistol from this range and that was why Khan had relegated him to minding the cultist. What he wouldn't have given for a Baneblade and its Demolisher cannon...

He watched as Khan and Adair desperately fought against the beasts. It was futile, he could tell. The xenos were starting to gain traction, scrabbling higher on top of each other on the undefended wall.

The xenos were going to win, he thought. Again. Except this time they would destroy the last people with the means to have stopped them, to have ended this and to have avenged the dead. And all he could do was watch. The adrenaline and frustration in his blood curdled into fury. His knuckles whitened as he gripped his laspistol. Useless, impotent as his last surviving comrades fought to their deaths.

'Incoming!' Khan yelled, wheeling her plasma pistol round to shoot just past Anditz at an encroaching alien.

'No!' shouted the cultist, arms outstretched, trying to throw herself in the way.

Anditz only just managed to tackle her to the ground as Khan's shot screamed over them. He felt the heat sear the back of his neck before the shot ruptured a statue atop one of the tombs, shattering obsidian shards onto the massing xenos.

'You've destroyed it,' the cultist cried. Anditz felt choking sobs rack her body beneath him.

'What?' he shouted, rolling her onto her front.

The cultist's face was screwed into a silent wail.

'What?' Anditz demanded. 'What was so important you nearly got us killed?'

'The statue,' she moaned, tears and mucus streaking her face. 'The statue of the founder.'

Anditz glanced up at the blackened remains of the stone figure. 'A piece of rock?' he said, his anger becoming icy. 'Billions of dead on this world, and you're crying for a broken stone?'

'You don't understand. We are our history,' Lamya said. 'Our culture.'

'What you are is nothing,' Anditz spat. 'What you are doesn't matter because in a few days, there will be nothing here. Do you understand? Nothing.' He stared at her. 'This planet will just be a rock. No atmosphere, no anything. Your art, your music, your buildings, your past – everything will have gone. The galaxy will forget you. Everything you have ever felt, or done, or thought, was pointless and will be lost forever. Unrecorded and unremembered.' Anditz caught his breath.

The cultist stared at him with dark, expressionless eyes. 'No.' She shook her head. 'No. Lazulai has existed for tens of thousands of years. We are cleverer than you. Better than you.'

Anditz laughed, a cold, spiteful anger gripping him. He wanted to hurt the cultist, make her see. Why should she comfort herself with a delusion? 'Your cities are dust, heretic. I wish the Imperium had ground them down, but you did this yourself. You called down the plague that has eaten your world.'

'Lies,' Lamya said, curling herself into a ball. 'Lies of the Imperium.'

'Back at the tower, before the cisterns,' Anditz said. 'Adair shot your precious moths, and their keeper. She did it out of kindness. To save them from the deaths that you brought to them. You killed them. You killed everyone. You did all of this,' he said, gesturing at the ruin surrounding them. 'It is you who brought the rot to the thing you loved.'

Lamya placed her hands over her ears, tears streaming down her face.

Anditz smiled. It brought him gratification to see her broken. 'All you have left to live for now is the final dismantling of what you were. Piece by piece. You have devoured yourself.'

He heard Khan shout and looked behind him. One of the great feeder-beasts was rearing up against the side of their ossuary.

Anger rose in Anditz's gut. He was damned if he was going to wait this out and babysit the wretched cultist. In that moment, all he wanted to do was kill.

He drew his power sword. 'For Cadia,' he said, cold fury in his heart. Then with a running leap, he dived off the edge of the ossuary and onto the back of the foul monster. He could hear Adair calling out behind him, but he didn't have time to reply.

He cleared the obscene mess of a maw and landed on the hard chitin plate of the creature's shoulders. It seemed to have grown in one piece as if it were a shield plate upon the alien's back. From it rose horns and protrusions that Anditz gripped between his legs for balance. This close to the creature he could smell a sickly-sweet scent of decay.

Raising his power sword high, he drove it hard down into the gap between the back plate and head plate, into the pale flesh around the tiny cluster of unseeing eyes. The creature juddered, but continued to move, grappling onto the pilasters around the ossuary. Anditz swore. Gripping the power sword as if it were a piton, he pulled out his laspistol. He pushed the barrel against the creature's skin and fired, again and again. It barely singed the hard leathery flesh.

There was a sudden jolt and steam vented forth from the set of bone chimneys on the creature's back. It stank like the foul breath of a carnivore, and Anditz ducked to avoid the scorching heat. As the steam died away, Anditz suddenly laughed as he realised what he must do. Reaching into his webbing pouch, he pulled out a frag grenade and slid over to the nearest chimney rising from the alien's spine, then pulled the grenade's pin. The chimney felt warm to the touch and slightly tacky with some foul excretion as he stuffed the explosive inside the obscene aperture. Then he scrambled away as fast as he could. Depending on the fuse, he had four seconds, possibly five, Emperor willing.

There was no time to recover his power sword. He stood at the highest point on the alien's snout and jumped towards the ledge of the ossuary. Adair was blasting her flamer with one powerful arm, and with the other, she hauled Anditz up.

'Get down!' he yelled, pushing her as the explosion blasted beneath them. Fragments of meat and bone shrapnel flew out of the bursting xenos in a terrible belch of fire.

Adair laughed in disbelief. 'We've got our way out!' The blast had cleared a route through the beasts.

'Where's the cultist?' Khan roared.

Anditz stared around. There was no sign of Lamya.

'Find her,' growled Khan.

Anditz ran to the side of the building where she'd last been standing. He saw to his horror that she'd climbed down the rooftop near to where the genestealer was curled in a pool of its own leaking ichor. It must have been more badly wounded than it first appeared.

'Get back!' Anditz shouted.

Lamya turned, eyes dark in her face. 'The angel's hurt.'

'It's a monster,' Anditz said.

Lamya didn't seem to be able to hear him. 'Do you know that it has come from beyond the stars? Through clouds of moondust and the coldness of dead galaxies?' She gazed at the xenos with adoration. 'To think I believed anything else mattered. To think I tried to deny myself this one-ness, to reject eternity.'

'Get back here,' Anditz said, thrusting out a hand.

'You were right, soldier. This world is dying. Everything I was, gone. But the angel can give me everything.' Lamya's eyes were wide. 'It is the way to absolution. I can see it now.' She crawled closer to the wounded genestealer.

Anditz pulled his laspistol and fired at the xenos. It hissed as the shots bored into its flesh. Lamya screamed and ran to it, shielding it with her own body, face pressed against its hideous visage.

Anditz heard Khan yell from behind him. 'We need to go! They're about to take down the structure.'

He swore and turned back to the others. Panicked guilt rose in his gut.

The corpse of the grenade-ruptured xenos had formed a bulwark against the tide of feeder-beasts who had turned their attention to devouring their kin. But the blast had also damaged the ossuary's supporting pillars.

'This way,' Khan called, dropping down in the lee of the dead xenos. They ran along the cemetery wall and scrambled up onto the next bone house.

They watched as the ossuary they had been sheltering on collapsed under the weight of the feeder-beasts, who rushed forward towards where Lamya and the 'stealer were. Lamya's face was turned inward, pressed into the chitin ribcage of the xenos. Anditz wondered if she was aware that she was about to be devoured. Just before the terrible raw-flesh-faced xenos fell upon them, the genestealer raised one scythe and gently pushed its bone-blade into the cultist, impaling her. And then they were both gone, consumed by the feeder-beasts.

'Come on,' Khan said. 'We need to get higher.'

'I don't know where the footway is, sir,' Anditz said, guilt twisting his stomach.

Khan shook her head. 'We'd have needed the cultist for access anyway. We have to revert to the original plan. Head for the bridge and hope the city-killer has left.'

They followed the mausoleum rooftops, clambering over carved skulls and gilded cherubs. Beneath them swarmed the xenos, now piling themselves into the sea of acid.

'Look out overhead,' Khan called, loosing a shot at a winged 'gaunt.

'They never travel alone,' Anditz said. 'There'll be more.'

Khan nodded. 'I know. Keep moving. We're not high enough.' The feeder xenos below were being joined by other forms now, some 'gaunts, others that Anditz had never seen before. And all of them were increasingly frenzied. 'Something's agitating them,' he said.

'Yeah. That big-headed bastard, I bet.'

Anditz felt a flood of horror as he looked up to see one of the floating xenos emerge slowly from the city. From this distance it appeared little more than a bone-plated head with a rictus grin and tiny, atrophied limbs. Mist roiled from it as it approached, hundreds of smaller xenos moving ahead of it.

'It's herding them,' Anditz said.

The City of the Dead terminated abruptly before them, dropping away to a steep gorge. Behind and to the right were xenos. To their left ran the maglev bridge.

Anditz's heart sank when he saw the vast city-killer xenos still patrolling the ground beside it. Far enough away to disregard the squad for now, but close enough to the bridge that if they tried to cross it, they would be seen. The thing's head was parallel to the rail. It would devour them all in one mouthful.

'Climb,' Khan ordered.

They scrambled up onto the rails of the maglev bridge's framework. The major looked around, seeking options, trying to discover avenues for escape. But Anditz knew there weren't any, and it was because of him. He swallowed hard.

'I'm sorry, sir. It's my fault.'

'The cultist got away. She was half mad. It was going to happen at some point.' Khan stared into the distance. 'This mission...' She shook her head. 'It was always going to fail. But I confess, I'd started to hope. When we made contact with the fortress and the Shrikes...' She broke off.

'The cultist didn't get away,' Anditz said. 'I drove her to it,' he added. 'I told her that everything was her fault. Forced her to break her delusion. I pushed her over the edge, sir. Intentionally. And then I left her alone.' He frowned. 'I left her alone because I wanted to fight. I wanted blood.'

Khan looked at him, disbelieving.

'I had to, sir. I've got to fight for the rest of my regiment now.' Even as he was saying it, he saw the coldness grow on Khan's face.

'So, it was about your pride,' she said. 'And with it you've doomed this squad. Doomed this mission.'

'I'm the only Cadian left, sir. The weight of their fight is on me. Besides,' he said, feeling his anger rise, 'it's what you do. Every Catachan fighting alone, for their honour. You talk about Marbo enough, you know what I mean.'

To his astonishment, Khan barked out a hard laugh. She shook her head. 'For all your training, all your intelligence, you still don't understand us,' she spat. 'Let me tell you something.' Her expression hardened. 'Sly Marbo works by himself, but he is *never* alone. None of us are. We stand shoulder to shoulder with every Catachan who ever lived and died. Behind us stand the ghosts of the first humans who learned to live on our death world – the first settler who killed a Catachan Devil, the first ancestor who fought a brainleaf and survived. Because of them, we know how to survive. We know we are never alone. Do you understand? Nobody can make it by themselves. We owe everything to those who went before us, and those who stand with us.'

She stopped and stared into the distance, the anger suddenly gone from her. She appeared drained, and it seemed to Anditz that her years had rapidly caught up with her.

Then she spoke quietly. 'Our survival says more about the people around us than it does of ourselves. That is the source of our pride, and if we forget that, we lose. We lose everything.'

She was right, of course. The Cadians had always stood together, just like the Catachans. His behaviour had been nothing more than self-destructiveness. He had been trying to convince himself that it was something more than a concealed desire for self-annihilation. Anditz felt a swell of self-loathing. At what he had done, at how he had lost control, and how he had failed.

'I'm sorry, sir.'

Khan shook her head, sombre. 'No,' she said. 'I'm sorry, soldier. I didn't lead you in the way you needed.'

There was a rushing, clicking sound. Anditz recognised it from the swarming of Opal Bastion. In moments, the xenos masses would rush out of the city and overwhelm them. At least they would die before the very air of this foul world devoured them.

'It's been an honour, sir,' Anditz said.

Khan nodded.

'Major,' Adair called from down the track. 'I reckon there's something coming.'

Anditz turned to look. A cloud of flying tyranids hung over

the city. A vast form flew in the centre of the monstrous mur-muration. 'They're coming this way,' he said.

'Yeah, but I mean something's coming down the rails.' Adair wrinkled her nose. 'Might be a shunt.'

They all looked at each other.

'Can't be them, can it?' Anditz said. 'Not after the spore-bombs came down on the city?'

'I would have bet the sergeant hadn't made it, sir, but Him-on-Terra's got a funny sense of humour sometimes,' Adair replied.

Khan squinted. 'Something's definitely coming. Looks like a shunt to me.'

Sure enough, Anditz saw a shunt emerging from the city, trail-ing smoke behind it. 'Looks like it's on fire.'

'It's still the best offer we've got,' Khan said. 'Even if it's going to drive us straight towards that city-killer.'

'How fast do you reckon it's going?' Anditz said.

'Too fast,' Khan said.

Anditz frowned. 'They probably can't see us. If it is them,' he added. 'Sir, do you have a flare?'

'No.' Khan drew her plasma pistol. 'But I've got this.' She fired the antique weapon into the sky. It belched out a great ball of blue plasma fire that streaked high above them. It would have been visible for miles around.

'Wasting munitions'll bring them to a stop if the Martian's on board,' Adair said with a grin. She slapped the side frame of the ladder-like metal structure that soared above them, supporting the bridge and running parallel above the rail. 'If we climb up here, we'll be able to drop down from above. Reckon that'll be easier than trying to get on from track level.'

The three clambered up onto the rail. Anditz felt the exhaus-tion in his limbs as he scaled the metal bars. Even Adair seemed to take her time hauling herself up the framework before settling atop the overhead line with her legs dangling down.

They watched the approaching vehicle.

'Does it look like it's slowing down?'

'No. And neither is the horde. Get ready to jump,' Khan said, holstering her weapon.

'Wait!' Adair said. 'Is that Ghost?'

Anditz saw someone with a pale face leaning out of the carriage on one side. They had a red bandana tied around their head. As the vehicle approached, the squad saw how much damage it had taken. There were burn marks and holes burst into the side. Some of the carriages were almost entirely denuded of roofs or walls. There was a sudden scream of metal and the shunt slowed. They had a brief glimpse of the tech-adept, Wrathe, in the driver's compartment, then Sergeant Haruto burst through a hole in the ceiling of the central carriage.

'Quickly!' he shouted, one arm outstretched.

Anditz jumped down onto the carriage's roof. The drop knocked his breath out of him, but he held on firmly, dragging himself across the roof against the wind resistance and down through the ragged hole onto the shunt floor.

Ghost helped him up and out of the way as Khan and Adair dropped in after him. The sergeant carefully lowered himself back down inside, struggling on a leg that was bloodied and bound and couldn't bear his weight. Anditz noticed that he was pale, sweat beading on his brow. Ghost barely looked much better.

'You stubborn bastard,' Khan said, gripping Haruto by the shoulders. 'It's good to see you alive.'

Haruto's normally dour expression lifted, and he embraced the major. 'You sent Ghost after us.'

'Yes,' Khan said. 'I wasn't going to lose any more soldiers to this damned planet.' Anditz could hear the emotion in her voice.

'And we won't lose you, sir. It's good to be back.'

Khan nodded. 'Look, there's a tyranid up ahead,' she said. 'A big one.'

'Orders?' Haruto said.

Khan raised an eyebrow. 'Following them again, are you?'

The sergeant grinned. 'Your turn to get us out of this one, sir.'

'I have an idea,' Anditz said. 'But we need to be going much faster. And we're going to need Trooper Adair's heavy flamer.'

'Anything else?' Khan asked.

'As many barrels of promethium as we can get.'

Haruto laughed. 'I like it, sir. Sounds almost Catachan in vision.'

Anditz smiled. 'Anything's a weapon if a Cadian's holding it, sergeant.'

CHAPTER FOURTEEN

Anditz crouched atop the moving maglev, laspistol readied. The swarm was chasing them, but their greater concern was approaching: the vast, spindled nightmare tyranid that seemed to be waiting for them towards the centre of the bridge they were nearing. They were so close to the excavation site now. So close to fulfilling their mission. They could not fall at the last hurdle, Anditz thought. Cruel as the universe might be, it surely could not allow all of the pain and suffering on Lazulai to be for nothing.

He frowned. Of course it could. But he would not allow it.

The stocky major stood right at the front of the vehicle, Adair's heavy flamer cradled in her bulky arms. She turned her head for a moment and gave Anditz a ferocious grin, the wind from the maglev's movement lashing the bandana around her arm. Then she refocused her attention on what was ahead.

The vast city-killer xenos was still a distant shape, but the vehicle was picking up speed, moving out across the high bridge, where it lingered. Adair crouched beside him, ready to sling barrels of promethium at the xenos once they got close enough. Khan's job was to light them as they struck, Anditz's to cover them. Ghost was stationed below with his long-las, ready to pick off airborne threats.

It would be a few minutes until they were far enough onto the bridge to see action. In the moments of waiting, he felt a flare of self-loathing. None of this would be necessary if he hadn't goaded the prisoner. If he'd guarded her properly. He'd seen soldiers shot for less.

'You sulking, sir?' Adair said.

'Trooper,' Anditz reprimanded, angry that she'd read his mood.

She ran a hand through her short pale hair. 'Dwelling on it won't do any good. We don't know if the heretic's route would have been open. We don't know if it even existed! Throne knows she was half mad at the end. Could have been a hallucination she was having.'

Anditz shook his head. 'I should have done better.'

'If we'd followed the other route, we might not have met the others. You think any of us would have made it through alone? Now we face what comes together.'

'I'm responsible for my comrades. Responsible for all of my soldiers who died.' He paused. 'Responsible for you.'

'I'm fine.'

'You might not have been. That's the point.'

'None of us has got very long, sir,' Adair said. Her eyes were clear, and she was earnest. Any sign of earlier mockery had gone. 'I mean here. In this life...' She gestured vaguely around them. 'It's damned short, sir. There's no time to dwell. Everyone fouls up sometimes. It's what you do after that matters. Turn it into something useful.'

'Sounds easy when you put it like that,' he said, one eyebrow raised. But something in her face and words pulled him back. To find the utility in grief – that, he could do.

'Incoming!' Khan roared as she raised the heavy flamer.

The back of the vast tyranid arched like a mountain above the track, its hideous head slung far below, and for a moment Anditz wondered if they might pass it without notice. Clouds of spores drifted from the chimneys on its back, and Anditz coughed as they filled his lungs. He pulled his rebreather up over his face, but his chest still felt tight.

As the forward carriage drew parallel, the terrible purple chitin-plated spine of the monster began to move, uncoiling into an upright position. With a dreadful inevitability, they were presented with a set of jaws the size of a tank as it reared level with them.

Luminescent bio-plasma was already rising in the monster's gullet as Adair hefted the promethium barrel at its face. With a manic grin, Khan shot a blast of flame after it, then skidded back down through one of the holes in the carriage roof even as the fire licked at the barrel. It burst almost immediately and shot thunderously through the side of the alien's head like a terrible missile, ripping off one of its jaws and blasting a hole in its serpentine neck. Gallons of plasma gushed from the wound, and it shook its head, spewing burning caustic liquid from its jaws as the maglev shot past.

Anditz pulled Adair back down into the carriage just in time to avoid them both being spattered.

'Watch out, sir,' Adair called, pulling him aside as gobbets of the fluid ate through the metal roof. They watched it drop down and pool on the floor before eroding it away, exposing the maglev track rushing past below.

'Report,' Khan barked, striding down the carriage, heavy flamer slung over her shoulder. 'Is it coming after us?'

Ghost was hanging out of the next compartment, looking back the way they'd come. 'I don't think so.'

'Did we take it out?' Khan asked.

Ghost shook his head. 'No.' He paused. 'No, actually I think there are more tyranids coming out of it.'

'What?' Khan snarled. 'Someone give me their magnoculars.'

Anditz handed her his. She stared through them for a moment.

'You're right. Half a dozen of the bastards just dropped out of it, and they're already after us. Wonder how long it took for it to cook those up.'

'We're moving faster now,' Haruto said. 'It'll take a few minutes before we're at full speed again.'

Khan nodded. 'How long until we reach the excavation site?' She handed Anditz back his magnoculars.

Haruto pulled out the map, little more than a tattered scrap now. 'Couple of hours, if we can keep this pace up.'

Khan nodded. 'Good. Ghost, take the forward defence. Lieutenant Anditz, Adair, take the rear. I want to know if anything's after us.' She turned to Haruto. 'Sergeant, you're going to sit down and rest that leg. No arguments,' she said. 'Go and talk to the adept about what we're going to do when we get to the excavation site. Seeing as it looks like we might actually make it now, I reckon it's time to think about it.'

Anditz turned to take up his watch post at the rear of the maglev. He tugged the rebreather mask down off his face, but his breath caught in his throat, and he coughed.

'Put it back on, sir,' Adair said. 'Air's getting bad.'

He pulled it back on, and found it was a little easier to breathe. 'You don't feel it?'

'Smells rotten all right. And it's too thick. But don't forget the atmosphere on Catachan's half poison anyway. We're used to it.'

Anditz nodded. Adair would be better to save her rebreather's filter for when it was really needed anyway. He stepped to the edge of the carriage, taking up his watch post at a charred burn-hole in the wall. The vast, spindling Titan tyranid was moving in the opposite direction now, towards the city. Not that there could be much of it left to destroy. The ground moved past far below, a blur of decaying vegetation, xenos flora and the occasional xenos. But the rail ran high enough to feel relatively safe.

He felt the rush of the air on his face, rifling through his hair. It was pleasant, better than the humid stillness descending on the planet. The intermittent red rain had stopped, and with it, the spore haze had slightly lifted. He put his magnoculars to his eyes and scanned the retreating horizon. Carnadine was too far away to see clearly now, but as he panned the magnoculars, something snagged his attention on the bridge into the city. It was at a great distance, but he focused on it as best he could.

What he saw sent ice rushing through his blood.

Something he recognised was coming from the direction of the city, walking along the high maglev rail after them. It was humanoid and moved with purpose, but it wasn't running or rushing. It was as if it knew it didn't need to. It stalked along the rails, the bridge framework rising high each side of it. It was in the very place that he, Khan and Adair had dropped down into the shunt.

Its silhouette was burned into the back of Anditz's mind. The four outstretched sabres, the sweep of spores blossoming out behind it like blood in water. He was taken back to the night his regiment had died. This was the xenos that had led the attack on Opal Bastion.

The leader-alien that he knew, in his heart, meant the end of everything was coming for them.

* * *

Khan stood at the front of the maglev, leaning one shoulder against a half-torn wall, gazing out at the livid pink landscape unfolding in front of her. Alien things flailed from the sky and yawned up from chasms tearing open in the ground. The vehicle rattled past them at high speed, smearing the nightmare tableau into a single pink, undulating blur. The wind buffeted hot in her face, and she was thankful for it. The sensation was the only thing that felt real now. It was the first time she had stopped for a long while, and the exhaustion had dropped onto her suddenly. She was physically tired, but more than that, she was tired in her heart. She had fought and bled on so many worlds and watched countless comrades die. She had known loss and tasted victory and the emotions had all bled into one. She could feel the jungle calling her back, but the Emperor wouldn't let her die. Maybe he had some purpose for her, or perhaps just a warped sense of humour.

'I don't know how much longer I'm going to be any use to you,' she muttered. She pulled out her last cheroot and lit it. All that mattered to her now was that she got her people off this planet. She'd have to deal with the tech-adept later, but she wasn't going to buy Mars their damned cogs with any more human blood. This world had taken enough, she thought.

She exhaled. She should probably feel guilty about disregarding General Kvelter's orders. The tough old Cadian officer had gone to her death believing it was for a purpose, that Khan would lead her squad to salvage something from this carnage. Well, Khan would salvage something, but it would be blood and bone. There was nothing more valuable to the Imperium than its people. The Imperium *was* its people. And you couldn't serve it if you were dead. The best way to fight was to survive, and that was what Khan intended to make sure the remaining Shrikes did.

Wrathe had been certain the magos had had a transport at his facility. If she wouldn't operate it for them, then Haruto could. Although whether he *would* remained to be seen. He'd taken up the Martian's cause when it came to the maglev all right, but when it came to the life or death of his own, she was almost certain he'd follow her orders.

Almost.

Khan rolled her neck, scratching the old knot of scar tissue there. Catachans didn't often tolerate commissars. They didn't need them. Catachans regulated themselves and would put down any soldier who was placing the others at risk. Anyone who put others in danger, who kept making bad choices, who was reckless or selfish. It's what kept Catachan commanders honest. You were only ever in charge for as long as you deserved to be. Nobody was above reproach, and nobody's word was law.

It was what made it so hard for Catachans to work with other regiments. You never knew if the officer giving you orders had earned their place through blood and sweat or was there simply because someone had stamped a docket saying they were in charge.

Khan took a drag on her cheroot. The wind whipped the smoke away into the filthy air. Lazulai's whole climate was falling over, she thought. The Cadian lieutenant was struggling to breathe already. The Catachans were faring better, but before long they'd need rebreathers too. She could feel the air itching at her lungs. How long the rebreather filters would last, she didn't know. They'd have to keep the masks for when they really needed them and pray it was long enough.

'Sir,' the Cadian reported briskly beside her, voice slightly muffled through his rebreather mask.

'Lieutenant,' she replied.

'There's a tyranid following us.' The Cadian's violet eyes were expressionless, but there was something wrong, she could tell.

'Report.'

'I saw this one back at Opal Bastion. It's different from the others. It's aware of us in a different way.' He hesitated. 'A leader, perhaps.'

'Show me.'

He led her to the back of the vehicle and passed her his magnoculars. Clamping her cheroot in her teeth, she squinted through the eyepiece at the disappearing speck in the distance. She could barely discern details from here, other than it was bipedal with a shroud of smoke flowing out behind it. But there was something purposeful about its movement, less animalistic than the other tyranids she had seen.

'This one brought down Opal Bastion?'

Anditz's face worked. 'Something like it did, sir.'

Khan nodded briskly and handed him back the magnoculars. 'If it comes near enough, you have the first shot. And if you're not there to take it, I'll frag the bastard for you. I swear that on the Shrikes.' She raised her arm, and they clasped hands firmly.

There was a sudden thud on the roof. Khan and Anditz pulled their pistols. Something was moving overhead. To land and grip in the headwind atop the shunt while it was moving at this speed, it had to be something big, and fast. Khan gestured to Ghost at the other end of the vehicle, signalling that there was an enemy above them. He nodded and shouldered his long-las.

Then a tentacle as thick as a human torso punched through the carriage roof.

Khan registered the movement too late to react, but the Cadian had seen it first and barrelled into her hard, shoving her aside. The stabbing tentacle missed her head by inches.

The purple spike withdrew as rapidly as it had appeared. It had a stinger with a bulbous sac the size of a human head swelling behind it.

'What in the hell was that?' Khan growled.

'Watch out, it's coming back, sir!' Anditz called.

There was the crack of a long-las, and the stinger burst even as it lunged through a window. Ghost's shot had ruptured the swollen sac, spilling a writhing mass of embryonic tyranids onto the floor. They were semi-translucent and thrashing in some foul-smelling fluid. Unborn, yet already fanged and furious.

'Throne's sake!' Khan exclaimed in disgust.

'Sir,' Anditz reprimanded automatically.

The damaged limb withdrew, spattering ichor as it did so.

'I've had enough,' Khan growled. It was as if the xenos were developing increasingly repulsive and obstructive variants as a slight against the few remaining humans on the world. The squad was less than an hour from the excavation site now – she wouldn't allow them to fail at this stage. She threw her cheroot down and pulled her Catachan Fang out.

'What are you doing, sir?' Anditz asked.

'I'm going to cut the filthy bastard in half. Stay here.' She clamped the knife in her teeth, and with a running jump, swung herself up out of the carriage and onto the roof.

The wind threw spores into her eyes and the tyranid came for her immediately. Khan ducked, dodging its lashing scythe, and stowed her knife. She was going to need her chainsword for this. The alien was bigger than she had thought, a flying form, but not a variant she'd seen before. She could now see that the limb they had damaged was its tail; whatever that foul incubation sac on the end of it had been intended for, she was glad they'd removed it. It lowered its seemingly eyeless head, the elongated forehead a flat sheet of purple ridged chitin, and leapt.

Khan pulled out her chainsword, swinging it under the monster's shield-like forehead and into the jaw as it descended upon her. The xenos slammed into the blade's screaming teeth, the force of the impact embedding the weapon into its skull and throwing Khan backwards. She skidded along the maglev's roof, arms braced, with only the chainsword between her and the xenos. She flung an arm out and grabbed a ventilation grate to stop herself being swept off the speeding maglev. With a furious howl, she held the monster back with her chainsword arm. She was almost face to face with the creature's rictus grin. Its inverted ribcage carapace pressed into her chest, crushing the breath from her. She needed to get the wretched thing off her.

Tyranid forms diverged wildly from each other, and from templates of life that existed elsewhere in the galaxy. Countless soldiers had met their ends thinking they understood where the weak spots of the xenos were. It wasn't clear if they even felt pain. This form appeared to be entirely made of jointed bone – apart from the fleshy tail from which the unformed xenos had spurted on being shot. Khan drove her knee hard into the base of the tail and the thing jerked. It was only a slight movement, but it was enough to allow her to move. Her chainsword was firmly stuck, however, rigidly protruding from the alien's sternum, and she rolled away weaponless. The xenos was after her immediately, lashing out with the stump where the venom sac had been. The seared limb thumped into Khan's legs, knocking her off her feet. Denuded of its spike it may be, but it was powerful. A blow to her skull and that would likely be the end.

The monster extended its wings and launched itself. Khan thought it was about to land on her, but it skimmed over her head and landed on the front carriage, above the driver's compartment. Then it raised its scythes and stabbed them down through the ceiling, right where the tech-adept was.

Khan swore.

The maglev was running faster now, wind screaming past, buffeting her and snatching her breath. She could hear shouts from the squad inside the carriage below. She gripped a panto-graph between her knees and pulled out her plasma pistol. The wind skewed her aim, but the blue ball of energy crackled into the alien's body, blasting off one of its claw-like lower limbs, and the remainder of its tail. Ichor and purple viscera splattered out of the wounds, and the xenos withdrew its scythes from the roof and lifted off once more, lunging at Khan as it flew back down the carriage. Khan rolled onto her back and raised her weapon as the monster flew overhead. It lashed out at her with a scythe, and she fired in the same instant as the xenos pierced her shoulder. There was a brief surge of pain and an explosion above, and Khan's gun flew from her hand. The xenos landed clumsily at the other end of the maglev, two carriages away from the driver's compartment. One wing was smoking and hung strangely.

Khan made to reach for her blade, but found her left arm wouldn't cooperate. She stole a glance at it, and saw it was covered in blood. She tried to clench her fingers, but they hung numb and limp. She gripped at a vent with the fingers of her right hand, now the only things stopping her from sliding off the maglev and to her death.

'You think this is going to stop me, you bastard?'

Robbed of the ability of flight by Khan's shot, the tyranid lowered its head and charged. The shield-like crown of bone atop its skull would impale Khan within seconds if she didn't act. She had one working arm, and no weapon that could kill it. With the wind screaming in her ears, she did the only thing she could, and let go of the vent.

She shot down the maglev towards her attacker, legs clamped together into a battering ram, good hand outstretched behind her, sped by the wind. As her boots struck the xenos hard in the chest, it was thrown backwards. Khan scrabbled for a handhold to halt her movement before she was thrown to the ground. Her fingers hooked into a tear in the roof, and she gripped it. The force of the stop jerked violently at her fingers and flipped her onto her front, winding her and cracking her face against the metal. But she held on. She saw the tyranid fall backwards off the shunt, tattered wings unable to prevent its descent as it vanished out of sight. Khan gritted her teeth and pulled herself forward with her good arm. Her feet couldn't find purchase and her other arm hung limply behind her. The wind felt as if it would drag her away, and the grip of her fingers was weakening.

She spat blood, and with a roar, summoned up her last reserves of strength and dragged herself towards the tear. If she could only make it that far, she could drop down into the carriage. Tears welled in her eyes from the effort. The torn metal of the roof-tear cut into her fingers. Then she was looking over the edge of the gap and down into the carriage. Adair appeared below, clambering up, lifting her down with strong arms.

Lights prickled at the edge of Khan's vision. She was aware of warmth trickling down her hand, and the dizziness the blood loss had brought. She sat down heavily on a supply crate as her comrade supported her.

Adair tore away the shoulder of her shirt and examined it. 'Looks nasty.'

'I can't feel anything,' Khan replied, panting as she recovered her breath.

'Reckon you've fragged the nerves then, sir. What was it?'

'Scythe,' Khan grunted.

'Lucky it didn't punch down to the lung.'

'Lucky? I'm feeling very lucky, trooper,' Khan said, glancing down at the blood pooling at her boots.

Adair grinned. 'I'll put it in a sling it for now and shoot some counterseptics into you.'

Lieutenant Anditz strode up, brows furrowed. 'Sir,' he said.

'Yes?'

He paused. 'Very nicely done.'

'Thank you. But we're not finished yet, soldier.'

The Cadian nodded. 'We're closing in, sir. If we can maintain this speed we'll be at the site within the half-hour.'

'Good. Keep focused on the mission.'

'Yes, sir. I've had a thought about the archeotech–'

'The archeotech?' Khan interrupted. 'The *squad*. I'm getting my soldiers off this damned rock if it's the last thing I do, Mars be damned. That's the priority now.'

The lieutenant looked as if he was about to say something, then thought better of it, and nodded stiffly. 'Yes, sir.'

CHAPTER FIFTEEN

Anditz had taken up watch at the rear of the maglev. Major Khan was speaking with Haruto and the tech-adept at the front of the shunt. She'd made it clear that despite their original orders, her priority was now to evacuate the squad. Anditz understood why, after everything they'd seen, after everything they'd been through. Although he wondered if it was even possible to escape Lazulai's orbit now, given the xenos horrors roiling in the sky.

And he couldn't in good conscience leave this world to incubate and nourish another fleet of xenos that would go out and devour regiment after regiment, system after system. If this archeotech, whatever it was, could be turned against the aliens, they would be duty-bound to use it. But he would have that argument with Khan when the time came. And doubtless so would the tech-adept. Although from everything Anditz had heard, the Martians hoarded and worshipped technology rather than used it, so he would likely have two fights on his hands.

He cleared his throat. The air he could taste through his

rebreather was sour. It caught in his lungs, and when he coughed there was a deep rattle in his chest. It felt acidic against his exposed skin too.

'You sound about as good as the maglev, sir,' Adair remarked.

He shot her a look. After the various onslaughts it had undergone, the vehicle's engine spluttered, and the whole thing creaked and groaned as it went.

'Everything just needs to hold together long enough to complete the mission,' he said.

Adair shrugged. 'I don't know. It'd be nice if you'd last a bit longer than that.'

'How sentimental of you, trooper,' Anditz said, one eyebrow raised.

Adair grinned.

Something caught Anditz's eye. 'You're bleeding,' he said. 'There.'

Adair touched her finger to her mouth. A fine line of red had appeared, tracing from her chin and over her lips up to her nose.

'It's your scar,' Anditz said. 'It's opened up.'

Adair frowned. 'Can't have done. Took that mark more than a year ago.'

Anditz pushed up his sleeve. He had an old wound there, an injury from years before. The once-pale mark had become livid.

'There has to be an explanation,' Adair said.

Anditz made his way to the front of the vehicle. Khan stood leaning in the open doorway of the engine chamber. Sergeant Haruto sat with his splinted leg stretched out in front of him. Wrathe looked tired, dark shadows smeared beneath her eyes.

'Sir,' Anditz said. 'Do you have old injuries opening up?'

'That's not the sort of question I like to hear, lieutenant,' Khan said, hazel eyes narrowed. 'After this long in the Emperor's service there's very little of me left that isn't old injuries.'

Anditz turned back his cuff and showed her the newly livid

scar on his forearm. 'That happened a couple of years ago,' he said. 'It looks fresh now. The mark on Adair's face has opened up too, and it was completely healed.'

'You will find, lieutenant, that an injury is never healed. Not truly. Your flesh works in a continuous process of knitting itself. A flaw in design,' the tech-adept said. 'It is not uncommon following poor nutrition for damaged flesh to come apart as it is unable to maintain its attempts at cohesion.' Her vox-grille sounded somehow grainy as she spoke, and Anditz wondered how her mechanical components were faring in Lazulai's conditions. He noticed a fine coating of rust speckling her silver cuirass.

'Fascinating.' Haruto frowned. He was examining something on his shoulder. Wrathe moved to look. 'A Catachan Devil slashed me here when I was a teenager. It looks fresh again.' He pressed his fingers to it. 'It's actually bleeding,' he said with interest.

'What does this mean?' Khan asked.

'It means we're coming apart,' Haruto said.

'I would posit it to be a pre-digestive function of the xenos,' the tech-adept added.

'So, the tyranids haven't managed to eat us yet, but now the planet's going to,' Khan summarised.

'They are very likely to be one and the same now, major.'

In his mind's eye, Anditz saw a brief flash of the miles of acid pools consuming flesh and metal alike, devouring regiments whole. He realised that it wasn't enough simply to kill the tyranids on the world. Lazulai itself had been infected, seeded with spores and turned into a tyranid-engine to perpetuate their filth. The whole planet had to die.

'I don't know how quickly it will accelerate,' the tech-adept was saying to the major. 'I suspect that deeper or newer injuries will reopen first. But that is only conjecture. I am not a magos biologis.'

'Not just injuries,' Haruto said. 'Augmetics.'

Khan winced. The same thought must have occurred to her as it had Anditz. Haruto's artificial eye was bad enough, but the tech-adept was largely mechanical now. Each of the incisions that had been made in her flesh to replace organic with artificial would start to slowly reopen, if they hadn't already.

There was a moment of silence as the group considered the implications.

'We'll be at the site in a few minutes,' Haruto said. 'We've made good pace, but I'd estimate we're only about an hour ahead of the city swarm.'

'If they're coming this way,' Khan said.

'They will be,' Anditz replied. He felt sure of it. 'Because of the leader. It's hunting us.'

Khan grunted. 'And that's the one we know about. Whole damn world's as good as a swarm now. We get in, we get the transport, we get out.'

'After recovering the archeotech,' Wrathe added, inclining her head.

'If there's time,' Khan said.

'Major?' Wrathe's voice sounded tight, even through the distortions of the vox-grille.

Khan shrugged. 'We can't hold off a swarm. There's no point dying in an attempt to do so.'

Two red spots appeared on the tech-adept's cheeks. A strangely human reaction, Anditz thought.

'Major. Your orders are to recover the asset,' she said.

'And my priority is this squad.'

'Tech-Adept Wrathe,' Anditz said swiftly. 'If I may, sir,' he said to Khan. 'Our standing order is to recover the archeotech. However, as I believe the major may be suggesting, if we are unable to do so then we should commence withdrawal from Lazulai.'

Khan made as if to speak.

'A reasonable approach, I would suggest,' Anditz continued quickly, 'given we have yet to gain ingress to Magos Stuhl's facility.' He shot a glance in Khan's direction.

Khan nodded, understanding. They had to keep the tech-adept onside if they were even going to be able to access the shuttle. The three of them might all want something different, but each of them needed to get into the site, either for the archeotech, or the transport. From his brief encounter with Stuhl, Anditz suspected that whatever security measures he had put in place, it would be impossible to navigate without a Martian.

'I concur, lieutenant,' Wrathe said, smoothing her robes. Anditz noticed a red Catachan bandana tied around one of her metal hands and wondered what had made Haruto give it to her. 'It has been a long while since I was in contact with Magos Stuhl, but he was always greatly concerned with matters of security. I believe it will not be straightforward to enter, if he has indeed expired.'

'Anything we can do to prepare?' Khan asked.

Wrathe shook her head. 'We must assess the situation on arrival.'

The maglev started to slow. They were descending into thick foliage now, fleshy pink xenos growth. Huge leaves the size of a human smashed against the vehicle, releasing thick clouds of spores into the air.

The tech-adept coughed, the motion racking her body.

Sergeant Haruto frowned. 'Isn't your vox-grille filtering the spores?'

Wrathe shook her head. 'The filter became overwhelmed some time ago.'

'Take a rebreather,' he said, offering his.

Wrathe reached behind her ears and unclipped the metal grille that covered the lower half of her face. Anditz had thought it was implanted, so was surprised to see that beneath, she was flesh and blood. Metal contact studs surrounded her mouth. There was a trickle of blood at the corner of her lip, and Anditz wondered how damaged the tech-adept was.

'Thank you,' she said as she took the rebreather. Her voice was just as blank and mechanical as it had been behind the vox-grille. She gave Haruto a stiff smile, an expression that seemed half forgotten to her.

He nodded as she placed the mask over her face, and her shoulders relaxed as she breathed more easily.

'Why didn't you say you were struggling?' Haruto asked.

She frowned. 'It is a matter of dishonour. Flesh is weak.'

'That's why it's important,' Haruto replied.

The tech-adept gave him a strange look. The light filtered dimly through the half-ruined walls of the carriage and lit up her pale eyes.

Anditz glanced away to the landscape outside. 'We're here,' he said.

The maglev track ran past the excavation site, by Stuhl's design. The route had been redirected to serve his facility and transport the tons of ferrocrete that had been required to build his lab complex out in this remote part of the world. All Anditz had seen of it had been the exterior – the vast, half-buried dome that housed the archeotech remnants, and the long rectangular lab complex that abutted it, built to the side of the ancient dome to provide access.

Wrathe moved to slow the vehicle, and they came to a grinding halt, smoke rising from the ruined maglev.

Anditz raised his magnoculars to examine the entrance of the excavation site. It was little changed since he'd last passed through with his battalion. Strangely unchanged, given the bristling of

tyranid flora everywhere else. In the centre of a wide, bare circle
of earth, a cairn of soil was heaped over a heavy ferrocrete lintel
with a solid metal door, the entrance to the laboratory complex that Stuhl had built. It was about half a mile away from the
ancient dome, half of which was buried under the soil, but the
visible part must have been a thousand feet across, built of a black
stone Anditz hadn't seen anywhere else on Lazulai. What passage
the tech-adept had created between that and the dome, Anditz
didn't know. The eccentric Martian hadn't admitted any soldiers
to the site, so what he had been doing inside remained a mystery.

Two underslung heavy bolters sat in defence cradles on each
side of the entrance door. There were corpses littered ahead of
it, suggesting they would receive a rather less warm welcome
than his first visit. And that occasion had ended in Reiner Stuhl
refusing to leave with them in the face of a tyranid invasion.
Anditz wondered whether they would have had an easier time
gaining access if the eccentric tech-priest was alive or dead – but
they would find out soon enough.

Major Khan jumped off the maglev and turned to offer Sergeant
Haruto a hand as he eased himself down stiffly. His splinted
leg was awkward to manoeuvre, and he winced as he dropped
to the ground.

They had halted in a clearing. Something about it set Khan's
nerves on edge. It was strangely empty, without even dead foliage.

'Something's not natural about this,' she said.

Haruto frowned. 'It doesn't smell like anything.'

'The jungle ends in a straight line,' Khan said, pointing. Haruto
turned to survey the division between jungle and clearing.

'Hmm.' He looked down at the bare ground. 'Nefeli,' he said
to the tech-adept as she emerged from the maglev. 'The soil
smells dead. Is it?'

The tech-adept shrugged her red cloak over her shoulders and jumped down. She picked up a fistful of earth in one of her metal hands and raised it to her face. Khan noted that the sergeant had used the tech-adept's personal name.

'The levels of xenos micro-fauna are greatly reduced compared to elsewhere,' Wrathe said, her eyebrows rising in apparent surprise.

Haruto leaned forward. 'Why? Is it because of the archeotech somehow?'

Wrathe gestured uncertainty. 'I don't know. There is no sign of any other organic life either. I cannot extrapolate the cause without further data.'

'Lieutenant Anditz,' Khan said.

The Cadian stepped forward. His violet eyes were bloodshot, and she could hear his chest rattle as he inhaled through the rebreather. She couldn't imagine she looked any better herself. Catachan physiology was robust thanks to the generational pressures of living on a death world, but there were limits to that advantage beyond a certain point.

'Can you give us any background on the excavation site from your posting here?' she asked.

Anditz shook his head. 'Very little. The actual archeotech is inside there.' He pointed at a smooth, black stone dome. Khan had never seen anything like it on Lazulai.

Wrathe stared. 'It is ancient,' she said. Khan thought she could hear reverence in the adept's toneless voice.

'The doorway in is new,' Anditz said. 'Stuhl built a tunnel underground to the base of the dome. As far as we could tell, that's the only way in. We were never permitted inside, and intelligence on the site wasn't considered a priority at the time. But the implication from the magos was that it was sufficiently guarded to defend him against a serious tyranid onslaught.'

'He may have been wrong about that,' Khan said.

'The doors appear intact,' Anditz said, looking through his magnoculars. 'Heavy steel, flanked with two heavy bolters. Active, by the look of the debris...' He paused, eyebrows furrowed. 'There appears to be some kind of contact pad by the door, but I can't see it clearly from here.'

He handed the magnoculars to Khan. She scanned the wreckage of flesh around the perimeter. The heavy bolters looked to be automatic from the spatters of blood that painted a neat tide-mark around the entrance. Anything that wandered into their firing solution would be dealt with swiftly – and had been, from the looks of the corpses littering the area. Mostly tyranid, but there were humans too.

'Well, that's as close as we can get.' Khan gestured at the arc of dried blood smearing the boundary of safety.

'About fifty feet?' Adair said. 'Reckon I can get 'em with a grenade.'

'No,' Wrathe said. 'If you destroy the access pad, it will greatly delay our entry. Wait. I will attempt to contact their machine spirits.'

She reached a hand under her hood and made a gesture Khan couldn't see. A low mechanical noise started up, apparently being produced from inside her head. It reminded Khan of the sound the tech-adept had generated back at Cobalt Fortress when she had wanted to conceal their first conversation. Wrathe closed her eyes and placed her hands over her ears. She trembled slightly and appeared to be in a state of deep concentration.

'Sir, look over there,' Ghost muttered in Khan's ear.

Khan glanced behind them. The sky was darkened with a cloud of twisting shapes that formed and re-formed constantly. They were distant for now, but moving as one towards them.

'I don't like the look of that,' Ghost said.

'No,' Khan agreed.

'Only ones I've seen that small are the little bastards that are mostly teeth.'

Khan nodded. 'But hundreds of thousands of them.'

Ghost scratched his chin. 'Maybe we *should* try the door with a grenade.'

There was a sudden spark from the heavy bolters, and the guns sagged in their cradles. Wrathe stumbled, and Haruto gripped her firmly by the elbow. As the tech-adept turned, Khan saw that a trickle of blood ran from her nose.

When she spoke, her voice was weak. 'The machine spirits are now at rest. It is safe to approach.'

'Are you sure?' Khan asked. A small light still blinked beneath the heavy bolters.

'Yes. I will go first,' Wrathe said. She stepped forward, Haruto following close behind. They crossed the line of safety, step-ping over the twisted body of a purple-carapaced xenos, and Khan found herself holding her breath, waiting for the sentry guns to whirr into life and track their movement. But nothing happened, and they closed the distance.

Khan gestured for the others to follow her. As she approached the tidal detritus of corpses, she saw the human faces among the xenos remains. Rich, poor, Ecclesiarchical and mutants alike had died here.

One couple caught her attention, a pair of young women. Affluent Lazulaians, by their dress. They must have died recently, as the heat had not yet begun to decay their skin. Or perhaps the strange vacuum of microfauna here had somehow preserved it. The couple lay close by, arms flung out towards each other, but not quite touching. Seeing that the tech-adept was working on the door's access pad, Khan paused. She looked down at the pair. One had skin the same tone as her own, the other was as pale as Ghost. One's head had been burst by the heavy bolter, but her companion's face was pristine. Lips slightly parted, hair tousled in the filth of the dead earth. They wore matching rings, the significance of which Khan did not know. She felt a sudden surge of emotion as she looked at the strangers, illuminated in the unearthly sporeglow of the sky.

It was impossible to feel the weight of a billion deaths. A person would go mad if they could – only Him-on-Terra knew or could bear such a burden. No single soul could comprehend the tragedy of Lazulai, the toll of the bright pinpoints of consciousness winked out, the single, brief chances of life granted to millions upon millions, extinguished in an instant. Life was a glimmer of light between two great voids of darkness, and for the people of this world, the darkness had fallen upon them much faster than it should. As a soldier, Khan dealt in death – but that did not mean she had to like it. And this small, personal tragedy had a weight she could feel.

She nudged at one of the women's outflung hands with her boot, gently pushing it so it met the fingers of her companion. For however long this planet lasted, their hands would touch. Khan completed the last single, desperate action they had tried to take before they died but could not. At least it was a quick death, she thought, raising her eyes and stepping over the bodies. Better than most of the people on this world had had.

An ember of anger burned in her heart. These people had come here in the hope of shelter, only to be cut down by the tech-priest's guns. Why had he done this? And why had he hoarded a weapon that could have stopped all of this? Khan hoped that they would find him inside, so that she could make him pay. Mentor or not, she wouldn't let Wrathe stand in her way.

She chided herself almost immediately. There was no benefit

to such thoughts. Anger begat irrationality, and she needed a cool head for what lay before them.

As she approached the squad, the heavy metal door cracked open, revealing only darkness beyond. Wrathe turned from the control pad.

'Binharic algebra,' she said. 'A simple plaything. Perhaps we will find access to the site less troublesome than initially anticipated.'

Khan grunted. 'Let's hope you're right. Lead on.'

They moved forwards into the darkness. Ordinarily, Khan would have preferred being out in the open, but the wide, tomb-like passage they entered felt like a blessing to her. Lazulai's sky hung dead above them. It moved, but it moved as a corpse did. Roiling with decay and writhing with the worms of rot. The xenos now visible in the lower atmosphere were semi-veiled by clouds and spore-effluence, pushing like intestines against a thin skin. It was oppressive and foul, and Khan was grateful for the screen of ferrocrete between her and the horrors above.

CHAPTER SIXTEEN

Anditz and Adair followed Wrathe into the excavation site's entrance gateway.

Sergeant Haruto slammed the heavy door behind them, and the silence closed in. Cold strip-lumens flickered to life in the long darkness ahead, illuminating the ferrocrete passageway. It was wide enough that you could have driven a battle tank down it.

Huge reinforced steel pillars stood at intervals down the tunnel, and Anditz wondered if the tech-priest had refused to admit the Astra Militarum lest they requisition some of the resources he had been stockpiling at a time of war. Throne knew what else he had hoarded in here – what other machines or knowledge that could have helped to turn the conflict.

The temperature grew cooler as they descended, and Anditz felt his sweat chill on his skin. The tech-adept moved ahead with the rest of the squad following behind. Adair walked beside him, gripping her heavy flamer. He could feel that the big woman was tense.

'What's wrong?' he muttered.

'We're underground, sir,' she whispered back.

'And?'

'And it's not natural.' She shuddered slightly, her broad shoulders moving like two great boulders. 'No way out, is there?'

'You've been underground before, trooper. You're not afraid of enclosed spaces.'

She tutted. 'I mean deep, sir. *Under ground.* A lot of stuff above us. And Throne only knows what blasted stuff the Martians have down here.'

'Nothing more frightening than you, I'm sure of it,' he said. It brought a smile to her face, although he knew what she meant. He experienced a flash of memory and for a split second he was back at Opal Bastion, sealed underground with the enemy slaughtering his comrades above him.

Adair's grin froze and she halted abruptly, head cocked. 'Something's coming,' she hissed.

Wrathe turned. 'I hear it too.'

Anditz drew his laspistol as Adair gestured for the others to halt. There was a second of silence before Anditz's ears could detect the sound, too – the growl of an engine coming down the corridor towards them.

'Fall back,' Khan said.

The squad moved behind the meagre cover of the support struts and readied their weapons. As the sound of the vehicle grew louder there was a sudden stench of ozone, and Anditz felt the hairs on his arms begin to rise. He glanced at the tech-adept. Her slim mechadendrites had unfurled themselves and were lifting, tiny sparks flashing from them.

Anditz saw a huge servitor trundling towards them. In the darkness between lumens, he could discern no detail, just that it was vast.

'Stay back! Arc weapon!' Wrathe said.

'What's that?' Anditz called. His mouth tasted of metal. Creed only knew what the Martians had cooked up – he'd never seen the tech-adept look this worried.

He got his answer before Wrathe had time to reply. A gun muzzle atop the servitor glowed, then a great crack of lightning momentarily replaced the darkness of the tunnel with a strange, clinical blue-white brightness. For a split second he saw the thing approaching them in horrible detail. A set of tracks like that of a small tank propelled a heavily armoured servitor torso with a huge, long-barrelled gun mounted on one shoulder. Built onto the other was a vast hydraulic claw that could easily crush a human. The thing's defences appeared impenetrable, save for a small sliver of skull not clustered with lenses or plating.

Adrenaline twisted his guts. 'Aim for the head, Ghost!' he yelled back to the squad's sharpshooter.

But in the moment it had taken him to speak, the battle servitor had fired again.

A screaming pulse of energy blasted past and shattered the outcrop that had been sheltering the others. Anditz's breath caught in his chest.

He stepped forward out of cover, laspistol raised. He was running on instinct now. He'd been dazzled by the blast, and in the blackness he'd only had his memory of the rolling monstrosity's position to rely on. Clenching his teeth, he took another step forward out into the darkness and shot blind at where he recalled the exposed skull to have been. He fired three times, rapidly, and prayed the Emperor would guide his hand.

There was a sudden scream from the servitor's engine, then the motor died. The burst of relief Anditz felt was momentary. Even as the tracked guard stopped moving, its arc weapon began sparking to life. In the flashes of light issuing from the arcane weapon, Anditz could see that the exposed segment of the servitor's skull had burst, and brain matter had splattered over its chestplate. However, the gun was still somehow active.

Anditz swore.

'Language, sir,' Adair admonished with a mocking tone. He turned to see her grinning as she drew her Devil's Claw, three feet of brutal hardened steel.

'Trooper? What are you doing?'

'Gutting it,' she called as she sprinted towards the stricken servitor.

Anditz started as he saw the gun rotating to target her. There were only seconds until the next shot. Without thinking, he rushed out, firing his laspistol.

The servitor's gun swivelled to target the source of his shots.

Anditz dived to the other side of the corridor just as the deadly arc weapon flared again, obliterating the section where he had been standing.

Then Adair was on the servitor, ignoring the sparking of the gun and leaping up onto the automaton's mighty tracks. She stabbed her blade into the coils of cabling in the machine's midriff and with a roar, tugged hard. Cables sheared away, spurting promethium and causing the torso to jerk. The arc weapon drooped, but a final surge of power threw Adair to the ground in a shower of sparks. Her knife clattered away from her hand. The battle servitor stood lifeless and silent above the motionless Catachan.

Anditz ran to where she lay. As he knelt, he saw that the blast had singed the pale hairs on her arms and eyebrows. He placed his fingers below her square jaw to feel for a pulse. To his relief, her heart beat as strongly as a grox. He put his hand on her forehead. Her eyelids flickered open, and she grunted, her face contorted in discomfort.

'Trooper,' Major Khan said, appearing at Anditz's elbow. 'Are you all right?'

'Fine,' Adair said, slowly levering herself up to a seated position. She shook her head as if to clear it and exhaled heavily. Anditz proffered her an arm and she clambered to her feet.

'Ready?' he asked.

'Yessir,' Anditz replied with a nod, and loosing her grip from his elbow, she recovered her weapons.

'Nice shot, lieutenant,' Ghost said, stepping up to inspect the servitor.

'A compliment indeed, coming from yourself,' Anditz said with a wry smile. The taciturn trooper had grown on him. Quiet and focused, he was completely unlike the usual stereotypes of the Catachan Jungle Fighter – as opposed to Adair, who fulfilled every one of them.

Although, through her, perhaps he had come to value those characteristics, too.

The squad continued down the tunnel, with the tech-adept in the lead again, although Anditz thought she moved rather more cautiously than before. He guessed they were a third of the way down the site tunnel now. That they'd already come so close to losing a soldier was not a good sign. Between that, the major's busted arm and Sergeant Haruto's leg injury, they would need to take more care.

Up ahead there was a dull blue glow. A bank of plasma generators rose up, installed down one side of the corridor. Waves of heat surged from them, humid eddies of uncomfortably warm, chemical-scented air.

A few steps on there was a sudden flare of light. The squad raised their weapons instinctively, but the light was only a flickering hololith rising from the floor. Anditz recognised the robed figure as Magos Reiner Stuhl himself. The projection held its hands behind its back and began to speak in a mechanical, aged voice. The face was mostly obscured with a hood, but Anditz thought he could make out the same filigree design that incised Wrathe's hands and torso on the metal face plates of the venerable Martian.

'If you are seeing this message,' the recording said, 'I am either absent or indisposed.'

Anditz saw Wrathe cross her arms. The gesture was uncharacteristically anxious, human.

'This is a warning to anyone who may try to access my facility,' the hololith continued. 'Don't. I speak especially to any excavists who may consider themselves rivals.' He cleared his throat with a contemptuous blast of static. 'And for anyone else who has proceeded thus far without realising your presence is unwelcome, you plainly need this spelling out very simply. Go back or find yourself annihilated.'

'Expect more guards, then,' Adair remarked.

'If you elect to persist and perish, be assured that your demise shall be recorded for future analysis. As the Fabricator Plutonis said, "The eyes of the Omnissiah are ever upon us."'

'That was your mentor?' Haruto asked with careful neutrality as the hololith flickered out of existence.

Wrathe nodded stiffly, unable to speak for a moment. 'I never thought I would see his likeness again,' she said, passing one of her metal hands over her face.

Haruto patted her shoulder awkwardly and looked around at the others with a grimace.

'For his sake, pray you don't see that pompous bastard here,' Khan said, jaw set hard.

'Elucidate on that statement,' Wrathe said, turning to the major.

'If I find him, I'm going to make that damned cog-worshipper answer for what he's done.' Khan's eyes narrowed. 'He's worried about rivals stealing his discoveries. That's what matters to him. He killed a world out of greed. Out of obsession.'

'Magos Stuhl did nothing,' Wrathe said.

Khan barked out a cold laugh. 'Exactly. He sat here, hoarding the knowledge that could have saved this planet.'

'The safety of the device comes before anything else, major. It is sacred.'

'Sacred. Unlike the lives of my soldiers?' She flung her good arm back towards the tunnel entrance. 'Unlike the lives of the civilians out there? And he failed, anyway. By shutting us out, all he did was ensure the device festered here. If he'd worked with us from the start, the whole war could have gone differently.'

'You do not understand. This machine is a part of the Omnissiah, an ancient, living spark of their presence.'

'Then when I kill the magos, he'll die in the presence of his god. That's better than he deserves,' Khan spat.

The tech-adept stepped up close to Khan, her white eyes unblinking. The diminutive Martian only stood as high as the major's shoulder, but she stared down the big woman without fear. Anditz halted, not knowing how to intervene without worsening the situation. Throne knew what the Martian was capable of, slight as she was.

'Sir,' Haruto called. 'Those plasma generators ahead… Recommend Adept Wrathe examine them before we proceed.'

Khan's gaze flicked to her sergeant.

'A sensible suggestion,' she said.

'Agreed,' Wrathe said before striding away towards the generators.

Anditz exhaled. They didn't have time for conflict. And they couldn't risk losing Wrathe before she'd shown them how to use the weapon. That was all that mattered now.

'Your instincts were correct, Sergeant Haruto,' the tech-adept called back. 'If the appropriate protocols weren't enacted before passing this area, the generator would have vented its plasma.'

Khan raised her eyebrows. 'How can you tell?'

'Easily. The magos left a warning in infrared.'

Khan grunted. 'Then we can knock our six lives from the ledger of his debt. Proceed.'

The corridor was uncomfortably hot as they passed the great plasma generators that flanked the left wall. The blue coils of the tanks rose above them, crackling with energy. A nest of pipes and tubes coiled up out of the top of the generators into the roof of the corridor, running in the direction of the excavation site.

Khan could see a black wall up ahead where the ferrocrete tunnel terminated and punched its way into the base of the ancient dome. They were so close now. She felt her heart thud in her chest. Whatever was inside that dome was the culmination of everything they and their comrades had fought for and died for on this mission. It had taken so much from them. But now, it offered hope. A chance of rescuing her surviving soldiers.

'This is it, sir,' Anditz said.

Khan glanced at him. The Cadian's eyes were fixed on the end of the corridor. This mission had changed him, she thought. When she'd first encountered him, the loss of his regiment had knocked him badly. But his grief had focused into anger, an emotion that when deployed correctly could be a powerful weapon. Albeit one that it was easy to wound yourself with, if you weren't careful.

'We need to get in first, soldier,' she said. 'We don't count our barking toads until they're hatched.'

Anditz nodded, but kept his eyes forward, pulling out his magnoculars. 'There's something up ahead, sir,' he said.

'Report,' Khan said as they came to a halt.

'There's an access door into the dome.' Khan saw him squint into the lens. 'Couple of gun towers each side. They look to be heavy stubbers. Servitor operated.'

'Recommendations?' Khan said, turning to the rest of the squad.

Ghost stepped forward. 'Reckon I could hit the servitors' skulls from here. It didn't wipe out the battle servitor, but it made it easier to neutralise.'

'That's a long shot,' Anditz said.

'You're about to see a master at work,' Khan said with a grin. 'The Shrikes have never produced a better sharpshooter. The rest of you, prepare to respond once Ghost has taken his shot.'

She watched the gaunt Catachan kneel on the floor of the corridor and wrap the sling of the long-las tightly around his arm before fixing the butt firmly into his shoulder. He put his eye to the weapon's scope to sight the target, then flinched.

'Sir.' He looked up at Khan.

Frowning, she bent down beside him.

'Sir. The gun-servitors.' Ghost spoke so only she could hear. 'They were soldiers.' He paused. 'Looks like one of them was Catachan.'

The shock hit Khan like a punch to the guts. Servitors were made from the living, not the dead. The magos had lobotomised living soldiers to create a defence for his excavation site. And amongst them, one of her people.

Khan felt her eye twitch. 'Take the shot,' she said.

'Sir?' Ghost said.

'Do it.' Khan felt the anger rising in her. The sooner they ended the half-life of these poor bastards, the better.

'Sir.' Frowning, Ghost looked down the scope of his weapon and exhaled, paused for a second then shot twice in quick succession. Khan saw the servitors' heads burst and the weapons' nozzles droop as promethium drooled from the punctured tanks.

'Impeccable,' she heard the Cadian say behind her.

Ghost nodded, an uneasy expression on his face.

'Lieutenant, give me your magnoculars,' Khan said. She needed to see for herself.

She held Anditz's magnoculars up to her eyes. One of the dead soldiers was unmistakably Catachan, despite the cables that had been bored into his body. On his cheek were tattooed Catachan kill-marks that matched Adair's. They stood out starkly against the ghoulish pallor of his dead skin.

Khan swore, then turned and snarled at Wrathe. 'Your damned magos is going to pay for this.' She flung the magnoculars back at Anditz and strode towards the disabled gun towers. There was silence behind her as the rest of the squad followed. She came to a halt in front of the dead soldiers, sagging at their emplacements, skulls ruptured. Ghost might have killed them, but they had died at the moment when the magos had drilled into their brains and removed the very essence of who they were.

Khan's breath caught in her throat. She felt Adair rest a strong hand on her shoulder. She turned to face the squad. A muscle worked in her jaw. She had regained control, but barely. Her voice seethed with emotion as she spoke to Wrathe.

'This soldier has been murdered, and his body desecrated. Explain.'

'Major, logically I cannot give you an explanation. I was not here when this servitor was produced.'

'If you want to live long enough to see your damned archeo-tech get off this planet, you'd better try.'

Wrathe clasped her metal hands. 'Perhaps they were injured severely enough that they would not survive.'

Khan shook her head. 'Or perhaps Magos Stuhl felt the cost of

sacrificing an organic subject worth paying to defend the artefact. I can see what we mean to you, Martian. So, which of us
will it be next? How much more of our blood will you take?'

Adair suddenly moved like a fury. Before Khan had fully registered what was happening, the woman was standing with one
massive hand gripped around the tech-adept's throat.

'Give me one good reason I shouldn't snap your neck,' she
growled, her face set in a ferocious grimace.

'I will give you three reasons,' the tech-adept said, looking up
at the giant Catachan.

'Adair,' Haruto said.

Khan watched silently.

Wrathe raised a hand towards him. 'The first,' she continued,
'is that you cannot do so, even with your strength. I am sure
you would try, but my spine is reinforced beyond even your
ability to break.'

She regarded Adair evenly with her blank eyes.

'The second is that you will regret it. You are not, I judge, a
cruel person, albeit you are an impulsive one. My death would
not restore your comrades.'

The anger began to drain from Adair's face.

'And the third,' the Martian continued, 'is that whilst you are
fast, I am faster. Even now, you will feel my pistol in your ribs.'

'So I do,' Adair said, one eyebrow raised.

Khan saw the glow of the gamma weapon where Wrathe
held it beneath her cloak. Adair wouldn't stand a chance if the
tech-adept wanted to kill her.

'I do not wish to fire,' Wrathe said. 'So, I would ask that you
unhand me.'

'Leave her, Adair,' Khan ordered. 'Now.'

Adair relinquished her grip and stepped back, shaking her
head.

'I cannot give you a specific answer as to "why", major,' the tech-adept said, turning back to Khan as if nothing had happened. 'All I can do is remind you of what is at stake here, and what Sergeant Haruto said when we first met. That recovering this artefact was worth a planet.'

Khan spat. 'He may have said that, but I never did.' She turned to Haruto. 'Is it worth it, sergeant?' She gestured at the dead Catachan. 'Is this a reasonable price?'

'No,' Haruto said. 'It's not. But it's one worth paying. You know what this could mean for the Imperium.'

'So much blood spent,' Khan said. 'Kvelter's crusade force alone...'

'Yes.' Haruto nodded. 'They all died so we could get through that door. So that's what we've got to do.'

He was right, she knew. 'We're going to cut these soldiers down first,' Khan said, her mouth held in a tight line. She walked across to the other servitor. Its head had been totally obliterated by Ghost's shot. Reaching up with her good arm, she pulled out the deceased trooper's ident tag. 'I don't know how they treat their dead on Savlar, but we'll do what we'd do for our own and burn her.'

Anditz stood at a respectful distance with Wrathe while the Catachans took the soldiers down and spoke some brief rites before commending the bodies to the white heat of Adair's flamer. Khan had placed her own bandana on the remains of the dead Catachan beforehand.

'Do you know how to open that door?' he asked the tech-adept.

'I believe so. There is a logic puzzle on it, beneath the mark of the trinity. A simple sequence of the prime numbers.'

Anditz nodded, although he didn't know what either of those things were.

'Right,' Khan said gruffly, approaching them. 'Get it open.'

Wrathe began working. Haruto remained with the tech-adept, while Ghost moved off to guard the rear. Adair stood, stolid and inscrutable, to one side of the door.

'She says it's a simple puzzle,' Anditz remarked.

Khan grunted.

'Are you all right, sir?' Anditz said. The question was inadequate for the circumstances.

'I don't think any of us are, lieutenant.'

'No,' Anditz agreed.

He watched the tech-adept move number blocks on the door. She had moved three so far, sliding them up to form a sequence. Now she gripped a block with the numeral seven on it and pushed. There was a grinding sound and the block stopped moving. Wrathe pulled her hands back, frowning.

'I do not understand,' she said.

Anditz became aware of a hollow rumbling sound. 'What's that?' he asked.

Khan looked up. 'It's coming from above.'

There was a brief moment of silence, then a juddering whine rose up. Anditz felt a prickle of anxiety run down his spine. 'Stop what you're doing,' he called to the tech-adept. Something was wrong.

There was a crash and then something vast slammed down from above them.

An enormous tracked battle servitor had dropped from the ceiling to land behind Ghost. An exotic weapon rested on its shoulder, a brass tri-segmented monstrosity with glowing red nodes. The barrel traversed to aim at the nearest target, glowed for a second, then flared. The air shimmered briefly, and the segments on the barrel spun.

As brief as the next second was, the image burned itself deep into Anditz's brain. Ghost was raising his gun to target the servitor's vulnerable skull, when the Martian weapon twisted. As easily as you might tear parchment, the Catachan was ripped apart.

CHAPTER SEVENTEEN

Khan felt as if she had been doused in ice water as she saw Ghost die. The effect of the weapon on the man was that of a balloon bursting. Suddenly, the viscera and fluid that had constituted his innards were on the outside, and the flesh-and-bone remains of the Catachan lay in three segments on the ground.

Khan had seen hundreds of people die up-close before – a career in the Astra Militarum guaranteed it. But there was something singularly terrible about this instance of death, the dreadful, thoughtless ease with which Ghost's life had been ended.

Through the disassociation, she scrambled for her weapon, and was aware of the others doing the same around her. But everything was happening too slowly, and the barrel of the gun was beginning to glow again, and they were all going to die in this terrible way, just as Ghost had died…

A pulse of glowing gamma radiation blasted past her, roaring into the servitor's chest and head. The blue rays seared a massive hole through the servitor's torso, severing its head and spinning the brass weapon into silence.

Khan turned to see the tech-adept holding her gamma pistol. A tear of blood rested on the Martian's cheek.

'What was that?' Haruto said flatly.

'A torsion cannon,' Wrathe replied, her voice quiet. 'A hallowed machine of dreadful power.'

'Hallowed,' Khan barked, and aimed her plasma pistol at the tech-adept. 'Hallowed,' she repeated. She felt her face contort into a mask of fury. 'Did you do this deliberately?' She shook her head. 'You're all the damned same.'

'No,' Wrathe replied, shaking her head. 'No. I am not my mentor, major.'

'Major,' Haruto said, stepping in front of the tech-adept, shielding her from Khan's wrath.

'Stand aside, sergeant!' Khan shouted.

'No, sir. We're all responsible for the things we do, but she didn't do this.'

'Where are your loyalties, soldier?' Khan spat.

'With you, sir,' the stolid Catachan said, holding her gaze. 'Always. That's why I won't let you do this. You're not thinking straight. You're not thinking about this mission.'

The realisation came like a gut-punch with Haruto's words. Khan felt separated from herself momentarily. In that instant she saw what was apparent to her sergeant. Her focus had narrowed to a tiny beam of hope, built on unstable ground. Her sole objective was to protect her troops. Her fury at the tech-adept was not logical. It only served to impair the safety of the soldiers she sought to save.

She felt the anger rush from her.

'You're right. I'm not thinking straight,' she said, shame pressing down upon her. 'Do what you need to do. Take command, sergeant.'

Haruto's scarred face twisted into a half-smile. 'No, sir. We choose our leaders. You don't get to step down.'

Khan nodded, exhaling heavily. Catachan leaders didn't get to choose. That was the point. 'As you wish. I'm sorry,' she said brusquely to the tech-adept.

'As am I,' Wrathe replied. 'The magos left this trap for my kind.'

'Can you open it?'

'I believed it to be Ashgar's divine sequence. A code of prime digits. But something was wrong – the correct answer triggered this hostile response.'

'Because you're still expecting the magos to be acting on your terms. What makes you think that he actually wanted to help you get through these traps?'

Wrathe was quiet for a moment, considering. 'Regardless of his motivation, I believe I can open this door, but it will take time to unpick the noospheric code.'

'I don't want to take that risk,' Khan said, frowning. 'Nor do we have the time. Let's force it.'

'You cannot. It is a blast door. It is not vulnerable to heat.'

Khan pointed at Wrathe's weapon. 'What about that?'

Wrathe glanced down at her pistol. 'Gamma radiation could render the material brittle, given sufficient time,' she acknowledged. 'But not enough to rupture it.'

'What about the hinges?'

Wrathe nodded. 'I could expose the door pistons and irradiate them. A plasma bombardment from your weapon may then be sufficient.'

'Do it,' Khan said.

'In the meantime,' Wrathe said, 'you may wish to attend to the trooper.' She paused. 'May he be commended to the Omnissiah.'

'Thank you.' Khan nodded curtly, and turned to the squad. Haruto's expression was unreadable, the Cadian's pinched. Adair stood tall, but a tear tracked down the big woman's face. These were the moments that every leader dreaded – to inspire in the face of despair – but the moments for which they were most required.

'Ghost went alone into the jungles of Catachan and survived,' Khan said. 'But he did more than that. When a Catachan braves solitude then chooses to return to their people, they are transformed. They return as the living jungle. And so when we fought alongside Trooper "Ghost" Hasan, a piece of our world fought with us. The ferocity of the Catachan Devil, the cunning of the Spiker, the stealth of the Death Cobra – all of the fear and fury of our death world fighting alongside us.' Khan looked around at the squad. 'We all carry a part of the jungle in our hearts. We carry a piece of Ghost with us. Keep that alive, and you keep him alive.'

Khan straightened. It wasn't as much as Ghost deserved, but it would have to do. She saw the tech-adept turn and gesture readiness.

'Adair, take my pistol and get that door open. And give me your flamer. We won't leave Ghost to the xenos.'

She heard heavy bolts clanking aside behind her as she doused Ghost's remains in burning promethium.

'I'm sorry we couldn't take you with us, trooper,' she murmured. 'May yours be the last Catachan blood to be spilled on this world.'

Anditz followed Haruto and the tech-adept through the heavy door into the archeotech dome. Khan's plasma pistol had blasted the radiation-damaged hinges away, and Adair had smashed down the door like a human battering ram.

He was barely aware of Adair walking beside him. They were approaching the objective he had fought for, had pledged to his dead regiment that he would hunt down. Somewhere in this dome was the means to fight back against the xenos, to deliver retribution to the tyranids.

He stared around at the cavernous space. It was carved of austere black stone, unlike the garish rainbow striations of jewels everywhere else on Lazulai. It spanned nearly fifteen hundred feet and rose to around two hundred, apparently unsupported by any reinforcing structures. At its apex was a large, tightly closed iris aperture. The space felt ancient, like a living presence, somehow. He knew instinctively that it had been built by unknown hands labouring in the darkness before the Imperium came. A strange and terrible thought.

On the far side Anditz could see that prefabricated structures had been erected by Magos Stuhl, portable laboratories flanked by mobile flood-lumens and tracked excavation servitors, which stood idle.

'Deus Mechanicus!' Wrathe fell to her knees with blood-tainted tears staining her cheeks as she beheld the scene.

Anditz followed her gaze to the ground at the centre of the dome. It sloped down to a wide ring of golden metal encircling a deep shaft. The size mirrored the aperture that sat in the ceiling above it. Anditz examined it through his magnoculars. The ring appeared to be roughly the height of a human, and was inscribed with strange, linear symbols. At one side rose a console of the same material. Rigged alongside it were Mechanicus machines, terminal banks and coils of wire and monitors crawling into and around the ancient technology. Above the ring and chasm rose a skeleton scaffold framework of Martian manufacture, clusters of flood-lumens illuminating the machine below, immobile servitors hanging in work cradles, and auspex arrays, inactive and silent.

On the far side of the dome sat an exotic shuttle painted in Martian livery. It didn't look much bigger than an Aquila lander. Anditz lowered his magnoculars.

'Pass me those, lieutenant,' Khan said.

Anditz handed them over. Khan examined the shuttle through the magnifying lenses.

In the meantime, the adept had got to her feet and was moving towards the great ring-device and console as quickly as she could, Haruto following close behind.

'That's what we're supposed to be shifting off the planet, sir?' Adair muttered to Anditz.

'That's what we're going to use to kill the tyranids.'

Adair gave him an uncertain glance as Khan approached.

'Shuttle's big enough for the squad,' the major said, slapping her hands together. 'I want us out of here and on the way to rendezvous with the rest of the Shrikes as soon as possible.'

Before Anditz could reply, a shout came from Haruto. The sergeant was waving them over to where he stood beside Wrathe at the centre of the dome.

Khan frowned. 'Come on,' she said, and started to make her way over to them.

As they jogged across the dome, Adair pointed. 'What's that?'

Across a blasted stretch of ground lay shapes, blackened remains as if something had been set alight. Some were clearly human, but others were tyranid. As they drew closer, it became apparent that the figures were twisted as if in agony, reaching out with claws and hands alike.

'Don't touch anything!' Haruto shouted. He was limping across to them from the centre of the dome. Khan could see Wrathe still huddled over a console next to the ancient machine.

'What's going on?' Khan asked.

'It looks like the device did this,' Haruto said.

Khan looked at the bodies. 'The device, or the magos?'

'I'm not sure, sir,' Haruto said.

Khan gestured at the archeotech. 'How are we supposed to get that off-world, sergeant?'

Haruto glanced back at Wrathe. 'I don't think we can. Even if it wasn't so big, I'm fairly certain it's embedded in the planet's core. That seems to be how it's powered.'

Khan raised her eyebrows. 'So why are we still here?'

'Can it be used against the tyranids, sergeant?' Anditz asked, his tone urgent.

'The tech-adept is still examining it,' Haruto said.

'We don't have time to wait,' Khan said. 'There's a mega-swarm converging on our position. If we can't use it or take it with us, we're leaving.'

Haruto shook his head. 'Come and have a look.'

'Quickly,' Khan said.

Anditz felt anxiety build in his stomach as they approached the vast golden ring. The floor sloped gently downwards to where the console stood. It was unmistakably strange, despite the familiar Mechanicus contrivances looping around it. A smell like hot, dry sand and amber rose from the metal.

As they approached, Anditz saw that Wrathe was enshrined in a nest of cables. Wires spooled out from her wrists and snaked into the machine, and her crown of mechadendrites furled upwards into the Martian monitoring array.

Anditz glanced at the display on the Mechanicus console. External vid-screens showed movement outside, a few flighted tyranids moving lazily around the dome. Not an active threat yet, but where the vanguard led, the rest was soon to follow.

'Report,' Khan said.

The adept's blank white eyes made it impossible to know what she was looking at, but Anditz had the impression that she was elsewhere.

'I have been able to access Magos Stuhl's records,' Wrathe said. 'You are in the presence of a mighty spirit, a sacred presence of a magnitude and power I had not envisaged.' She gripped the control panel hard. Energies ran through her, and fluttered the hem of her scarlet robe. 'This mission may have brought us to the most significant discovery made by my peers for centuries.'

Satisfaction began to replace the anxiety in Anditz's stomach. The struggle was over. Finally, he could bring oblivion to the enemy, to crush them as they had crushed his comrades.

'Well? What does it do?' Khan said, impatient.

Wrathe turned to the major, trembling slightly with what could have been stress or fatigue. 'It is nothing less than an engine of creation. As we speak, I am communing with the machine spirit that engineered this very planet.' Her face was rapt, the blood tracks painting her cheeks like the tears of some beatific, unseeing saint.

Anditz struggled to understand her words.

Haruto exhaled sharply. 'It's a world-maker.'

'Yes.' Wrathe smiled. 'A wondrous blessing from the Omnissiah.'

Anditz felt as if he was falling. 'It's not a weapon?'

'No,' Wrathe said. 'It is not a weapon. It is an engine of creation, not of destruction.'

Anditz's vision swam. A cold numbness spread over him. For a moment, he barely registered what the others were saying.

Khan was gesturing at the huge golden ring. 'Let me get this straight. We can't kill the bastards with it, and we can't get it off-world as is?'

The tech-adept slowly shook her head.

Adair broke the silence. 'For Throne's sake,' she snarled, tears welling in her eyes. 'We've come all this way for nothing? Ghost, dead for nothing?' She slammed her fist into a tracked servitor beside her. The machine rocked with the impact of the Catachan's mighty blow.

'Soldier,' Khan said. 'Keep yourself together. The rest of the

Shrikes at Jasper Fortress need you. Our mission is to survive. All of us. Now we don't need to worry about the device, we can get the hell out of this place and get to our comrades.'

'We cannot leave the machine,' Wrathe said. Anditz imagined that he heard desperation in her toneless voice.

'It's not going to fit in the shuttle,' Khan said. 'What do you want me to do?' She gestured at the vid-screen showing the external view. 'Swarm's nearly on us. We get on that shuttle now, or we die.' She turned away.

'Wait!' the adept said. 'You must allow me to salvage as much as possible.' She looked around and ran her hands desperately across the golden console. 'Some data, any removable components.'

'There's no time,' Khan said.

'Sir.' Haruto stepped forward. 'I'd like to help Adept Wrathe take what she can. If we get anything usable back to the Imperium… It has the power to make dead worlds live. Think of every world in the wake of the hive fleet that came here, every place they scoured to nothing. With this, they don't have to stay dead. We can bring them back. Besides' – he gestured upwards – 'we need to get the roof iris open before we can get out.'

Just then, the dome shook, and the ground underfoot trembled.

Adair leaned over to look at the vid-screens. 'Incoming, sir. Flighted xenos are attacking the dome, and…' She squinted. 'It looks like we've got enemies entering the front door.'

'And we just disarmed all the defences for them,' Khan said. 'Adair, Anditz. Hold the entrance. Use the heavy stubbers at the gun towers where we disarmed the servitors. Haruto, Wrathe. Your first priority is to figure out how to get the dome open so we can leave. Recovering any of the device is a secondary priority. I'm going to prepare the shuttle.' She gestured. 'Go.'

Anditz followed Adair towards the entrance wordlessly. He felt separated from himself. The device wasn't a weapon. The mission had failed. He had failed. His regiment had died for nothing. He couldn't avenge them. The tyranids had won. They had lost the world. They had struggled for nothing. His continued existence was without purpose.

'Sir.' He felt Adair grip his arm. 'Can you hear me?'

'Yes,' he replied. His voice felt strange in his mouth.

'Right.'

He detected concern in the Catachan's voice, but he was too far removed to register an emotional response. He felt certain he would die here. There was some comfort in that. He had come here for an ending. One way or another, he would receive that.

'I'll work on the iris, you work on the relic,' Haruto said.

The tech-adept gestured acknowledgement as her filigreed fingers moved across the console like lightning. Haruto didn't understand her faith, but he knew that this was something sacred to her. He was a heathen treading in her temple.

'Nefeli,' he said, then paused for a moment. 'About the machine. It's not what we thought it was, but what about the anti-tyranid properties that Magos Stuhl reported?'

'It was an erroneous assumption, based on incomplete data.'

He watched her continue to work. 'And the bodies out there?'

'You are referring to the organic matter in the test bed.'

Haruto glanced at the fenced-off patch of twisted bodies. 'The burned remains?'

'They are not burned.'

'Well?'

Wrathe reluctantly gestured at the console, and Haruto leaned across to see what she indicated.

'Disassembled.'

'The device took them apart?' He frowned at the scrolling

sigils on the console. 'Both humans and tyranids. But it started with the xenos. Why?'

The tech-adept exhaled with a crackle. 'The purpose of the machine is to terraform, to create a suitable environment from an unsuitable one. It starts by using the material furthest from the life it is designed to support, but it will eventually work through everything at its disposal to complete its function.'

Haruto nodded. 'So the initial results would have made it appear it was targeting the tyranids.'

'Correct. The magos siphoned off a tiny fragment of the device's energy to experiment with. He evidently discovered in a terminal way that it cannot be actively directed in such a manner.'

'I'm sorry for his loss.'

'Thank you.'

Haruto paused. 'Look. About the device. You're telling me it's designed to create, but that process is a destructive one.' Haruto scratched his face. He thought of something that Lieutenant Anditz had said to him back on the shunt. That anything was a weapon if a Cadian was holding it.

'Nefeli–'

'No,' she said, turning to him sharply.

'You don't know what I'm–'

'I can predict what you are considering. And my answer is no. Magos Stuhl's research revealed instabilities in the machine that require careful renovation before use, or otherwise risk destroying it.'

Haruto frowned. 'Do you mean no, the machine can't be used like that or no, you don't want to use it like that?'

Wrathe didn't reply.

'It's going to be destroyed anyway. We're about to leave it to the tyranids.'

'I am aware of that,' she snapped with a blurt of static. 'But that is entirely different to my setting a sequence to destroy it.'

'You could do it?'

Wrathe stepped over to him, face upturned to meet his gaze. 'Please,' she said. 'I implore you. Do not make me desecrate this spirit.'

'I have no choice.'

Wrathe crackled angrily. 'I thought you understood. I was clearly incorrect. Besides...' She gestured towards Khan. 'Your major wants to save her regiment. How can she do that if you have destroyed the world? The machine cannot be triggered from afar.'

'I assumed as much.'

Wrathe clenched her fists. 'You would both doom your comrades and betray the Omnissiah. Where do your loyalties lie, sergeant?'

'Not with any one person, Nefeli. My duty is to do the right thing. And this is the right thing.' He straightened. 'I need to talk to the major. Prepare what you can to take with us, but make sure we can activate the machine at the end.' He made as if to leave, then turned back. 'I am sorry. Truly.'

He knew that the words weren't enough. That nothing ever could be.

Khan examined the control panel of the shuttle. It was indecipherable Martian babble to her, all cogs and brass and arcane glyphs. But she had managed to get the vessel warming up, that was the main thing. It was Mars-manufactured and growled like a predator. Khan fancied the machine spirit sounded ferocious – that was what they were going to need to escape this wretched planet. Now she just had to make contact with the Shrikes.

Khan felt a rising elation. She was going to do it. She was actually going to get what was left of her regiment off this bloody rock.

'Sir.' Haruto stooped to come aboard the shuttle.

'Good timing, sergeant.' Khan grinned at him. 'I can't find the damned vox. I need you to patch me in to Captain Thorne at Jasper Fortress.'

Haruto squinted at the cockpit. 'The vox is here, sir,' he said, pointing at a panel. 'But I need to tell you something first.'

Khan glanced at her sergeant. His face was unreadable.

'What's wrong?' She swivelled in her pilot's chair to fully face him.

'It's not that anything is wrong...'

'Out with it.'

Haruto's craggy face rearranged itself. 'The machine isn't a weapon, but it can be used like one.'

'Explain.'

'It builds new things by taking old things apart. We can use it to destroy this world, and the tyranids on it.'

Khan didn't understand the sergeant's reticence. 'Good.'

'We cannot do it remotely, sir,' Haruto continued. 'Once we set it going, it will unmake everything. There won't be time to rescue anyone. There may not even be time for us to escape. We'll need to set the iris opening as we launch and hope we make it out before either the tyranids get in, or the machine takes us apart.'

Realisation rushed over Khan. A sick, stomach-dropping lurch that felt as if it ripped her guts out.

'You're asking me to kill everyone left on this planet. Your comrades.' Khan stared at Haruto. 'You're asking me to kill a world.'

'To put a world out of its misery, sir.'

'What you're suggesting is, in effect, Exterminatus.' Her voice rose. 'The complete death of a planet. We're not qualified to deal that judgement, sergeant. Do you understand the weight of that decision? Why ordinary soldiers like us aren't granted the powers to make it?'

'If we don't hit the xenos fleet here, we condemn a whole system to Exterminatus. Do you think the rest of the worlds in the system stand a chance against what's coming?' Haruto said. 'The choice you have now is between ending one world that's already doomed, or ending dozens with a chance of survival.'

Khan growled and slammed her fists onto the console.

Haruto stood calmly, watching her. It was as if he knew what she'd decide. Of course he bloody did, he'd known her long enough. It was between the lives of her regiment and the lives of billions of citizens. What else could she do? The hope that had risen in her slipped away like morning mist over the jungle.

'I thought I could protect them,' she said, her voice a rasp. 'I thought I could save them.' Through the tear-streamed haze of her vision she saw Haruto lean forward, and felt him grip her arm.

'I'm sorry, sir. It's an impossible choice.'

'Emperor damn you, it's no choice at all.' She wiped her arm across her eyes. 'Go and get everything ready for us to leave. I need to send a message.'

Haruto left, and she was alone. The shuttle's vid-screen showed the vanguard of the tyranid horde outside amidst the ruins of the world. Khan sighed heavily. Leading always came down to this. Being alone, making the decisions nobody wanted to make. She rubbed her eyes and wished she had a smoke.

Then she tuned the vox to the frequency of Jasper Fortress. It crackled to life.

'Jasper Fortress, this is Major Khan.'

'*Major Khan, this is Captain Thorne. It's damned good to hear your voice. We were beginning to think you'd forgotten us.*'

'Thorne, do you have space-worthy transport there?'

There was a pause. '*Negative, sir.*'

Khan closed her eyes. Even if she had made it to the fortress, Thorne's force would still have been doomed.

'*Do you, sir?*'

Khan paused. 'Yes.'

After a moment of loaded silence, Thorne spoke. '*I understand, sir.*'

In the privacy of the shuttle, Khan let her face crumple.

'*Have you completed the mission?*'

'We'll be doing so shortly. Thanks to you, captain. Thanks to everyone still holding the line against the xenos.'

'*Sir. Thank you, sir. And your orders are for us to continue to fight?*'

'Yes,' Khan said, somehow keeping her voice from breaking. 'You're doing Catachan proud.'

'*As are you, sir.*' He paused. '*Keep fighting for us,*' he added.

Khan closed her eyes, tears running down her craggy cheeks. She knew that Thorne understood what she had to do, that the world was in its final death throes. But somehow that made it worse. 'Always, captain.'

'*May the Emperor speed your way, sir. Thorne signing off – I think we've got time to take a few more of the bastards out.*'

Then he was gone, and Khan was left alone in the darkened shuttle with only the hiss of the vox-static.

CHAPTER EIGHTEEN

Anditz felt the wet spatter of ichor against his cheek. He had, almost unconsciously, been letting the oncoming tyranids in the corridor gradually get a little closer to the circle of light cast by the heavy stubber's muzzle flare each time before shooting them.

The flickering light illuminated the bursting of their monstrous skulls. *Die,* he thought calmly as another 'gaunt ruptured under the relentless hail of bullets. *Die. Die.*

The 'gaunts were advancing in waves through the entrance tunnel. As they emerged, he and Adair shot them down from their respective gun towers.

The rhythmic rattle of spent casings filled his ears. His finger had lost sensation from the pressure of squeezing the trigger. The familiar tang of fyceline wove through the air.

He felt calm.

Killing was easy. It was what he had been trained to do. Death without end.

What was there to fear, here?

Another burst from his heavy stubber, another rank of tyranids flayed apart. Bone visages shattering. Bodies piling upon bodies. Rictus grins surging closer and closer through the dark.

He would have died to avenge his regiment. He had already willed his life away, so perhaps he had already spent it. He would end for them here. A last stand as an agent of death.

'Sir,' he heard Adair shout. 'We've got to keep them back.'

He glanced at her across the nightmare slaughterhouse of the corridor, across the mounds of dead bone and flayed meat, and vivid xenos flesh.

Atop the gun tower, the Catachan gripped her heavy stubber with her mighty hands as if she was throttling it. Teeth gritted, face set in a wild scowl, white-blonde hair spiked with sweat, she sprayed the xenos with bullets. Vital, vengeful, powerful.

She was life, and he was death, Anditz thought.

The Catachan's gun abruptly stopped firing. 'Throne,' she swore, staring round at him, wide-eyed. 'Lieutenant, cover me! I need to reload.'

Anditz swung his heavy stubber around to shoot down the oncoming aliens while Adair clambered to the back of her gun tower to fumble with the belt feed. There was a lull in the oncoming tyranids. Anditz picked off the stragglers with short, precise bursts of fire.

'Bastard!' Adair suddenly shouted, jerking the ammunition belt. 'It's jammed.' She thumped the side of the gun in desperation.

As Anditz watched, from the corner of his eye he saw something moving rapidly towards them. A flying tyranid, barrelling down the tunnel and heading directly for the unarmed Adair.

He knew instinctively it was above his gun's firing solution.

It was going to kill her.

Something sparked inside him, a brief flash of feeling. *No it bloody wasn't.*

He roared, teeth bared, and took a running jump directly at the flying tyranid. He hadn't thought about what he would do when he hit it. He felt only an overwhelming desire to stop it reaching Adair.

Anditz smashed hard into the side of the tyranid mid-air, just before it got to her. He crashed to the ground alongside the monster, and barely managed to roll away from its scything talons. It was the size of a human, with a sleek bone-horned head and rictus-clenched maw. It lashed a powerful wing at him, apparently seeking to pin him under the leathery appendage.

'Gun's live!' Adair yelled. 'Stay down, sir!'

Anditz crawled towards the base of the gun tower. Adair wasn't messing around. Almost immediately her heavy stubber rattled out a cacophony of shots that sang just over his head. The bullets tore into the grounded tyranid, rending open the alien's body cavity and exposing viscous, crawling organs.

'Come on up, sir,' Adair called. Anditz reached for her hand and she pulled him up onto the emplacement.

His muscles resisted, bruised and aching from the fall.

'What the hell was that?' she said, searching his eyes.

'What?'

'Wrestling a xenos in mid-air? That's something only I'd be stupid enough to do.'

Her jibe belayed the concern in her gaze. Anditz felt as if she could see straight through him, see the black core of nothingness that had opened up inside him.

'Stay with me, sir.' She gripped his hand.

He nodded.

'Throne!' Her head snapped around. 'Incoming!' she yelled. Before Anditz knew what was happening, Adair had pushed him against the wall. There was an explosive impact, and her body pressed hard into his, enveloping him for a moment.

Then she had turned with a roar and was back at the heavy stubber, pelting round after round into their attacker, a stocky tyranid with a ridged spine. It advanced with a huge living missile launcher held aloft.

Anditz saw that the Catachan's back was torn and bloodied from where she'd shielded him from the tyranid's attack. She moved more slowly than usual, and he knew she'd sustained some serious damage. The heavy stubber on the opposite emplacement had been totally destroyed. The gun was twisted and wrecked beyond repair. Shards of bone protruded from the walls, the same shrapnel that had injured Adair.

'Cook the bastards, trooper!' Anditz yelled.

Grinning, Adair reached for her flamer and Anditz took over the heavy stubber.

By muzzle flare and flamer-light they fought, hitting the chitinous monster until its back burst. The smoke the thing generated was acrid, and the corridor stank of burning hooves.

Anditz could smell it through the rebreather. He coughed. Little flecks of blood spattered the inside of his mask. He felt his fingers tremble, and readjusted his grip on the weapon. He could see from his hands that the usual brown of his skin had taken on a sickly grey undertone. The spores that were devouring the world were in his blood now, disassembling him from the inside. He tried not to think of the miniscule tyranids that the tech-adept had seen in the blood-rain, tried not to imagine them consuming his organs at the microscopic level, turning him to liquid as they had his comrades in Carnadine's City of the Dead.

'*Come in,*' Sergeant Haruto's voice came over the vox.

'Sergeant,' Anditz said.

'*We're nearly ready to leave. Get back here, now.*'

Anditz frowned. He could see shapes moving at the end of the corridor. 'We can't leave. We still have hostiles incoming. They'll swamp you. But I'll send Adair back.' He closed the channel.

'You won't, sir,' Adair said.

'We're down to one gun, soldier. No point us both dying here.'

'No, there's not. But I'm staying.'

'No,' Anditz said abruptly.

Adair toasted a couple of smaller xenos with her flamer, then looked down at him. 'It's not really a suggestion, sir. It makes the most sense.'

'I disagree,' he said, feeling a tightness in his chest. 'And I outrank you.'

'You know by now it doesn't work like that,' she said with a half-smile. 'Look,' she said, and passed him something she drew out of her fatigues' pocket.

Anditz stared in disbelief at the small item she had placed in his palm.

'Well?' Khan snapped. She was leaning inside the Martian shuttle, watching Haruto operate the console vox from the command chair.

Haruto shook his head. 'Lieutenant says he's staying to hold the tyranids off. Reckons he'll send Adair back.'

Khan shook her head. 'No.'

'No?'

'I'm done with losing soldiers, Rutger. I'm going to bloody well bring them both back.' Haruto saw a glint in the major's eye. Manic, furious. He'd seen it before.

She drew her plasma pistol. 'Be ready to leave.'

He watched the stocky Catachan jog towards the entrance of the dome. When the major was in a mood like this, she'd tear down mountains to get what she wanted, and woe betide anything that got in her way.

Haruto moved briskly back to Wrathe's station. The tech-adept had been studiously ignoring him while she worked, and didn't look up as he returned.

'Nefeli, I need to get the iris open,' Haruto said, staring at the Martian interface. 'But I can't see a way of doing it without physically standing here and triggering it. As soon as it's open the tyranids are going to be pouring in. We'd be swamped before I got back to the shuttle.'

Wrathe gave a crackle which Haruto took as an impatient tut. 'I will examine it in a moment. In the meantime, you will shortly remove this component and stow it on the shuttle.' She gestured at a gold block to the side of the ancient controls.

Haruto stepped forward.

'Not yet,' she snapped. Turning her attention to the console, she ran her filigreed fingers across a tangle of glyphs.

There was a deep clang somewhere underground, then a soft drone started up far below them.

Nefeli breathed in sharply. 'It wakes!' she said, her tone reverential, her anger forgotten.

A warm wind rose up from the shaft like the breath of the world and ruffled Haruto's hair. The air smelt of ozone. Haruto felt a thrill of excitement.

'Was that the ignition?'

'Yes. It is powered by the planet's core. The heart of Lazulai itself.'

They watched the great device for a few seconds. Haruto thought he could see little flecks of gold light shimmering among the rings.

'I am sorry,' he said. 'I know that this isn't what you wanted.'

'More than that, sergeant. It is a violation of everything I believe.'

'You don't want to see it work?'

Wrathe's vox crackled. 'I shouldn't.'

Haruto nodded. 'But it is beautiful.'

Wrathe watched the living machine, the shimmering of the golden lights reflected in her pale eyes. 'Yes. It is,' she said quietly. Then she straightened. 'You may take the activation unit now. Then ensure the shuttle is ready to depart before I initiate the next stage of the inversion. There will be little time to spare and you must be ready to launch.'

'You're not going to pilot?'

Wrathe paused, then shook her head. 'No. I will be occupied with recording as much data as I can in the final moments.' She rested her hands on the console and looked up at him. 'I have every faith that you are sufficiently capable, sergeant.'

Haruto wondered at the tech-adept's words as she turned back to her work at the console. 'What about the iris?' he asked.

Wrathe glanced up briefly. 'I have identified a remote trigger. Everything is in place now.'

Haruto nodded, and bent to lift the activation unit. 'See you on the shuttle.'

Anditz stared down, unbelieving, at the thing he was now holding in his hand. Adair had given him the small, battered tin that had been the pride of his regiment, which had held the soil of Cadia, and which he had abandoned back at the necropolis in despair. He looked up into her eyes.

'How?'

She shrugged. 'I didn't think you meant to throw it away. Not really. Scooped up as much as I could. There might be some of Lazulai as well as Cadia in there now. But that seemed right.'

Anditz caught a flicker of movement down the corridor. He stowed the tin and squeezed the heavy stubber's trigger. The tide of xenos seemed to have reduced down to a trickle. Were they massing for something?

'You can't stay,' he said, keeping his eyes fixed ahead. 'I'm sick, trooper. Likely dying. You're not.'

'I was hit pretty bad, sir.' She winced, and pressed a hand to her side. Patches of blood soaked her vest where the bone shrapnel had sliced her.

Anditz eyed the lurid bruise already colouring her shoulders. 'It's nasty, but they'd have to try harder to end you, trooper. You'll recover.'

Adair shook her head. 'You need to get out, sir. Tell command what they need to do, how to learn from this. Reckon I'm better at stories than you, but you're better at words. They're not going to listen to a thug like me.' She waved away his protests. 'It's true, sir. That's how the galaxy is. We all have a different duty to see through.'

'My duty is to stay, trooper,' Anditz said. 'To give every breath in service is what it means to be Cadian.'

The vox crackled. *'You better hurry,'* Haruto said tersely. *'Major's coming down there to bring you back.'*

'The major'll understand, sir,' Adair said. 'She'll take you with her while I hold the xenos off. I'm sorry, sir. Really, I am. But I'm not afraid.' She turned to watch the tunnel.

Anditz stared at Adair's face in profile, at her strong jaw and clear eyes. There was no mockery in her now and she was absolutely calm. His heart sank. He knew that she had already relegated herself to the countless ranks of the dead. She was terrible, and primal, and magnificent, and she was going to die. For a moment, he saw all of the ghost legions of Catachan standing behind her, every Jungle Fighter who had lived and died and learned to exist on a world of death calling her back, reaching out their arms to carry their kinswoman home.

'Incoming,' Adair called.

Anditz saw a pair of the xenos forms that had destroyed his heavy stubber advancing down the corridor. He squeezed the trigger of the gun, but nothing happened. 'Damned thing's stuck again!' he shouted, frantically dropping to examine the belt feed.

The projectile orifices on the tyranids' organic muzzles were beginning to engorge and flush fluorescent. Adair wouldn't be able to get to them with her flamer to stop them before they launched, he realised. They would lose the second gun, and with it, their lives.

Then there was a familiar hiss from behind him and a roar of blue light as the pair of xenos were enveloped in a ball of plasma fire that melted their flesh and burst their projectile organs.

'What in Throne's name are you doing?' Khan roared from behind them, plasma pistol still smoking. 'We're leaving.'

'I'm staying, sir,' Adair said. 'I'll hold the xenos back so the rest of the squad can get out.'

'Sir,' Anditz said, his breathing laboured, 'we've already decided who will remain. My physical condition makes me the most expendable. I'll stay.'

Khan's brows were furrowed low over her craggy face. 'I don't give a shit what you think you've decided. Either of you. *I've* decided I don't want to lose any more soldiers today. Get to the dome.' She jerked her head.

'Sir,' Anditz protested.

'No.' Khan glared. 'You're one of mine, son. You're coming with me.'

The vox crackled. *'You need to get out of there now,'* Haruto said. *'I'm looking at the vid-feed and there's a few hundred xenos about to enter the end of the corridor.'*

'See, sir?' Anditz said. 'You two need to leave.'

Khan looked around, then a sudden, manic predator grin appeared on her face. 'Get back to the doorway,' she said. 'We're going to stop these bastards in their tracks.' Then she marched away from them, down the corridor.

'Where are you going, sir?' Anditz called.

'Blowing the plasma generators!' she shouted.

'Oh, Throne,' Adair said, eyes widening, pulling Anditz back towards the dome.

'She can't be serious,' Anditz said. His legs were weak, his lungs felt as if he were breathing through gravel. In the darkness behind them, he heard a rising whine. 'Cadia's Gate. That's a plasma pistol overloading,' he said.

Adair hooked her arm in Anditz's, supporting him as they rapidly retreated. He glanced behind them. Down the corridor a light was growing in intensity until it was painful to look at. And in the centre, the dark silhouette of Khan running towards them at full pelt, her good arm pumping, the other still strapped to her chest in a sling.

The whine rose to a scream and then there was a blast that nearly knocked Anditz over. When he glanced around he saw that Khan had been thrown down, but was already getting to her feet.

Behind her he could see glowing plasma gushing from the ruptured tanks, spitting out geysers of luminescent blue spray so hot that it ignited the air. The plasma pooled on the tunnel's floor, creating a wall of bright fire with them on one side, and the enemy on the other.

Khan walked towards them. She was singed, but laughed a deep, throaty laugh, satisfaction writ large in the set of her shoulders.

'Bloody hell, sir,' Adair said.

'Just in time.' Anditz indicated behind the major.

On the other side of the flickering wall of blue fire, a mass of tyranids were gathering.

'That's put a stop to them,' Adair said.

'Wait.' Anditz frowned. 'Look. They're trying to get through.'

Like a ghastly shadow play, they saw the shapes of tyranids flicker and distort as they threw themselves into the flames, relentless. Trying to attack the squad even as their bodies were melted down to thrashing armatures of bone in the roiling flames of plasma. The grisly deaths of their fellows held no fear for the xenos. They simply continued to fling themselves forwards for immolation.

'Reckon they could choke that fire out?' Adair said doubtfully.

'There's enough of them that it's only a matter of time,' Khan said. 'Come on.'

'We're going to get the rest of the Shrikes now, sir?' Adair asked.

Khan's shoulders fell as she walked. 'No, trooper. We're not. We could try and save them, or we could blow up this bloody rock along with all the xenos on it. We can't do both.'

Adair rested a hand on her commander's shoulder. 'They'd want us to frag the bastards, sir,' she said gravely.

Khan nodded. 'It's what the lieutenant wanted, all along. You were right,' she told Anditz wearily. 'We have to try and damage their fleet. We set the archeotech to blow, then leave.' She shook her head. 'But damn me, it still feels like running away.'

Anditz walked behind them. He knew the major meant she felt as if she was running away from her regiment. But Anditz felt as if he was running away from his own death. He had wanted to destroy the world. But now he realised that he had wanted to be part of the destruction. To cease to exist, to end as the Cadian 82nd had.

How could he continue to live like this?

From the pilot's seat in the shuttle, Haruto saw Anditz and Adair barrel into the dome after Khan. He grinned. Of course the major had done it.

'Nicely done, sir,' he voxed.

'We have to move out, now,' Khan voxed back. *'Swarm incoming through the corridor!'*

'Understood,' Haruto replied. There was nothing more to prepare in the little shuttle. They just needed the squad aboard.

Something caught Haruto's eye in the mid-section of the dome. Frowning, he brought the area up on the shuttle's vid-display and enlarged it.

Pale, human-sized xenos were trying to force themselves through small wire ventilation grates overhead. They could not fit through in one piece, but instead were pushing themselves through in fragments. The grates were starting to buckle under the pressure, and Haruto could only imagine how many hundreds of aliens were lined up behind their fellows to continue the process.

'Sergeant...' Khan arrived at the shuttle breathless. Adair was half carrying the Cadian officer, his respirator mask flecked with blood.

'Strap in,' Haruto said. Then he pressed his comm-bead to his ear. 'Nefeli. Quickly. We're ready. When you're in the shuttle we can open the iris.'

The tech-adept remained where he had left her beside the archeotech, metal hands moving like lightning across the console.

There was a sudden inorganic scream from above. Frowning, Haruto leaned out of the shuttle's open door hatch to see where the sound had come from. With a stab of shock he saw that the great circular aperture in the dome's ceiling was slowly irising open. Something must have triggered it early. The enlarging star of putrescent sky it revealed was so filled with xenos that the heavens appeared to be boiling above them.

'Nefeli,' Haruto called. She wouldn't have time to get to safety before the tyranids began pouring through. He swung out of the shuttle and gestured to her across the distance of the dome.

She glanced up at him for a moment, then back down to the console. Haruto felt the panic in his gut settle into a painful clench of realisation.

She wasn't coming.

'You need to leave, sergeant,' she voxed.

Haruto stared at her from across the great distance. 'Why did you open the iris?'

He saw Wrathe pause for a moment. *'To force you to leave. Someone must remain to activate the device. I did not wish to argue with you about who it should be.'*

'What about the remote trigger?'

'I am the remote trigger. I observed some time ago that the mechanism has failed and would require manual operation. Sergeant, I estimate that you have approximately a minute to get into the shuttle and commence take-off, otherwise you will be condemning the rest of your squad to death.'

'Dammit, Wrathe!' Haruto roared. His clenched fists were slick with blood from reopened scars. 'It wasn't your decision to make.'

'And yet I did,' the tech-adept said, looking up at him from across the dome.

From this distance he could barely make out the bright tears of blood that tracked down her face. She looked like a painted icon, Haruto thought. Beautiful and cold and unreachable.

'Duty is more important than loyalty now, sergeant. And your duty at this moment is to serve the Imperium. You must in turn allow me to serve the Omnissiah by preserving this knowledge.'

A chasm of emptiness opened in his chest and took his anger with it. Dazed, he turned and climbed into the shuttle, mechanically triggering the take-off procedures. The engine growled as it warmed.

'Sergeant,' Wrathe said in his ear. *'I need you to capture as much*

*data as possible about the device's operation now that I have awak-
ened the machine spirit.'*

Haruto glanced at the centre of the dome. The ancient machine
was indeed now moving, the vast disc spinning up. He could see
a heat-haze rising from the deep shaft, and brightening flecks
of golden light above it.

'The shuttle will record environmental data,' he said numbly.

'Insufficient,' Wrathe replied. *'You must synchronise my visual
input with the shuttle.'*

Haruto frowned.

*'You will see what I see. The precision afforded will be superior to
the onboard instruments by an order of magnitude.'*

'Sergeant.' Khan leaned across from where she was strapped
into her shuttle seat. 'We've got to get this bird off the ground.
Fast. The aperture is nearly wide enough for us to get out, which
means it's nearly wide enough for the xenos to get in.'

Haruto glanced at the shuttle's rear vid-feed, which showed
the opening iris. He could see in the distance that long tendrils
were descending out of the lower atmosphere and connecting to
the beleaguered world. Spores fell down through the open roof
like dirty snow, huge flakes of drifting alien biomatter.

'Please, sergeant. It is the last thing I will ever ask of you.'

Haruto pressed his comm-bead to his ear. 'Tell me what to
do. Quickly.'

Wrathe told him.

Haruto had expected something like a vid-feed to appear on the
shuttle's console display, but instead realised that Wrathe was
sharing not just what she saw, but how she saw. An image of the
shuttle tinted green appeared before him amidst soft streams of
data and symbols. Wrathe blinked, and the shuttle was suddenly
enlarged. Haruto felt a strange jolt of recognition as he realised

he was looking at himself through the front windscreen, sitting in the pilot's chair, brow furrowed low, his expression stony. *Is that how I look to her?* he wondered.

He could see strands of light weaving around himself and Khan, and behind them, around Adair and the Cadian. But they were most brightly tangled around him, illuminating him in Wrathe's vision like a white-hot star. Bright little tags of meta-data scrolled and flickered around his shoulders, unfurling calculations and estimations and projections that he couldn't understand. He reached a hand forward to the shuttle's control column and saw the light play around his fingers.

'What is this?' he asked.

'It is how I visualise the Motive Force. The power that animates all life, organic and mechanical. Omnissiah willing, I will return to it when I die.'

Haruto could feel the terrible psychic pressure of the millions of tyranids massing outside, all closing in on the tiny red-robed figure of the tech-adept far below, still at her station.

'Then you will continue to exist,' he said.

'In a manner of speaking, yes.'

'I will see you again, Adept Wrathe.' He swallowed. 'In all things.'

There was a crackle over the vox. *'This would be most satisfactory to me, Sergeant Haruto.'*

Wrathe turned away to look at the ancient device. Through her eyes, he saw that a golden cloud was forming above the chasm. The tyranid spores seemed to be clearing above it. Haruto didn't know if it was his imagination, but the boiling sky outside also appeared to be diminishing directly above the iris.

'I posit that now would be the optimal time for your departure, sergeant.'

Even from inside the shuttle, he could hear the sound of the oncoming tyranid swarm outside the dome, the hushing of chitin and the rising clatter of a billion claws. And he could hear something else, something like the sound of choir song rising from the ancient device as it began the process of dismantling the pieces of the planet around it.

Haruto squeezed the control column and began to raise the shuttle. His heart felt like a stone.

Wrathe glanced from the device to the shuttle. In her projected vision, trails of light streamed from the little vessel like tears as it flew up out of the dome and into the roiling sky, before disappearing.

'May the Emperor and the Omnissiah protect you, Nefeli.' Haruto gritted his teeth as he piloted the shuttle upwards, his last glimpse of the tech-adept a tiny speck of red in an encroaching sea of horror.

As the shuttle rose, Anditz saw the tiny figure of the tech-adept in the machine's light as if she were surrounded by stars, robed in a firmament of beautiful destruction.

The view changed as they lifted above the dome. The tyranids were almost at the excavation site now, a super-swarm converging on it from all sides.

He had a brief glimpse of a lone tyranid moving in a space between the others, smoke billowing from its shoulders, sabre-scythes held aloft. It paused to look up at them for an instant before they had risen too high to see it. Anditz felt a clench of horror in his guts at the sight of it that was replaced with cool satisfaction that the bastard was almost certainly about to die.

Terrible appendages and tentacles hung from the sky around them, but the shuttle rose through a slim column of clear air cleansed by the beam rising from the machine below, a narrow beacon of possibility for escape.

The glow from the excavation site was becoming brighter, and a tremendous roar sent vibrations through the shuttle. Anditz didn't know if it was from the device or the tyranids.

'Two minutes to orbit,' Haruto said.

As the machine stripped the planet below of all features, the movement of the tentacles in the clouds was becoming more agitated. Then they reached the upper atmosphere above the clouds and the true nature of the vast feeder-tyranids was revealed. Titanic armour-plated parasites the size of continents floating in space, sucking the planet dry with grotesque, peristaltic motions. If any of them were aware of the shuttle, they could have destroyed it in an instant. Could, most likely, have done so unknowingly.

The sergeant glowered with concentration as he navigated the turbulence and thrashing horrors around them. With his massive fists clenched around the shuttle's control column, he flew the little vessel as surely as any bird.

Below them the final unmaking of the world and everything on it unfolded. Anditz closed his eyes, momentarily blinded as Lazulai ended not in blood and bone, but radiant light.

Then something ruptured off to one side, rocking the little shuttle violently.

'It's one of the tyranid vessels!' Adair shouted.

Anditz stared as another of the xenos burst in a cascade of gold light, streaming fragments showering back down to the planet.

All around them, the fleet was withdrawing feeding pipes from the world. Vast intestinal tubules uplit by the glowing planet waved stiffly in the sky below, but many already seemed damaged by the ancient terraforming device.

'It's working,' Adair said gleefully.

But Anditz felt only a strange emptiness at the sight of the glowing ball of energy that the planet had become. The battlefields and places where he and his regiment, where humanity had struggled were all gone, all unmade. Even the device itself, the terraforming machine that had made Lazulai what it was, was now disassembled, and nothing but light was left.

'Did we win?' he found himself asking.

'That's up to us, lieutenant,' Khan said. 'But for the Cadian Eighty-Second and the Catachan Night Shrikes and all of the others who didn't get out, we're going to make damned sure we did.'

'We've got the trigger, but not the rest of the device,' Anditz said. 'What can anyone do with that? How can it be used as a weapon?'

'Maybe the cog-worshippers can do something with it. Maybe they can't. But we've damaged the hive fleet. Given the rest of the sector a fighting chance.' Khan turned in her chair, her face twisted into a half-smile. 'And anyway, you're forgetting what the real weapon is we're carrying.'

Anditz shook his head. 'I don't understand.'

'It's you,' Khan said. 'And it's me. And it's Adair and Haruto. It's this story. The story of a squad who rode into the mouth of the beast and survived, who stole victory from the jaws of the tyranids. It's a story that will be told by sector command and repeated by troopers round fires and on battlefields and in habs and passed on to children to help them believe the Imperium will win.'

'How can that be worth it?' Anditz said. 'Worth everything?'

Khan shrugged. 'I can't tell you that it is,' she said. 'But I can tell you what hope means. What it spurs people to do.' She paused. 'Whatever else we wanted, whatever else we think should have happened here, that we survived matters. Whether you think we should have or not is something you'll need to learn to live with.'

She held Anditz's gaze for a moment.

He nodded.

'Sergeant Haruto,' Khan said. 'Get us to the nearest Imperial ship, outpost, or world. What's left of the hive fleet is reeling now, trying to figure out what's going on, but it won't last. Just get us out of here. Whatever the nearest place is I can get a half-decent smoke.'

'I'll do my best, sir.'

'Sergeant, at this point I'd take a cheroot from an ork.'

Haruto nodded briskly and scanned the star charts. 'Iridian will be our best bet,' he said, pointing. 'On the edge of the sector. Unless we can intercept a vessel on the way. It won't be a short trip.'

'Anyone know any songs?' Adair said cheerily.

'Sir, I refuse to pilot this craft if Trooper Adair is going to sing,' Haruto said flatly.

'Poetry, then?'

Anditz frowned. 'I thought that was a joke.'

'Oh no,' Khan said, eyes twinkling. 'Catachans never joke about poetry.'

Anditz glanced at the piece of archeotech they had salvaged, stowed at the back of the shuttle. The life of an entire planet had bought it – how could adequate worth be placed on such a thing? He had been ready to end his struggle back on Lazu-lai, but now had to find it in himself to continue to fight. He looked down at his hands. Was Khan right? Could the squad change the fate of worlds?

He balled his hands into fists. They must find the strength in themselves to ensure it did.

The tiny, vulnerable speck of the Martian shuttle moves between the drifts of scattered xenos and out into the starfields beyond.

The wounded hive fleet drifts away, gathering the remaining masses of individual xenos into a single, terrible shoal that slowly swims off into the darkness of space, its destination unknown, leaving their corrupted dead to float in orbit. This is not a victory. Against the Great Devourer there can be no such thing, only the postponement of oblivion. The death of this world might buy the neighbouring system a little longer until eternal night falls. Perhaps, for the brief flicker of a single human lifespan, this is sufficient for hope.

On Lazulai, darkness falls and the dust begins to settle. Amidst the nothingness, something moves, for in all endings can be found the forces of beginnings.

ABOUT THE AUTHOR

Victoria Hayward is a trained historitor who spent
her youth serving as an acolyte in a Games Workshop
store. She writes about black holes and the palaces
of despots in her day job as a science communicator
and her favourite corners of the 40K universe
are those occupied by the Inquisition – which is
all of it. Her work for Black Library includes the
Warhammer 40,000 novel *Deathworlder*, and the
short stories 'The Siege of Ismyr' and 'The Carbis
Incident'. She resides in Nottingham, where she
keeps birds and practises printmaking.

An extract from
Cadia Stands
from the Omnibus *Minka Lesk: The Last Whiteshield*
by Justin D Hill

Below them, the planet was poised half in light and half in darkness.

Major Isaia Bendikt could not tell if a new day was coming on, or if the night was falling. He stood with Warmaster Ryse and his posse of command staff on the viewing platforms of the *Fidelitas Vector* and remembered how he'd left Cadia over twenty years before.

In those twenty years, he'd had more than his fair share of benighted ice-worlds, void-moons and jungle worlds with bloodsucking nanobes that dropped onto you from the branches above.

He'd seen the worst of the galaxy and now, looking down upon Cadia, he remembered his last moments on his home world.

A young Whiteshield, without a kill to his name.

* * *

Bendikt's father had never got the chance to go off-planet. He was one of the one in ten Cadian Shock Troopers whose draft drew them as a territorial guard. It was his life to stay at home and stand ready to protect Cadia. But war had not come, and that uneventful career was a shame that had discoloured his life.

When the sixteen-year-old Isaia Bendikt drew an off-world draft he was both proud and envious of his son. It was a hard thing for a dour father to express, so he'd done what many fathers had before him – bought a bottle of Arcady Pride and got both himself and Bendikt drunk.

Bendikt remembered the night clearly. They had been sitting at the round camp table that stood in the middle of the small sub-hab central room of their home. His father had drawn up the camp chairs and slammed the bottle down between them, set two shot glasses on the table.

He had forced a smile as he unscrewed the top, crumpled it up in his hand and threw it back over his shoulder, where it had rattled in the corner of the room. His mother had left them a few plates of boiled grox-slab and cabbage on the table. Bendikt had tried to line his stomach as his father poured them a shot glass each.

'Here,' he'd said and held out the brimming glass.

They'd tapped the rims against each other and tipped the glasses high. Shot by shot they'd drunk and slowly knocked the bottle back. When the muster bell rang there was only a little amasec in the bottom of the bottle. 'To your first kill!' his father had slurred. His mother, a thin, worn, earnest-looking woman, had joined in with the last toast.

It was a short walk to the muster point, where other White-shields were being loaded onto rail trucks, their apprehensive faces staring out from under their Cadian-pattern helmets. All the tracks led straight to the landing fields outside Kasr Tyrok.

Bendikt and his parents pushed through the crowds to find his truck. Both his mother and his father had last words for him, though he was damned if he could remember them. He was only sixteen and so drunk he could barely stand. There were no tears. It was poor form to show sadness when a Cadian was sent to fight. It was part of the rhythm of life: birth, training, conscription, death. It was natural that a young Whiteshield would go and kill the enemies of the Imperium.

Bendikt had imagined himself many times taking the straight route south, and never seeing his home again. Before climbing aboard, he checked himself one more time to make sure that in his drunken state he had not forgotten anything.

He had boots, webbing, jacket, belt, combat knife, lasrifle, three battery packs, Imperial Primer in his left breast pocket, water canteen in his right. He pulled in a deep breath. He was ready, he told himself, to face anything the galaxy could throw at him.

'So,' Bendikt said. They said goodbye to one another, and his mother briefly embraced him and stuffed a packet of folded brown paper into his jacket pocket. 'Grox-jerky,' she whispered.

She was a tough woman, brought up on a planet where the only trade was war, and little given to expressions of emotion.

'I want to thank both of you for giving me life. I promise you I will be all that a Cadian should,' he said. It was a speech he had prepared, but being drunk he stumbled on his words and left much of it out.

Then he saluted and turned to climb aboard the truck. He looked out to wave goodbye to his parents, but darkness was falling and they had already turned for home. That was the last Bendikt had ever seen or heard of his family. For the next twenty years, other Guardsmen had been his brothers and sisters, and the Emperor his father.

Bendikt found it hard to remember his father's face but had never forgotten the hug his father had given him, and feeling his father's thick arms wrap around him, his broad, rough hands on his back. His mother's voice had never left him; he could recall her whispering 'grox-jerky' into his ear, and those words stayed with him, and somehow came to mean 'Look after yourself', and even 'You are well-loved, my son.'

As Cadia revolved beneath them Warmaster Ryse put both hands to the carefully tooled brass railings and leaned forward, his breath misting a little on the chill of the foot-thick glass.

He wanted to mark this moment with something momentous, yet poetic and memorable. Something that could go in his memoirs when, and if, retirement came. As if sensing its moment, the Warmaster's servitor-scribe, an emaciated body with augmetic stylus right arm and waist-mounted scroll, shuffled forward, knocking a few other sycophants out of the way.

The scribe had come with the title of Warmaster and Ryse seemed to rather like having his every word taken down for posterity. And now that there was no more Deucalion Crusade for Ryse to lead, it had occurred to many of them that perhaps Ryse might not be a Warmaster much longer.

Perhaps, many were thinking, Ryse's star was on the wane, and it was time for them to find one that was rising.

Ryse coughed to clear his throat, then his bass-baritone rang out, 'We have returned to our mother in her time of direst need.'

There was more, and Bendikt thought the Warmaster's speech could have been better, but the Warmaster finished with a flourish, like an Imperial preacher waxing lyrical. 'Men shall not say that we forgot our duty, nor that we forgot from whence we came.'

As he spoke, there was the scratch of stylus on vellum, leaving a trail of precise minuscule, in neatly justified blocks of text.

Bendikt could not help reading over the scribe's shoulder while Ryse paused as if waiting for it to catch up, letting the words ring through his head.

Bendikt looked away. The Warmaster turned, and as if picking him out for not paying due attention, asked, 'What do you think, Major Bendikt?'

'She looks peaceful enough to me,' Bendikt stammered.

Ryse smiled indulgently. 'Yes. Cadia sent out the call and we have returned. Her need has not been forgotten.' The motors of the Warmaster's bionic arm whined gently as he patted Bendikt on the back. No doubt he had meant this to be a human gesture, but Bendikt did not find the crude press of metal fingers comforting.

'How long until we disembark?' Ryse asked a thin, pale officer with a shock of white hair.

The officer snapped his heels together. 'Governor Porelska has sent his personal barge to bring you down, Warmaster. *Sacramentum* is being loaded onto it as we speak. As soon as it is stowed down, I will let you know, sir. The freight captain did not think it would be more than a few hours.'

Sacramentum was Ryse's Leviathan. A brass-worked marvel of gunnery and armour and engineering that had spearheaded at least two assaults on the hive world of Owwen.

'Good,' Ryse said. 'Good.' He was one of those men who liked to fill silences with his own voice. At that moment one of the adjutants touched the Warmaster's sleeve. The commander of a battalion of Mordians had arrived on the viewing deck. They were standing by the lift in a formal and uninviting group, waiting for an introduction.

'Ah!' Ryse said as if a passing chat with the Mordians was all he wanted in the world, and nodded to them all. 'Excuse me, gentlemen.'